CROSSROADS
of GRANITE

MICHAEL REIT

ISBN (eBook): 978-3-903476-06-6
ISBN (paperback): 978-3-903476-07-3
ISBN (hardcover): 978-3-903476-08-0

DISCLAIMER

This is a work of fiction. Names, characters, businesses, places, events, and incidents are either the products of the author's imagination or used in a fictitious manner. Any resemblance to actual persons, living or dead, or actual events is purely coincidental.

Title Production by The BookWhisperer.ink

Cover Design by Patrick Knowles

Part One

RAWICZ PRISON, RAWICZ, POLAND, MAY 1944

CHAPTER ONE

Waking up to the stomping sound of heavy boots had become all too familiar. Christiaan Brouwer squeezed his eyes shut, trying to ignore the incessant clanging as the guard tapped his metal-tipped baton on every cell door he passed. *Clang.* Christiaan turned his face to the wall to avoid the harsh lighting that would soon spring into life. He grunted as his back cracked from an uncomfortable night spent on the concrete slab of a bed.

In his three months in the prison, his discomfort had only grown —pain radiated from his neck down to his lower back. And if it wasn't his body keeping him awake at night, the guards often found a way to rouse the entire hallway.

The electric buzzing of the lights in the hallway meant it would be seconds until the single bulb in Christiaan's cell ended the comfortable darkness. He pulled his knees to his stomach and shivered. It was late May, the Polish nights were cold, and his cell was unheated. The guards had made it clear that the prisoners were fortunate they could even shut their windows. Christiaan had soon found out it was indeed a privilege that could just as easily be taken away. A few days after their arrival, a prisoner upset one of the guards when he asked for a blanket. The guard had mocked him and said he hadn't experienced true winter yet. He removed the single small but precious window separating the prisoner from the outside elements. The man had survived the first night, but when a cold snap had temperatures dropping well below freezing point, he was found frozen to death in his cell the next morning. There had been no more complaints about the cell temperatures after that.

Christiaan reluctantly opened his eyes to the faint glow of the light bulb warming up. *Clang.* Less than five minutes to get ready for roll call. He swung his legs out of bed and grimaced as he reached for his shoes, placed neatly on the far side of his bed. An intense cramp shot through his left calf and he flung himself back on his bed, stretching to relieve the searing pain spreading through his leg. His eyes watered and he cursed inwardly. The cramps were new; food and water rations had steadily declined the past week, and he went to sleep every night thirsty and hungry. His strength was waning; he had likely lost at least a fifth of his weight since arriving in the prison four months ago. Or was it five? He couldn't remember.

The pain passed, and he stood in his prison uniform. He hadn't bothered undressing for bed; he needed every layer of clothing during the cold nights. There was movement in the hallway and he moved toward the cell door. He could hear the guards opening the doors of the other cells, and a few seconds later, his cell door swung open. An imposing guard wearing the dark green uniform of the SS motioned for Christiaan to step out. He did as instructed and glanced to his left, where he spotted his friend, Max. He gave him an almost imperceptible nod, relieved he appeared in relatively good shape. The guards opened the last cell door before the men were marched upstairs, toward the roll call area.

Christiaan followed the man in front of him, keeping his gaze firmly on the ground, making sure he didn't leave too much space between them. Moving too slowly was considered loitering, and Christiaan had seen men getting a severe beating for the offense. Christiaan was determined not to give the guards any excuse to administer the dreaded morning wake-up call.

The walk to the roll call area in the yard in the middle of the complex took five minutes as they made their way through the labyrinth of the prison. He could vividly remember his arrival from the Assen prison, in his home country of the Netherlands. The journey had been uncomfortable, and thirst had plagued them; a sign of things to come. Christiaan's group of fifty-five men had boarded a train in the middle of the night, and they had traveled east for two nights, making frequent stops on sidetracks as freight trains thundered past.

When they stepped off the train, they were escorted through the center of what turned out to be the city of Rawicz in Poland. Snow covered deserted streets, but Christiaan had spotted curious faces peering through the drawn curtains of the homes they passed. The walls of the prison appeared out of nowhere in the middle of the city. Christiaan had glanced back before entering, the snow already covering their footsteps. As the gate closed, he realized it would be his last glimpse of life on the outside.

They reached a short flight of uneven stairs, and he focused on making sure he didn't trip. Even though there was a handrail to his right, he didn't even consider using it. The guards enjoyed nothing more than to punish minor infractions. The image of the frail, older prisoner getting pulled out of line and forced to sprint up and down the stairs until he collapsed was fresh in his mind.

They reached the top of the stairs and entered the main hallway on the ground floor. Their cells were in the basement, isolating them from most of the regular prisoner population for all activities but roll call. Groups of men merged from side corridors to form a neat procession heading for the yard. Christiaan hardly had a chance to speak to the other men, but he knew they came from all corners of

Europe. Poles, Germans, Frenchmen, and even a few Americans were interned in Rawicz Prison. All had taken different paths to end up here as enemies of the Third Reich. And that was enough for the SS guards running the prison to treat them as subhuman. For the prisoners, it meant they were all in the same situation.

The temperature dropped sharply as they approached a large open door leading to the yard. Christiaan braced himself, pulling his thin sweater up to his chin to stay a bit warmer. Nearing the door, a familiar, sweet smell entered his nostrils. He peered past the men in front of him. A light drizzle had started to fall. With a heavy sigh, he stepped outside to see dark clouds looming overhead. The guards would be delighted to have a roll call in the rain.

Christiaan found his spot in the middle of the yard, lining up alongside the other Dutch men. He looked around as the last of the prisoners filed into the yard. The guards seemed nervous, their eyes shifting between the prisoners. Some held automatic rifles. The men that ruled Rawicz normally made do with batons. Given the condition most prisoners were in, that was more than enough to keep order. He glanced at Max, who looked worried. He gave Christiaan a quick shake of the head. *What's going on?*

They didn't have to wait long. The gate to the yard was closed, and but for a few suppressed coughs, it was silent for about a minute. The dark clouds were directly overhead, and thick drops of water were pelting down. Christiaan could feel the water seeping into his uniform and shivered involuntarily.

A side door opened, breaking the silence, and attracting the attention of all those in the yard. A thousand pairs of eyes shifted in the direction of a man wearing the gray-green uniform of an SS officer. Accompanied by a guard holding an umbrella over his head, he rushed to the small platform in front of the group of prisoners. Christiaan recognized *Hauptsturmführer* Anton Winkler. He swallowed hard. Winkler oversaw the prison but was seldom seen. From what Christiaan heard, the man preferred to leave the day-to-day running of the prison to his underlings while he lived in a villa on the outskirts of town. For him to make an appearance in front of the entire prisoner population could only mean something was very wrong.

Winkler raised a microphone to his mouth. "Prisoners. I apologize for the inconvenience of having to stand out here in the discomfort of this weather." The metallic distortion of his voice did nothing to hide the insincerity of his words as he scowled at them. "Unfortunately, this is the most efficient way to resolve this situation." Winkler let the words hang in the air for a few seconds. Without exception, the prisoners lined up in front of the SS officer had their gazes fixed firmly on the ground. The rain intensified and a wind picked up, and Christiaan's teeth chattered.

"I've caught rumors of a group of prisoners planning an escape," Winkler continued, a hint of indignation in his voice. "I can't tolerate even the mention of this ridiculous plan." He snapped his fingers at the guards lining the walls, who pulled out their batons and took a step toward the prisoners. The guards looked confident and determined, some softly patting their batons on their free hands.

"I'll give anyone who knows anything about this escape thirty seconds to step forward," Winkler said as he glanced at his wristwatch. "I give you my word you'll be spared if you tell us the truth."

Nobody in the yard moved as the seconds ticked away to the sound of thick raindrops landing in puddles forming between the prisoners. Christiaan kept his head low but glanced around. He knew nothing about an escape, but he was excited to hear of the initiative. If what Winkler said was true, the men looking to break out of the prison weren't doing it without outside help. He sometimes overheard prisoners talking about the efforts of the Home Army taking the fight to the Nazis on the streets of the Polish cities. It gave him hope that perhaps one day, the men and women of the Home Army would storm the prison.

"Nobody, then?" Winkler's voice startled Christiaan back to the present. "That's a pity." With a flick of the wrist, he signaled to the guards. The uniformed men raised their batons and moved toward a group prisoners on the far side of the yard. Other guards were standing a few meters back, their rifles aimed at the prisoners. Some of the prisoners took a step away from the armed perimeter, unsure of what to do. Unfortunately, this decision proved fatal. The guards rushed forward and grabbed the men who had tried to distance themselves. In less than sixty seconds, twenty men had been separated and badly beaten by the guards as they moved them to the front.

Winkler stood looking down from his elevated position. His facial expression hadn't changed, and he patiently waited for the guards to finish lining up the men. They stood facing the rest of the prisoners, every man accompanied by a guard standing close behind him. Even from a distance, Christiaan could see the pistols strapped to these guards' belts. When they were done, Winkler gave a curt nod and raised his microphone.

"Since no one came forward, I thought we should expedite our search for the perpetrators. I don't have all day. Each of the men in front of you is worth thirty seconds."

A sinking feeling overcame Christiaan as he listened to the warden's words. The energy in the yard changed. Some hadn't understood Winkler's words and looked around in confusion. Most, however, understood the words perfectly, and their faces had turned ashen. Only two looked unshaken, their faces etched with determination.

"This is your last chance to come forward and avoid unnecessary bloodshed," Winkler said, his eyes slowly scanning the crowd. "Otherwise, what happens next is on you."

The yard remained quiet.

"Very well, then. Let's proceed." Winkler waved at the guard standing behind the prisoner on the far left.

The guard's voice boomed across the yard as he started counting. "One. Two. Three." He sounded calm and composed, emphasizing each syllable, perfectly timing every second. Christiaan looked around, hoping someone would end this madness by stepping forward. "Eight. Nine. Ten."

There was no movement around the group, as no one even dared shuffle their feet. Christiaan's eyes went to the condemned man, who had closed his eyes and stood shaking as the guard continued his count.

"Twenty. Twenty-one. Twenty-two."

Christiaan considered the possibility that Winkler was just carrying out a cruel exercise in prisoner discipline, that there were no rumors of an impending escape, and that the men at the front of the group would soon be released after this scare.

"Twenty-eight. Twenty-nine. Thirty."

It was silent as the guard finished his count. He turned and looked to Winkler. Christiaan held his breath. Winkler nodded, and the guard unholstered his pistol. The sound of him cocking the hammer reverberated through the yard. Christiaan looked away, just before a single gunshot shattered the silence. A dull thud followed almost immediately as the condemned prisoner's lifeless body unceremoniously hit the ground.

Without missing a beat, the next guard started counting. "Three. Four. Five."

Christiaan's stomach churned. He wanted to help these men, but his body screamed for him to stay put. The second guard finished his count, and as the next prisoner crashed to the ground, there was nothing he could do.

Another gunshot rang out in the front, but it hardly registered in Christiaan's mind. The only way to survive this prison was to keep his head down. If there really were plans for an escape, surely the execution of twenty innocent men would only expedite them?

Ten minutes later, Christiaan passed through the large gate, back into the prison. He was soaked but hardly felt the cold. They had been forced to march past the bodies of the murdered prisoners, and Christiaan had felt a fury he didn't know he possessed when he glimpsed the SS guards in charge of the execution. They stood at a

distance, casually chatting with each other while they smoked cigarettes. Some even grinned and pointed at the lifeless bodies strewn
haphazardly in the yard. At that moment, Christiaan knew there was
only one way he could ever get back at these men. He would survive
and get his revenge one day, no matter what they threw at him.

CHAPTER TWO

The tall man placed his crutches next to the wooden bench. His dark brown hair was cropped short, and he sat down with a sigh.

"You feeling okay today, Flo? Do you still need those crutches?"

Floris Brouwer turned to his friend and smiled. "The nurse wouldn't let me leave without them. I can do all right on my own." He waved his hand at the stunning landscape. "They still come in handy when climbing the hills around this place, though. How are you doing? Did you get your check-up this morning?"

Anton's hand automatically went to his left shoulder, a habit he had picked up since the incident, and shrugged. "I can't really complain. The doctor said I should be ready for action soon enough. He asked me if I wanted to stay a bit longer, but I told him I would rather get back, make a difference, you know?"

Floris nodded. He knew exactly what his best friend was talking about. They had arrived in the hospital four months ago. He could still remember the day they were struck down in some Russian town whose name he couldn't remember. The memory of the Russian tank lingered in his nightmares, and he could still recall the force of the blast when it fired upon them from only fifty meters away. He looked at Anton, who sat on the bench next to him with his legs crossed, looking down on the city below. They had been overrun by Soviet soldiers, and when they had to abandon their position, Anton had been struck in the middle of the street. If Floris hadn't ignored orders and gone back for his downed friend, he was certain they wouldn't be sitting here together. Caught in the eye of the storm of the raging battle, Floris had searched frantically for a safe spot for his injured friend. When the shelling started, the air in the streets had filled with dust, and Floris had blindly wandered around with his friend slung over his shoulder.

"Shall we head back to the barracks via the *Wanderweg*?" Anton interrupted his thoughts, pointing toward a small trail running parallel to the hill and back to the Waffen-SS base. The trail Anton referred to offered spectacular views of the Austrian city of Graz and was often frequented by the locals on the weekends. It was slightly more strenuous than the regular path, but Floris agreed they could both use the exercise. Besides, it was a beautiful day, and he had nowhere else to be. He took his crutches and carried them under his arm, determined not to use them on the way back. *I'm strong enough for duty.*

The path was well trodden, and Floris found it easy to match Anton's moderate pace. He suspected his friend was moving a little slower for his benefit but accepted he would never be able to walk completely unhindered anymore. His mind wandered back to the eastern front.

When the orange-grayish dust cleared, Floris and Anton found themselves on the wrong side of town. There was heavy fighting all around, and it was only a matter of time before other soldiers would pass through their safe house. Soviet soldiers of the Red Army would be horrendous. His prayers were answered when fellow Waffen-SS soldiers came running by. They, however, were more concerned with saving themselves, and Floris was unable to keep up while carrying Anton. That's when he heard the crunching of debris behind him, and the Russian T-34 tank appear from nowhere. When the operator fired the deadly shell, Floris and Anton were forced to the ground.

The next thing he remembered was waking up in a dimly lit tent with doctors and nurses fussing over him. The pain had been excruciating, but they had to operate. He had passed out again, and the following weeks had been a blur as he drifted in and out of consciousness.

Finally, he had woken up in a real bed, and the nurse told him he was in Graz, in the SS training hospital, to recover from a broken shoulder and, worse, a broken shinbone. She had made it clear his recovery would be long. Worse, he needed to understand he might never walk without support again.

From that moment, Floris decided he would do everything humanly possible to walk on his own again. Progress had been agonizingly slow. In Floris' darkest moments, when he wanted to tell the doctor he was ready to give up, Anton took him to one of the other wards. They found soldiers who had just come from the eastern front. A few of them had been struck blind, unsure if they would ever see again. Others lost hands and feet, with severed arms and legs. These men had no chance of ever walking again, never mind serving in the Waffen-SS. Floris owed it to them to recover and return to the front.

They reached the end of the path, the hospital barracks coming into view. They continued on the main road for the final two hundred meters and Floris caught up with Anton, who raised his eyebrows as his gaze fixed on the crutches still under his arm.

"I saw you didn't have to use those once on the path. I think that's a first, no?"

Floris had been so caught up in his thoughts that he'd forgotten about the crutches. He also realized they hadn't exchanged more than a few words on the half-hour hike. "I suppose I really don't need them anymore," he said, before a sharp pain shot through his calves and he did his best to suppress a grimace.

After getting to the barracks, they found a few of their

comrades lounging in the sunshine. It was a pleasant day in late May, with just enough warmth to be comfortable, provided there wasn't too much of a breeze. One of them, a Berliner who had been recovering from shrapnel damage in both his knees, waved them over. "You're both to report to the admin building right away."

Floris cocked his head. "Said who?"

"Some messenger came looking for you about an hour ago, just after you left. I told him you'd be back before noon, wouldn't miss lunch." He chuckled. "The boy said you should report to the administration before lunch. Sorry."

Floris' stomach growled, but he ignored it. Whatever they needed from him at administration, it meant something was about to happen. Would he finally return to the front?

———

Floris and Anton were directed to a small office in the back of the administration building. They had never been here before, and Floris felt a flutter of excitement in his stomach. He was in high spirits after completing the hike that morning. Even though it was only a short distance, hardly comparable to the march-filled days on the eastern front, he knew Hitler's armies were struggling in their battle with the Soviets. Experienced soldiers like him and Anton would be invaluable.

"He'll be with you in a moment—take a seat." The young clerk pointed at two simple wooden chairs before closing the door, leaving Floris and Anton on their own.

They sat down and Floris couldn't contain his excitement any longer. "We're going back, I'm sure of it, Anton. They must've waited for both of us to be strong enough to return to the unit."

"I'm not so sure, Flo," Anton said, but Floris interrupted him, waving his finger.

"No, it can't be a coincidence that they're calling us in here when you just had your check-up this morning, and I've been walking around without crutches."

Anton looked hesitant, his eyes shifting between Floris' leg and face. "Do they know you're walking without your crutches yet? Wasn't this the first time now?"

"You wait. I'm sure they're sending us back." The door behind them swung open, and they turned to find the doctor treating Floris and a high-ranking Waffen-SS officer walk in. Floris and Anton shot to their feet and raised their right hands. *"Heil Hitler,"* they belted out in unison.

The officer returned their salute half-heartedly, mumbling the words as he indicated for them to sit down again. He had the rank of *Sturmbannführer*, a major, and he exuded all the confidence his rank required.

"Gentlemen, I'll get right to the point. Your recovery has taken quite some time, but we"—he signaled to the doctor alongside him —"have been impressed with your dedication in building up your strength. I've witnessed soldiers displaying less determination while recovering from lesser injuries. Especially you, Brouwer. You've not given up."

"Yes, sir." Floris inclined his head, barely concealing his delight at the officer's words.

The Sturmbannführer shuffled through some papers and placed them in front of Floris and Anton. "After consulting with *Herr Doktor*, I'm pleased to share you can return to active duty." A thin smile spread on his face. "You must be thrilled to leave this place."

Floris felt elated as he gripped the sides of the chair. He was returning to battle! He nodded enthusiastically and wanted to reach for the papers when the officer raised his hand.

"There is, however, one thing." His eyes shot to Floris' leg for a split second before picking up the papers and handing them to Floris and Anton. "Despite your incredible recovery, the medical staff has advised against frontline duty." Floris' heart sank as he took the paper from the Sturmbannführer. Were they assigning him behind the lines, in charge of supplies? He clenched his teeth; he wanted to fight. *I've earned this!* He was about to protest when the officer continued. "That is why you've been assigned as guards in one of our camps."

Floris looked up, his eyes going between the doctor and the officer. "Camps, sir?" The doctor looked uncomfortable and averted his gaze. The officer nodded and pointed to the bottom of the paper Floris was holding.

"You're going to join the SS regiment of guards at one of the most important prisoner and labor camps of the Reich and see that everything runs smoothly. It's an honorable and important job."

For Floris, it felt the complete opposite as he scanned the page, the words dancing in front of his eyes. He hardly registered what he was looking at until he reached the bottom. *Konzentrationslager Mauthausen*—concentration camp Mauthausen.

The name meant nothing to him.

CHAPTER THREE

The Receiver Room was buzzing. Nora was used to people looking over her shoulder, but this morning was different. As soon as she walked in for her shift at eight, she knew today would not be just another day. When she entered the Receiver Room, she was slightly overwhelmed to find not the usual team of five operators, but another half-dozen men and women in officers' uniforms crowding around. Machines lining the walls and the area directly behind Nora's desk made the room feel cramped in normal conditions. Now, with the officers jostling for space as well, Nora felt herself flush. She forced herself to take control of the situation as she sat down at her workstation and placed her headset over her ears, muffling the voices of the officers behind her.

Nora's eyes went to her screen, where a horizontal line appeared, interrupted at regular intervals by little blips pointing downward and constantly refreshed. At the top of her screen was a series of numbers from "0" to "100" showing distances in miles. The little blips were airplanes, and the closer they appeared to the left, to the zero on her screen, the closer they were to her station of Bawdsey, on England's southeast coast. This morning, Nora watched her screen filled with blips moving steadily to the right. These were the American bomber squadrons making their way across the North Sea, heading for targets in Germany. It had been like this for the past months, and Nora kept her eyes focused on the blips for ten minutes. When she was satisfied there were no unusual movements in her section, she removed her headset and turned to the woman next to her.

"Hey, Mary, what are the bigwigs doing down here?" She spoke in a low voice. "It's the first time I'm seeing so much interest in our work. And they're not asking us anything either?" Normally, whenever visitors appeared in the Receiver Room, they were guided by one of Nora's commanding officers, who explained what the young women were doing. Outside this room, they weren't to breathe a word of what went on inside.

Mary shrugged. "Don't know, and I'll tell you something else, I don't really care. I don't really fancy explaining what I'm doing here for the umpteenth time." She pointed at her own screen. "Looks like the first American planes have reached the Dutch coast. I wonder where they're going today."

Nora glanced at her own screen again, making sure everything was still in order. All but a few of the blips had moved almost entirely to the right of her screen. Soon, they would disappear from range, and she would have to wait for them to return in a few hours. Even though that technically meant her work would be a bit easier, it also meant she had to be extra vigilant not to lose her concentration. When their own planes left for Europe, their paths were predictable and easy to track. She was more concerned about the planes heading in the other direction, toward Britain. The Nazis had started launching unmanned airplanes, called V-1s. Even though they flew a lot faster than the regular airplanes of the *Luftwaffe*, they were also more predictable, for they flew in straight lines and at a consistent speed. Nevertheless, as soon as Nora or one of the other women in the Receiver Room spotted one, they needed to act swiftly to give the pilots of the Royal Air Force a chance at intercepting them. Some of the pilots involved had come down to Bawdsey to see how the women tracked the V-1s. One of the pilots had shared their approach in disabling the rocket planes. They would position their own planes just ahead of the V-1, then allow it to catch up and tip its wing to send it crashing into the sea.

She eyed her screen again, and just as she confirmed most of the American bombers had left range, she saw a blip appear slightly off the middle of her screen, indicating it was some 60 miles out. She frowned as she sat up straight and put her headset back on. Had she missed the plane in the crowd of bombers heading in the other direction? She scoffed; that would be reckless. Nora impatiently stared at the screen, waiting for the blip to move. There was something else that bothered her: the plane wasn't sending out the required IFF signal, which, in the case of the American and British planes, would mark it as a friendly craft on her screen.

Her screen refreshed and Nora let out a sigh. The blip had moved farther left. It was heading toward Britain, and still unidentified. Nora turned around in her chair, took off her headphones and walked over to her supervisor. Wing Officer Anna Lewis, standing near the group of visitors, was patiently explaining how they plotted enemy aircraft.

"Ma'am, sorry to bother you, but might I borrow you for a second?" Nora spoke politely but firmly. She didn't salute her superior officer; Lewis had made it clear to the women under her command that such formalities were not required in the Receiver Room, where time was often of the essence.

Lewis picked up on the polite urgency in Nora's tone and quickly excused herself from the group, following Nora to her screen. "Did something happen to the bombers?"

Nora shook her head, returned to her seat, and placed her headset over one of her ears. "No, ma'am, I tracked them all the way across the North Sea. It's this blip I'm concerned about." She pointed at her screen, where the plane had moved farther left, now some 45 miles from the English coast.

Lewis' eyes shot across Nora's screen, and without missing a beat, she said, "Where is its IFF designation? Was it part of the group heading out?"

Nora hesitated only for a second before replying. "No, ma'am, I would've picked up the abnormal signal."

"Are you sure?" Lewis' gaze shifted from the screen to Nora. "In between those hundreds of bombers heading out, it's possible to miss one with a malfunctioning IFF system. Did you see it turn around?"

"I did not see it turn around, ma'am." Nora spoke softly, slightly ashamed of missing the plane earlier. "It appeared on my screen at sixty miles out."

Lewis kept her eyes glued to the screen. When the screen refreshed, the plane had hardly moved, the blip between 40 and 45 miles out. Lewis frowned. "That's odd. Has it been moving this slowly all the time?"

The observation startled Nora. She had been so focused on fixing her mistake that she hadn't noticed the plane's airspeed was abnormally low. Feeling her cheeks flush, she caught herself before answering. "It does seem off." At this speed, she dismissed the threat of a V-1, then corrected herself; it could be a V-1 with a busted engine.

"Have you tried contacting them?" When Nora shook her head, Lewis pointed at her radio. "Try that now." Lewis looked worried, and Nora cursed herself for not thinking of that earlier. She turned to her radio and sent out a neutral message. "British mainland calling unidentified plane bearing two seven zero, at forty miles out, identify yourself."

Nora held her breath as she listened to the static crackle from her headphone. Her heart pounded in her chest as she kept her eyes fixed on her screen, praying the pilots heard her. After thirty seconds, Nora repeated the call. Again, there was no response. She turned to Lewis.

"Do you want me to instruct the AA crews on the coast to look out for the plane?" The antiaircraft guns were posted all along the coasts, and it wouldn't be the first time Nora relayed suspicious air traffic to the men and women scanning the skies. The last time that they had shot down a number of V-1s on Nora's observations, they had celebrated the win with her in a pub in London when on leave together. Nora had great respect for the men and women manning the big guns, for they were prime targets for the Luftwaffe.

Lewis shook her head. "Hold off on that for one second. Something's wrong with this plane. Even though we can't identify them, they must know we can see them, or at least will when they reach the coast. Why would they risk it?" She rubbed her nose for a moment, her eyes distant as she weighed her next words. Then she turned to Nora. "We should intercept. Contact Newchurch and tell them to get eyes up there."

"Yes, ma'am." Nora changed radio frequency and was soon in contact with Royal Air Force Station Newchurch, located some 80 miles south. Lewis stood behind Nora as she spoke to Fighter Command. Nora kept her eyes on her screen and relayed the position of the plane. She thanked the dispatcher and turned to Lewis. "They're on their way, ma'am. I should have contact with them as soon as they're airborne."

For the first time that morning, Lewis looked a little shaken. "I pray we made the right decision, Brouwer. If this is a trap, we're sending those boys right into it."

Nora returned her focus to her screen. If the plane continued at the same speed, and the RAF planes were airborne within five minutes, they should be able to intercept it at least ten miles from the British shore. That left them enough time to shoot it down without any civilian casualties on the ground.

As she waited for the pilots to make contact, she considered her own journey to England. It had been less than half a year ago when she arrived in England by plane from Gibraltar. She had traveled across the continent from her home in Amsterdam to Gibraltar with three strangers. At least, that's what Katja, Arthur, and Lars started out as. Somehow, they hadn't been caught, despite several close brushes with the Nazi authorities. Upon arrival in England, Nora and her friends were subjected to a long questioning by British intelligence, and for a while she wondered why she had been so determined to come to England in the first place. After the agents appeared satisfied with their reasons for coming to England they were moved to London. The friends were soon offered different assignments. Much to her delight, Katja was accepted to the Dutch merchant fleet. Arthur's limited medical background proved enough to earn him a spot in a London hospital. Lars signed up to join the small division of the Dutch Royal Air Force in England. They promised to stay in touch, but Nora knew the reality of the war meant that would be nigh impossible. Whatever happened to them, Nora prayed they would somehow meet again. She'd formed a strong bond with her fellow *Engelandvaarders,* England sailors.

Nora initially moved in with Lisa Abrahams, her brother-in-law Christiaan's girlfriend. After a few days, Lisa handed her an invitation to one of the RAF's London offices, telling her a mutual friend would like to talk to her. Startled and more than a little curious, she had reported to the offices to find a young man welcoming her. He introduced himself as Gareth and explained Lisa and Christiaan had smuggled him from Geneva back to London, and he owed them his life. He said Lisa had asked if there was anything Nora could do to contribute to the fight against the Nazis, and Gareth asked if Nora was interested in keeping the skies safe. Gareth had suggested she join the Women's Auxiliary Air Force, the WAAF. With her knowledge of German, she had quickly been assigned to radar operations, and that's how she ended up in the Receiver Room in Bawdsey.

There was static in her headphones, followed by a voice. "Big Ben, Firebirds Able and Baker on our way, ma'am. Please provide coordinates."

Nora relayed the position of the plane and waited. Soon two blips appeared on her screen, showing the RAF Tempest fighters at 60 miles out. The pilots on the other side of the connection were mostly silent, occasionally requesting confirmation they were still headed in the right direction. Nora was continuously plotting the course of the unidentified plane, but it was easy; it continued following the same predictable course, never changing speed or altitude.

It took less than ten minutes for the Tempests to make visual contact. "It's a big one, ma'am. Looks like a bomber, but I can't quite make out the shape from this far away. We're closing in."

Lewis had sat next to Nora and also plugged in a headset. The two women looked at each other. Without saying a word, Nora knew they were both thinking the same thing. Were the Germans bold enough to send a large bomber across the Channel on its own, hoping they wouldn't detect it? It was madness. Nora leaned forward in her chair, the blips on her screen now almost overlapping. Soon, the three planes would merge to form one blip.

Her headphones crackled. "Umm, this is a bit odd, and I'm not entirely sure, but I think what we're seeing is one of—" The pilot's voice was abruptly cut off.

Nora frowned and checked her radio. It was functional, the dials showing her set was receiving signals. "What happened?" She switched her attention to her screen, which refreshed to show the two Tempests merge into the signal of the larger plane. Nora swallowed hard. She pressed the transmission button. "Firebirds Able, Baker, report. What do you see?"

Nora felt her neck burn. Without a radio connection, she was unable to make out what happened to their Tempests. Lewis let out a frustrated sigh but kept her face composed.

"Call them one more time. If there's no response, we inform the antiaircraft stations and Fighter Command."

Nora did as she was told, even though she knew Fighter Command was aware of what was happening. They were on the same frequency and heard everything. After thirty seconds, there was still only static on the headset. Lewis pushed back her chair and stood.

"I'm calling Fighter Command; something is clearly wrong." Lewis moved across the room toward a telephone.

Nora stayed in her seat and felt her stomach turn. She worried about the pilots of the Tempests that had been in her ears just minutes ago. What had happened? Had they been shot down by the unidentified plane? Even though she didn't want to consider the possibility, there was little other explanation for the sudden radio silence. She transmitted her request one more time as she eyed Lewis on the phone with Fighter Command. Her superior officer would instruct them to send out more Tempests, as well as have the antiaircraft crews on the coast on full alert.

"Big Ben, this is Firebird Baker. Do you copy?"

Nora could hardly believe her ears as the unfamiliar voice of the Firebird wingman crackled through her headphones. She almost slammed her hand on the transmit button. "This is Big Ben; you're coming in loud and clear. What happened?"

The response was immediate. "Not sure, Big Ben, but sure happy to hear your voice. Seems like we lost the connection for a bit there. Requesting permission for a high-priority escort to Woodbridge."

For a moment, Nora had trouble processing the words. *Escort?* She looked up to find Lewis standing next to her, eyes questioning. She decided the pilot had priority. "Escort for what, Firebird Baker? Is Able operational?"

"Roger that. We've identified the other bird. It's one of our Lancasters, but it's pretty banged up, struggling to keep altitude. Their radio has been blown out, and I'm pretty sure so has their IFF. We've got visual contact with the crew, though."

Another voice came over the air. "Firebird Able, Baker, this is Fighter Command. Permission to escort and land at Woodbridge granted. Big Ben, please hand over to Woodbridge tower."

"Roger that, Fighter Command. Cheers, Big Ben, thanks for the ride."

Nora took off her headset and watched the blips disappear from her screen.

"Good job, Brouwer." Lewis' voice startled her as she turned to the wing officer. "You kept your composure in a rather stressful situation."

Despite her frayed nerves, Nora smiled at her commanding officer's understated way of describing the situation. Nora felt she had lost control after her brief lapse in concentration. She didn't recall feeling more anxious than a few minutes ago, when they lost radio contact with the Tempests. But she wasn't going to tell Lewis that. "Thank you, ma'am. Permission to take a break?"

Lewis laughed out loud. "Yes, Brouwer, go get yourself a cuppa. You deserve it. I'll see you in half an hour."

Nora handed over control of her section to a new operator, and she quickly made her way toward the exit. She opened the door and breathed in the fresh sea air.

CHAPTER FOUR

Sixty miles to the south, in London, Lisa Abrahams furiously scribbled to keep up with the men talking in rapid succession. The large conference room of the *Bureau Inlichtingen*, the Dutch government's intelligence branch, was packed. Lisa sat next to her boss, Jan Marginus Somer. One of the British agents was explaining the mechanics of something she didn't quite understand, and Somer leaned toward Lisa.

"Don't worry too much about these details," he whispered. "What the Americans are about to share will be more interesting."

Lisa smiled gratefully while she continued to jot down her notes, hoping they would make sense after the meeting. Somer had always been a great boss to her, especially after she became his personal secretary. He involved her in all the important meetings and often asked for her opinion. She was especially pleased to be in the current meeting, and she couldn't deny she was impatient to hear what the Americans had to say. She eyed the two men on the far side of the table, who had spent the first half hour of the meeting politely listening to the brawny British agent hogging the conversation. He kept emphasizing the importance of his country's intelligence network in the preparations for Operation Overlord. Lisa suppressed a chuckle, remembering how last year Somer and she had uncovered a particularly disturbing bit of evidence on the Special Operations Executive's functioning.

Unbeknown to British intelligence, the Germans had compromised the SOE's network of Dutch spies parachuting into the Netherlands. As soon as the young men touched down on home soil, the Nazis would be waiting for them. It was Lisa who spotted that a suspiciously high number of messages—supposedly sent from their agents in the Netherlands—were missing their safety checks. This coded communication was unique to each operative, and verified the message was sent by them without duress. Their suspicions were confirmed when word came from Somer's new, uncompromised network. Two captured spies had escaped from a prison holding nearly fifty Dutch agents and had contacted Somer's Amsterdam-based resistance cell. The SOE network was compromised, they said; they should stop sending agents.

When Lisa and Somer presented their findings to their British colleagues at the SOE, they were quick to dismiss their claims. From that moment, Somer decided to use only his own, smaller network for communications with the Netherlands. So Lisa was one of the first people to know what was happening back home, as agents communicated directly and exclusively with the Bureau Inlichtingen.

It was thanks to this network that she could keep track of how Christiaan was doing. He was one of the first agents sent back to the Netherlands through Somer's network. His mission was to connect with the many resistance cells back home and find a way to unite them. The plan was to create a unified resistance network that prepared for the Allied liberation of the Netherlands.

As always, things didn't turn out quite how they had hoped, and Lisa felt a stab of pain in her heart. Christiaan's last message had been over six months ago—he had vanished, and no one knew where he had gone. He hadn't shown up for a meeting with one of the resistance leaders. Soon, rumors surfaced of his arrest. If Christiaan was arrested, the chances of his brother Floris being involved were frightfully real. The brothers had been on opposite sides ever since the occupation, with Floris choosing the side of the Nazis, while Christiaan covertly joined the resistance.

It had been Christiaan who saved Lisa when her hiding spot was discovered, managing to move her only hours before the Nazis broke down the door and took her parents away. When Floris found out about his brother's involvement in the resistance, there was no other option but to flee the country.

Christiaan and Lisa had made it to the safety of Switzerland, and everything had been wonderful at first. They found jobs at the Dutch consulate in Geneva and helped other Dutch refugees find their feet. But after a few months, Christiaan became restless. He wanted to do more, he wanted to fight the oppressors. That's when he and Lisa helped smuggle a British pilot to Spain. After arriving in England, Lisa started working at the Bureau Inlichtingen, and Christiaan started training to become a spy, dropping back into the Netherlands last summer.

"Lisa, would you mind recapping our recent efforts around FUSAG?" Somer's voice brought her back to the conference room in London. She looked up to find all the men at the table looking at her. She felt flushed for a second, then shuffled some papers and found her composure.

"Certainly, sir." Lisa cleared her throat, buying a few extra seconds to catch her train of thought. "We've kept communications around the preparations of General Patton's army at a steady pace. I've asked our radio operators to send our embassies and consulates on the mainland classified updates on new troop movements around Ipswich and Little Waltham, focusing on the US Fourteenth Infantry divisions." She smiled as she saw the surprised looks of some of the men in the room. She knew by heart the names and positions of the army corps and divisions that made up General George Patton's First United States Army Group, FUSAG.

"And we're certain these broadcasts are picked up by German

intelligence?" one of the British agents asked. Lisa suppressed a smile when she saw one of the American officers grin.

"Yes, sir, absolutely. We're utilizing several channels we're certain are compromised." She gave a knowing look to Somer, who kept his face impassive.

"Such as?"

"We have German double agents feeding information to Berlin. Apart from them, we know a small number of our consulates have been known to, umm, leak certain information."

"Most importantly, the information sent by our Dutch allies has been consistent with other methods of misdirection in Britain." One of the American agents stood up and moved toward a map of Britain and the coastline of western Europe. He moved his finger from Dover across the narrow body of water separating Britain and France. "Hitler continues to assemble more troops in the Calais area, confirming our FUSAG approach is working. They are clearly expecting our invasion across the Strait of Dover."

Lisa listened as the officer explained how the buildup of German troops in Calais diminished the Nazis defensive strength across the rest of the western European coast. Operation Quicksilver appeared to be paying off. When Somer asked her to assist in a top-secret operation designed to misdirect Nazi defenses, she was delighted to be able to make a big difference to the war effort from London.

The First United States Army Group they were discussing wasn't real. Instead, the Allied forces had deployed phantom armies across the south coast of England. Cardboard tanks, landing craft, and massive tent camps had been erected for the benefit of the Luftwaffe spy planes flying high overhead. Even though Lisa had never been to one of the sites, she had seen the photos. She had to admit that, even from a distance at ground level, the military vehicles looked damn convincing. From the sky, the FUSAG looked every bit the army it was pretending to be. The scheme was so elaborate that tractors created simulated tank tracks under the cover of darkness.

"Taking everything into consideration, this means we should

intensify communications to the highest level." The American sat down again and there was tangible excitement in the room as the men pondered the man's words for a moment. Lisa felt a tingle in her stomach as the magnitude of the man's words hit her. *It's happening soon.*

———

The other men had filed out of the room and Lisa was cleaning up, collecting empty coffee mugs on a tray. As the only woman in the group, that task unfortunately still befell her. Her eyes fell on the map on the wall, and she wondered where the invasion would take place, if not Calais. It really was the most logical place to cross, with less than fifty kilometers of water between Britain and France. She considered the brilliance of the plan and hoped the intelligence about Hitler building up his forces at Calais was correct. She always worried the Germans had seen through their ruse and were simply responding in kind. The German counterintelligence's success in infiltrating the Special Operations Executive's Dutch spy network had her questioning everything, all the time.

"Lisa, are you all right?"

She looked up to find Somer standing in the doorway. She straightened her back and forced a smile. "Absolutely. Just tidying up here."

"I think you can leave those. We'll get someone else to clean up later," he said as he stepped into the room and closed the door. "I was impressed with your quick analysis just now. And I could see the others felt the same. Especially the Americans."

"Thank you," Lisa said, and she meant it. "But I've been working with Josh and Stan for so long now that they know what to expect, I think."

"Regardless, I'm pleased it went so well. You've never let me down." Lisa could think of a few instances where she had, but she kept her lips pressed together. "That's why I would like you to initiate the next phase in the communications plans."

Lisa put her hands on the large conference table and looked at her boss. "Really? I thought you would want to brief the women in the radio room yourself. This is a big deal."

"That's exactly why I want you to do it. Nobody in this building has been more involved in Quicksilver than you." Somer smiled broadly, a rarity.

She felt herself blushing. "When, sir?"

"Right away, of course. The sooner they think we're launching a full-scale invasion at Calais, the better."

"Can I ask you something?" She shuffled on her feet.

"Come on, Lisa. We've been working closely together for over a year now. You know you don't have to ask me permission to speak your mind."

"Apologies, sir." She smiled weakly, realizing she had just sat in perhaps the most classified meeting of the year. "Do you think it's happening soon? The actual invasion? This is the first time we're scaling up to this level of communications. I mean, I realize we're pretending FUSAG is going to attack, but do you think the actual armies will be making their way toward the mainland?"

Somer didn't immediately respond, but leaned on the back of one of the large chairs. "I can't say for sure, but I think we're on the eve of the great invasion. Even though we've been involved mostly in Quicksilver, it's impossible to miss the troop buildup all around the country, isn't it? And it's not just the American bomber squadrons. Even on the streets in London, I hear the American and Canadian accents all the time. I spoke to a few of them the other night, and they were certain they would set off for the mainland soon." He stepped back from the chair, a look on his face Lisa couldn't quite place. "But those men in here today, they're high up. They know a lot more of what's going on than what they're sharing with us. And if they tell us it's time to communicate that we're preparing to move out FUSAG, then I believe the actual invasion can't be far away."

Lisa nodded, pleased to hear Somer confirming her own thoughts. "Thank you for being frank with me, sir."

"Always, Lisa. Now, come on, let's get the message out. General Patton's First United States Army Group is preparing to ship out!" He winked at her before turning on his heel. "That should get the attention of the Nazi commanders."

CHAPTER FIVE

Floris admired himself in the mirror. He was clean-shaven, his eyes were clear, and he felt fresh after a good night's rest. The field gray SS uniform felt familiar, even if the markings on his shoulder straps differed from his previous Waffen-SS uniform's. He felt the same pride as he nodded at himself in the mirror and left the bathroom.

He stepped out of the barracks and shielded his eyes from the bright June morning sunshine. The mountain air felt crisp and clean. After his stay in Graz, he had come to appreciate the Austrian landscape, especially the mountains. Floris puffed his chest, a little surprised to find himself looking forward to starting his new job in Mauthausen today. Anton had been right, after all.

Floris had been disappointed with the new assignment. He'd considered going back to the SS officer and doctor and asking if they would reconsider him for duty on the eastern front. He would even be happy to assist behind the lines, peeling potatoes, cooking, or whatnot. Anything to be involved in the war effort. Anton had convinced him it was a terrible idea. He had sat Floris down and explained the doctors were right; they were in no condition to serve.

Had Floris ever seen a frontline soldier with a limp? And had he forgotten about the overwhelmingly powerful Red Army? They survived only by pure luck. Floris had protested, but he knew his friend was right. It wasn't just their close brush with death in the city when the building collapsed onto them. They had suffered plenty of setbacks on their campaign, on the battlefields. And when they were recovering from their injuries in Graz, news from the front was hardly encouraging, as the German armies were pushed back west every day. Floris shook his head; he had been lucky to be assigned guard duty at this camp in the heart of the Reich.

"Ready for the first day?"

Floris turned to find Anton: he looked sharp in his neatly pressed uniform.

"It'll be good to have something on our hands again, right?" Floris started walking down the main camp road. They had arrived by train the day prior, and most prisoners had been at work outside the camp. The guard welcoming them had pointed out the administration block and the guards' quarters before informing them their shifts would start the next day. They only had to pick up their uniforms and could use the rest of the day to get acquainted with their surroundings. They would learn the rest they needed to know about life at Mauthausen the next day. It won't be hard, he had ensured them.

They arrived at the administration building, where a dozen guards milled about. Floris noticed they all had the same rank as him and Anton and felt his confidence growing. Even though the hospital in Graz was filled with Waffen-SS like himself, he had never felt a need to bond with any of them. Most passed through within weeks, and Floris had soon given up on trying to make meaningful connections. In Mauthausen, looking at the men wearing the same uniform and carrying out the same job, everything was different. Here, he could work himself up the chain of command, perhaps find a new career.

Floris and Anton joined the group, and some of the men

acknowledged them, but none gave a hint of being interested in conversation. Floris turned to Anton. "Did you speak to anyone yesterday?"

"Just the two guys sleeping across from me. Told me not to worry too much about the first few days' assignments. They said they will show us how it's done."

"Yeah, same," Floris said while scanning the area. The main road was relatively quiet, although Floris could hear men going to the latrines and preparing for roll call on the other side, where the prisoner blocks were located.

The door of the administration building opened, revealing a tall, bulky man wearing the uniform of an *Untersturmführer*. The guards outside sprang to attention and saluted him, and Floris and Anton joined in. The officer returned the salute and signaled for them to be at ease. Floris was surprised by the man's youthful appearance. He looked to be in his midtwenties, yet exuded the confidence of a seasoned officer as he inspected the men with calm, calculating eyes. Floris made an effort to hold the man's gaze but found it impossible to make out anything from the piercing blue eyes staring back at him.

Apparently satisfied, the officer clapped his hands. "Right, gentlemen. Welcome to Mauthausen. On behalf of camp commander Ziereis, I'm glad to have you join us. There is much work to be done here, and the number of prisoners has only been growing. We can certainly use your help and expect you'll be putting in your best efforts in keeping the prisoners of Mauthausen in line and motivated."

The officer spoke in a condescending tone, the way a teacher would speak to a group of schoolchildren on their first day of classes. Floris bit his lip to keep his face neutral as he struggled to contain the scowl forming behind the mask he was putting up.

"My name is Untersturmführer Herchenbach, and I'll escort you to roll call today." He glanced at the clipboard in his left hand. "But before we leave, I'll share your assignments for the day. After roll call, you'll join a group of experienced guards as they take out the work details. They'll bring you up to speed on what is expected of a guard in Mauthausen."

Floris was one of the first to receive his assignment, which turned out to be the same for all but a few of them lining up. They would accompany the largest group to the *Wiener Graben*, the Vienna Quarry, just outside the camp. As the group of new guards followed Herchenbach to the *Appellplatz*, the roll call area, he explained that the quarry was one of the most important elements of the camp, providing granite for the entire Reich. In fact, he was proud to mention as he pointed up to the walls surrounding them, this camp was built using the very granite they mined down there.

With every word he spoke, Floris found his dislike for the Untersturmführer grow. He was relieved when Herchenbach told them to report to the guards who would be taking them along today. As Floris and Anton did, they were told to simply stand to the side and observe.

"You're welcome to join in the activities later this week," one of the older guards said with a grin. "Now stand to the side; the prisoners will be here any minute."

It was silent for a few minutes, and Floris looked around. The grim features of the other guards sent a shiver down Floris' spine. Overhead a single hooded crow circled the area, cawing. The bird's call was followed by the sound of hundreds of feet shuffling down the main granite-pebbled road. A seemingly endless column of men wearing a ragtag assortment of clothes entered the roll call area. They kept their gazes focused firmly on their feet, avoiding any form of eye contact with the guards. Their clothes hung either too loosely or fitted too tightly around their bodies. Their heads were shaven, but that wasn't what caught Floris' attention. The creatures lining up in neat rows of ten could hardly be called men. One of the prisoner's eyes were sunken unnaturally deep in his face, and it took Floris a few seconds to realize it only appeared that way because of his hollow cheeks, his jaw sticking out like he'd never seen before. As his eyes scanned the crowd, he found few prisoners in a better state. These men were walking skeletons, clinging onto life in name only. He wondered where his work detail was, for he couldn't imagine any of these wretched creatures chipping away at granite.

Roll call stretched into an hour, and it proved too much for at least two dozen prisoners. Without warning, their legs gave out and they landed on the ground with loud thuds.. No amount of threats or beatings by the guards convinced the men to rise, and they were unceremoniously dragged away.

Another hour later, the guards leading the roll call were finally satisfied, and Floris walked along a column of prisoners heading toward the camp's gate. He looked at the men he would need to guard today and decided this would be the easiest job he ever had. These men wouldn't be able to run fifty meters if they wanted to.

———

It was almost eight when they reached the quarry, the sun steadily making its way up in the sky, and the quarry ridge basked in the sunshine. Floris followed a small group of guards stationed at the bottom of the quarry. As they made their way down and into the shade, Floris could feel his hairs stand on end. He looked at the prisoners, who appeared relieved to escape the sun. They picked up their tools and were soon chipping away at the towering granite walls surrounding them. As Floris observed from a distance, he marveled at the size of the quarry, and the number of prisoners slaving away. He stood with the rest of the guards who were chatting and appeared indifferent to the masses of slave laborers. Weren't they supposed to make sure the prisoners weren't slacking off?

It took less than a minute for a cry of agony to echo between the walls of the quarry. Floris turned to the source of the sound. In the middle of a group of prisoners a man lay on the ground, his pickax on the ground beside him. Another prisoner was flailing him with a large piece of wood. The man dishing out the beating was in a fit of rage, his cheeks flushed red, while yelling at the man on the ground in a language Floris didn't understand. Floris glanced at the other guards, who looked on with amused expressions.

"You see? The prisoners take care of the weaker ones. We don't really have to do much," one of them said. "If you want, you can take a closer look, see if he's still alive. I doubt it, though."

The man on the ground was no longer resisting. His arms were by his sides while the other man bashed the now-bloody piece of wood into his skull. Floris stood frozen. Nearby prisoners continued working, apparently oblivious to what was happening only a short distance away. Finally, the man dropped his piece of wood and looked around with an air of accomplishment. He wore a prisoners' uniform like the others, but with one important added accessory. Prominently displayed on his right arm was a white armband. In red letters it read *"Kapo."* Floris approached the man, who was inspecting his murderous handiwork, leaning over the downed man's face to check if he was still breathing. When he noticed Floris, he sprang to attention.

"Sir, I caught this man skipping work. He was resting on that stone over there, while the other were working." The man spoke in heavily accented German, and Floris suspected he came from the east. There had been plenty of Ukrainian soldiers serving the Waffen-SS on the eastern front, and the man's accent was familiar.

Floris looked at the broken body on the ground. The dead man lay in an unnatural position, his face and head permanently distorted by a gaping wound that bled profusely onto the ground. The force of the blows had been so strong that it had broken the bones within the man's skull and crushed them like eggshells. Before Floris could say anything, another guard appeared next to him.

"Get some others to put his body on one of the carts over there," he said to the Kapo while pointing at a cart farther down the quarry. Floris caught four men lifting another corpse onto the cart. The four men the Kapo picked out hardly seemed bothered as they lifted the body and headed toward the cart in an apathetic stupor.

"That's what the Kapos are here for. They make sure none of the prisoners get any ideas," the guard said nonchalantly. As he turned back to his group of friends, he added, "Welcome to Mauthausen. You'll get used to it."

With the guard's words echoing in his head, Floris had a feeling the casual murder of one prisoner by another only scratched the surface of what this camp was about. Suddenly, he wasn't so sure he wouldn't rather be on the eastern front.

CHAPTER SIX

L isa reported to the office earlier than usual. She normally arrived at eight, but Somer had asked her to come in at six. Today might well be the day. Crossing the hallway she looked into the radio room. The ladies were already there, and her pulse increased. She waved at Linda, who yawned but smiled and returned the wave, bleary eyed.

It had been a busy week. After Somer had asked her to increase communications, Lisa had set the women to work, providing numerous messages they were to send to their embassies on the mainland. Lisa had prepared the messages months in advance and felt proud as she stood listening to the women tapping and talking away on the wireless. After they had notified the official channels, they moved on to their agents, hiding and spread throughout the Netherlands. The messages sent to these men were slightly different. Even though there was no sign any of their agents had been compromised, Somer and Lisa wanted to make sure they didn't endanger the agents or their missions. They told the men that the invasion was due to start any day now, and they should prepare accordingly. It was code for getting their cells ready to blow up German communi-

40

cation and railway lines when the Allied forces reached the Netherlands. Lisa suspected that might take a few months, even if the
initial landing went according to plan. But if the Germans expected
FUSAG landing in Calais, it wouldn't take long to make it north to
the Netherlands. It all made sense.

The door to her boss's office was open, and she quickly rapped
her knuckles on the doorway while she entered. Somer looked up
from his desk, littered with papers and files.

"Morning, Lisa. Good to see you. Hope you had a proper rest; it's
going to be a long day." He signaled to a chair opposite. "I want to
show you why I called you in early today."

She sat down but couldn't contain her curiosity. "It's happening
today, isn't it?"

"It already has. The first ships left port a few hours ago, and more
are leaving as we speak. These are the slower ships, and it will take
them the whole day and night to make it to the rendezvous points."

A jolt of excitement shot through Lisa's body. They had been
working toward this point for over half a year, and even though
every meeting indicated things were moving forward, those in the
know always appeared hesitant to commit. Even after carrying out
her plan of increased communications the past few days, she knew
the operation could be called off at any time. To know the first boats
were on their way to the European mainland gave her hope beyond
measure. "What would you like me to do, sir?"

Somer picked up a large folder and slid it across the table. "This
is the planned timeline of Operation Overlord." He chuckled as he
handed it to Lisa. "Well, everything they want us to know, I suppose.
What you're about to read is highly classified, and you're not to
breathe a word of it outside this office."

Lisa leafed through the thin document, scanning some of the
first pages. The writing was compact, the sentences short and
written in the functional military style she'd become used to. It made
it easier for her to plan her actions. There was no fluff, and very little
chance of misinterpretation. Somer picked up a folder of his own,

and they sat in silence for fifteen minutes while Lisa soaked up the information. Even though she knew this would be a massive operation, her mind boggled at the numbers on the pages. She had to double-check the number of planes involved. More than ten thousand. When she finished reading, she closed the folder, carefully placed it back on the desk, and looked to Somer.

"So, what will you have me do? I assume we're sending more messages to Europe?"

Somer nodded. "I'd like you to instruct the radio room to send messages of the invasion forces moving out in a few hours. That should give you some time to tweak your message based on this information, yes?"

"I don't think I need to change much. The messaging this week has been clear about the planned landing at Calais. A few of our agents reported back, saying they picked up increased German communications about the impending invasion. I think our ploy is working just fine."

"So, it's only a matter of doubling down."

"Exactly, sir. I'll go and grab the message and you can see if you require any changes." She stood from her chair, anxious to get started. "Was there anything else you needed?"

A nervous smile appeared on her boss's face. "You know, Lisa, when you joined the Bureau in the typists' room, I knew you were different. Not many Jewish refugees reaching Geneva would take the risk of making another crossing through France and Spain to get to England. It would've been easier for you to stay put and wait for the war to end."

Lisa was taken aback but recovered quickly. "It wasn't just my decision. Christiaan was very passionate about coming here, and it was always his intention to take the fight to the Germans back home." She paused for a moment as the face of the man she loved flashed in her mind. She prayed he was alive, wherever he was. Her eyes shot to the briefing document on the desk. *We're coming for you.*

Somer picked up on her emotions. "Christiaan has been invaluable in setting up the very network we're using to communicate with home," he said in a softer voice than usual. "He's smart and resourceful. I know you worry about him, and I do too, like I do about all my agents, but we need to trust he's working in the shadows."

"I know, sir, and I'm proud of him. Jumping out of that airplane with the likelihood of the Germans waiting for him on landing was heroic." She took a deep breath and composed herself, rolling her shoulders. "The thought of him returning to me alive is what keeps me going, and what motivates me to push just that bit harder in everything I do around here. I'd like to believe it's no coincidence that I'm doing what I am today."

"I know it isn't, Lisa, and I'm glad you're here, on my team."

"Thank you, sir. I'm just glad to be working on something so important." She suddenly felt awkward standing in the middle of the room. "Shall I just go and grab that message for you?"

Somer nodded, and Lisa hurried to her own little office across the hallway. She opened a drawer and picked out a thin brown manila folder. As she turned back to hand it to Somer, her head was buzzing. They were on the brink of something that would change the course of history, and she was in the middle of it.

CHAPTER SEVEN

It was close to midnight and the area around the Bawdsey radar station was covered in darkness. The plain-looking concrete building hid a beehive of activity inside.

Nora was glued to her screen in the Receiver Room, where all stations were manned. Each of the ten operators had an additional WAAF support person, making sure there was plenty of backup available. Nora was so mesmerized by what was happening on her screen that she didn't notice the officers circling the room, observing the screens, and overhearing the conversations the women had with the radio operators on board the countless planes and warships making their way across the North Sea and, to the south, the Channel.

When she left her shift the night before, Wing Officer Lewis had told her to make sure she was well rested for the next day. She shared an apartment with Phyllis, another radar operator. Even though they weren't supposed to discuss work outside Bawdsey's walls, they agreed something was about to happen. Phyllis had just returned from London, where she spent her two days off. She'd never seen so many army vehicles making their way through the city. The soldiers in the trucks were kitted out in full uniform, and there was no doubt they were heading for the ports dotted on England's southeastern coast.

Now, an hour into their shift, Nora's and Phyllis's suspicions were confirmed as Nora struggled to keep up with the massive number of planes in her section. It was hard to tell the exact number, and she was grateful that she didn't have to communicate with all the planes at the same time. They flew in large formations and had their targets set. Nora's job was to keep an eye out for potential German responses. So far, there had been none, and Nora tracked the American bombers as they continued their southern course, sticking to the relative safety of the sea for as long as possible. They would soon line up for their targets on the French coast.

Fifteen minutes later, the airplanes left her section and disappeared from the screen. It was odd to have an almost empty screen, and it gave Nora some time to think about what the men in those airplanes were about to do. Lewis had briefed the operators in the Receiver Room just before they started their shift. Tonight's planes didn't carry their usual payload of explosives like in the months prior. Instead, their fuselages were filled with men ready to jump and deploy their parachutes. They would land behind German defenses on the French coast and set up beacons for the ships making their way across the Channel. Nora wondered how it must feel for these young men as they sat in the planes' hulls, waiting to jump into the darkness of the night, praying the wind wouldn't blow them off course and into the vision of the German defenses. These men carried out some of the most dangerous and crucial jobs of the invasion. Without the beacons, the approach of the thousands of ships making their way toward the Normandy coast would be severely handicapped. Even though Nora wasn't religious, she caught herself whispering a prayer.

"All birds have left range." It was the familiar voice of Wing Officer Lewis. "They've all gone dark. Now we wait." Despite completing the first part of the mission, there was no cheer in Bawdsey's Receiver Room. All those present knew the most difficult part of the night was before them, and there was nothing they could do about it. They had played their part. It was up to the flight and paratrooper crews some sixty miles away. Nora was suddenly very tired and felt the need to stretch her legs. She motioned for the woman next to her to take over.

She was relieved to see she wasn't alone as more women stood up and headed for the door. "Take fifteen minutes, ladies. Let's make sure we're ready when they return. We don't know what may have happened on the other side," Lewis said as the women filed out.

Nora made her way to the canteen, where she was pleased to find Phyllis pouring a cup of coffee. Phyllis noticed her roommate and grabbed another cup. "I'm sure you can use one as well," she said as she handed the cup to Nora.

"I feel like I've already spent an entire shift, but it's only been two hours. I've never seen anything like the number of planes heading over tonight," Nora said as they found a spot in the middle of the room. "It's funny—normally I can make out the planes in my section. But today I couldn't count the individual planes anymore. And to think they're carrying all those paratroopers with them. There must've been thousands of men crossing tonight."

"Don't forget about the ships." Phyllis took a sip. "The entire fleet has left Britain. There are tens of thousands of men preparing to land in the morning."

Nora blew on her coffee and checked the clock on the wall opposite her. Ten minutes had passed. Had the paratroopers jumped by now? Were they on their way down, rifles in hand and ready to start the liberation of the Continent? Christiaan had done the same nearly a year ago. She wondered how he had felt when his feet touched the ground. Lisa had told her he made contact a few days later, with no evidence that he had been caught by the Germans. But then he had disappeared, and Nora had a sinking feeling her husband Floris was involved. If Christiaan was walking around Amsterdam again, Floris would hear of it sooner or later.

There was a tap on her shoulder. One of the women from the Receiver Room stood next to her. "Are you coming? It's been fifteen minutes."

Nora nodded and smiled at Phyllis. "I'll see you at home."

Her roommate returned her smile. "Whenever that may be."

———

Thirty minutes later, the first blips appeared on Nora's screen. She felt a jolt of adrenaline as she identified them as friendlies. After a few minutes, her screen filled with planes returning to Britain. With every squadron that appeared, she heard another set of pilots reporting in to Bomber Command. The message was the same every time. They had dropped their cargo and had encountered little to no resistance, except for some expected antiaircraft guns dealing only minor damage. The flight crews reported little wind on approach and expected most of the cargo had landed near the planned drop zones.

This time, there were a few small cheers in the Receiver Room, men and women pumping their fists as nearly all the flight crews reported in, and the blips moved steadily to the left of their screens. Soon, they would land, and the men could give more detailed reports of what happened on the other side of the Channel. Nora felt a wave of optimism wash over her. They had carried out their mission successfully, and it was almost two in the morning. Normally, her shift would end at seven, but Lewis had already informed all the operators involved in the night shift that they would finish around five today, handing over to a fresh crew. Nora was reluctant to leave her post, for she knew the battleships and troop carriers were only hours from the French coast. She wanted to be here when General Eisenhower brought down the hammer on Hitler's *Atlantikwall*.

CHAPTER EIGHT

L isa had had less than five hours of sleep, but she was back in the Bureau's radio room bright and early at five thirty in the morning. She had spent most of the prior day in the same room, listening in to the operators sending out her message informing their embassies, consulates, and foreign agents that the First United States Army Group was shipping out for the liberation of Europe. It had been rewarding to listen to the energy in the women's voices. Most of them had been working in this room for over two years, and while most thought they had experienced it all, this announcement carried a whole new level of excitement. Even though they didn't know they were sending out deliberately false information, they knew they were part of something big. Lisa understood how they felt, and she was proud of them. She had started her career at the Bureau Inlichtingen in the same room, transcribing incoming messages on her typewriter. Independent-thinking women were of tremendous value to the Allied war effort.

As the women filed into the office this morning, Lisa briefed them on what was happening on the French coast. When she revealed the invasion force wasn't headed for Calais, but three beachheads on the coast of Normandy instead, they were stunned. If they were fooled, then the Germans must surely have been, too. Lisa explained they would serve as a secondary contact center for the two solitary Dutch gunboats participating in Operation Overlord. Nicknamed *the Terrible Twins* for their relentless bombardments in the Mediterranean theater of war, the relatively smaller gunboats *Soemba* and *Flores* would attack the German coastal positions alongside the American battleships. Lisa was proud of this Dutch contribution to Overlord, and she wanted to make sure they had every chance to impress and succeed. If that meant providing communications backup to the Supreme Headquarters Allied Expeditionary Force, Lisa and her team would do exactly that. It also gave them a direct connection to the battle, and Lisa was eager to hear the plan unfold.

She didn't have to wait for long, as the *Soemba* reported coastal bombardments of Omaha Beach, one of Overlord's five landing spots, had started. Lisa could hear the rumble of the ship's cannons in the background as the operator's voice crackled over the radio.

"The first landing craft have left the troop carriers a few minutes ago. They're approaching the beach, but we haven't taken out all the German bunkers yet." There was either a pause, or the connection dropped, as there was only static for a few seconds. Then the voice returned. "Those boys are in for a rough reception. We're increasing the rate of fire on coastal targets."

Lisa swallowed hard as she imagined the men in the landing craft as it broke through the surf. They must be terrified, the very first soldiers landing, the machine gunners in the bunkers surely licking their lips in anticipation. *No,* she then thought, *these men are the bravest and most capable in the world. There's a reason they are the first to set foot on the beaches.*

"Copy that, *Soemba*, fire at will," came the response from the Allied headquarters. "Air support is inbound; they should be there shortly."

"I can hear them roaring over ahead, sir. Much appreciated."

Lisa couldn't resist a smile at the understated reaction. Even though he was in a relatively safe position a few miles from shore, he also knew what the men in the landing craft were up against.

The radio went silent, and Lisa scanned the room. Two operators each were connected to the *Soemba* and *Flores*, mostly listening in. Even though they were ready to assist in any request for intelligence, most of the communications were restricted to the Allied headquarters leading the assault. Operators maintained contact with a number of important posts on the European mainland and Britain. There was a direct connection to Queen Wilhelmina's offices at 77 Chester Square in London—Lisa was certain the monarch was following the invasion closely.

The women in the room were going about their tasks in a calm and efficient manner. She wondered how long it would take for the Allied forces to break through the defenses. With the number of men and amount of material committed to the invasion, Lisa could hardly imagine the German soldiers defending the beachheads holding out for long, especially after reports from planes returning early in the morning that there was no evidence of additional forces moving toward the Normandy beaches. Instead, the French Resistance reported increased activity around Calais. Lisa was jubilant: the Germans bought into their phantom army ruse!

The voice of the radio operator on board the *Soemba* crackled through her headset again. The first soldiers had landed on Omaha Beach, taking heavy fire. Lisa listened to the man's words and a sliver of doubt entered her mind. She was proud of what she had accomplished here in London, Operation Quicksilver her finest moment. But as she listened to the battle raging 150 miles away, she suddenly felt very detached from the operation. While young men risked their lives on the beaches of France, she sat in a comfortable, safe office in London.

She thought of Christiaan, who hadn't hesitated for a moment when asked to risk his life to drop back into the Netherlands. Wherever he was, it was on the other side of the Channel or the North Sea, taking the fight to the Nazis. Lisa was certain that, even if he was in captivity, he would sabotage their operations. She didn't even want to consider the possibility that he was no longer alive.

Word from the *Soemba* confirmed two German bunkers had been taken out, and the number of landing craft racing toward the French shoreline was increasing. Small boats dotted the sea ahead of the *Soemba*, struggling against the strong surf. Despite the tough conditions, the operator sounded optimistic.

His positivity spread across the radio room as the women shared his latest update with the other stations in Europe. Lisa stood, buoyed by the news, yet she couldn't shake the knot in her stomach. It wasn't that she doubted the mission; her confidence was growing. But she knew once Operation Overlord was over and they had established a beachhead in Europe, she would need to reconsider her role. She was watching from the sidelines, and she could no longer accept that.

CHAPTER NINE

Christiaan looked at the bowl and plate on the small tray. The bowl contained a watery substance that was supposed to pass for soup, but he knew better than to expect any taste. On some days, it contained one or two pieces of indistinguishable vegetables. Today he wasn't so lucky. He took a bite of a stale slab of bread and washed it down with what tasted like little more than lukewarm water.

It was quiet in his corner of the prison. The other men were no doubt struggling through their breakfast as well. Even though they had long accepted the food was inedible, it was the only way to survive. Because the cells of the Dutch prisoners were in the cold basement, the guards weren't too keen on staying for long. That meant they were able to talk with each other once the guards had passed on their hourly rounds. During roll call, they were kept from the other prisoners, and if any of them dared reach out to the other men, a baton-wielding guard would be on them in a flash. The other prisoners had soon learned to give the Dutch a wide berth.

He dipped another piece of bread in the soup, keeping it there for a few seconds to let the moisture soak in. When he took a bite, the bread was somewhat easier to chew. As he did, he cast his mind back to the roll call a week earlier. It was only the second time the prison had gone into lockdown. The last time it was because of an actual escape by two prisoners. They had soon been found hiding in a farm outside the city. After their capture, they were interrogated for weeks before they were unceremoniously hung in front of the rest of the prisoners during roll call. Christiaan wondered if the men involved in the new escape plans had been part of the first, and if they had somehow gotten wind that their plans were compromised. He was certain the resistance had people working for them inside the prison. Either way, nothing had happened in the past week, and Christiaan had to admit he missed the roll calls, if only for the opportunity to breathe some fresh air and stretch his legs.

His thoughts were interrupted by movement in the hallway. He put down his soup and listened to the quick footsteps making their way past rows of cell doors. This wasn't a regular patrol: they were coming for someone. In the first months of their captivity, all fifty-five men in the basement were taken for interrogations multiple times a week. Yes, they came from the Netherlands, but they most certainly weren't spying for the British. They had all received training on how to handle interrogations, and the number one rule was never to admit to being a spy, no matter what. A tremor went down his spine when he thought back to the early interrogations and torture. He had never experienced pain quite like what the sadists in the dark room on the other side of the prison inflicted on him. But if he admitted to being a spy, his life would be over. Worse, the SS animals running the prison would most likely execute every single one of them. After no one talked and they endured the interrogations for two months, they had suddenly stopped. Now it appeared their captors were happy for the men to rot away in the basement.

The footsteps neared Christiaan's cell door and he held his breath. One of the guards grunted something to the other, and Christiaan felt his heart skip a beat when he heard a key jingle in his door. *Shit, they're coming for me.* Instinctively, he grabbed the soup and downed the bowl just before the door swung open, revealing two bulky guards he didn't recognize. *Not a good sign.*

"Come with us," the largest grunted, already looking annoyed as he motioned for Christiaan to stand and turn. Christiaan did as he was told, feeling the cold metal handcuffs cutting into his wrists.

They escorted him through the hallway and up the stairs, and as they stepped out of the basement, Christiaan almost automatically turned to the right, toward the interrogation section of the prison. One of the guards roughly grabbed his elbow and turned him in the opposite direction. They took him through a maze of well-lit hallways. It was much brighter than he was used to, and small black spots clouded his vision as they turned into a broad corridor. Harsh concrete made way for carpeted floors, and even some plants lining the hallways. The guards shoved him through one of the doors and into a neat office. A man wearing an SS officer's uniform sat behind a desk. He was reading a file and didn't acknowledge Christiaan's presence.

"Sit down," the bulky guard said, pointing at a chair opposite the SS officer.

Christiaan did as he was told but found it uncomfortable with his hands behind his back. The guards looked unconcerned as they stood on either side of him, focused on the man behind the desk. The officer's eyes quickly scanned the sheet, and Christiaan could almost hear his mind working as he turned to the next page. It was obvious the man was unfazed by the arrival of the newcomers, and Christiaan knew he should just sit and wait patiently. When the guards took him from his cell he hadn't expected to be escorted to a comfortable office.

The SS officer took another minute, closed the file, and placed it on a neat pile on his desk. He looked up, meeting Christiaan's eyes. The officer's eyes went to Christiaan's arms, and his attention switched to the guard to Christiaan's left.

"You can take off his handcuffs; I'm sure he's not going to be a problem." He spoke with a deep voice, expressing a confidence that befit his rank. The guard undid the handcuffs and Christiaan felt the blood returning to his fingers. "You can wait outside. Mr. Brouwer and I are going to have a civilized chat. I'll call for you." The officer dismissed them with a flick of the wrist, the guards making themselves scarce.

Christiaan rubbed his wrists as the man opposite him stood from his desk. To Christiaan's surprise, he held out his hand.

"I'm Obersturmführer Wessels, and you must be wondering why you're in my office, and not in your usual surroundings." His tone was neutral, and as Christiaan reached to shake his hand, he was struck by the man's firm handshake. It almost felt normal to shake this Nazi's hand, as if they were about to conduct regular business together. He simply nodded, and the German motioned for him to sit back down as he did the same. "I realize your stay in Rawicz has hardly been comfortable. I'm afraid that's just the nature of how these things work. You understand? When you're caught spying for the Brits, well, that complicated matters."

Wessels clipped his words but spoke without any distinguishable accent, and Christiaan found it easy to understand him. Despite his civil tone, there was no mistaking this was no casual chat between equals. Wessels had already established he considered Christiaan a spy. He wanted to respond, but Wessels offered him no opportunity.

"I remember when you and your colleagues arrived six months ago. We were told you would only stay here for a few weeks, as Berlin considered what to do with you next. More importantly, they tasked us with finding out everything about your motivations, your missions, and to learn what information you might've sent back to London prior to your capture." He chuckled and cracked his neck. "It's funny, in a sense. You'd already had months of interrogation in our facilities in the Netherlands, and then they send you to Poland for further interrogation? You must've wondered why you weren't sent to a concentration camp, where they would kill you within a week." The man's voice had risen in volume, slightly cracking the calm and composed exterior facade.

Christiaan cleared his throat. "Sir, I'm not sure what you want me to say. I'm not a British spy." His eyes went to the stack of files on the officer's desk. "I can't tell you anything that I haven't shared in the conversations with your colleagues." He was careful not to contradict anything the man said other than his accusation of being a spy.

"Right. And what about the others?"

"I'm not sure I understand, sir."

"The other men in the basement. Your compatriots. Are they spies?"

"I don't know all of them, but from the ones I've spoken to, I would be very surprised if they were." From his training, Christiaan knew he needed to keep his answers as concise as possible, but still add enough detail to give the man sitting across from him the impression that he wasn't lying or making things up.

The man nodded. "That's interesting, because I've spoken with several in the past few days, and they had a different take." He patted the stack of files on his desk. "They admitted a large number of you were working for the British government before you were captured."

Christiaan's blood ran cold but he forced himself to keep a neutral expression. His mind was racing as he processed Wessels' words. He was certain none of the agents in the basement would ever admit to being spies so easily. They had held out for over half a year, for Christ's sake. Why would they cave now? He looked at the Obersturmführer, who eyed him confidently, a thin smile on his face. Wessels didn't wait for his response.

"You don't believe me, Mr. Brouwer? Perhaps you'd like to see the files? You think I'm trying to trick you, is that it? I can assure you I'm not. The thing is, I don't really need your confession anymore. I've only invited you here to give you an option to come clean."

Christiaan's mouth went dry as the realization hit. He swallowed hard. "How so?" he managed in a croaking voice.

The grin on the officer's face spread into a smile. "Those men that confessed to being spies, they also shared other useful information with me. For one, that you are most certainly one of them. The game's up, Mr. Brouwer. I know you're a spy."

Christiaan held the man's gaze. The man was either an incredibly gifted liar, or some of the other agents really had confessed. He knew all the men from their time in the Dutch prisons, where they shared yard time together. These men had withstood numerous threats to their life already. It didn't make sense. He raised his chin and looked the SS officer in the eye.

"You're bluffing. You don't have any confessions. I'm not a spy."

For a moment, the German appeared caught off guard, his confidence wavering. An instant later, it returned, along with that all-knowing smile. "You know, when I mentioned those concentration camps earlier, I saw you flinch. Does the thought of being sent there frighten you?" His voice was icily calm and he continued without waiting for a reply. "In the end, it doesn't matter if you confess, because I've gathered enough evidence to know you, and the other fifty-four men in the basement, are spies. And you won't stay in Rawicz forever. In fact, I can guarantee you'll be transferred to one of those concentration camps next. And I'm quite certain you've heard about the conditions there. They make Rawicz seem like a five-star hotel."

"I can't confess to anything I'm not, sir."

"Yes, you've mentioned that a few times now. The problem is, though, that I don't believe you. I'm going to give you one more chance to come clean. In fact, if you do, and you cooperate with me, I might be able to keep you off the list for the transport to the concentration camp, and you can stay here, in Rawicz. I might even be able to transfer you to the general population once the other spies are shipped off." He paused for a moment, pretending to give Christiaan time to mull over the proposal. He then raised his hand, as if suddenly remembering something. "Oh, and before you decide, let me tell you this. If you decide to take your chances in the concentration camp, you should know you'll be marked as a political prisoner. Do you know what that means?"

Christiaan shook his head.

"Your chances of making it past the first month are slim to nonexistent. The only group of prisoners that have worse survival rates than political prisoners are the Jews. I'll give you twenty-four hours to decide." He stood and clapped his hands. "Guards! Take him back to his cell."

CHAPTER TEN

The morning roll call went a lot faster than usual. Floris watched as the other guards walked along the rows of prisoners. This was his second week in Mauthausen. He hadn't participated in any of the beatings and was content to leave the dirty work to the Kapos. His reluctance to beat the—in his opinion—pathetic excuses for human beings, was a matter of honor. Despite his new role as guard, he still considered himself, first and foremost, a police officer. In all his years on the force, he had never physically abused his power. Sure, there had been times when he had been a little rough, but he had never beaten someone who had clearly surrendered or was unable to fight back.

The guards had almost completed their count, and it appeared they were satisfied with the numbers. Floris let out a silent sigh of relief. He was keen to finish roll call and get out to the quarry, where he could catch up with Anton. After the first week, they had been assigned to guard the same work detail, and it meant the friends could stick together. Floris had been especially pleased about that, as it had proved difficult to make friends in Mauthausen. Floris and

Anton were once again consigned to the *Ausländers*, the foreigners. They were going to need each other.

There was movement in the front, where it was announced all prisoners were accounted for, and that they could collect their breakfasts and prepare for work. The prisoners filed out of the roll call area with blank looks. Their breakfast consisted of little more than a tiny piece of sausage, cheese if they were lucky, some jam, and a very thin slice of bread. It wasn't nearly enough to sustain them through the day's labor.

He noticed a dozen prisoners on the far side of the yard. They walked apart from the others, appearing like sheep lost from the herd. Floris immediately saw why; their uniforms were marked with yellow triangles. They didn't have the haggard look of the others and didn't walk with what he called the *Mauthausen slouch*, with shoulders hunched forward and faces focused on the ground, barely able to take ten steps without tumbling over. These Jews were new, and they had already been left to find their own way. They hadn't escaped the notice of the Kapos eyeing them from the other side. These men would most likely return from their work details piled in the back of a cart this evening.

"Brouwer." A voice startled him, and he found one of the senior German guards in his detail standing uncomfortably close to him. His expression was neutral, but he stood impatiently tapping his right foot. "You're wanted in the *Kommandant*'s office."

Floris was surprised. "Now? Aren't we supposed to head out to the quarry in half an hour?"

"Yes, so you better get there quick because there's no way you're missing your shift. I need you down in the quarry today." He looked up into the clear sky, the sun already making its way up behind the hills to Floris' back. "It's going to be a hot one today, and you know what that means."

Floris nodded, glancing at the group of new Jews as they moved from the roll call area. There would be plenty of weak prisoners joining them on the carts to the crematorium before the day was over.

––––––

When he arrived at the Kommandant's building, Floris was surprised to find himself immediately directed to a large office at the back of the building. He was told to wait, as *Herr Schutzhaftlager-führer* would be with him shortly. Floris wasn't certain if he'd heard correctly, and asked the clerk if he had perhaps misunderstood who he was meeting. The clerk shook his head.

"No, you heard correctly. *Hauptsturmführer* Bachmayer will be with you shortly."

If the mention of a personal meeting with Bachmayer wasn't enough to alarm Floris, the look on the clerk's face was. Floris felt his chest constrict.

Georg Bachmayer was one of the most powerful men in Mauthausen. While technically a Hauptsturmführer, a captain, it was his position as Schutzhaftlagerführer of Mauthausen that really mattered. It made him responsible for all prisoners in the camp, with the smooth operation of the quarries his top priority. He exercised his responsibilities with a zealous dedication Floris hadn't witnessed before. Unlike most other highly ranked SS officers who preferred to leave the dirty work to their underlings, Bachmayer was keen to dish out punishment himself. Floris had witnessed the man beat several prisoners to death for not lining up properly at roll call. His policy shaped the attitudes of the guards and Kapos.

Floris stood in the middle of the room while he looked around. The office was spacious and richly furnished. Behind the ornate wooden desk stood a comfortable chair. The walls were lined with bookcases and photos of Bachmayer with various senior Nazi Party members. Floris recognized Bachmayer alongside Heinrich Himmler, the supreme commander of the SS, touring the Vienna Quarry. Floris took a deep breath and wiped his sweaty palms on the sides of his pants.

The door opened and Floris turned to recognize Bachmayer. He quickly saluted the senior officer, who nodded at him as the door slammed shut. He stormed across the room, sank into his chair on the other side of the desk and looked up at Floris impatiently. "Sit down, I'll keep this short." He waved at one of two simple chairs.

Floris quickly took a seat, his hands trembling. He clasped them together and hoped Bachmayer didn't notice his anxiety as he sat on the edge of the seat, his spine straight and shoulders pulled back. Bachmayer reached for a sheet of paper and quickly scanned it, giving Floris an opportunity to eye the officer from up close for the first time. He was young for his position, perhaps only a few years older than himself. Despite their minimal age difference, the man on the other side of the desk had the power to make or break Floris' career. He put the sheet of paper down and focused his attention on Floris.

"I know you've only been in my camp for a few weeks now, and you must be wondering why I've called you in today." Floris nodded meekly, sensing Bachmayer didn't expect more of a response. He was right, as the officer continued almost immediately. "Normally, I wouldn't summon you to my office, but in your case, I thought it was prudent. I understand you fought on the eastern front. With Wiking?"

"I did, sir." Floris thought he detected a hint of admiration in the officer's voice.

Bachmayer's eyes went to the sheet of paper. "And I see you were injured in combat when you tried to save a fellow soldier?"

"We were ambushed in one of the cities, and my friend Anton was hit while our squad was retreating. I went back for him."

"Right, I see that in your file." Bachmayer nodded, and Floris' anxiety lessened, his confidence growing. "An admirable move, if it wasn't for the charge of insubordination."

Floris dropped his head to hide the anger building up inside him. If he hadn't gone back, Anton wouldn't be alive today. The order to abandon him had been bullshit. Yet, here it was again, haunting him far beyond the battlefield. He took a deep breath and composed himself before lifting his gaze back to Bachmayer. "Sir, I am aware of the charge, but if you don't mind me asking, why is that relevant today?"

"I've received reports of your performance since arriving at Mauthausen. There are some questions about your dedication to keeping the prisoners in check."

The words hit Floris like shots, and he racked his brain to place what Bachmayer said. "My dedication, sir?"

The Hauptsturmführer stood and took a few steps to the side of his desk. He was suddenly consumed by one of the photos on the wall and didn't immediately respond. Then he turned back to Floris and spoke sharply. "I want you to know I respect your record at the Waffen-SS. Serving on the eastern front is no small feat. But I think it's important you're aware of your responsibilities as a guard in my camp. Perhaps you haven't been briefed properly."

"Sir?"

"I only care about reaching our granite quotas from the quarry every day, Brouwer." He pointed at the photo of himself and Himmler. "And so does *Reichsführer* Himmler. And the reality of the matter is that we have too many mouths to feed in Mauthausen. There are too many expendable prisoners, leeches on the population. Your job is to make sure they are weeded out. I don't care how you do it, but all I've heard so far is that you've been negligent in your responsibilities."

Floris listened to Bachmayer in amazement as the words sank in. *Who has reported me?*

"These men are worthy of life only when they help reach our quotas. That's my responsibility to Berlin. You, as a guard, are responsible when they're at work. I need to know you'll take appropriate action when they aren't up to the task." He waved a hand at the window. "We have fresh prisoners coming in every day. Let's make sure we have enough space and food to accommodate them. Get rid of the unworthy. Do you understand what I'm saying, Brouwer?"

Floris nodded. Bachmayer had made his job description crystal clear.

"Good. You better hurry to the gate; they'll be heading out any minute now. I expect I won't be receiving any more reports questioning your commitment to the cause." It wasn't a question.

"No, sir. Thank you for clarifying this. I will not let you down."

"I'm sure you won't. Dismissed."

———

Floris reached the gate just in time to see his work detail heading out. He spotted Anton walking in the back and caught up with him as the last prisoners passed underneath the camp's imposing granite gate.

"I thought you weren't going to make it. What did they want from you?" his friend asked, an inquisitive look on his face.

Floris looked around, making sure none of the other guards were within earshot. "You're not going to believe it. It was Bachmayer."

"What do you mean?" Anton's eyes went wide, and Floris could see his friend making the connection. "The Schutzhaftlagerführer wanted to see you? Why? What could he possibly want from you?"

"I was just as surprised. In fact, I didn't think he knew about my existence." They walked on alongside the high walls of the main camp, and Floris caught Anton up on the conversation while they kept their eyes on the prisoners. When he finished, Anton shook his head.

"Who would report you like this? And, why would it go all the way up to Bachmayer? Doesn't he have more important things to worry about?" Anton kept his eyes on the prisoners to their left, but he looked genuinely worried. "You know, you should watch your back, Flo. Did you piss anyone off?"

Floris shook his head. "I thought about that, too, but I really can't think of anyone. I suppose we'll just have to— What's going on over there?"

Something had happened within the ranks of prisoners. As they moved to and from the quarry, the men would walk packed closely together, like sheep trying to avoid standing out. Now, a gap had formed in the middle, where prisoners sidestepped around a figure lying on the ground. Most passed him silently, averting their gazes, but one or two appeared to mumble something to him. It didn't matter, for the man appeared apathetic, indifferent to his surroundings.

"Perhaps you should see how he's doing," Anton said with a knowing look. Floris made his way through the group of prisoners, who readily made space for him. He reached the man on the ground and instantly identified him as a *Muselmann*. The term was reserved for prisoners who were so emaciated they resembled only the shell of a man. There was little he could do for the man, but he had to get him back in line somehow.

"Get up!" he shouted at the man, loud enough for everyone to hear. Nearby prisoners pretended not to notice yet took a few extra steps to the left and right of the scene. There was no response, and Floris prodded him with his baton. "Get up, damn it! You need to get to work. You can't stay on the ground!" Floris looked around and saw some of the guards farther ahead had stopped and turned. A few looked on with amused expressions, curious to see how Floris would handle this. It confirmed what Floris had suspected; the complaints about his performance had come from the men in his squad. *Bastards.*

Anger built up inside him, and he gripped the baton in his right hand tighter. He looked at the man on the ground, clenched his teeth, and brought his arm up. A second later, he smashed his baton into the man's back with all the force he could muster. "Get up!" he roared, and some of the nearby prisoners jumped. Floris brought the baton down again. "Get up, you useless piece of shit!"

Floris found himself breathing hard as the man on the ground clutched the side of his stomach with one hand. With the other, he slowly lifted himself onto his right knee, and then his left. Floris felt relief. Perhaps the beating had stirred some life back into the man after all. The Muselmann lifted his face, lifeless eyes staring up at Floris. For a moment, Floris was back on the eastern front, standing atop the ditch, his rifle aimed at the defenseless, silent man below, while his superior yelled at him to shoot the damn Jew.

This time, the man on his knees wasn't silent. He spoke in a barely audible whisper, in a language Floris didn't understand. Floris' eyes went to the black triangle with a prominent *U* inside. It marked him as an antisocial from Hungary. Floris told the man to stand up, but the man simply shook his head and repeated his earlier words. This time, however, he pointed at the pistol strapped to Floris' belt, and then at his forehead.

Floris felt conflicted. This man was no enemy of his. He wasn't a Jew; he wasn't a Soviet prisoner of war. Yet, even without looking up, he could feel the eyes of his fellow guards burning into him, waiting for him to make his decision. He thought of Bachmayer's words and knew what the man at his feet was. *Expendable.*

In a daze, Floris unholstered his pistol. The sound of prisoners marching past him faded into the background as he cocked the hammer. He looked down at the Hungarian, eyes closed, leaning slightly forward. Controlling his trembling hands, Floris gently placed the muzzle against the man's exposed forehead. He saw the man flinch only for a moment, then he pressed his forehead into the muzzle. Floris squeezed the trigger, and all the sights and sounds of his surroundings rushed back to him at the force of the explosion. The Hungarian's body slumped to the ground, blood trickling from the small hole in his forehead.

Floris forced himself to look up and meet the other guards' eyes. He saw a mix of surprise and admiration. That was all he needed to know. He focused his attention back on the body at his feet. The dead man's expression was oddly serene. As the other prisoners marched on either side, Floris realized the man on the ground was now at peace, freed from the daily terrors of Mauthausen. Floris' own hell had only just started.

CHAPTER ELEVEN

Lisa admired Lyons' Oxford Corner House as she waited to cross Tottenham Court Road. She loved this part of the city, and this was one of her favorite places to window-shop, to admire the goods on display as she passed by the large facade. She crossed the street and entered through the building's grand main entrance. It was lunchtime, and Lisa jostled for space with patrons making their way to the building's numerous cafes and brasseries.

She felt a tingle of anticipation as she joined the short queue for the Mountview Cafe. It had been nearly three weeks since she'd seen Nora, the woman who had become something of a sister to her. When Lisa needed to escape Amsterdam a year-and-a-half ago, but wasn't able to fund the journey south, Nora hadn't hesitated to provide her with the money. Even more impressively, Nora had risked her own life by stealing the money from her husband Floris' chest of ill-gotten treasure. Lisa was certain she wouldn't be alive today if it wasn't for Nora Brouwer. When she heard Nora had made her own journey south six months ago and was stranded in Spain as she waited for a visa to travel to England, Lisa had used all her connections at the Bureau to expedite Nora's journey. With the help of her boss, who also recognized the value of having an experienced resistance fighter like Nora, she managed to get her on a plane to England. Lisa still remembered the day Nora walked out of the Royal Victoria Patriotic School, after she had been thoroughly grilled on her intentions in coming to Britain. Lisa knew what it was like, having experienced the interrogations herself. But all that was forgotten in an instant as the women embraced on the street outside. Lisa had been delighted to have Nora in London, especially since the man they both deeply cared for was lost in the Netherlands.

She reached the front of the queue and stated her name. A young woman escorted her through the crowded room where men and women of all walks of life enjoyed lunch. Waitresses wearing their distinctive black-and-white *nippy* uniforms flashed across the room, carrying heavy trays loaded with all sorts of delectable cakes and pastries. Despite the lunch-hour rush, the women seemed unfazed, and Lisa was impressed. She wasn't sure she'd be able to navigate the busy room with the same grace.

"Here we are, ma'am. I hope this is okay for you?" The waitress pulled a chair from the table in the corner and Lisa sat, nodding her thanks.

"Absolutely, thank you very much."

The woman disappeared and Lisa scanned the room. It wasn't her first visit to the Mountview, but she was impressed by the grandeur of the establishment. The large art deco pillars in the center of the room created an intimate space. Combined with the low ceilings it made for a cozy dining experience. The tables were packed close together, further adding to the feeling of sitting in someone's dining room, albeit a very grand one.

"I hope you haven't been waiting for too long?"

Lisa was delighted to hear Nora's voice and hurried to embrace her. "I've only just arrived, don't worry about it." Nora looked stunning as always, her light green coat perfectly accentuating bright green eyes and dark hair. She took off the coat and draped it over the back of her seat before sitting down with a smile.

"How have you been, Lisa? I can't believe it's been three weeks."

Lisa leaned forward in her chair, elbows on the table. "So much has happened. The last time you were in London you thought you'd be back by the weekend, and we could go dancing together."

Nora giggled. "I'm planning on going tomorrow evening; my next shift is on Monday afternoon. I can take the early train back."

"Sounds great," Lisa said, and she realized she hadn't been out for two months. "Work has been taking up all my time. It would be nice to let my hair down, especially with you."

"I know, I'm sure it's been as crazy for you as it has for me." A waitress appeared at the table and they both ordered tea and cake. When the woman left, Nora leaned forward. "So, tell me, what was it like to be at the Bureau during the invasion?"

"It was exhilarating and terrifying. We could hear what was happening aboard the Dutch ships in real time. When they announced the first landing craft had reached the beach, I couldn't help but wonder how many of those men would leave that beach alive." She sighed, and they were quiet for a moment, as both women considered the incredible loss of life on both sides during Operation Overlord. Lisa felt a knot twist in her stomach as a wave of sadness passed over her.

"Well, at least they didn't die for nothing. The Mulberry harbors at Omaha and Gold Beaches are fully operational. We're working round the clock to make sure they cross the Channel safe and sound." Nora's eyes twinkled as she spoke.

"I've heard the first British troops have surrounded Caen, and when they take it, the road to Paris will be free," Nora continued, optimistically. "At this rate, they should liberate Paris within a few weeks."

Lisa nodded, not sure she shared her friend's optimism. Their waitress returned and placed their tea and Battenburg cake in front of them. Nora immediately dug in, and looked to Lisa as she took a sip of her tea.

"What's going on with you? Have some cake." She pushed the

plate with the colorful, pink-and-yellow checkered cake toward her. Lisa forced herself to take a bite, the sugar rush lifting her mood. She turned to Nora.

"You know, ever since listening in on the invasion, I've been thinking about the soldiers risking their lives on the other side of the Channel."

Nora put down her fork, her face turning serious. "Are you thinking about Chris?"

"Of course, I think about him every day, and I can't wait to see him again, but it's not just about him."

"I know it's hard, but we can't lose hope." Nora reached out over the table and took Lisa's hand. It felt good. "You know Chris. He's smart, and he's a hell of a lot smarter than those Germans stationed in Amsterdam. Trust me, I know."

Nora's eyes were sparkling again, and Lisa felt a bit better. Nora's experience avoiding the Germans in Amsterdam during her time in the resistance spoke for itself. Nevertheless, she also suspected Nora was hiding her own worries about her brother-in-law to make Lisa feel better.

"I know, I know," Lisa said, gently squeezing Nora's hand. "But it's not just about Chris."

Nora tilted her head a little. "What do you mean?"

"When the radio operator of the *Soemba* reported on what was happening at Omaha Beach, I realized I wanted to be more involved. I didn't know how, but I felt that if Overlord was completed success-fully, my job at the Bureau was perhaps ..." She paused for a moment, searching for the right words. "Completed as well."

"Are you saying you want to leave the Bureau?" Nora was unable to keep her astonishment out of her voice, although her features were composed. "You're so integral to their operations. What do you think Somer will say?"

"Somer can't wait to activate his network of agents back home. From what I can tell, he's itching to follow the soldiers to the main-land." She looked at Nora and frowned. "And I want to do the same. I want to do more than keep our embassies informed. I want to help the troops as they make their way through Europe, to do something, you know?"

Nora didn't immediately answer, her bright eyes studying Lisa with interest. Then a smile crept onto her face. "So, why don't you just ask him? He might well have a use for you as well. Maybe not today or tomorrow, but I'm sure he would want his trusted assistant by his side when he does cross the Channel."

Lisa nodded, understanding Nora's words of caution. But as she savored her cake, Lisa could feel the frustration bubbling up inside her. She didn't want to wait; she wanted to take action. She was ready to help today. As she lifted her cup of tea and took a large sip, she decided there was only one way she could make that happen.

————

Lisa returned to Bureau Inlichtingen to find her boss's office door closed. She knew better than to interrupt him, and she took her seat in her office across the hall. Somer's door opened and two men in suits scattered out. Lisa didn't recognize them, which was odd because she was involved in nearly everything her boss did. She checked his calendar and was surprised to find this meeting was unscheduled. She stood and crossed the hallway, softly rapping her knuckles on his door. Somer looked up in surprise, then quickly waved her in.

"You're back early; was lunch not what you expected? You were meeting Nora, weren't you?"

Lisa couldn't suppress a smile. She wasn't the only person in the room aware of the other's schedule. "It was lovely, actually, but you know how it can be at the Corner House during lunch."

"A bit too busy. Were they trying to get the next customers in?" Somer opened a filing cabinet in the corner of the room, his finger flicking through the files as he spoke.

"Something like that, yes. Can I help you with something?"

"Already found it, thanks. I am still able to find some things by myself, Lisa." He waved a file at her. "We don't have anything scheduled, do we?"

Lisa took a deep breath, bracing herself. This was not going to be easy. "We don't, sir. But there is something important I wanted to discuss with you, if you have a few minutes."

"Of course, I always have time for you." He waved at the chair opposite his desk and waited for Lisa to sit before he did the same.

"Now that the Mulberry harbors are established, and with the reports of the armies making good progress, I was wondering what is next. I mean, we've been so involved for months, but it appears activity in our radio room has significantly quieted down. We're mostly keeping the embassies updated, but I haven't seen many messages go out to our agents."

Somer nodded but didn't immediately respond. Instead, he leaned back in his chair before answering. "I agree it's been a bit of a change of pace. The Brits are pushing east and surrounding Caen, and the Americans have made great progress in the west. They've already liberated a number of cities, and morale is high. It's important we encourage that confidence in our agents and embassies, and also in our compatriots back home."

Lisa nodded. She listened to Queen Wilhelmina's broadcasts on *Radio Oranje*. The monarch didn't need any encouragement in sharing the American victories in France. "I understand, sir. But why are we not communicating as much with our agents? They must be wondering what they can do, hearing of the successes in France? Don't you think they're getting restless?"

"I understand your concerns, but they need to lie low just a little bit longer. Once the armies secure the north of France, they'll push through, and our agents will be activated. With a little bit of patience, the Germans will be so overwhelmed by the force of the liberating armies that they won't have enough resources to keep track of our agents back home. That's when we strike, and we hit them hard. But we'll only get one shot at doing this right."

Lisa was impressed; she hadn't looked at it like that before.

"But that's not all you wanted to ask me, is it? It seems like there's more to your question." He spoke calmly, his eyes studying her.

"There is, sir. After Overlord, and especially when listening in on the invasion, I felt I wasn't contributing quite enough. I felt detached from the action. That was fine when we were preparing for Overlord. I'm forever grateful for your trust in me and for including me in all the preparations. But now, I feel restless, like I'm in the wrong place to contribute to the next phase of the war. The part where we liberate the Netherlands, and Europe."

"You want to be more involved." It was a statement, and Somer's voice was even. Lisa couldn't read his thoughts. "I understand, Lisa. I feel the same way. I long to go home and connect with our agents. These men have lived in mortal danger for months. Hell, some of the SOE men we haven't heard from in years. I want to find them, to activate them when we drive the Nazi filth from our country. This network is my legacy, it's what I've been working for these past years." His shifted forward in his chair, and there was genuine pain in his eyes. "I also know some of these men have been captured. We discovered this together, yet I refuse to believe we've lost all of them. If they are still in that prison in Haaren, I want to be there when we liberate it."

"You want to go home as well, sir."

"More than anything. But even though the initial reports from France are encouraging, I also know there's little use in me going back now, when the route is still blocked. For now, I've accepted I need to stay in London a bit longer. But I sense you feel differently."

"Sir, I don't want to be on the sidelines. Working with you this past year, I was in the thick of the action. I was communicating with our agents; coordinating with the Americans and Brits as we prepared for D-Day. Now, I feel hamstrung, useless even."

"You're not useless."

She shook her head. "I know, but you understand what I'm

saying, right? I need to help, and I believe I can help on the other side of the Channel now."

Somer was silent for a moment, then nodded. "This is about Christiaan, isn't it?"

"He's part of it, yes, sir. He's there, fighting in some capacity. I wish I knew where he was, or what he's doing. But he's one of the hundreds of thousands of men risking their lives for our freedom. And I can't sit by idly." Lisa felt a sharp pain in her heart as Christiaan's face flashed through her mind. She focused on controlling her breathing as Somer stood and moved to her side of the desk. To her surprise, he knelt next to her.

"I can't say I'm too surprised. When you became my assistant, I knew you were special. And I understand what you're saying. If I were in your position, I would feel the same." He chuckled. "Actually, I think we've already established I do."

Hope and relief filled Lisa's chest. "Are you saying I have your blessing?"

"Of course you do." Somer looked surprised, a bit taken aback. "I'll miss having you around, but I soon hope to make the journey myself as well. There's just the small matter of what you'll do, though."

Lisa hadn't thought of that yet. She had been so consumed by getting her boss's approval first that thinking a step ahead hadn't crossed her mind yet. She felt flushed, realizing her preparation had, for once, been inadequate.

Somer appeared to read her thoughts. "Have you considered joining the *Vrouwen Hulpkorps*, the VHK?"

Lisa looked at him in surprise. She hadn't even thought about applying for the only female division of the Royal Netherlands Army.

"I expect they will be mobilized soon," Somer continued. "They won't be a fighting unit, but they will be near the front lines, assisting soldiers and civilians. I think it's your best chance to contribute on the other side."

Lisa had never considered herself a soldier, but then she wasn't an intelligence officer before joining the Bureau, either. And she had adapted to that well. The VHK provided the perfect opportunity to ship out to Europe. Lisa looked at Somer and nodded.

He rose and smiled. "Let me make some calls."

"Thank you, sir." Lisa stood and headed for the door, her mind racing with possibilities. She opened the door but turned as Somer cleared his throat.

"I'm proud of you, Lisa."

She inclined her head and left her boss's office. Her heart was bursting, her knees weak from excitement. She was going home. And she was going to find Chris.

CHAPTER TWELVE

The wind tugged at Lisa's scarf as she walked up to the gatehouse. The guard slid down the window and waved her through, directing her toward a nondescript gray building down the main road. She gripped her small suitcase tighter, passing several barracks. The door of one of the buildings opened and a group of laughing women wearing smart uniforms stepped out. One of them spotted Lisa and gave her a friendly smile. Lisa returned the gesture and walked on.

It had taken Somer almost two weeks to arrange her transfer. It had given her time to consider her future, and sometimes she'd questioned if she had asked for the right thing. She knew nothing about fighting, nursing, or the army. No, she corrected herself, that wasn't entirely true. The past six months especially had given her a thorough insight into the workings of the armed forces. When her boss walked into her office two days ago, informing her she would need to report to this army base, she knew there was no way back. Now that she was here, the doubts came creeping out.

She opened the door to the gray building and stepped into a brightly lit reception area. Fluorescent overhead lighting buzzed as

Lisa approached the small counter in the middle of the room. A young woman was sorting papers and looked surprised to see Lisa. She quickly recovered and forced a smile. "Can I help you?"

"My name is Lisa Abrahams; I was told I needed to report here. I'm starting with the VHK today."

"The what?" The woman scrunched her face, but before Lisa could say anything, her eyes went to a list of names on her desk. "Ah, yes. Abrahams. Please follow me." She stood and led Lisa down a long hallway. The doors to most of the offices were open, and Lisa noted people in various uniforms working and chatting. It reminded her of the Bureau office in London, and she again wondered if she was making the right decision. The woman turned into one of the offices, where a man and woman stood talking near the window, their backs to the door. They turned on hearing Lisa entering. The woman escorting Lisa disappeared quickly, closing the door behind her.

"Miss Abrahams, welcome. Please take a seat." The man waved her toward a chair. Lisa immediately noticed his twangy American accent as he drawled her surname. She was further surprised to find him wearing a US Army uniform. She'd seen enough of those in the past months to identify him as a captain. The woman next to him looked especially striking in her gray-blue uniform, the insignia on both sides of her jacket collar stating "*A.R.C.*" in bold black print. The patch on her sleeve left no doubt to her affiliation as it read "American Red Cross." Lisa was now thoroughly confused, and it must have shown, for the woman gave her a reassuring smile as she sat and smoothed her skirt.

"We want to thank you for your time, and I suppose you're surprised to find us welcoming you on your first day at the VHK. My name is Heather Madison, and I'm with the Red Cross." Her voice was soothing, and it had a calming effect on Lisa. She nodded at the man next to her. "And this is Captain Rogers with the US Army."

"Pleased to meet you both," Lisa said, finding some of her confidence returning. She moved forward in her chair a bit and placed her hands on the desk between them. "You're right, I am a little lost."

"Allow me to explain, Miss Abrahams." Rogers appeared keen to speak, perhaps stamp his authority on the meeting. "We were informed of your intentions to join the VHK, which is both a brave and honorable thing to do, considering your position." He paused, and Lisa folded her hands on the desk, encouraging him to continue. "Right, let me just get to it. We want to offer you an alternative to the VHK. Don't get me wrong, we think it's a great initiative, but we're not sure it's the best place for someone with your skills and knowledge."

Lisa sat up in her chair and frowned. "How so, sir?"

"Well, for starters, the VHK won't ship out for a few months. The way it looks now, they'll be sent across the Channel once we've secured ports in Belgium, and well, that's not happened just yet. Once they've landed on the European mainland, they will provide assistance to civilians and refugees. A noble task, goes without saying."

"But they won't be traveling with the liberating armies," Madison joined in. "They will be far away from the front lines, operating solely in liberated, relatively safe areas." She looked at Lisa inquisitively. "From what we've heard, that's perhaps not what you're looking for."

Lisa studied the faces of the Americans across the table. They appeared genuinely interested, clearly set on recruiting her. "Why me? Don't you have your own people coming in from the United States?" She had seen plenty of young American women in their Red Cross uniforms on the streets of London in the past weeks.

Rogers leaned forward in his chair. "Miss Abrahams, how many languages do you speak?" The question caught her off guard, and she didn't immediately respond. "From what we've heard, you're fluent in English, Dutch, French, and German. Is that correct?"

Lisa slowly nodded. "I wouldn't say completely fluent in French, but I get by."

"And you've worked in military intelligence for the past year and a half," Madison said as she smiled at her. "How many of the women in my organization do you think can claim the same? You're unique, Miss Abrahams."

"What would you have me do?" Lisa felt herself blushing and spoke quickly, hoping it would draw the attention away from her burning cheeks.

Captain Rogers' eyes sparkled as he laid out his plan. "You'd join one of the American regiments in France and travel with them as they push the Germans back east. We consider your language skills alone invaluable. You would be able to speak to civilians we encounter along the way, converse in their own language, and gather intelligence. But also, the German soldiers. We have them on the run, Miss Abrahams, and soon those boys will start surrendering. We'll need people on the ground that speak German and are knowledgeable about the reality of the war. We believe having you travel with the US Army under the cover of the Red Cross would be of immense value."

Lisa's stomach fluttered listening to the Americans. They were right about one thing; when she entered the base that morning, she hadn't expected this.

"So, what do you think, Miss Abrahams?" Heather Madison's voice interrupted her thoughts and her eyes shot back across the table. Rogers appeared relaxed; his eyebrow was twitching ever so slightly. The corners of Madison's lips were curled upward into a soft smile.

Lisa thought of what she had told Somer in his office almost two weeks ago. This was what she had asked for, wasn't it? She would no longer be on the sidelines, but actively fighting to end the war. And the sooner it was over, the sooner she could go home and find Chris. She took a deep breath, faced the Americans, and spoke with a trembling voice. "When do I start?"

Part Two

UNKNOWN LOCATION, 6 SEPTEMBER 1944

CHAPTER THIRTEEN

The train slowed down, and Christiaan tried peering through the small gaps in the walls of the car. The midday sun glared. Through the cracks he saw colorful houses slowly rolling by. They left Rawicz two nights ago, and this was the third time Christiaan had traveled in a cattle boxcar. He wondered, had they had finally arrived at their destination? The man interrogating had been quite clear; if he didn't confess to being a spy, or rat out his fellow Dutch prisoners, he would be on his way to a concentration camp. Even from his limited perspective inside the car, he could see this was no such camp.

Christiaan hadn't said a word after returning to his cell. The twenty-four hours came and went, and a guard stopped by to ask if he'd changed his mind. Even though he was terrified of being sent to a concentration camp, he would not be able to live with himself if he betrayed the men in the surrounding cells. Besides, he doubted the SS man would keep his word. He suspected a confession would only hasten his death; he hoped the other prisoners felt the same.

Evidently, they did. All were taken from their basement cells the next morning. It was still dark outside when they were marched through the city of Rawicz, the streets deserted, its inhabitants fast asleep. Upon arrival at the city's train station, they were taken to a small sidetrack, where a train with a single boxcar stood waiting. A familiar sight, by now. The men were loaded into the narrow surroundings without a word. When the train left, Christiaan was certain they were heading for one of the nearby camps. Instead, the train continued through the night. It crossed back into Germany, but when they passed through the mountains the next day, Christiaan realized they were going south. He knew there were camps in Germany and Poland, but nothing of any farther south.

The train stopped, its wheels creaking, the engine letting out a loud sigh. Through the cracks, Christiaan could see the outline of a station. The space in the car was very limited, and the men remained in their places. They were tired and thirsty, their water bucket empty since the evening before. For the first few minutes, nothing happened, and Christiaan thought this must just be another stop. He listened for the sound of another train approaching. A stop was usually followed by a freight train passing them, no doubt transporting goods essential for the war effort. Now, however, it remained quiet.

Then voices rapidly approached from the far end of the platform. They were male, and speaking German. There was more movement in the car now as the passengers looked at each other. *I suppose we've arrived after all.* The men reached the train car and soon the handle locking the door was moved with a clank. An instant later, the door slid open, the bright sunlight blinding those inside. Christiaan held his hand before face, his eyes quickly adjusting to the brightness. Crisp air flooded into the boxcar. Even though the cracks in the car's walls and roof provided some basic ventilation when they were moving, it had not removed the stench of some fifty sweaty bodies packed close together. Not to mention the bucket used for excrement. Christiaan took a deep breath and regained a bit of energy despite his tired, hungry state.

"Everybody out, now! Come on, *schnell, schnell!*" The uniformed soldiers on the platform started shouting, clearly in a hurry, or at least in no mood to give the men in the car any respite. They did as they were told, and within a minute, Christiaan stood lined up on the platform. Surrounded by a dozen men wearing the grayish-green uniforms of the SS, he held his breath and avoided their gaze. All but a few wore the skull-and-bones emblems of the *Totenkopfverbände*. Christiaan was confused; the SS guards and officers primarily wore the emblem in concentration camps. Yet, as he looked around, he saw only the houses of the village around the tracks. *Where are we?*

One of the soldiers produced a piece of paper and, without prelude, called out Christiaan's name, only glancing up when Christiaan didn't immediately answer.

"Brouwer, if I have to call your name out one more time, you'll regret it!" His tone left no doubt as to the sincerity of the threat, and Christiaan quickly raised his hand.

"Yes, sir, apologies."

When all prisoners were accounted for, the SS man put away the list and turned around. At that, the other soldiers started shouting at the men. "Two abreast and stay close together. Let's go! Come on, we don't have all day!"

Christiaan caught Max's look as they fell in line. Max had been the first person Christiaan met when he arrived in Haaren almost a year ago. In Rawicz, Max was in the next cell, and they built up a friendship, talking in hushed tones when the guards weren't around.

"Where do you think we are?" Max whispered, his eyes on the guard walking a few meters away. "Did you see any landmarks?"

Christiaan had scanned the station for an indicator of where they were, but like at most stations, the signs indicating the station names had been removed. He shook his head. "We must be in southern Germany, or even farther south, after crossing all those mountains." They exited the station and stepped into a small square. The two-story houses all looked alike with their shuttered windows. They differed only in the colors of the exterior walls. The square was a colorful mix of bright yellow, dark orange, and off-white houses.

There was some activity on the square as several people appeared to be out doing their grocery shopping, carrying small bags. The scent of fresh bread coming from one shop made Christiaan's mouth water. He didn't get much time to savor the normalcy, for the SS soldiers were already yelling at the prisoners to keep moving.

The eyes of the villagers followed Christiaan and his group as they made their way through the small town. Some stopped to stare, talking among themselves in hushed whispers. They seemed almost indifferent to the unfamiliar faces passing through, as if this sort of thing happened every day. Christiaan felt his body shudder, and he glanced at Max, who silently nodded.

They marched on through the narrow main street, and soon the number of houses thinned. Despite the chilly air, Christiaan was sweating, the muscles in his legs protesting. Panting, he focused his energy on putting one foot in front of the other. They walked along a winding road for another fifteen minutes, passing small farmhouses, before they reached a fork in the road. The soldier leading the group turned right, and as Christiaan looked up, he saw the road making a sharp incline. He sighed, his mouth parched, his body screaming for water. He looked at the guard closest to him. The young man looked well fed, a canteen dangling from his belt. For a second, Christiaan considered asking the man if he could get some water, but then he thought better of it. At best, it would result in a beating.

The pace of the group slowed considerably as they made their way up the winding road. Surprisingly enough, the guards appeared fine with it, only occasionally yelling at one of them to keep up. After another half hour of the grueling climb, they turned to find the valley behind them opening up. Rolling hills stretched as far as the eye could see, and a large river glistened below. It reminded him of his life with Lisa in Geneva, where they would often go for walks near the lake. He strained to remember her beautiful face. His tired mind made it harder to remember, and he cursed inwardly. Lisa was everything he had left, and knowing she was safe in London was the only consolation in his wretched life. Lisa was the reason he wouldn't give up. He made a promise, and he would be damned if he didn't do everything to keep it. *I will return to her. I will survive whatever these bastards throw at me.* He glanced again at the guard, who had taken out his canteen and took a large sip. When he caught Christiaan's look, he screwed the top back on and gave a wicked smile. "What are you looking at, you piece of shit?"

———

After an hour climbing the winding roads, the path straightened out, revealing a steep incline. Christiaan's legs ached, but he kept going. Excited voices came from the top of the hill, like men playing in a sports match. *My mind must be playing tricks on me.* He glanced at Max, who was sweating and wheezing. His face was pale, and Christiaan feared his friend might not last much longer. *It can't be far now, hold on.* The first prisoners reached the top of the hill, and the guards suddenly became restless. One of them stepped toward a prisoner and started yelling at him. Christiaan recognized the prisoner. He had spoken with Kees a few times in Rawicz.

"Come on, hurry! We need to get you processed before roll call!" He took out his baton and hit Kees in the ribs. He doubled over and coughed violently. The prisoner walking next to him reached out to help but received a vicious blow to the arm. The guard showed no patience as he took a step closer to Kees, who was clutching his stomach. "Are you going to just stand here, or are you walking on? It won't end well for you if you don't start moving now!"

Kees straightened himself and, with an effort, continued. It wasn't the first time Christiaan witnessed violence by guards. In Rawicz, intimidation and fear ruled. The only thing that surprised him since stepping off the train was that it had taken so long for the men wearing the skull-and-bones uniforms to exert their authority the way they knew how.

Christiaan reached the top, where the road flattened out, and the sight that greeted him some two hundred meters ahead almost made him stop in his tracks. The structure resembled a medieval castle, the smooth walls rising at least seven meters. Watchtowers were perched atop at regular intervals, and even from a distance, Christiaan could spot the soldiers manning machine guns, their gazes fixed on what was happening below. The castle looked out of place atop the grass-covered hill they had ascended.

He looked to his left and saw the source of the excited shouts. A group of men in smart-looking sports outfits were playing football in the meadow below. A little beyond the field stood two rows of barracks surrounded by barbed wire. People moved about the camp slowly, and even though it was hard to make out their faces, their blue-and-white striped garments unmistakably identified them as prisoners. *What is this place?*

Christiaan's group walked on toward the large structure, passing the men playing football. They were in good shape and looked relaxed, like men who didn't worry about a thing. These were no prisoners. They were guards enjoying their time off.

They neared the castle and turned left. The road under his feet changed into a gravel, the tiny stones crunching under his feet. They walked next to the towering walls. Christiaan noticed the walls weren't as smooth as they looked from a distance. They were built from large, irregularly pieces of stone with pink, black, and white flecks. *Granite?*

"Keep moving, come on!" came the command from the guard at the front. In the distance ahead he heard clanging sounds of industry, as if hundreds of people were chipping away at something. Following the guards down the narrow road, he had a sinking feeling the tiny pebbles crunching under his feet, the granite walls of the castle, and the sounds ahead were no coincidence.

CHAPTER FOURTEEN

Floris stood at the camp's main gate. He closed his eyes for a moment, savoring the late summer sun on his face. He sucked in a whiff of fresh mountain air and exhaled contently. It had been a good morning. Roll call had been quick and easy, and the men in his work detail had set off for the quarry on time. Floris, however, would not join them in the dusty pit today.

"You seem in a good mood!" Floris opened his eyes to the smiling face of Anton. "Something to do with our assignment today?"

"I'm just happy we're spared spending the day down there." Floris looked up at the cloudless sky, the sun making a steady ascent. "It'll be boiling hot in a few hours, and with any luck these new arrivals won't give us too much trouble."

"From what I heard they've made quite a journey. I'm sure they'll be too tired to try anything funny."

"Well, that's nothing new, is it? I've never seen anyone arrive here all fresh-faced and rested," Floris said with a dry chuckle. He scanned the road running up to the gate, but there was no sign of the new arrivals yet. "Where did they come from, anyway? Straight from home?"

Anton shook his head. "Some camp farther east, I think. It surprised me they assigned us; it's not like the clerks really ask them that many important questions."

"Well, in case anyone gets cocky, we'll be there to set them straight, I suppose." Handling the new arrivals was usually undertaken by the more experienced German guards. They had their way of making sure new prisoners in the camp were quickly vetted, as they called it. Floris had never witnessed the ritual, but some of the other guards spoke gleefully of when they were assigned this particular duty.

"I think that's them." Anton pointed down the road, where a group of sorry-looking men slowly approached. They wore shabby clothes, and even from a distance Floris could see they were exhausted.

"I don't think they'll pose much of a problem. We should have them processed and into their barracks before midday." Floris caressed the pistol on his hip as he walked back through the gate and informed the other guards their prisoners had arrived. Their leader, a grumpy guard named Kahler, barely acknowledged him and waved him off.

"We'll take care of it, just secure the other side of the gate and observe."

Floris nodded and pretended not to notice the condescending tone and walked back to Anton, who gave him a smirk. "Arrogant bastard," Floris muttered under his breath, in Dutch.

They stood inside the camp on one side of the large gate. Floris wondered how the men approaching the camp felt. It was an imposing sight, the high walls, the two guard turrets above the gate. He looked up to see the guards looking on somewhat boredly, unconcerned about the new arrivals. And why would they be? Thousands of prisoners passed through these gates every day, posing no threat. Even if they managed to wander away from the main camp, there was no way they would make it past the many SS barracks unseen, let alone the guards with dogs walking the outer perimeter. And if by some miracle they made it past them, their emaciated bodies wouldn't survive outside the camp for very long.

The first guard walked through the gate, nodding at Floris. "Take them to the showers first?"

Floris nodded at Kahler and his cronies. "Check with them."

The guard gave him an odd look but walked on. Floris caught a first glimpse of the prisoners as they followed the guard. Some looked up at their new surroundings, their tired eyes taking in the camp's main thoroughfare, which doubled as Appellplatz, or roll call area. This would be the center of their world for as long as they were in Mauthausen. Looking at the men, Floris almost felt sorry for them, but he quickly reminded himself these men were enemies of the Reich, just as much as the Jews working a few hundred meters down in the quarry.

The escorting guard yelled for the men at the front to follow him as he moved toward the *Wäscherei*. The first floor of the building housed the camp's large laundry run by prisoners, but it was the underground level where these new prisoners were going. They were led toward a steep single flight of stairs leading into the basement. Gripping the rickety railing as they descended, they were careful not to slip on the uneven steps. Floris watched the prisoners silently enter the camp. They had barely enough energy left to raise their feet, and they kept their heads down. As he waited for them to descend, one walking at the back caught his attention. There was something about the way he moved, his gait oddly familiar. The man's light hair was cropped short, prison-style, and he looked much like the men surrounding him. As the prisoner passed the gate, the sun momentarily blocked, he looked up for a fraction of a second. As he did, Floris felt the blood drain from his face. The man quickly scanned the broad thoroughfare lined with barracks, then dropped his head again, waiting his turn to descend into the basement.

Floris stood frozen at the gate. He felt as if he had been hit by a truck. *It can't be him.*

"Are you okay? You look like you've seen a ghost." Anton's voice sounded distant, and it took Floris a second to realize his friend was talking to him.

"I'm fine, my mind drifted for a moment."

Anton looked at him curiously but didn't push further. The last prisoners disappeared down the stairs, and Floris felt himself breathe a little easier.

"Kahler said we should wait on the other side of the basement; in case the clerks have trouble communicating with the new prisoners. Said we'd finally be useful."

"Screw him." Floris scowled, his hands shaking. Was his mind deceiving him, or did the ghost of his past really walk into the camp? There was only one way to find out. "Go ahead, I'll be right there. I just need to check on something in here."

———

The door to Block 1, the administration block, slammed shut behind Floris. He walked into a large open space where around twenty-five prisoners sat at small desks. Some were clacking away on typewriters, while others organized paperwork, or whatever other things these clerks spent their days working on. Floris didn't care, he just needed to find the person in charge of the new arrivals. He approached the man sitting closest to the door, who appeared very focused on the papers he held, not immediately noticing him. Floris was instantly annoyed at the prisoner's blatant flaunting of etiquette. He kicked the man's desk, and the man almost fell from his chair in surprise. He immediately realized his mistake and took off his cap and sprang to attention.

"Apologies, sir, I was so caught up that I didn't hear you come in." There was genuine terror in the man's eyes as he cowered before Floris. "Please forgive me, sir."

Floris enjoyed the man's squirming, and he would normally have milked it a bit longer, but he didn't have time for it today. "Be more alert next time, or you might find yourself working in the quarry tomorrow. As part of the penal unit." The man's face went pale as a sheet, and Floris felt a flutter of excitement in his stomach. They both knew assignment to the penal unit meant the man wouldn't see the sun set the next day. "I need the names of the new arrivals."

"Certainly, sir. Let me get those for you." The man practically ran across the room, talked to one of the other clerks in a rushed voice, snatched a pile of papers from his desk, and rushed back to Floris. "We have two shipments coming in today, sir. One from Rawicz, the other from Auschwitz."

Floris took the papers. The list from Auschwitz had more than a thousand names, and he quickly checked the other list. Forty-eight names. He didn't need to scan far down. At the top, his fears were confirmed.

CHAPTER FIFTEEN

Christiaan shivered as he took off his shirt. Mold covered the walls of the drafty room; the floor was covered in mud and other filth. He searched for a place to hang his clothes but found none.

"Leave those on the floor. You won't need them anymore," a guard said with a wicked grin. "Just make sure you hold on to your shoes. Now hurry up." To reinforce his point, he took Christiaan's shirt and tossed it on the floor like a rag.

Some of the other men had already finished undressing and had moved to the adjacent room. Christiaan was one of the last to enter. The cramped room had a low ceiling with six support pillars spread throughout. A network of pipes with basic showerheads was installed on the ceiling, a simple tiled floor punctuated by drains completing the massive shower room. Christiaan stepped down into the sunken shower area, where the other prisoners stood shivering. One of the guards at the front of the room opened a valve and the sound of water being pushed through the pipes above their heads could be heard. When the water reached the first showerheads and rained down, all but a few of them let out shrieks.

The water was ice cold. The men were soon involuntarily dancing from the shock to their already heavily battered systems. Christiaan struggled to stay on his feet but raised his face toward the showerhead and opened his mouth. He didn't care that his hands were numb from the cold, or that the water tasted like rotten eggs mixed with copper; he just needed to quench his thirst. It was the first time in almost two days that he had a chance to drink, and he wouldn't let it go to waste. He wasn't sure when he'd get another opportunity.

With his eyes closed, the freezing water numbing his senses, he tried to block out his surroundings. He heard the guards howling in laughter, the curses of his fellow prisoners, but their voices were distant, and Christiaan tilted his head a little, allowing the water to enter his ears, momentarily blocking out all sounds as the cold cleared his head.

An instant later, his body was on fire. With a yelp, he jumped away from the heat, only to find it replaced by similar blasts a few steps to his left and right. The water's temperature had turned scalding hot within seconds. The men in the showers ran around, searching for cover they couldn't find. It was impossible to escape the streams of heat raining down. Christiaan felt his skin burning, his heart pounding hard, struggling to process the sudden changes in temperature. He was having trouble breathing as the room filled with steam.

The guards controlling the valves roared with laughter, and some of their companions from the changing room peeked in. They had the same amused looks on their faces, but they soon left. This was nothing new to them.

The water temperature changed again, and this time the freezing water was welcome as it soothed his scorched skin. The relief was only temporary, for seconds later Christiaan felt his skin tingle from the chill. A thousand little pins pricked all over his body, making him shiver, his teeth chattering uncontrollably. He felt faint, and as he looked at the men around him, he saw their faces and upper bodies turning a faint blueish hue. Some sank to their knees, moaning and crying as the torture from above continued relentlessly.

Christiaan looked to the guards controlling the temperature. They were no longer laughing but eyeing the men on the ground with calculating looks. It was at that moment Christiaan realized that whatever he did, he must stay on his feet. One of the guards turned the valve again, and he braced himself, closing his eyes and clenching his jaw. *Don't show them your pain.* When boiling water flowed from the showerheads, he experienced a pain so intense, he clenched his hands into fists with such fury that he feared he would break his own skin. He opened his eyes, the water running down his face masking tears of pain. The guard controlling the temperature had his gaze fixed on him. Despite the scorching water raining down, Christiaan was chilled to the bone. The man's eyes were pure evil. He had truly arrived in hell.

———

When the guards grew bored of their game, the showers ceased spraying out their torturous downpour. The men pulled themselves off the wet floor and helped each other back into the changing room. Christiaan found it hard to get dressed in the new prisoners' uniform handed to him, his entire body numb. His shaking hands made it difficult to tie his shoelaces.

They somehow made it back up the stairs and into the mild September afternoon, the feeling in Christiaan's extremities slowly returning. They were led into a large room where four men wearing the same prisoners' uniforms confirmed their identities from a list. Christiaan went through the procedure in a daze, undressing for the second time in an hour. He hardly noticed the blunt razor cutting into his skin as the hair on his head was scraped off. He followed the other prisoners, all dressed identically, their heads shaved and bloody as their guards escorted them to their barracks at the back of the camp.

He vaguely registered passing yet another gate and walking alongside high walls with barracks to his right until they reached an isolated building. The door opened and Mauthausen's newest forty-eight prisoners marched inside.

The room was crowded, but Christiaan didn't care. He looked around for an empty bunk in vain. Thoroughly exhausted, he slumped against the wall and slid to the floor. He didn't care what happened next, so long as he got some sleep.

CHAPTER SIXTEEN

F loris and Anton reported to the commander's office outside the main camp early the next morning. They had been informed Bachmayer wanted to speak with them specifically before roll call. Floris had spent the night tossing and turning in his bunk. With the arrival of his brother, it couldn't be a coincidence that he was picked out by the man responsible for all prisoners. There was no doubt in Floris' mind that Bachmayer had inspected the list of new arrivals. With the men in Christiaan's group marked as political, these were exactly the kind of high-profile prisoners Bachmayer would take an interest in. *He's seen a familiar name at the top of the list.*

When they arrived, he was relieved to find the rest of the guards of their work detail waiting outside the office building as well. They, too, were surprised to be there so early, but they seemed less bothered than Floris. Most stood quietly waiting, bleary eyed, smoking cigarettes in the pleasant light of dawn.

Bachmayer walked out at exactly four thirty, looking surprisingly fresh. The men gathered around while he stood, slightly elevated, on the stairs. "Gentlemen, I'll keep this short." Bachmayer's gaze went over the group, and as they paused on Floris, his hands went clammy. His temples throbbed while his mind raced with all the punishments the German officer would come up with for the crime of being related to a political prisoner. To his relief, the Schutzhaft-lagerführer's eyes moved on as he continued. "Some of you will know about the arrival of several political prisoners yesterday. In fact, I believe our Dutch colleagues were part of the welcoming committee." He looked at Floris and Anton neutrally, and Floris nodded nervously. "They will join your work party after roll call, and you should be aware of their position in the camp. They are British spies, and they've spent the night in Block 20."

Floris barely hid his surprise. *Christiaan is a British spy?* The mention of Block 20 chilled Floris' blood. Also known as the Death Block, primarily reserved for Russian prisoners of war isolated from the rest of the camp population. Men in Block 20 did not survive Mauthausen for long.

"No doubt they've spoken to the Russian prisoners, but, unlike them, they won't stay inside. I want them to join roll call this morning, and then they'll join you in the quarry." A grin appeared on Bachmayer's face. "They'll think they've escaped the fate of the Russians, that they won't be left to die in Block 20. And they'll be correct. But I don't want to see these men returning to the camp this evening."

The guards looked at each other and nodded. Plenty of them shared Bachmayer's macabre views on prisoner management, and even though they needed little encouragement in their daily murder sprees, the Schutzhaftlagerführer's orders would ensure none of the Dutchmen would emerge from the quarry alive that afternoon.

Floris thought of his brother, the man who'd plotted with his own wife to bring him down in Amsterdam. A man who betrayed his own blood in his ill-guided belief that he, Floris, was the monster. Christiaan didn't understand the ways of the world. He didn't see the danger the Jews presented. They had stealthily taken control of the wealth of the country, and when Hitler had finally shown them for what they were, parasites of society, Floris had been certain the rest of the world would see it, too. But people like Christiaan and Nora clearly didn't. Instead, they sabotaged Floris at every turn, stabbing him in the back.

And now Christiaan was in Mauthausen, a British spy, captured and soon under Floris' control. He deserved every bit of punishment that came his way in the brutal camp. But did he deserve to die?

"I take it everything is clear," Bachmayer said from the front. "Any questions?" The way he spoke the last two words made it clear he didn't expect any. He waited for a few seconds before waving his hands at the men. "Very well. Have some breakfast and get ready for roll call. Dismissed." The officer turned around and disappeared into the building.

Floris stared at the door, vaguely aware of the other guards leaving, mumbling among themselves. If his brother really was a spy for the Brits, death was the only penalty. Floris considered the possibility. Sure, his brother had been part of the resistance in Amsterdam, but he couldn't imagine Christiaan linking up with spies from that position. He didn't have the network. Or did he? *Have I underestimated my little brother so badly?* Had Christiaan really become so influential, such a big player in the resistance, without Floris' knowledge? Had Floris unknowingly provided him with information when they were both still in Amsterdam?

Then it clicked. It was Nora. She was the key to Christiaan's rapid ascent in the resistance. When Floris had found out his wife spied on him, he thought she and Christiaan were somehow connected. But now it all made sense. Nora wasn't the one leading the operation; she was working for Christiaan. He felt a little dizzy as he put the pieces together.

"Hey, Flo, shall we get something to eat? Roll call is in less than an hour. I'm hungry, and I need some coffee." Anton stood next to him, and Floris looked at his friend, who frowned. "Are you okay?"

"I'm fine. Let's go." Floris and Anton passed the other SS barracks, where more guards made their way toward the mess hall.

Nora's deceit had been even bigger than expected, and his brother's role in the resistance was far more significant than he thought, making him both elated and downcast. Nora was out of his grasp, but his brother was right here, a prisoner going nowhere. And if Floris was right, Christiaan was an important player in the resistance, someone with significant connections. His little brother was valuable, even if Bachmayer didn't know it. He thought of everything he could extract from his little brother, blowing open the entire Amsterdam resistance. *Or more. Who says Christiaan wasn't operating outside the city by now?* Christiaan was his ticket home, a way to repair his broken reputation. But for that to happen, his brother needed to stay alive long enough to tell Floris everything he knew. Floris glanced at the man walking next to him, his best and only friend, for over a year now. Anton must've felt his gaze as he looked up inquiringly.

"I need your help. It's risky, but if we pull this off, those German bastards won't be snickering behind our backs anymore."

CHAPTER SEVENTEEN

The roll call area that was nearly deserted when he arrived was now packed. Christiaan stood among the other prisoners about halfway down the thoroughfare. SS guards walked between the rows of prisoners, counting them for the second time this morning. They had spotted a problem with the initial count, which meant the process was repeated from the start. It was a familiar procedure for Christiaan, who spent plenty of hours on his feet in Rawicz's prison yard.

He glanced around, doing a quick count of the prisoners on the Appellplatz, and he estimated there were at least a couple thousand men in ill-fitting, mismatching prisoners' uniforms. He'd spoken to some of the Russians in his block, and they told him the clothes used to belong to their comrades. Christiaan didn't have to ask what happened to them.

One guard passed by, and Christiaan kept his eyes straight ahead. He felt his stomach grumble as the man walked by, mumbling his count. They were given no food the night prior, and his knees were shaking, his head throbbing from hunger. *After roll call, surely.*

Christiaan's heart lurched as two guards broke away from their count and stepped into one of the lines. Out of the corner of his eye, he could make out a figure on the ground convulsing wildly—too wild to be a natural movement. The guards screamed something at him, but there was no response—only more violent thrashing. He turned his head enough to get a better look, just in time to see one of the guards lash out with his baton, again and again. Then, in an instant, an agonized wail surged through the air and the man stopped moving. Christiaan felt his hands shaking as if he were being struck by that same baton.

"Shut up and get back in line, or else!" the other guard shouted, loud enough to interrupt the counting of the other prisoners. It got the attention of the officer at the front. He had been leading the roll call and made his way over. He took a quick look, snapped his fingers, and flicked his hand toward the platform at the front. The two guards unceremoniously dragged the barely conscious man from the lineup. The man's moans echoed through the silent Appellplatz. Even though Christiaan was too far away to make out his eyes, he could make out the apathetic expression, one of surrender.

The officer reached the platform, and it soon became clear what was happening. Two of the guards lifted the person onto a small platform, then two more arrived with a thick rope in hand. They tossed the rope over an iron bar that hung three meters above the platform; it was attached to two large columns on either side. Christiaan felt nauseous witnessing their familiar movements as they brought their plan to fruition.

The prisoner was held upright as they placed the rope around his neck. He was now close enough for Christiaan to see the hollow expression in his eyes. His clothes hung loosely around his frame; he was severely malnourished and unaware of his surroundings. One guard forcefully tightened the noose around his neck, and a flicker of realization appeared on the man's face. It passed a second later as he continued his soft wailing.

"This is what happens to useless prisoners." The man in the officer's uniform spoke evenly, his voice booming across the Appellplatz. Behind him, the guards took a few steps back, pulling the rope taut. The men holding the prisoner relaxed their grip on his arms, and then the officer nodded. With a grunt, the guards pulled on the rope, lifting the man off the platform. They quickly secured the rope on a small wooden beam behind them.

Christiaan watched in silent terror as the man on the rope stirred from his limp state. The fear of an imminent death was etched into his face, his bulging eyes almost popping out of their sockets and his cheeks becoming a shade of scarlet. His hands clawed frantically at the rope while his feet kicked against air, hoping to find a miracle foothold. In no more than thirty seconds, what felt like an eternity, he hung suspended, lifeless, head bowed and body still.

For a few seconds, the Appellplatz was silent. Not even the guards on the platform moved, as if they were waiting to make sure the prisoner was dead, and there wouldn't be any final death throes. A powerful gust of wind made the prisoner swing eerily on the gallows, and Christiaan closed his eyes. When he opened them, he saw the guards continuing their counts as if nothing had happened.

When they moved out for work fifteen minutes later, the dead man's body swung lightly on the rope, his bulging eyes an unmistakable warning to the living marching past. Life was worthless in Mauthausen.

Christiaan passed the gate in a daze, following the footsteps of the man in front of him, his head down. Even though the Russians in the barracks had warned him, he hadn't expected a hanging before the day had properly started. But what had he expected? The surrounding prisoners wore expressions not unlike the man murdered at roll call. There was no hope. They passed the SS barracks lining the road on either side. Christiaan wondered how long it would take before the camp would break him as well; until he would walk in the same unremitting daze. Would he die like the man at roll call?

It hadn't even been twenty-four hours. *This is how you lose hope, this is how the camp gets you.* They neared the edge of the quarry and the procession turned. Guards walked on both sides of the group, their hands unconsciously resting on the sides of their belts. The morning's showing proved the guards were more than capable with their batons. Christiaan made a note to avoid catching their attention at all costs.

His stomach grumbled again, followed by a sharp stab of pain. It was becoming harder to ignore the hunger pangs. He couldn't remember his last meal, but he felt more sluggish with each step, his eyes hurting as the first rays spilled between the trees on the other side of the quarry. *Keep going, Chris, they'll have to feed you at some point.* He tried to keep his spirits up, but one look at the men around him, in their loose-fitting uniforms severely dampened his expectations. He would need to find another way to get food, and he would need to do it fast if he wanted to survive the camp.

Christiaan felt a nearby presence and turned his head. As soon as he did, he wished he hadn't. A guard walked uncomfortably close by, his eyes following Christiaan with interest. *What did I do to catch his attention?* Unsure what to do, Christiaan turned his face away from the man, hoping that would be enough. He was not that fortunate.

"Listen to me." The man spoke urgently. "If you want to live, you need to do exactly as I say."

Christiaan turned his head in surprise. Was his tired mind playing tricks on him or did the guard address him in Dutch? He wasn't sure how to respond and decided to pretend not to have understood the man. *Is this a trap?* His thoughts went back to the hanging at roll call. *The guards can't be trusted. Whatever it is he's doing, he must be tricking me. He doesn't even know me. Why does he care what happens to me?*

Yet, before Christiaan averted his gaze, he saw something in the man's eyes he couldn't quite place. Was it genuine concern? Interest? *It doesn't matter. I can't trust him.*

The guard grabbed his shoulder, forcing him to slow down somewhat. "Look, you can ignore me, but if you do, you'll be dead before noon. Think about the men in your block. The Russians. They're not here, are they? It's just you and the other Dutch agents." *Agents. He knows who I am.* His surprise must've shown, for the guard nodded at him, a weak smile appearing on his face. "Why do you think you were placed in that block with the Russians last night? Did you get a good look at them?"

Christiaan met the guard's eyes but didn't respond. The Russian soldiers looked worse off than most of the men at roll call. They told him they hadn't been outside their block for two weeks. They didn't say why, but Christiaan had his suspicions.

"It's a death block. They're starved to death. They're isolated from the other prisoners. And if you were bunked with them last night, and you're walking out here now, what do you think that means?" Christiaan's throat constricted, the guard's words chilling him. The man let go of his shoulder. "Slow down if you want to live, Christiaan. And not a word to anyone else. Just you."

He opened his mouth, but the guard was gone, moving back in the stream of prisoners. He looked around and found his friend Max looking at him curiously.

"What did he want?"

"I'm not sure."

Christiaan pondered the guard's words as they neared the quarry's entrance. Was the man genuine, or was he being set up?

CHAPTER EIGHTEEN

Floris secured the rear of the procession and watched Anton make his way back. He hadn't been able to pick out anything from Christiaan and Anton's conversation as both men had their backs to him. Christiaan continued walking at the same pace, staying in the group of condemned agents. It was concerning.

"I'm not sure he believed me," Anton said as he fell in line next to Floris. "I couldn't have made the danger any clearer, but he seemed oddly detached."

"Did he say anything?" Floris felt his frustration grow. Even the explicit threat of death didn't stir his brother. *Damn, why must he always be so stubborn?*

"No. But he understood me; I could see it in his eyes."

Floris grunted in frustration. The first prisoners walked into the quarry, and as soon as Christiaan did the same, it would be almost impossible for Floris to separate him from the other agents. The guards were keen to carry out Bachmayer's orders, and Floris had overheard them talking about how they would do it on their way to roll call. In the monotone life of the guards, the arrival of these special political prisoners—no, spies, even—was an exciting event.

Bachmayer's orders had been clear, and Floris knew the men were eager to carry out their murderous task. Normally, Floris didn't care much for the executions. This morning, however, he had to make sure his brother survived. He scanned the prisoners in front of him. Christiaan continued moving at the same pace. *I'll have to go get him myself.* Floris gripped his baton and upped his pace, about to push aside the first prisoners between his brother and him.

"Hey, what do you think you're doing?" Anton grabbed his elbow, his eyes shooting up toward the guard towers fifty meters ahead. "They'll be watching. How do you think it'll look when they see you pull him from the group? The other guards will notice, too."

"Let go, Anton. I need to get him out of there. I'll be quick, they won't see." Floris shook his arm, but Anton held firm.

"You can't take the risk, Flo! You know these guys are waiting for you to make another mistake and report you to Bachmayer again. And what do you think will happen if they find out you're brothers? How will that look, huh?" Anton peered at him with determination. "Trust me, I tried my best. If he didn't get the message, he obviously doesn't want to."

Anton's words were hard to process. Christiaan was so close, but Floris knew his friend was right. He had been lucky no one had made the connection between them yet, and he couldn't afford to draw attention to himself. Not with Christiaan. He felt anger bubbling up inside him, the muscles in his forehead constricting as he ground his teeth in frustration. There was nothing he could do but hope for another opportunity before they assigned Christiaan to *mule duty*. He felt his hope fade with every step toward the wide-open space of the quarry floor.

He focused on his brother, who, for the first time that morning, turned his head. Floris frowned, urging his brother on under his breath. *Come on, Chris. Slow down, move toward me.* Up on the ridge of the quarry, Floris spotted two guards. They were facing the other way. *Now, Chris.*

It was as if his brother heard him as he slowed his pace, allowing other men to overtake him. Even though Floris couldn't see his eyes, he could see his brother's head moving slightly to the left and right, monitoring the guards walking on both sides of the procession. Floris eyed them too, and he saw with relief that the mass of prisoners was too large to make out any movement in the middle. The guards didn't care too much about what happened in the prisoner detachment, so long as nobody tried to break from the lines.

"Looks like he got the message, after all," Anton said, watching Christiaan. "Smart man. I wonder how he'll respond when he sees you."

If his brother made a scene, it would mean the end for both of them. Floris would have no way to explain why his brother had broken away from the group. But if Christiaan really was a spy, Floris had to believe his brother would understand Floris was the only person who could help him in this camp. It was why he'd sent Anton to talk to him. Christiaan made his way through the other prisoners and looked alert in a sea of fearful faces.

Christiaan was now only five meters away. Almost all the prisoners ahead of him had turned into the quarry. The dusty, dry air of the quarry floor filled Floris' nostrils. Soon they would be out in the open, where it would be nigh impossible to hide from the omnipresent gazes of the Kapos and guards, ready to pounce on any infraction. There would be no chance for Floris to pull his brother from the group of spies. *Come on, Chris, hurry up.*

Floris inched forward, this time pushing a few of the prisoners out of the way as Christiaan came within reach. His brother paused his walking again, and Floris grabbed the back of his shirt, yanking him, not letting go of his shirt as they entered the quarry.

"Not a word, and don't turn around!" Floris snarled in his ear. Christiaan stopped dead in his tracks. Despite Floris' warning, Christiaan pivoted his head, his gaze locking with his brother's, his shock and confusion clear as day. He opened his mouth to speak, but Floris fiercely shook his head and dug his fingers into Christiaan's ribs. "Do what I tell you if you want to stay alive."

CHAPTER NINETEEN

Christiaan's entire body was shaking as he followed the rest of the prisoners to the center of the quarry. Drills, pickaxes clanging, and men hammering away at the slabs of granite faded into the background as he felt his brother's hand burning in the small of his back. Was it really Floris walking behind him, or was he so hungry that he had gone mad? He didn't dare look back a second time.

His head was swimming as the group of prisoners stopped. The guards moved to the front, and the first smaller groups broke away for their day's assignments in the quarry. Floris moved next to him as they did, and Christiaan realized it really was his brother. He looked bigger and stronger than the last time he'd seen him, and he stood proudly in his SS uniform. Christiaan had so many questions, but he kept his lips tightly pressed together.

"When I call out my prisoners, follow me," Floris said from the corner of his mouth. "And don't look back."

The group was rapidly shrinking, and Christiaan noticed the other Dutch agents were kept apart. He wondered if the guards would notice he was missing, that they were a man short. He spotted Max and felt a pang of guilt. Even though he didn't know exactly what was about to happen, Floris' warning had been clear enough. He looked around and took in the bustle of the quarry. Hundreds—no, thousands—of prisoners slaved there, pushing carts, drilling, or chipping away at the granite walls towering twenty to thirty meters high. Guards kept watch at regular intervals, with more patrolling the grounds, some with dogs. It wouldn't be easy to escape. In fact, as he looked up at the guard towers lining the ridge, he decided it would be impossible.

"Okay, detail one-one-four, come with me." Floris' voice boomed in his ear, and about fifty men moved toward Floris, who gave Christiaan a small shove in the direction of a large shed. "Be quick with your equipment—we've got a lot of work to do."

None of the men making their way toward the shed took notice of Christiaan. They moved mechanically as they collected their pickaxes. Christiaan accepted one as he heard his brother warn the men to return their tools in the afternoon. "Anyone without one will face severe punishment." The men didn't respond as they moved to a site near the walls. They were soon chipping away, and Christiaan did the same. His shirt was drenched within minutes, the muscles in his arm aching from the unfamiliar task. A trickle of sweat ran down his forehead and he used his shirt sleeve to wipe it away, catching his breath as he rested on his pickax for a moment.

"What do you think you're doing? Did I say you could take a break?" Floris' harsh words in German sounded behind him, and Christiaan turned around. His brother moved toward him, waving his baton menacingly. "You're new, aren't you? Come, I'll show you what happens to prisoners who think they can take breaks."

Christiaan felt the eyes of the other prisoners working the wall on him, even if they kept picking away at the same rhythm. He turned and walked toward Floris, catching the gaze of the man next to him. His wrinkled, sunburned face and emaciated body made him look years older than he was. But it was the eyes that caught Christiaan's attention. Bright blue and filled with terror. The man quickly averted his gaze as Floris neared.

"Take your pickax and follow me." He swung the baton back and landed a blow on Christiaan's shoulder. Floris then muttered something to the other guard, the one that approached Christiaan earlier, and moved away from the group.

Christiaan rubbed his back but didn't say anything as he followed Floris. They walked alongside the quarry wall, and it was then that Christiaan first noticed the limp. *When did he pick that up?*

They reached the other side of the quarry, where a steep slope curved up around the edge. At the bottom of the slope, Christiaan spotted a group of about two hundred men gathered around a large pile of rocks. They had wooden carriers strapped to their backs, and several prisoners without the carriers were loading rocks onto these packs. It was an odd sight, and Christiaan was confused when Floris halted at a quiet spot about a hundred meters from the incline. On closer inspection, Christiaan spotted the uneven steps carved into the incline. It was a very steep staircase running from the bottom to the top of the quarry. Christiaan could see why they hadn't taken this route this morning; thousands of laborers making their way down the stairs would take far too long, not to mention the danger of someone missing a step.

"Take a look at the men in that group," Floris said, his voice back to normal. "Recognize any of them?" He leaned against a large boulder.

Christiaan had a sinking feeling in the pit of his stomach. He soon recognized the other Dutch agents, the men with whom he'd spent the past year. They all had wooden carriers strapped to their backs.

"You must be wondering what they're doing," Floris said, clicking his tongue. "That's the penal squad. They'll be carrying rocks up those stairs all day."

Christiaan remembered the effort it took to lift his pickax minutes ago. He was grateful Floris interrupted his work. He couldn't imagine the guards near the staircase affording their prisoners the same luxury. The first men moved toward the steps, their carriers half-full. Despite that, it was clear they were having difficulties as they gripped the leather bands on their shoulders tightly, evidently struggling with the weight of the rocks tugging at their backs. Slowly, the men ascended the stairs, others following closely behind, harried forward by guards ascending the steps, unhampered by additional weight.

"There are a hundred and eighty six steps. I've climbed them myself a few times." Floris spoke matter-of-factly, his eyes on the group. The first climbers were almost halfway up. "Even without the burden of those rocks, it's difficult to keep your balance."

Christiaan looked on with bated breath as the first of his comrades started the climb. He turned to Floris, his voice uneven. "What's the point? Isn't it quicker to use the carts running along the quarry?"

"Just watch. It'll soon become clear."

It took ten minutes for the group to reach the top. They disappeared from sight, and Christiaan turned back to his brother. "Why did you separate me from the group? How did you know I was here?"

Floris didn't immediately answer, his gaze on the steps. Christiaan didn't push, instead inspecting his surroundings. He couldn't imagine Floris saving him from hard labor without a reason.

When the first men returned and took their initial careful steps down the stairs, Floris spoke up. "Did you see how their packs were only half-full on the way up? That will be a bit different now."

They reached the bottom and the process of loading their packs was repeated. As Floris predicted, the packs were now filled almost to the brim, and most men now keeled backward as they struggled toward the steps. As soon as all prisoners made it to the bottom and had their packs filled, the guards forced them back up.

Floris stepped away from the boulder and stood next to Christiaan. "It won't be much longer now."

Christiaan's dread intensified. The staircase was filled with men packed closely together, their groans loud enough for Christiaan to hear. Then it happened. A man in the middle of the group lost his balance. The weight of the boulders in his carrier pulled him backward, setting the first rocks flying down. They landed squarely in the face of the man behind him, who tumbled backward, taking the man behind down with him. He tried to catch himself, and in his panicked state reached for the men to his sides. Seconds later, more than a hundred men had toppled down the stairs like human dominoes. Christiaan watched in horror as the mangled bodies lay at the bottom of the stairs. Most were still moving, their cries of pain echoing through the quarry. Others no longer moved, their limbs pointing at unnatural angles. Nausea rose in Christiaan's throat as he watched the injured men pushing the dead—their heads joggling freely on their broken necks—away from them. He turned to his brother, who looked at the scene without emotion. *He's seen this many times before.* Christiaan opened his mouth, but no words came out. Floris pointed at the horror scene below the stairs.

"It's not over yet."

Reluctantly, Christiaan turned back. Guards swarmed on the stricken men, feverishly beating and kicking them. Within a few minutes, none of the men at the bottom of the stairs moved. Almost a hundred men had been reduced to a heap of bones and boulders within a minute.

The remaining prisoners had made it to the top. They too looked back in horror. Christiaan couldn't imagine how they felt. There was no doubt they realized this was their fate as well. When those at the front started moving away from the staircase to unload their packs, the guards stopped them. *What are they doing?*

To his shock, Christiaan recognized Max as one of the men called over by the guards. Along with four others, he was told to line up on the side of the stairs. The guard pointed at Max, then at another prisoner. Even from a distance, Christiaan could see the shock and horror on his friend's face. Without taking his eyes off the situation, he asked, "What are they telling him, Floris?" He wasn't sure he wanted to know.

"Just watch."

Max shook his head at the guard, taking a step back. He caught himself just in time, for he stood close to the quarry edge. The guard appeared to repeat himself, and Max raised his hands pleadingly this time, shaking his head. The guard then nodded, and without warning, shoved Max.

"No!" Christiaan gasped as time slowed down. Max lost his footing and stumbled backward. He desperately tried to regain his balance, arms flailing, but the guard's push had been too forceful, the rocks on his back taking care of the rest. He tumbled over the edge and crashed down to the quarry floor thirty meters below. Christiaan closed his eyes and flinched as his friend landed on the stony ground with a dull thud. A few seconds later, another body landed.

"That's what I saved you from." Christiaan turned away from the stairs and faced Floris, who looked at him with a neutral expression. "Your group was marked for death the moment you arrived." A scream pierced the air behind Christiaan, abruptly cut off a couple of seconds later. Floris cocked his head and took a few steps in the other direction. "Come, let's get back to work."

Christiaan followed his brother in a daze, his mind struggling to comprehend what he'd witnessed since waking up that morning. He was now completely on his own in the camp. Whatever reason Floris had for keeping him alive, it wasn't out of brotherly love. They reached their work detail, where the other guard stood anxiously waiting.

"Flo, two of the prisoners collapsed."

"Perfect. Did you take care of their bodies the way we agreed?"

The other man nodded. "They're behind those enormous boulders there. Out of sight."

"Thanks, Anton, I'll take care of it." Floris turned to Christiaan, his eyes urgent. "Come."

The brothers reached the boulders and Floris quickly glanced around to make sure no one was looking. He then signaled for Christiaan to follow him. Behind the large stones lay two prisoners of around the same age as Christiaan. They appeared asleep, but the conversation between Floris and Anton had made it clear they were anything but. Floris inspected the men's shirts and prisoner emblems sewn onto their left breast pocket. Both were German prisoners, the only difference in the color of their badges; green and black. Floris didn't hesitate and pointed at the man with the green badge. "Swap your shirt for his."

Christiaan didn't immediately respond, and Floris grabbed his arm, pulling him toward the dead man. "Chris, you need to take his shirt, now." He pointed at Christiaan's badge, a red triangle with the letter *N*. "You're dead. You died on the stairs just now. Take his identity and live. That green triangle means he's a criminal prisoner. I'll find out his name and why he's in here, but from now on, you're no longer Christiaan Brouwer." Floris was already stripping the corpse. Christiaan had no other option but to do what his brother said. He slid the shirt over his head and shuddered. Perhaps because he was wearing a dead man's clothes, or because he would soon find out why his brother had saved him.

CHAPTER TWENTY

L isa emerged from the large tent and yawned. It had been a long shift, and she was looking forward to getting a cup of coffee and a slice of toast in the mess tent. She walked along one of the main paths through the camp, passing neatly positioned identical-looking tents. Voices sounded from a few, the flaps firmly shut on this cold October morning. She smiled as a chorus of laughter greeted her from the mess tent. No matter the time, the improvised mess hall was always crowded, even outside mealtimes.

She entered and headed toward the food counter, scanning the tables for familiar faces. Her night shift had been especially busy, and she looked forward to catching up on gossip and listening to the men's stories from home. The mess hall was a good place to forget about the war for a bit. She picked up a large mug and filled it to the brim, savoring the smell of fresh coffee. After slathering a thick piece of toast with jam, she headed for a crowded table in the back.

"Hey, Lisa!" One of the men moved over, patting a spot on the bench next to him.

"Steve, when did you get back? Haven't seen you for a few days," Lisa said, smiling as she squeezed between him and another soldier.

As she bit into her toast, her legs tingled, and she massaged her calves. She'd been up all night, assisting the Red Cross doctors as they made their rounds. Even though they'd been stalled near the German border for a few weeks now, General Patton had made it clear to his troops that they should remain ready to move out as soon as possible. It was why the Third United States Army hadn't set up any more permanent dwellings, living and operating in their tents instead. It didn't matter, for the soldiers were sent on frequent, round-the-clock sorties. Even if the army didn't have enough fuel to push farther east, Patton made sure his troops didn't get bored, and more importantly, that the Germans never had a chance to catch their breath and get comfortable. The experienced general's approach worked. Morale was high, despite the temporary halt in their push from the French coast all the way to the western German border.

"Came back early this morning. Didn't see much action, but it was a good chance to stretch our legs and explore the riverside a bit. I heard some of the other squads ran into Jerries, though, chalking up some victories." Steve raised his mug and took a large gulp. "What about you? Keeping busy in the hospital? Hope you don't have too many of our boys coming in?"

"It's not too bad. Just making sure everybody is comfortable. I don't really see the severe cases until they're doing better." Lisa spoke candidly. She was happy working as a nurse and traveling with the Third Army. Her training in London had been swift, even if they'd only taught her the basics. Her job went beyond her Red Cross nurse's uniform, even if only a few people in the camp knew. Like Steve. She'd joined his squad a few times when they needed someone to talk to the French villagers. He'd been curious about how she joined the Red Cross, and she'd told him about her work back in London. Well, the basics, anyway. In return, he spoke candidly about his life as a soldier, and they often met in the mess tent to exchange stories. Steve loved to talk about his wife and one-year-old daughter at home.

"Say, if we're chalking up victories along the Saar River, do you think we might push on soon? Did your platoon commander tell you anything?" After two weeks in one spot, Lisa was getting a little restless.

"Not really. In fact, I heard we might be stuck here a while longer. Story is that Allied command is hesitant to send us more fuel. Something about a big operation happening somewhere else soon, and they're saving all the gas for that one."

"I'm sure the general isn't too pleased about that."

Steve whistled through his teeth. "That's putting it mildly. From what I hear he's royally pissed off, giving Ike hell every day, telling him we can end this war by Christmas if we're only given the things we need."

"And what do you think?"

"Hey, whatever General Patton wants to do, I'm down. He hasn't been wrong before, has he? We've made it to the border within two months. Give us another two and we'll be in Berlin." Some of the other men at the table raised their mugs in agreement, and Lisa smiled. She hoped Patton could convince the Supreme Allied Commander soon enough, and they would be on their way. The sooner they crossed the Saar River, the sooner they'd be able to kick on. She was convinced if they kept moving east, Hitler would have no choice but to start peace negotiations.

A man approached their table, his eyes focused on her. "Lisa Abrahams?" She nodded, and he made a gesture indicating she should stand up. "You're wanted in the command tent. Please come with me immediately."

Lisa stood, no longer tired, a flutter in her stomach. A summons to the command tent only meant one thing. She was needed for something beyond her Red Cross duties.

———

An hour later, Lisa walked in the middle of a group of soldiers. They had left the camp fifteen minutes ago, and Lisa was buzzing with excitement. When she had reported to the command tent, she was immediately told she needed to join a patrol headed for Saarlouis, one of the larger cities on the banks of the Saar River. The Third Army recently drove the Germans from the city, resulting in the capture of many German soldiers. It was essential for these men to be interrogated as quickly as possible, and they could use Lisa's help. There were also many civilians left, and they too could have valuable intelligence about the area.

"So you speak German and French?" the soldier walking next to her asked. When she nodded, he clicked his tongue and smiled. "Where did you learn that? I only barely speak English."

"We learn a bit of everything in school, but when the Germans invaded our country, I had little choice." She thought back to life in Amsterdam right after the occupation. Initially, not that much had changed, other than the many German patrols across the city. As a Jewess, before she knew it she was hiding in a dusty basement with her parents. Her heart ached at the thought of her parents. Lisa still felt guilty for leaving them behind that New Year's morning when Christiaan took her to safety. The next day, the house was raided, and her parents were taken to Westerbork. From there, Lisa knew it was only days until they boarded trains headed for the camps in the east. She choked back tears as she composed herself. She was alive, and she was part of the liberating forces. The Nazis hadn't beaten her.

"When I arrived in Geneva, it was only natural to learn the language." They continued along the side of a narrow road, the soldiers constantly scanning their surroundings. Even though this area was secured by the Third Army, it was always possible the Germans sent ambush squads behind the lines. General Patton did the same, to devastating effect. It was why the Third Army was able to capture so many positions along their side of the river.

"Well, I'm glad you did," the soldier said as the first houses appeared farther up the road. "The people in this town have been stuck in the fighting for months, and I'm sure they'll respond better to someone speaking their language." He patted his jacket. "Although I did bring chocolate. That usually helps break the ice."

The number of houses lining the road grew as they passed the outskirts of Saarlouis. Lisa imagined the city used to be beautiful, quaint even, before the war. Now, as they carefully made their way farther into the city, the traces of war were evident everywhere. Windows were blown out, holes from bullets scattered along steps and walls, roofs had collapsed under mortar fire. They passed piles of rubble that used to be people's homes, gardens that were surely kept in immaculate shape now mounds of mud and dirt. But most of all, Lisa was once again struck by how quiet it was. At first, when she arrived in France two months ago, the absence of people had surprised her. The soldiers explained most people fled the fighting, either trekking farther east, or hiding in nearby forests. When the fighting ended and the Germans fled, the inhabitants slowly returned, hesitant at first at the sight of new soldiers passing through their cities. Even though Lisa knew what to expect, the experience of being among the first to trek through these deserted battlefields that once were people's homes remained hard to get used to.

She was comforted by the sight of more American soldiers at the entrance to a number of collapsed apartment blocks. Behind them lay an expansive square, seemingly vulnerable to an attack, but more American soldiers had spread out across the square, guarding the narrow streets. She observed some activity within the ruins on either side of the area and was taken aback to see civilians bustling around the remains.

"They're inspecting what used to be their homes, hoping to salvage anything of value." A huge person wearing a captain's uniform approached Lisa; his name tag read "Samuel." His face was square and solid, and she involuntarily took a step back. But then he smiled, a bittersweet expression on his face, and he didn't seem so intimidating anymore. "Unfortunately, I don't think they'll find much. Whatever was there, food, jewelry, or money, I'm sure the German soldiers took. They spent more than a month holed up in this town, and we only took the square last night. You must be Lisa Abrahams."

"I am," Lisa said, shaking the man's outstretched hand. "I hear you've got the Germans on the run. They're no longer in the city?"

"Most of them fled across the river, yes. I'm sure some are still hidden or stuck inside the city, but they would be fools to show themselves without any backup. We've got most of the western side of the city secured. Besides, we've got several of their comrades. I doubt they would try anything that would endanger them." He waved across the square, where a group of some twenty German soldiers sat on their knees on the ground floor of a shot-up building. They were guarded by half a dozen American soldiers, who looked relaxed as they chatted among themselves. "I need you to talk to those boys over there. These are the ones that surrendered. Most of them aren't much older than twenty. They're scared, and I think a woman's face might put them at rest."

Lisa nodded. "What do you need from them?" She had an idea, but she wanted to make sure she didn't waste this opportunity. It would be the first time she spoke to the enemy, and she felt a mix of excitement and anxiety rising inside her.

"We need to know what's waiting on the other side of the river. Ask them if their commanders were confident about defending the other side of the city, or if they perhaps planned to fall farther back. I'm not sending American men across the bridge without that intel. Heck, Patton would kill me if he heard me even considering it. Can you do that, Lisa?"

She nodded, her eyes drifting to the bound soldiers on the other side of the square. Despite Samuel's confidence, she felt apprehensive about crossing. He appeared to sense her unease, for he called two soldiers to his side.

"Escort Ms. Abrahams to the POWs and wait for her there. Don't stand too close to them; give her space to talk."

The men nodded and Lisa felt more secure as she crossed the square between the two well-equipped American soldiers. She'd insisted on wearing her Red Cross uniform when she left the camp, and she was glad she had. It felt safer to be marked as a nurse rather than a combatant.

They reached the German POWs without incident and the soldiers hung back with the other guards gathered around a small fire. Lisa took a few steps inside the building. It was cold and drafty, and water leaked from an unknown source above their heads. She approached the German POWs, their hands tied behind their backs and secured to a rusty pipe. It would be impossible for the men to run, although judging by their calm demeanor, it didn't look like they were much of a flight risk. They had surrendered, after all. The young men looked up at her as she sat down across from one of them.

"My name is Lisa," she started in German. "I'm with the Red Cross, and I'm here to check on you. Are you all right? Have you been treated well by the Americans?" Even though she was part of the American army, she knew it was important to build trust with these men. They were captured, helpless, and surrounded by enemies. Lisa imagined how they must feel, and she could only come up with one word: terrified. She'd heard stories of how the Russians treated their POWs on the eastern front, and there was no doubt the young men tied up before her had heard the same.

At first, none answered. Some turned their faces away, while others looked back at her uncertainly. Then, one of the men shifted, drawing Lisa's attention. His bright blue eyes met her gaze—glazed with sadness and despair.

"We're thirsty and hungry," he said, licking his parched lips. "We haven't eaten in over twenty-four hours. Can you help us with that?"

Lisa was surprised by his soft-spoken manner. The way he clipped his words reminded her of some of her classmates back home when she was still allowed to attend university. She nodded. "I can help you with that if you tell me a few things first. I promise I'll bring you food and water. Our camp is nearby, and from what I've seen, the road into the city is secure. But before I can do that, can you tell me if that's correct? Is the road secure?"

The soldier looked at her for a moment, then nodded. "You must've approached Saarlouis from the west? Where the Americans are based?" Lisa nodded, and he continued. "We held the last position on this side of the river here, in the city. The American attacks in the open areas north and south of the river were too strong, and we were forced to withdraw to the city." He nodded at the soldiers tied up around him. "We were told not to abandon our position, whatever happened. But we didn't know the other squads had retreated from the city in the past twelve hours. We were left to fight the Americans on our own." He hung his head, and Lisa wondered whether it was exhaustion or shame. "When we saw the Americans approach from all sides of the square, we knew we didn't stand a chance, and we surrendered."

Lisa was surprised to feel sorry for the young man across from her. He was abandoned by his superiors, left to fight an impossible battle. "So, you're saying the rest of your army has fallen back to the other side of the river?"

He nodded. "The other side is heavily fortified. It's nothing like this side. They've abandoned us."

They've set up an ambush on the other side. Or is this soldier part of the ruse? "I need to know you're speaking the truth."

The young man fervently shook his head. "I swear it's the truth. We didn't want to join the army. We didn't want this war, but we have no choice. Every able-bodied young man in Germany has been called up." Several of the men around him nodded. "We're just fortunate we weren't sent east. Do you think the Russians would have brought the Red Cross? They would've executed us on the spot. In a few months, this war will be over, and Hitler will have gone. And maybe we'll be allowed to rebuild our country."

Lisa listened to him. Even though he was tied up and would say anything to save his skin, she believed he was sincere. He was only a few years younger than her and, while technically the enemy, he had the same hopes for the future as her. He wanted the war to end, and to resume life, a normal life.

"I'm going to talk to the captain and tell him you're willing to cooperate. I'll also recommend we provide you with some food and water. I'll be right back. Thank you ... what's your name?"

For the first time, a smile spread on the young man's face. "Theodore, ma'am. Theodore Wessels."

———

Samuel listened without interrupting as Lisa relayed Theodore Wessels' words. "I don't believe he was deceiving me, sir. He appeared genuine. You were right; they're just boys."

"Very well. We'll need to relay this back to command." He signaled to one of the soldiers carrying a radio. "I'll also ask for some extra supplies for the POWs. I suspect they'll open up even more once they've had something to eat. Would you mind hanging around a bit longer, Lisa?"

"Not a problem, sir."

Samuel took the receiver from the radio operator, dismissing Lisa. She approached a group of soldiers sitting next to one of the buildings. One of them offered her a piece of chocolate, and she took it gratefully—perhaps they realized she wasn't just a nurse. Soldiers were observant.

She was about to take a bite when she heard an odd whistling sound in the distance. She didn't get a chance to see where it came from, for the men around her immediately sprang into action. The soldier next to her grabbed Lisa's shoulder and pulled her to the ground. A few seconds later, the top floor of one of the buildings across the square was blown away in an explosion of concrete and dust.

Lisa kept her head down but had an unobstructed view of the square. The area where she had calmly walked back to Captain Samuel less than five minutes ago had transformed into a battlefield. The soldiers guarding the German POWs had taken cover in the next-door building, leaving the young Germans completely unguarded. It didn't matter, they were securely tied up.

The whistles of incoming mortars ripped through the air, sending shock waves through Lisa's body. Buildings across the square roared as they collapsed inward, raining rubble and debris all around. The intensity of the barrage was unbearable, and Lisa's heart was thumping in her chest. The soldiers scanned the square as everyone scrambled for safety. Suddenly several shells landed in the middle of the square, bouncing around before erupting into a deafening hiss that filled the sky with acrid smoke.

"As long as they're firing artillery, they won't commit men." The soldier next to Lisa spoke calmly, keeping his rifle trained at the smokescreen in front of them. "They're just trying to rattle us."

Well, it's working. Lisa's fingers tingled and her heartbeat pounded in her ears. The bombardment continued for another ten minutes, explosions rocking the ground underneath her. With every whistle she prayed the Germans on the other side of the river didn't adjust their aim.

A soft breeze picked up, clearing the smoke from the square. The whistles stopped, and the ground stopped shaking. *Is it over?* The soldiers around Lisa got back to their feet, and she shakily accepted an outstretched hand.

"Don't worry, this happens all the time," the soldier said with a wry smile. "They just want to show us they're still here. We do the same to them."

Lisa put on a brave face and watched the last remnants of smoke clear from the square. She was relieved to hear American soldiers yelling the all clear from the different corners of the square. But when she looked directly across, she had trouble believing her eyes. One of the buildings was completely blown away. She felt a stab of sorrow in her heart. The building where she had talked to Theodore Wessels, the young German soldier who couldn't wait for the war to end and rebuild his country, was no longer there. In its place raged a blazing fire amid piles of debris. The young soldiers hadn't stood a chance.

CHAPTER TWENTY-ONE

Christiaan stood waiting his turn, counting the men ahead of him. There were only six, and he sighed softly, making sure none of the Kapos hovering around heard. He resisted the urge to bend forward and rest his hands on his knees for a few seconds. One of the other prisoners had done so that morning, immediately catching their attention. The men had descended on him, raining powerful blows with their leather-covered truncheons. The prisoner was dragged away minutes later, unceremoniously thrown on the pile of bodies in a nearby cart. That cart was headed toward the crematorium halfway through the morning. The new cart was rapidly filling up, and it wasn't even noon.

The dusty, gray world in front of his eyes was spinning, yet he was grateful for the clouds hanging overhead. He'd been in Mauthausen for a month or so now. He wasn't entirely sure, as the days blended into one another. But he was still alive. The same couldn't be said for many of the men in his block. When Floris saved him from certain death, Christiaan did his best to blend into the general population. He worried about his new identity, and the threat of someone calling him out. It never happened, and he now went through life in Mauthausen as Max Oswald. According to Floris, the deceased German had attended a communist rally in Berlin. They had both been surprised he'd been given a green—criminal—triangle. Usually, it would have been the red—political—triangle. Floris suspected someone in the administration had made a mistake, and Max had been smart enough to keep his mouth shut. Criminal prisoners generally had a longer lifespan than political prisoners.

The line crept forward as the man in front of him turned around. Two prisoners loaded granite rocks into his carrier under the watchful eye of a Kapo. The carrier was almost full and the man grunted under the weight. The prisoners stopped filling the carrier, but the Kapo was relentless. He picked up a piece the size of a football and dropped it into the man's carrier. The prisoner keeled backward, almost losing his balance, and even though Christiaan was tempted to help him, he knew better. The man recovered just in time, leaning forward with all his might to stay upright. Even though the effort had strained him immensely—his cheeks were red, he was breathing hard—the alternative would've meant almost certain death. The Kapo stood and hit the man across the back of his head, like one would spring a mule into action. "Off with you, get moving, we don't have all day!" Without a word, the prisoner moved from the small shed, and Christiaan took his position. He turned around, avoiding making eye contact with the Kapo, and gritted his teeth while his own uncomfortable wooden carrier was loaded. Worn leather straps dug into his shoulders, the pressure on his chest restricting his breathing, but he closed his eyes and focused on not showing any pain. He waited for the inevitable smack across the back of his head, but it never came. "Off you go. Get moving." Perhaps the Kapo needed a break from his sinister work. It gave Christiaan an unexpected respite as he took determined steps toward the stairs only a few paces away.

He looked up at the uneven steps he was about to mount for the sixth time today. It was hard to keep track of anything in

Mauthausen, but counting the number of times he survived the Stairs of Death was essential in making it through the day. He didn't know why he'd been picked for stairs duty today; he had done nothing that warranted the task normally reserved for those in the penal block. Christiaan knew better than to question the guards and Kapos, though. He drew a deep breath and took the first steps. His calves burned, the stones in his carrier shifting as he leaned forward. He focused on the steps ahead, constantly scanning for the uneven parts that had sent hundreds, if not thousands, of men tumbling to their deaths.

He swallowed hard as he approached the halfway point. The backbreaking work combined with the dusty surroundings had him parched. Some prisoners sucked on pieces of rock, claiming it helped fight the thirst. Christiaan had tried it but found little relief. To him, it served as a constant reminder of his thirst. His body was screaming for water, but he knew there would be none until the short break at noon. *With a bit of luck, I might get away with only one more trip up the stairs.* He labored on, reminding himself he needed to survive the current climb first. His vision was clouded, and he made the mistake of looking up. From the halfway point, the top of the stairs appeared discouragingly far away, and Christiaan generally avoided it. This time, it was a good thing he looked up, for the prisoner crawling the last steps had attracted the attention of one of the Kapos. As soon as the prisoner reached the top of the stairs he struggled to get up. The Kapo said something, then casually pushed the man down the stairs. The exhausted prisoner with fifty kilos of granite in his carrier had no chance. He fell backward, landing on the back of his head. A sickeningly crunch confirmed the man's skull was split. Christiaan rushed out of the way, narrowly avoiding the man tumbling down the narrow stairs. The life had already left the man's eyes as he slid past Christiaan and down to the quarry floor.

Christiaan moved on, keen to avoid the attention of the Kapo. But his head throbbed, and he felt dizzy from the small black specks dancing in front of his eyes. He'd almost become used to the perpetual hunger and thirst. This time they combined to sap almost all his energy on the middle of the stairs. He considered the dead man at the bottom. He was freed from the constant pain and torture. Perhaps he was the lucky one? Christiaan looked up, eyeing the Kapo who stood talking with one guard. Perhaps Christiaan should take that way out as well? He was just extending his suffering, after all. Of all the men in his block, only a handful had been there before him. In the end, everybody perished.

He climbed on, almost delirious from thirst. *I will not make it up and down another time.* He glanced to his side, into the quarry pit. Perhaps he could jump from the top? Plenty of men had done it before, voluntarily, or otherwise. Christiaan hadn't heard of any surviving the thirty-meter drop onto sharp and uneven stones.

Christiaan reached the top, more black specks clouding his vision. *Were those there the last time I climbed up?* He didn't know for certain. *Where is the Kapo?* The man stood a few meters away, his back to Christiaan. It would be so easy now. Just pick a fight, and it would all be over soon. Maybe he could even take the Kapo down with him. Christiaan took a step toward him, the rocks in his backpack shifting yet again. The Kapo turned and frowned.

"Where do you think you're going? Get those stones to the camp. Hurry up!"

Christiaan was about to open his mouth when a loud blaring sound came from the main camp. The camp siren brought him back to his senses. The Kapo and guard sprang into action, shifting their attention to the men returning from the camp and making their way down for another grueling, death-defying climb up.

"Get back up here now! Return to the camp immediately! Come on, let's go, let's go!" The Kapo turned to Christiaan, his face filled with urgency. "Drop your carrier here, we'll pick it up later!"

Christiaan could hardly believe his ears. He lost the cumbersome backpack and felt like he could breathe again. His shoulders ached, but he didn't care. Something more important than carrying boulders up the Stairs of Death was happening at the camp. He didn't know what was going on, but the timing couldn't have been better.

———

Returning to the camp, the prisoners were immediately herded onto the roll call area. The siren was still blaring, and Christiaan was certain the powers that be kept the incessant noise going on purpose. He didn't care as he lined up in his usual spot. Prisoners hurriedly returning from all directions joined, and it took another fifteen minutes for everyone to complete the required rows facing the platform where whoever ran this additional roll call would address them from.

Christiaan stood silently in his row. His legs felt heavy, and he ached to sit down, but standing for roll call beat another few rounds up and down the stairs. He tried to tune out, forcing himself to think of better times. He'd become good at daydreaming with his eyes open, giving the impression of being present while escaping in his own thoughts.

Lisa's face drifted into his consciousness. Her radiant smile warmed him and gave him strength, even if her face wasn't completely clear. His memory of her faded with every passing day. Christiaan was certain it was his mind and body going into survival mode. Despite that, he fought hard to preserve the image of the woman he loved. She was the only reason he was still alive, and he felt guilty for almost succumbing to the temptation of giving up on the stairs. He clenched his hands into fists, nails biting into the soft skin. *You promised you'd come back.*

There was movement at the front, and Christiaan snapped back to the present. The familiar figure of Georg Bachmayer made his way to the platform, flanked by henchmen guards. Christiaan looked around and searched for his brother. Floris was usually not far away, but he hadn't seen him for a few days.

Bachmayer mounted the platform and took the microphone. He

tapped it lightly, causing the feedback to ring around the Appellplatz. Christiaan flinched, and then the SS officer's voice boomed through the speakers spaced throughout the roll call area.

"As you're all aware, I'm not a fan of interrupting your work. But today, unfortunately, I was left with no choice." Bachmayer's voice was cold, distant, and factual. He droned on, not blessed with impressive public speaking skills, even if he thought otherwise.

A door in the block behind Bachmayer opened. It was the penal block, and six men were marched out by the same number of guards. The prisoners stumbled along with bowed heads and had their hands tied in front of them. It was unusual for prisoners to be shackled; most were too weak to resist even if they wanted to. Few had enough mental, let alone physical, strength to consider the option. Christiaan watched with interest as the unfamiliar men were lined up in front of Bachmayer. Two of them raised their chins, their faces bloody, eyes swollen. Their uniforms were stained with dark patches of dried blood. Some of the men had discolorations running down their pants.

"This morning, it came to my attention that a number of men in the administration block were planning an escape." His gaze went over the six men standing below him. "I don't think I need to remind you all that such an exercise is both pointless and criminal. However, because of the actions of these men, we had no option but to recall every one of you, and make sure the culprits are weeded out. You will return to your blocks after this roll call and await further instructions. If you were in any way involved in this ill-conceived plot, you can expect a visit. The men placed in front of you have forfeited their lives, and you will witness what happens to prisoners abusing their privileged positions." He snapped his fingers, and the guards reached to the pistols on their belts.

A knot of tension formed in Christiaan's gut. He was desperate to turn his eyes away, but he knew if any of the guards spotted him, they would not hesitate to lash out at him. So, he kept his gaze straight ahead, pretending to follow the proceedings while he stared at the wall of the penal block instead.

It was impossible to miss. The guards kicked the men's already frail legs, and they sank to their knees. To their credit, the prisoners remained quiet, some closing their eyes, but others staring fiercely ahead, no doubt looking to meet the gazes of their friends in the crowd. The guards placed the barrels of their guns in the small of the men's necks. One of them turned his head to Bachmayer, who simply nodded. The guard turned back and counted to three. Six guns went off simultaneously, and the lifeless bodies fell to the ground of the Appellplatz.

Five minutes later, Christiaan was in his block. He found his bunk and lay down, ignoring the man with whom he shared his uncomfortable sleeping place. He didn't want to talk to anyone and closed his eyes. Bachmayer was fanatical about the daily quotas of granite, and today's interruption meant missing more than half a day of work. *It must've been a big operation.*

"Oswald, 143231, report!"

Christiaan was shaken from his thoughts at the mention of his name. He thought he'd misheard, but then the Kapo at the front of the block repeated his name and number. His heart went cold. Being singled out was bad enough on a regular day, but Bachmayer's words still echoed in his head. *If you were in any way involved in this ill-conceived plot, you can expect a visit.* Did they think he was involved in the escape attempt? He considered not responding, but that would only make things worse. The Kapo would lock the block down and they would find him soon enough. Reluctantly, he got up and walked to the front of the room. The Kapo eyed him with a scowl, his eyes checking his prisoner number.

"Next time, don't make me wait so long," the man said, fingering his baton.

"Apologies, sir. It won't happen again." Christiaan's voice was shaky, and he swallowed, steadying himself. "What do you need from me, sir?" He held his breath as the man frowned, checking a sheet of paper.

"They want you to report to administration tomorrow. There are some vacancies, and someone suggested you would be an able replacement." The Kapo spoke without emotion. "You know where the administration block is, yes?"

Christiaan's shoulders sagged with relief. "Of course, sir. Block 1."

"Good. Make sure you're on time. They expect you there immediately after roll call." He handed Christiaan the sheet of paper. "Take this and show it to the foreman."

"Of course, sir, thank you," Christiaan said to the back of the man, who was already on his way out of the block.

———

Christiaan shuffled some papers on his narrow desk. He glanced around the room, scanning the faces of the other clerks. They all appeared focused on their tasks, the furious clacking of dozens of typewriters reverberating through the room. This room was where all camp administration was handled, and the prisoner clerks made sure their records were kept up to date. With plenty of new arrivals every day, they were kept busy, and stress hung over the room like a heavy blanket, despite the absence of baton-wielding Kapos. There was no fear of a sudden blow to the head or ribs because a Kapo spotted a supposed infraction of the rules. Here, the head clerk—also a prisoner—ruled the room with words. For the people in this room, it worked. Christiaan wondered if a different approach from the vicious Kapos and guards outside might yield better results. He shook his head. The people in this room knew how fortunate they were to work indoors, their fingers dancing on the keys of the typewriters, rather than suffering the relentless assault on their bodies from hammering pickaxes away at the never-ending granite walls in the quarry.

"Hey, new guy, come with me." A man of similar age rapped his knuckles on Christiaan's desk and motioned his head in the direction of the door. When Christiaan hesitated, he stopped and spoke more urgently, "It's okay, we just need to grab some files from the other room." The man spoke heavily accented German. *Russian? Surely not. They were either kept in Block 20, or worked in the nearby Gusen quarry.*

Christiaan got up and followed the man down the narrow hallway and into a small room. There was no door, and the man let him pass while he remained standing in the door opening. He looked up and down the hallway before turning to Christiaan.

"How's your first day going? I'm sure it's all a bit overwhelming after yesterday."

Christiaan calmly eyed the man. "I was surprised to be selected, but I'm glad to be here. You said you needed help?" He looked around the room; the filing cabinets were on the opposite wall. "Files, you said?"

"Sure, but I wanted to ask you a few things first," the man said, leaning against the door post.

The hairs on the back of his neck pricked up. *I better be careful with this one.* Christiaan survived the past month because he kept to himself, not talking to other prisoners unless absolutely necessary. To have another clerk approach him hours after his arrival at administration was suspicious at best.

"Your name is Max Oswald?" He sounded almost casual as he asked the question, as if he already knew the answer. *Of course, he knows. He probably looked me up as soon as I came in. Or even more likely, before I arrived.* Christiaan nodded and forced a smile.

"You looked me up?"

The man's eyes narrowed, and he took a step toward Christiaan. "Not really, I didn't need to." He spoke with confidence, and Christiaan felt uneasy. "I was there that morning in the quarry, when the Dutch agents were killed."

Christiaan felt as if he'd been punched in the gut, blood draining from his cheeks. Had this man seen what Floris and he had done? Had he seen him change into Max Oswald's clothes? The smile returned on the face of the man, who glanced into the hallway once more.

"I see I have your attention. I don't know who you are, but you're not Max Oswald."

He doesn't know who I am. Christiaan felt a bit of hope that his identity was still safe, and he scratched his throat. "What are you saying?"

The man didn't immediately answer while he studied Christiaan's face. Then, he slowly nodded. "How long have you been in the camp?"

"Almost two months," Christiaan said, remembering what Floris had told him about the man whose clothes he wore. "You?"

"The same. And Max would've been here for two months as well, so you would've passed this test with anyone who only read Max's file and didn't know him." Christiaan felt his knees weaken. He knew the man's next words. "But anyone who knew Max would be very surprised by his sudden change in appearance." He looked away for a moment, then he fixed his hard stare on Christiaan. "Max Oswald was my friend. Perhaps even my best friend, if one can say anything like that about a fellow prisoner in this godforsaken place. And you are not him."

The way the man spoke left no doubt that he was speaking the truth. "You're right. I'm not Max Oswald." As Christiaan spoke the words, he felt his throat constrict.

"I know you're one of the Dutch agents that was supposed to die that day in the quarry. Instead, you somehow survived, and Max died." Oddly enough, there was no anger in the man's voice. *He knows I didn't kill his friend. But how?* Christiaan opened his mouth, but the man continued. "I was walking behind you on the way to the quarry. Saw that guard pull you from the group. You wouldn't be alive today if he hadn't."

Christiaan looked at the man in shock. "I didn't see you there." His mind went to that morning. The only thing he recalled was Floris and the other Dutch guard walking at the back of the group. *Were there more prisoners walking behind?* He shook his head. His memory was hazy, and he couldn't be sure. His head was spinning.

"I know you weren't involved in Max's death, though." The man's voice jerked him back to the present, and Christiaan looked at the man in shock and relief. "I saw the Kapo that beat him to death." His mouth twitched and he looked shaken for a moment. "Filthy animals, every last one of them."

"I did what I had to, to survive." Christiaan spoke softly. "But what do you want from me?" *Is he going to blackmail me?* The diminutive, well-spoken man now posed the biggest threat to his survival.

"I want you to tell me the truth. Are you one of the Dutch agents?"

Christiaan knew there was no sense in denying it. This man had seen Floris pull him from the group, and he knew he wasn't who he said he was. Even if he wasn't certain about his real identity, what he did know was enough to send him to his death. He met the man's eyes and saw no malice, only curiosity. He nodded. "Yes. I was part of that group."

There was compassion in the man's eyes. "So, you saw all your friends die that morning?"

"I will never forget."

The man looked at him for a few seconds, then extended his hand. "We both lost our friends that morning. My name is Petr. I will keep your secret, for we have a common enemy."

"Christiaan." He shook the man's hand. "Why did you seek me out? You could just as easily have reported me."

"Why would I do that? You're a Dutch agent. That means you're useful."

"Useful?"

Petr gave a wry smile. "Those men that were executed yesterday, they were trying to free the men from Block 20."

"The Russians?"

"You met them, didn't you? They're all soldiers and officers. If they'd been successful, they would've been quite the problem for the SS." He looked disappointed. "But someone betrayed them."

Christiaan saw the fire in Petr's eyes and heard the pain in his voice. It reminded him of the brave men and women in the Amsterdam resistance. "Were you involved?"

"Not really." It was the first time the man's response was shaky, and Christiaan didn't believe him. It must've shown, for he added. "I only pointed them in the right direction when they couldn't find some of the documents they needed."

"But you knew what they were going to do."

"Of course. It was obvious to anyone paying attention."

So it was someone in the administration that betrayed them. Christiaan made a mental note to be very careful. "You still haven't told me why we're talking."

A smile formed on Petr's face. "I did. It just seems you don't understand me yet. Working in the administration means you have access to almost all the information in the camp. That's the difference between survival and death." He waved his hands in the direction of the quarry. "If you were still in the quarry, you would most likely be dead in a few weeks, tops. Yet you find yourself here now. Keep your eyes and ears open and pay close attention to what's going on in the room next door."

There were heavy footsteps in the hallway, and moments later a guard poked his head around the door. "What are you two doing in here? Get back to work!"

Petr held up his hands, then yanked open one of the filing cabinets. "Apologies, sir. I was just showing this new guy our filing system. We'll be back in the main room in a minute."

The guard grunted something unintelligible, then left. Petr waited for the footsteps to fade, then turned back to Christiaan. "There's more to the clerks working here than meets the eye, Christiaan. You'll find out soon enough."

CHAPTER TWENTY-TWO

Floris stood at the edge of the sand pit in St. Georgen. Much to his chagrin, he had been assigned to oversee new prisoner arrivals at the nearby Gusen II camp this week. It was only fifteen minutes from Mauthausen, but it might just be the other side of the world. Floris had no access to Christiaan, and he felt restless. He hadn't been able to talk to his brother since he got him assigned to the administration block almost a week ago. It would be much easier to talk to Christiaan there. He could pretend he needed his brother to find him some files or look up information. Instead, Bachmayer had assigned half of Floris' group of guards to Gusen II. The only good thing about his transfer was that it was supposed to be temporary. Anton had also been assigned there, and his friend was now approaching, shielding his eyes from the bright October sun.

"How long do you think these new guys will survive?" Anton's voice was flat, devoid of emotion. Floris had noticed the change in his friend's demeanor and wondered if he had become numb to the suffering around them. He had to admit he felt the same; the prisoners forced to perform their grueling labor in the quarries and sand pits surrounding the camps were replaced weekly. Floris hardly acknowledged their faces and just got on with his job. He shrugged while he monitored a group of four men carrying large stones from the sand pit. In contrast to the prisoners mounting the stairs in the Vienna Quarry next to Mauthausen, these men carried the stones in their hands instead of on their backs. It meant they carried less weight, but it made their job harder as they constantly had to read-just their grip without dropping the stones. When they did, the Kapos circling nearby would be on them like hyenas. Few survived the attacks, evident by the pile of bodies on the far side of the pit.

"We'll be fortunate if a quarter of them survive long enough to receive their bread in the evening," Floris said. "They don't look like they've done much manual labor in their lives. This is tough enough for the strongest of men."

"One of the guards who's been here for two months says they've been getting more and more shipments from the camps farther east for months now."

Floris had heard the same stories. "These came from Auschwitz, didn't they?"

"Yeah, apparently the Russians are making good progress in the east. They're worried they might reach Auschwitz soon."

They needed to ship off these Jews. Floris was surprised at the number of prisoners with yellow stripes on the front and back of their uniforms. He'd imagined they would've been killed in Auschwitz by now. Instead, they were moved to Mauthausen and Gusen to work in the quarries and the underground factory they were building a little farther down the road. *Things must be getting desperate if we're moving useless Jews over here.*

A few meters away, near the top of the sand pit, one man carrying a pile of large stones tripped and fell. The stones spilled from his arms and rolled a small distance away. The man landed face first, and Floris noticed the yellow stripes on his shirt. Other men slowly trudged past, but the man did not try to get up. Two Kapos hurried toward him, their batons raised. When they reached him, one of them kicked the man in the ribs. There was no movement, and it was clear he wouldn't get up. Floris turned away as the Kapos finished the man off with blows and kicks to the head. It had all become normal, just another man going through the camp's meat grinder.

———

That evening, after escorting them back from the quarry to the Gusen II camp, Floris oversaw the handing out of food to the surviving prisoners. When they left the camp that morning, almost two thousand men had marched the dusty two-kilometer road between Gusen II and St. Georgen. Now, less than half of those stood in line for the single piece of dry, dark bread they had earned with the day's labor.

The line moved quickly, and Floris looked at the tired men. Their eyes were hollow, and all but a few had their heads bowed as they shuffled forward. Kapos hovered nearby, ready to beat anyone foolish enough to speak. Not that these men had any energy left to do anything but move toward their meager rations.

Floris' mind wandered off. These men weren't threats. He wondered if they would be part of the labor force required once the underground Messerschmitt factory was fully operational. They had run into numerous delays as tunnels collapsed, killing hundreds of workers and setting back delivery by weeks. Things appeared to be picking up, and Floris overheard that engineers were installing the house-high hydraulic presses required to create the aircraft fuselages. Floris could hardly believe they would soon assemble Germany's warplanes in the tunnels of St. Georgen. He focused his attention on the prisoners shuffling by. The supply of slave labor across the Reich seemed endless. *Why worry about the weak ones dropping out?*

"Hey, ready to grab something to eat ourselves?" Anton stood next to him, clearly keen to get away. "It will be a helluva lot better than what they're getting."

Floris noticed the queue had almost cleared, with the prisoners making their way to their barracks. "Let's go. I'm sure the Kapos can look after them on the way to the blocks."

They walked along the main thoroughfare of the camp and passed the prisoner blocks on their way to the guard quarters. Floris noticed prisoners queuing to get into their blocks. Two Kapos stood at the door, demanding the famished prisoners' bread rations. One prisoner in the back broke off a piece of bread and quickly stuffed it in his mouth. One of the Kapos caught him and jumped down from the doorway. The prisoner was still chewing his bread when the Kapo reached him. Without warning, he punched him in the throat, causing the man to spit out the bread. He reached for his throat as he let out a gargling sound, but the Kapo was too quick. He punched him in the face and kicked his knees. The man fell and immediately rolled into a fetal position on the ground. The assailant now took out his baton and rained down blows on the man's exposed back, side, and neck. Floris and Anton observed from a distance. Despite Floris' indifference to the killing of the prisoners in the sand pit earlier that day, he felt disgust at what was happening here. The prisoner had survived his trial of strength, and the piece of bread was his only chance of survival. For it to be so cruelly stolen by the Kapos seemed outrageously unfair.

Floris considered intervening but realized it would only draw unwanted attention to him. The rules in Gusen II were different. Kapos were rewarded for killing prisoners. In fact, they were handed a quota of ten dead prisoners a day. This Kapo probably hadn't met his numbers yet.

The man on the ground no longer moved, and the Kapo seemed satisfied with his work as he slid his baton under his flimsy belt. He wiped his forehead and bent down, picking up the piece of bread next to the dead man.

———

It was close to noon when a Kapo approached Floris near the entrance of the tunnels.

"Sir, I have a problem with some of my prisoners." The man looked annoyed. "They all seem to have diarrhea. Can't hardly work for more than a few minutes at a time before they have to run to the end of the tunnel."

"What do you want me to do about it?" Floris snapped at the man. "That's your problem, not mine."

The Kapo shuffled on his feet. "I know, sir, but do you want me to take care of them here, or do you want to take them to the *Revier*?"

Floris considered the man's words, then nodded. "Take them to the Revier." Short for *Krankenrevier*, it was an infirmary only in name. Floris had never been, but he'd heard the conditions were worse than the regular barracks.

"Sir, with all due respect, I can't leave the tunnels on my own. I need someone with more authority to accompany me back to the camp." Floris thought he spotted a smirk on the Kapo's face and considered reprimanding him, but let it go. He looked around and found he was the only guard. For a second, he considered telling the Kapo to take care of the men, but then decided he didn't mind getting away from the dusty tunnels for a few hours. The walk back to the camp might do him good. He waved at the Kapo dismissively.

"Get your prisoners. I'll take you."

───────

The walk back took more than an hour, as the dozen prisoners needed plenty of stops in between. The Kapo hadn't exaggerated about the men's conditions. *That's what eating less than half a loaf of bread a day and filthy water does to a man.* The St. Georgen tunnel site didn't have access to clean water, and they had hastily constructed a connection to the nearby Danube River. Even though it made them sick, the prisoners had no option but to drink the dirty water.

Floris was pleased when they walked back into the camp and

made straight for Block 13, the infirmary. He was hungry and he realized on the way over that he would be able to have a warm meal in the main camp before heading back. It certainly beat his usual St. Georgen rations of bread and sausage.

"Come on, hurry up!" he shouted to his prisoners as he opened the door to Block 13. The stench almost floored him, and he gagged before taking a step back. He motioned for the Kapo. "Keep an eye on them while I find whoever is in charge in here." He took a deep breath and stepped inside.

The conditions were even worse than he'd heard. Men were squeezed in thee across on the regular hard wooden bunks. Few had blankets, and the coughing was incessant as Floris made his way to the back of the block. He covered his mouth with his hand and caught some faces of the prisoners peering at him from the bottom and middle bunks. He shuddered at the gaunt faces, cheekbones sharply protruding, their eyes glassy, eyelids drooping. Next to every bunk was an overflowing bucket, serving as a communal bedpan.

Floris rushed through and was relieved when he reached the back of the room and stepped into a narrow hallway. The stench was not as intense here. The first room housed the latrines and was normally the least pleasant-smelling room in the blocks. Here, they appeared almost clean, and Floris realized few of the bedridden men had enough strength to make it to the latrines. He heard voices farther down the hall.

The door was open, and Floris entered. Six prisoners sat on their knees on the floor to his right. Their hands were bound behind their backs, and some wailed softly. Two had their eyes closed as they rocked back and forth on their knees. Floris turned to the other side of the room and, for a second, was sure his eyes were deceiving him. Two guards stood on either side of a tub of water, their backs to him. Between them a prisoner was on his knees, screaming and pleading for mercy as they held him with an iron grasp. Without warning, they plunged his head into the water. As the man thrashed and bucked, Floris could hear muffled cries from underneath the water.

The man's body convulsed as he fought to break free, but the powerful hands of the guards kept him submerged. Finally, his motions ceased, his head bobbing on the surface.

It was then when one of the guards noticed Floris. He frowned and dried his hands on a towel. "Can I help you with anything?" The other guard turned and gave Floris a curious glance. It took Floris a moment to compose himself as he struggled to look away from the lifeless man's head now floating limply on the water's surface.

"What is going on in here?" Floris managed to stammer.

The guard on the left looked at him in amusement, his gaze going between Floris and the barrel, clearly unshaken. "Oh, you mean this? We're just making space for new prisoners. You walked through there, didn't you? We don't have room for everybody, so we need to purge the weakest every day." He pointed at the men on the ground next to Floris. "They're next. They don't even know what's happening around them anymore."

Floris glanced at the men lining the wall. Their faces were stricken with fear. The man at the front was shaking and sobbing. He felt pity for the creatures, even if they were useless. No man deserved to die like this, having to witness his own impending execution in a filthy tub. He felt disgust for the executioners. They reminded him of the *Einsatzgruppen* he'd encountered near the eastern front. The men in those killing squads had no conscience either, murdering women and children without another thought.

"Well, what do you want? We're a little busy here," the second guard said, interrupting his thoughts. The other guard had taken the drowned prisoner from the tub and dragged his body to the corner of the room. Floris realized there was nothing he could do for the condemned on their knees. And why would he? He was part of the same organization as the men drowning them.

"I have several sick prisoners. Where do I report them?"

The other guard was making his way across the room toward the next prisoner and laughed. "Just tell them to find a bunk. We'll come check on the live ones after we get done with these. But it probably won't take much longer for them to draw their final breath here, either. Our recovery rate isn't too great." He broke into another laugh as he grabbed the prisoner by the scruff of the neck and hauled him toward the tub. The man tried to resist, and the guard kicked him in the chest. A small crack could be heard, and the prisoner wheezed as he almost collapsed to the floor. The second guard caught him, and as the man's wheezing broke into a cough, the guards dunked his head underwater.

The room went quiet but for the soft whimpering of the men watching their impending doom. Floris left without another word, nausea building up in the back of his throat. *This is not what I signed up for.*

CHAPTER TWENTY-THREE

Nora waited in the hallway in Bawdsey. She had just finished her shift and was looking forward to going home. It had been a busy day in the skies, with plenty of supply planes making multiple journeys across the North Sea and the Channel. In addition, she and the rest of the team were still always on the lookout for the V-2s coming from Germany. These new rockets were faster and harder to intercept than the V-1s. Thankfully, sightings of the V-2s were steadily decreasing as the Allied forces on the mainland advanced farther north and east, taking out the launch sites. Yet, the threat of aerial attacks remained, and Nora and the other radar girls stayed vigilant.

A door opened and the familiar face of Wing Officer Lewis appeared. She waved Nora into her small but tastefully decorated office.

"Thank you for your time, Nora. I'm sure you're eager to get home, but I'm afraid this couldn't wait." She waved at a seat opposite her and sank into her large desk chair. She had dark rings around her eyes, betraying the many hours she spent at Bawdsey. Nora admired the woman. Lewis always remained calm in the midst of the adversity of the Receiver Room. Where less capable men and women might crumble under the pressure, Lewis would always stop and think. Having worked with the woman for almost a year, Nora hoped some of Lewis' approach had rubbed off on her. Nora gave her commanding officer a friendly smile.

"That's not a problem, ma'am. I'm intrigued to hear what you wanted to speak to me about."

Lewis rubbed her temples as she reached for a piece of paper on the side of her desk. "Nora, I've been thrilled with your performance since arriving and joining the Receiver Room. It's always harder for foreign agents, or nationals, whatever you want to call it, joining us. Besides learning to operate the equipment, you had to catch up with our lingo in an unfamiliar language. I wasn't sure you'd be up to it in the first weeks, if I'm perfectly honest." She quickly gave Nora a reassuring smile. "But you've made me very proud. Your knowledge of the German language and the Dutch coastline and geography was essential in intercepting many hostile planes." Lewis paused for a moment, and Nora felt herself blushing. Her British superiors didn't dish out false praise, so when they did recognize someone, she knew it was sincere.

"Thank you, ma'am, I try my best," Nora managed to stammer.

Lewis waved her hand dismissively. "Please, there's no room for false modesty here, Nora. You were a fantastic asset to the WAAF."

Were? What's happening?

Lewis' face turned serious. "Unfortunately, this was your last day at Bawdsey, for now."

"Ma'am?"

"It wasn't my decision, that's for sure." Lewis slid the piece of paper across the desk. "This is a summons from your government in London. They're requesting your immediate return."

Nora took the paper, noting the royal Dutch crest at the top. She scanned the lines, her surprise mounting with every word. "Is this all you received?"

Her commanding officer nodded. "Unfortunately, yes. I can't tell you anything more because I simply don't know. The only thing that was very clear was that they want you back right away. The message was delivered an hour ago." She folded her hands on the desk and smiled wryly. "I guess we're not the only ones who value you, Nora."

The gears in Nora's brain were turning. As much as she appreciated the summons from London, she didn't want to leave Bawdsey. The place had become like home to her, dark and covert as it was. She enjoyed going to work every day, and she knew her work directly impacted the success of the Allied armies sweeping through Europe. She wasn't quite as convinced that whatever the Dutch government in London wanted from her would allow her to have the same impact. "I suppose there is no other option?"

"What do you mean?"

"Can I refuse these orders and stay at Bawdsey?"

Lewis stood, her smile more genuine now, and shook her head. "I'm afraid not. We've booked you on tonight's train to London. You better pack your things. Your country needs you, Nora."

"It's been a privilege serving with you, ma'am." Nora stood and saluted the wing commander.

Lewis returned the salute, then moved from beyond the desk and, to Nora's surprise, hugged her. "I'm sure they have a very good reason for recalling you. And whatever they need from you, I'm sure you'll ace it. Take care, Nora."

———

It took Nora a few minutes to reacquaint herself to the bustle of the London morning traffic. It had been over a month since she'd been in the capital, and the pace of life in the much smaller seaside town of Felixstowe was a lot slower. The way people went about their business on the London sidewalks, it almost seemed as if there was no war going on. That was, if one ignored the bombed-out ruins of buildings visible on every street corner.

After saying goodbye to her friends at Bawdsey, Nora had packed the few things she owned and hurried to catch the train.

On the ride down to London, she'd wondered about what the Dutch government needed from her. When she arrived in England, they had been quick to place her with the WAAF, which stationed her at the Bawdsey radar station. She hadn't heard much from her compatriots in the meantime, and now they needed her to pack up lock, stock, and barrel and race down to London overnight. *This better be good,* she thought as she checked the address.

She rang the doorbell, and a man maybe a few years older than her opened the door almost immediately.

"Mrs. Brouwer?"

She nodded, and he stepped aside to let her enter a short, narrow hallway leading directly to a steep flight of stairs. "Follow me, please. They're waiting for you." He sounded rushed as he took the stairs two steps at a time. Nora had trouble keeping up with him. *I'm well on time, aren't I?*

"I'm sorry, could you tell me who I'm meeting with?" she asked when they reached the top of the stairs, revealing a more spacious, well-decorated hallway. There were some nice Persian rugs on the floor, and mismatching paintings hung on the cream-colored walls.

He didn't answer her question as he stepped through an open doorway. "In here, please, Mrs. Brouwer." Nora frowned and followed him, stepping into another nicely decorated room. A large oak conference table dominated the space. At the far end sat two men, who stood as Nora approached. They were all smiles as they extended their hands and introduced themselves.

"So glad you could make it on such short notice, Mrs. Brouwer," said the one who introduced himself as Kuipers. He wore a fancy, expensive-looking suit that had seen better days. "I'm sure you were surprised to hear from us." He sat down and waved at a vacant chair.

"It would be a great start if you could tell me where I am, to be honest," Nora said, not taking the proffered seat. "The summons was a bit vague. Not even my CO at Bawdsey knew what was going on."

Kuipers appeared surprised by her response, and the other man, Veerman, took over.

"Of course, you're absolutely right, and we're sorry for the secrecy and rush in getting you back to London," Veerman said, his tone apologetic. "You're at the Bureau Inlichtingen. I believe you're aware of what we do around here?" The sides of his lips curled up in a nervous smile. "You were close with one of our colleagues, Miss Abrahams?"

Nora couldn't help but return his smile at the thought of Lisa. "How is Lisa doing?"

Veerman turned to Kuipers, who looked uncomfortable. *They don't want to tell me. Or they can't?* A cold feeling gripped her heart. *Has something happened to her?* The men looked undecided for a moment, then Kuipers spoke up. "I'm sure you're aware she joined the American forces on the Continent?" Nora nodded. Lisa had been excited to join, and they had met in London right after she'd finished her Red Cross training and was bound to ship out. That had been almost half a year ago, and she hadn't heard from Lisa since.

"Is she okay?" Nora held her breath, almost dreading the answer. To her relief, Kuipers nodded.

"Based on our latest information, the Third Army is holding their position near the German border at Saarlouis. Lisa is part of the Red Cross detachment working behind the lines. The American army has been steadily pushing back the Germans, and Lisa will be kept far away from the fighting. She's fine, Mrs. Brouwer."

Nora listened to the intelligence jargon she'd become so used to over the past year. Reading between the lines, she understood these men didn't know for certain what was going on in Saarlouis, but they had received no indication that Lisa had been hurt. That was good enough for now. "Thank you. Well, perhaps you could tell me why you needed me back here in such haste?" She sat opposite the two agents and placed her hands flat on the table.

"Very well, straight to the point." Kuipers stood and took a jug, pouring her a generous glass of water. "As I'm sure you're aware, the Allied advance north has been steady."

Nora nodded. "I've been following the reports. Last I've heard, Eindhoven was liberated?" Eindhoven was the largest city in the south of the Netherlands, and an important symbolic, but not necessarily strategic, victory for the Allied forces.

"The liberation of Eindhoven has given us a solid base for our operations back home," Kuipers said, a hint of pride in his voice. "The head of our division, Colonel Somer, has returned home to lead the Bureau's efforts from Eindhoven."

"What efforts?" Nora asked, taking a sip of water.

Veerman stood up. "We need to establish communications with the resistance cells farther north. They're essential in the Allied efforts to liberate the rest of the country. However—" He pointed at a map of the Netherlands, his finger outlining a stretch of rivers in the middle of the country. They were known as *De Grote Rivieren*—the Large Rivers—and formed a natural obstacle dividing the north from the south. "The German defenses around the bridges have halted our advance."

Nora remembered what Lisa had told her about Christiaan's mission of uniting the different resistance cells in the Netherlands. It all made sense now. "So why don't you simply activate the resistance cells farther north?"

The two men looked crestfallen. "Because we're unable to contact them. Our network isn't operating as expected."

"What does that mean? Are the Germans jamming your communications, or have they infiltrated the network?"

"We're not entirely sure. But that's where you come in. You're already asking the right questions."

Nora was confused. "What do you need me to do?"

"We want you to go back home and establish contact with the resistance cells. We need you to find out what happened to the network."

"And fix and activate it," Veerman added. "You're one of the few people with knowledge of the resistance's workings as well as transmission equipment."

Nora looked at the men in silence, processing their message for a minute. When she left Bawdsey the previous night, she was convinced she would be moved to an office somewhere, upset she wouldn't make nearly as big an impact as on England's southeastern coast. Now, these men were telling her they wanted her to return to occupied territories to assist the stuttering Allied liberation of her country.

"I'm sure this is a lot to take in, Mrs. Brouwer." Kuipers voice interrupted her thoughts. "But we'd really appreciate a decision from you, so we can make the required preparations for your return to the Netherlands."

Nora narrowed her eyes as pride swelled in her chest and she clasped her hands together. "When do I leave?"

CHAPTER TWENTY-FOUR

Christiaan and Petr followed the guard out of the administration block. The man took large strides down the camp's main thoroughfare. They passed the prison block to their right, where the wails of those locked up could be heard through the barred windows. Christiaan was grateful he was unable to hear what was happening in the windowless basement. He glanced at Petr, who looked oddly calm as he followed the single guard.

The guard had come into the large clerks' room a few minutes earlier. He'd gone straight to Petr and told him to follow him. He was needed in Block 20, where the Russian prisoners of war were held in isolation. When Petr asked what he was needed for, the guard had barked at him not to ask questions, but Petr had insisted he needed to know what was required of him. The guard relented and told him he'd need to document the prisoners in the block for a special operation. Petr then said he needed help and had volunteered Christiaan. Before he could protest, the guard barked at him to join them.

They neared the single gate to the walled-off quarantine area of the camp. The two SS troopers on guard stepped aside without a word. They first passed the regular quarantine blocks. These were used to separate newly arrived prisoners deemed valuable enough to have something resembling proper dwellings. Christiaan knew there was no way to house all new arrivals in these quarters, and those who didn't end up in these sheltered, somewhat decent blocks were unlikely to survive beyond their first, maybe second week. The people crowding around the congested space looked at them with interest; their appearance was the only break in their monotonous lives. There was nothing to do in the quarantine area but sit and wait. Christiaan didn't envy them.

They passed through another gate and reached Block 20, the Death Block. Christiaan had spent his first night in the camp here, and stepping into the walled-off section brought back memories. Faces of the other Dutch agents flashed through his mind. Time had faded most of their features, but it almost felt as if they were present. It was worse than he remembered. Inside, the smell almost made Christiaan gag. Men piled from the overcrowded bunks, with dozens more lying in the narrow spaces between the bunks. Few wore the official striped camp uniform. They were invisible to the rest of the prisoner population and were treated as such. They wore their unwashed, ragged Red Army uniforms.

The guard turned to Petr and Christiaan. "Pick thirty of the healthiest-looking prisoners and take down their numbers. That's all I need from you today." He wrinkled his nose as he moved toward the door. "I'll be outside. I expect you back out there in ten minutes. Healthy looking specimens only!"

Christiaan felt his spine tingle at the use of the word *specimen* and turned to Petr. "Whoever we choose is not going to be happy. Do you know why we got this assignment?"

Petr shook his head. "What, you think he'd tell me? He only asked us because he doesn't want to spend any time in here, which I quite understand." He looked uncomfortable, his nose twitching as he scanned the room. "We better get started, though. He won't be pleased if we take too long. Why don't you walk along that side of the room, and I'll take this side? Just jot down their number if they look somewhat fit. It'll be challenging enough to find thirty."

Christiaan nodded and set off between the bunks. The hierarchy meant the strongest men were always in the top; they didn't risk bodily fluids of sick or deceased prisoners trickling down onto them in the middle of the night. It was the sad reality of the camp that many of the men who survived the daily abuse of the guards and Kapos often didn't make it through the night.

He soon found his approach wouldn't work. The block was too crowded. Men slept on the floor, and he was unable to get through. He turned around, the bright light streaming in from the open door catching his eye. It was only noon, and the fittest men would surely not be inside this cesspit but catching whatever sunshine and fresh air they could.

He stepped to the door, where Petr evidently had the same idea. They found their escort outside, talking to a few other guards. He frowned at them, but Petr quickly explained their thinking, and he nodded before lighting another cigarette, continuing his conversation with the other men. "Just hurry up."

They spotted a group of around a dozen young soldiers standing in the corner. Their clothes looked somewhat less worn than those of the men inside. Petr flicked his head at them. "Follow me, let's get their numbers."

The soldiers spotted them from a distance, and by the time they arrived, the group's attention was on Petr and Christiaan. The stinging eyes felt uncomfortable, but Christiaan reminded himself he was a prisoner just like them, albeit wearing a different uniform, and not in isolation. Petr looked more at ease, greeting the men in their native language. Christiaan couldn't understand the words, but he saw the soldiers respond favorably. Petr spoke for a few minutes, and then the men nodded, turning toward him.

"We can take down their numbers; they're okay with whatever is asked of them," Petr said as he started jotting.

"Do they realize it might be strenuous?"

"I told them, but they said they'd rather volunteer than put their weaker brothers through it." Petr turned back to Christiaan. "They have a strong sense of pride, of what's right and wrong."

More curious men approached, and they soon had their thirty names. Petr said something and clasped a few hands, and then Christiaan and Petr set off across the yard, back to the SS guard.

"What do you think they signed up for?" Christiaan asked as he scanned the list of numbers on his sheet of paper. "Did they ask?"

Petr shook his head. "It could be anything. A transfer, a tough assignment in the tunnels or quarries, or they might simply want to thin out the population. Most of these men know what being placed in Block 20 means by now. We'll find out soon enough."

———

They didn't have to wait long. The same guard collected Petr and Christiaan after morning roll call two days later. Instead of another trip to Block 20, they were taken outside the main camp and into the guards' quarters. Christiaan was surprised, and judging from the expression on Petr's face, so was his friend. *That's a first.*

Christiaan had never been in the guards' encampment before, and the contrast with their own dwellings was night and day. The areas between the barracks were lined with grass, and comfortable benches and tables were placed outside. Not that the soldiers would be using them now, but Christiaan could see how the area would be very comfortable in warmer temperatures. Their guard walked at his usual ferocious pace, and they soon reached a large building. He opened the door, and as they entered, the comfortable mix of warm air and a smell of grilled meat embraced them.

Christiaan blinked as he took in the scene. The thirty Russian prisoners stood, motionless, in the center of the room. They were dressed in brand-new Mauthausen prisoners' uniforms that fit them perfectly, their faces freshly shaven. On their feet were shoes made from soft leather instead of the uncomfortable clogs that the other prisoners wore. The smell of fresh bread and mouthwatering cold cuts and cheese wafted through the air from a table near the far corner of the room, making Christiaan's stomach rumble. Suddenly, music filled the room as the camp orchestra, who were also dressed in clean clothes, began to play a joyous Russian polka.

One of the SS guards yelled something at the Russian prisoners, clapping his hands and dancing. The men looked confused, but when one reluctantly started dancing, the rest joined in. Christiaan couldn't believe what he was witnessing. In the madness of Mauthausen, this was the most baffling display yet. Petr gently poked him in the side.

"See that cameraman over there?" he whispered, pointing at a man in civilian clothes. He balanced a large camera on his shoulder while he navigated between the Russian soldiers. The men danced with bemused expressions on their faces. One of the SS officers watching from the side yelled at the orchestra, slicing his hand across his neck. The music abruptly stopped, and the Russian soldiers froze in place, ending the surreal picture in the middle of the room. The officer stomped forward, his face red with rage.

"Dance like you damn well like it! Smile!" He was in the face of one of the Russians. "You're supposed to be having fun! If you don't smile, you get nothing." He pointed at the table of food.

The Russians looked at the screaming officer in confusion. One of them responded in Russian, and Christiaan looked to Petr. The Czech shook his head and rubbed the base of his nose before stepping forward.

"Sir, they don't seem to understand. Would you like me to translate?"

Christiaan held his breath. To his surprise, the SS officer nodded.

"That would certainly expedite things. I take it that's why you're here. Tell them. We don't have all day. And make sure they realize they won't get a single bite of food until we're happy with the recordings."

Petr did as he was told, and soon the Russians were dancing

again. The cameraman appeared happy after fifteen minutes, and the Russians were instructed to grab a chair each from the side of the room. They lined them up in front of a small makeshift stage. As soon as the men sat, the lights were dimmed, and four actors appeared on the stage. They were fellow prisoners, dressed up in nice clothes and they acted out a scene, accompanied by the orchestra. They repeated the same scene four times as the cameraman hurried about, creating shots from all angles.

The actors cleared the stage, and the lights went back on. As the Russians placed their chairs back to the side of the room, a door opened. Four men carrying large trays of roasted pork knuckle walked in, and Christiaan's jaw almost dropped to the floor.

The SS officer signaled for Petr to approach. "Tell them to eat, but slowly, so we can film them. Tell them they can finish everything once we have the shots. That's a promise."

Petr translated to the dumbfounded Russians, who barely managed to control themselves as they each grabbed a plate. The cameraman swerved around the men as they loaded up their plates, and the SS officer walked over to Petr and Christiaan.

"That's all we need from you today. One of the guards will escort you back." He snapped his fingers and the same guard from the morning appeared. As they left the otherworldly scene, Christiaan glanced back one more time. Some of the Russians were unable to control themselves and were already gorging on the food, much to the delight of the cameraman, who made sure to catch everything. Christiaan stepped back into the cold air outside and wondered what madness he'd just witnessed.

———

Christiaan was at his desk the next morning when a guard dropped a single sheet of paper on his desk. "Process these accordingly. I want the updated sheet in half an hour." He didn't wait for a response as he stomped out of the room. Christiaan glanced at the paper while he cleared the sheet he was working on from his typewriter. The list looked much like those he processed every day, except this one contained an unusually low number of names. All had a cross next to their prisoner numbers on the left, marking them deceased. Christiaan loaded a fresh piece of paper into his typewriter and cracked his fingers. He started with the name at the top of the list and paused. A lump formed in the back of his throat. His eyes went down the entire list. There were only thirty names. And they were all Russian. With horror, he realized what he was processing. These were the men he'd seen dancing and eating the day prior. Now, they were all dead. He looked around and considered seeking out Petr, who was only a few desks away. *No, I need to finish the list first.*

He continued with shaking hands, the smiling faces of the dancing soldiers haunting him as he typed their names, dates of birth, and date of death in neat rows on the clean, white paper. It took him less than fifteen minutes, and as he inspected the sheet, he took a deep breath. The work had become mechanical, and he could type the data without thinking about it. When he started, his mind automatically calculated the ages of the deceased, but he'd learned to block that out. His mind kept going back to that warm, comfortable block where the SS cameraman shot his propaganda film. How many times had the cunning leaders of the camp done this before? It didn't take long for Christiaan to realize how the men had died. The mountain of food. The Russians hadn't eaten for weeks, and now their systems were overloaded. He shook his head and tried to block out the thought of the men suffering an agonizing death when they returned to their block. *They probably died overnight if they made it that far. Stop it!*

"Hey, are you all right?" Christiaan looked up to find Petr standing by his desk. "You look like you spotted a ghost."

"I suppose I did." Christiaan slid the piece of paper over to Petr. His friend scanned the page and sighed. "Those are the Russians from yesterday. I was afraid this would happen."

"You knew?"

Petr shrugged. "I had my suspicions. I mean, they took us away before they allowed them to gorge themselves to death. In a way, I'm glad they didn't ask us to stay. At least we didn't witness what happened. Or worse, we may have joined in."

"We picked them, Petr. It's our fault."

Petr grabbed him by the arm and took him into the small filing room. "You can't blame yourself for this! We only did what we were told, and those men volunteered. You were there. There was nothing we could do for them."

Christiaan stood shaking on his feet. "I know, but still. We could've warned them, maybe?"

"How, and what would you have said? Don't eat the food? Watch out, or you'll kill yourself? What do you think would've happened to them if they didn't die from overeating? They would've been shot if they were lucky. As soon as they were part of that film, they were done. That's how it works. You've been in the camp long enough to know this."

Even though he knew Petr was right, Christiaan struggled to accept it. Worse, no matter what Petr said, he felt responsible. His cheeks burned and he dropped his gaze.

"Listen, remember when I told you why some of the clerks were executed before you started here?" Christiaan nodded as Petr's words slowly came through his foggy mind. "They weren't the only ones trying to do something. Many of the men working in the room next door try to make a difference to the lives of the people in the camp. They can be small gestures, like changing work orders to give them an easier assignment for a day or two, allowing them to regain some strength. Or they can be bigger, bolder. Like trying to organize an escape. You can imagine how some things are harder to accomplish than others, and how some efforts draw attention."

The haze in his mind cleared as Christiaan listened to Petr. "What are you saying? Everybody is part of it?"

Petr wagged a finger. "Not everyone, and I'm not telling you who, but just know that we're all very aware of the power we have working here."

"How have you been involved? Didn't you say you were partly involved in that escape attempt?"

"Partly, yes. But it's about not getting caught." Petr smiled. "But in the end, we are prisoners, and we need to know our boundaries. Escapes are hard, if not impossible. But we can do other things. This war won't last forever, and we know the Russians are making good progress in the east. How do you think they would respond if they learn about the thousands of their comrades who've been murdered here?"

"The camp leadership would erase all traces of evidence before they made it here."

"Exactly. And that's where we come in. Information is power." His eyes went to the filing cabinets lining the walls of the room. "We come and go, Chris."

"Hey, I was looking for you!" The guard had returned and stood in the doorway. He looked annoyed as he pointed his finger at Christiaan. "You better have that sheet of paper processed for me, or else."

"Of course, sir, just a minute." Christiaan squeezed past the man and ran into the main room, grabbing the neatly typed list from his desk. He presented it to the guard, who inspected it, counting the number of names out loud, ignoring Christiaan and Petr in the confined surroundings of the filing room. When he was satisfied, he signed at the bottom and flung it at Christiaan. "File this and get back to work."

"Yes, sir," Christiaan said to the man's back as the guard was halfway out the door. He turned to Petr, still holding the list. His friend grinned, took the piece of paper, folded it twice, then hid it in his pants before neatly tucking in his shirt.

"Information is power, Chris."

CHAPTER TWENTY-FIVE

Walking through Eindhoven's city center felt odd. Technically, the south of her home country was liberated, but the marks of war were still evident on every street corner. A group of Canadian soldiers passed by, one doffing his cap to her. She smiled and walked on, but she couldn't help but compare the situation with when the Germans were still occupying her country. There had been soldiers everywhere as well. She crossed the street, then shook her head. This was completely different. These men were on their side, here to help drive out the Nazis.

Her journey from London had been relatively smooth, even if she had to wait a few days longer than the Bureau men had promised. There had been some complications clearing her passage to Belgium, and she had finally boarded a merchant vessel headed for the Belgian town of Antwerp the day before yesterday. It had taken her mind back to her escape from Portugal when the British destroyer picked her up. She wondered how her young companions from the journey through Europe had fared. Especially Katja, who had been proud to join the Dutch merchant fleet on arrival. Nora had even done a tour of the ship as they crossed the North Sea, hoping her friend might be on the same vessel. She smiled at the silly thought; she, of course, hadn't found Katja on board. Now that the Allies had secured the passage between Britain and most of Europe's west coast, hundreds of vessels—merchant and navy—ferried goods and people across.

Nora had taken a train from Antwerp to Eindhoven and had been struck by the normality of her journey. But for a small number of Allied soldiers at the train stations, everything felt much like it had in peacetime. It was a far cry from the last time she took a train in Belgium, jumping on board a speeding car to avoid a patrol. She chuckled at the thought as she reached a rather plain-looking three-story building. She double-checked to find this was indeed Willemstraat 54. She rang the bell and rubbed her hands; there was a slight chill in the air. Or was it just her nerves?

The door opened and Nora was surprised to see a familiar face.

"Colonel Somer." Her voice was a little shaky, and she quickly coughed, clearing her throat. "I didn't think you'd open the door yourself."

"Mrs. Brouwer, shall we dispose of the formalities?" He opened the door wider and stepped aside to let her in. "It's good to see you again."

The last time they met was when Nora had just arrived in England. This man had played a vital role in the final part of her journey, coming up with the field hockey scheme to get her out of Spain and into Portugal to board the British destroyer. He had been waiting alongside Lisa when she landed at the Whitchurch airfield. Their meeting had been formal, not least because of the MI6 agents hovering around, waiting to interrogate her, as she would later discover. But Nora had expressed her gratitude to him nonetheless, for she knew, even back then, that he had pulled many strings in bringing her to England. She was secretly delighted to be working with him. It almost felt as if repaying a debt.

"Come, let's get you something to drink, and then I can update you on everything that's happening here. You must be tired from the journey." Somer led her down a long hallway with offices on either side. It was busier than Nora had expected, with people carrying stacks of files as they went between the offices, other poring over papers on their desks in silence. It felt like a regular workplace. Then she realized it was. This was the Bureau's Dutch office, and it was no longer in occupied territory. She followed Somer into a small kitchen, where he picked up a pot. "Coffee? It's the real stuff, courtesy of our American friends." He didn't wait for her response and poured two large mugs. "Come, my office is just down the hall."

They entered Somer's office, and he closed the door while waving at one of the comfortable chairs arranged around a coffee table in the corner. "Please, Nora, have a seat. We have a lot to talk about, but first, tell me about the situation in London. How are people feeling?"

She placed her mug on the table while she sank into the soft chair. "What can I say. I wasn't in London long between rushing down from Bawdsey and boarding the steamer for Antwerp." She smiled. "But people seemed optimistic. The liberation is real, isn't it?"

Somer nodded. "Reports from the various battlefields are encouraging. The Germans are being pushed back, or at least not gaining significant ground, in most territories."

"How confident are you that they won't regain the lost ground? I mean, try to retake the south?"

"There are no guarantees, but American and British intelligence are confident Hitler is more concerned about stopping the advances in the Ardennes and farther south at the French-German border."

Nora's interest was piqued at the mention of the French-German border. "Along the Saar River?"

"You're concerned about Lisa." A gentle smile played on Somer's face. "So am I. But we shouldn't worry too much about her. She's with the strongest army on the Continent. Their progress has been truly remarkable, and General Patton's steamrolling run through France has only been halted momentarily. I'm sure they'll be moving soon. For now, they are well fortified and, from what I've heard, making life extremely uncomfortable for the German troops stationed in their vicinity."

Nora took a sip of her coffee and savored the bitter taste. Setting the mug down, she returned her focus to Somer. "What about Christiaan? Any news?" Even though the words came out almost casually, she felt her hands tremble.

"Unfortunately, no," he offered as the smile disappeared from his face. "He's been off our radar since shortly after arriving in Amsterdam. He managed to make contact with the Ordedienst in Amsterdam, and his confirmation of the SOE's infiltrated network saved a lot of agents' lives. But when an asset has been offline for such a long time, I fear for them. I'm sorry."

Nora's eyes stung, and she looked away, studying some of the simple art on the walls. Somer's words were no surprise, but she had hoped he would have better news. She refused to believe her brother-in-law—and one of her best friends—was dead. With every passing day, however, hope began to fade. She squeezed her eyes shut, trying in vain to stop the tears from falling, while part of her refused to believe it. She took a deep breath and met Somer's eyes. "Let's talk about what you need from me, Mr. Somer. Your agents in London gave me a quick overview, but none of the specifics."

He leaned forward and clasped his hands. "Very well, Nora. I asked for your return because you're one of the very few people with deep knowledge and experience in radio transmissions, and you know how the resistance operates."

"I haven't been involved in the resistance for over a year."

He held up his hand. "I know, I know. But among all the people at my disposal, there is no one with your combination of knowledge on both subjects. And there's one other very important thing." Nora raised an eyebrow, and Somer shook his head. "You're an Engelandvaarder, an England sailor. You traveled all the way from Amsterdam to Barcelona on your own, through occupied territories to make it to England."

"I wasn't entirely on my own. I had help along the way." The face of Nicolas, the man who sheltered them on arrival in Belgium, flashed through her mind. She still remembered the night the Gestapo raided his home, and he had put up a brave fight while Nora and her companions escaped through the tunnel.

"Of course, but it takes remarkable courage to make the journey, and exceptional perseverance to make it to England successfully." There was admiration in Somer's eyes. "It's no small feat, Nora."

She had no response to that, and she picked up her mug, cradling it between her fingers.

"What I'm about to ask of you is many times more dangerous than your journey south, and even though I hope you'll accept the mission, I want you to know you are free to say no. Even though you served with the WAAF, you are no soldier in the Royal Netherlands Army, and you are under no obligation to carry out what is asked of you—"

"I'm here for a reason, Mr. Somer. I wouldn't have traveled home if I didn't intend to undertake the mission. Please tell me what you need me to do."

He looked at her for a moment, his mouth open. Then he smiled and nodded, leaning back in his chair a little. "The Germans have halted the Allied advance at the Waal and Schelde Rivers. As you've been told in London, I've spent the past year setting up a network of radio operators connecting the resistance cells in the country. Many of them are positioned farther north, beyond the rivers, and the Germans along the front."

"You need them to attack the Germans rearguard."

"Exactly. And while we've established contact, we're unable to reach the most important and influential ones. I don't know what happened but mobilizing them would make the assault across the rivers much more secure. The groups could attack across the occupied areas, stretching the German army's resources, and hopefully taking some focus away from the river areas."

Nora could see the sense in the plan. "This was what it was all about from the start, wasn't it? This was why you sent Christiaan back?"

The tall man across from her nodded. "Yes, and whatever happened to him, we owe it to him, and the other agents, to get the plan in motion."

"What do you need me to do, exactly?"

Somer took a deep breath before answering. "I need you to cross the Waal River and make it past enemy lines."

Nora's breath halted as the gravity of the words sank in.

"Once you've made it across, you will make your way to Amsterdam and reach out to the Ordedienst, who should have the best equipment for you to carry out the next part of your mission."

"Which is?" Nora's head was swimming.

"Seek out the resistance cells across the country and restore communications. A woman traveling the country will attract much less attention than a male agent would."

Nora didn't immediately answer as she stood, her legs a little wobbly. She walked to the window looking out on the street. Outside, people went about their daily business carrying small grocery bags. She noticed a young mother carrying a baby wrapped close to her chest. Nora felt her heart ache, remembering the children she smuggled from the crèche in Amsterdam. It felt a lifetime ago, but she remembered every single one of them. If she'd been caught back then, she would most likely have been killed, but not before a series of grueling interrogations by the *Sicherheitsdienst*. She thought about what was asked of her today. Was it really that much different? The dangers were the same. If she were caught, she'd be interrogated and killed, although it was possible there would be no interrogation. But if she succeeded, it could—no, it would—end the war much sooner, and drive the Germans from her country once and for all. And wasn't that why she joined the resistance in the first place? The woman and her baby turned the corner, leaving the street empty. Nora knew there was only one thing she could do.

"How do I get across the river?"

The water was pitch black, the boat a lot smaller than she'd expected. The clouds above blocked the sliver of light coming from the nearly new moon. They had picked their night well, and Nora was certain it was no coincidence she was crossing tonight. The two soldiers behind her silently paddled in a regular rhythm, leaving a silent trail of rippling waves behind that carried the scent of rain and wet wood. The bow rose ever so slightly with every forward paddle motion, taking them closer to the other side of the river.

Nora strained her eyes trying to make out the far shore. Her eyes had long since adjusted to the darkness, ever since she stalked down toward the muddy riverbank. The soldiers had been waiting, silently acknowledging her before pushing off. The distance between the shores was less than three hundred meters, but it was a cold and foggy night, and Nora was unable to see the other side. Even though it unnerved her not knowing how far along they were, it also meant whoever might be paying attention on the other side wouldn't be able to see them until the very last moment. Or not at all.

Somer had been confident tonight was the ideal night to cross the Waal River. After agreeing to take on the mission in the Eindhoven office, she had been moved closer to the river. They had intentionally avoided areas where the river narrowed for their crossing. Patrols were bound to be more frequent there. She pulled on her jacket, putting the collar up and hiding her mouth, breathing warm air into the jacket. It helped a little, and she tried to relax by focusing on the soft paddling sounds around her.

Nora closed her eyes, mentally preparing for what she'd need to do once they reached the other side. If they weren't discovered, she would need to move quickly. There was a small town a few kilometers from where she'd land. This area had a lot of farms, and she would make her way to one of those and find shelter for the night in one of the barns. According to Somer's intelligence, the Germans hadn't requisitioned any of the farms, instead putting up their own camps farther downstream. She should be safe, but she needed to be extra careful.

There was a gentle tap on her shoulder. She didn't need to turn around to see why the soldier had prompted her. They glided through the fog into heavy stems of reed. In summer, these would provide ample cover as they screened most of the water close to the riverbank, but now they were barren, merely marking their imminent arrival on the other side. Nora turned around to the soldiers. One of them had exchanged his paddle for a rifle, pointing it at the fog ahead of them. The other soldier had slowed his paddling to a minimum as they approached silently, waiting for the boat to either run into the sandy bottom or bump against the riverbank.

Nora's heart pounded in her throat as she prepared to leave the boat. Her muscles tensed as the fog continued to restrict her vision. All of a sudden, the fog cleared, and the riverbank rose up in front of them. The soldier was no longer paddling, and they came to a soft yet abrupt stop. For a few seconds, none of them moved, each straining their ears for sounds from the riverbank. This was the moment of truth. If the Germans had somehow heard them approach, it would all be over in the next few seconds. Nora held her breath and counted to ten, as she was instructed. Then, she turned to the soldiers, who looked back at her calmly but urgently. One of them raised a thumb and inclined his head.

Without another thought, Nora climbed from the boat, feeling the cold dirt of the riverbank between her fingers. As soon as her feet hit the ground, she heard the boat softly whooshing away. She looked back just in time to see the bow disappear into the fog. She stood and collected her thoughts, waiting for her heart to slow down. She could hear it pounding in her ears while she listened for any signs of movement around her. All remained quiet. Slowly, she started to relax, and she became more aware of the sounds of the night around her. The water gently sloshing against the riverbank, a bird flapping its wings overhead. *It's time to move.*

Nora climbed farther up the riverbank. It was only two meters, but the fog at the top was less dense. She walked on, the ground underneath her feet changing from sticky clay to sand. She took a few more steps and saw a narrow road ahead of her. She breathed a sigh of relief; Somer had mentioned a road. She was to follow it west. The first farms would be no more than a kilometer's walk. Careful to stay clear of the road, she decided to move alongside it, staying in the muddy area still somewhat obscured by light fog. She took a few paces, remembering what she would say if she were discovered by a farmer. *Tell him I was lost and needed a place to stay. Simple.*

The cover provided by the fog gave her confidence, and she took a deep breath, closing her eyes for a moment. Nora didn't see the strong hands emerging from behind, gripping her arms and pulling her down. She landed painfully on her shoulder as she hit the cold, hard ground next to the road. She opened her eyes and let out a scream, which was quickly cut off as the hands gripped her throat, cutting off her breathing. Terror struck as she looked into cold, calculating eyes. "Shut your mouth, or I'll cut your throat."

CHAPTER TWENTY-SIX

The prisoners slowly moved along the gravel road. Floris walked to the side, loosely holding his rifle as he kept an eye on the men. Not that he worried about any of them stepping away from the column unless they were suicidal. A guard walked about ten meters ahead of Floris, another the same distance behind him. There was no chance for any of the prisoners to escape. And even if one managed to get away unseen, where would they go? The surrounding hills were covered in snow, winter making its appearance a week ago.

Floris rubbed his gloved hands together and puffed his cheeks, breathing a watery cloud. The ground was hard and razor sharp with frost. The cold was manageable, though, and they would soon be at the worksite in St. Georgen, where he would oversee the workers in the tunnels. Prisoners shivered in their ragtag mix of torn uniforms and other pieces of clothing they'd somehow managed to get their hands on. The camp uniform didn't distinguish between seasons, and these uniforms were only mildly comfortable in summer. Many of the prisoners working outside became victims of the cold, many of them dying of pneumonia. It was hardly a problem, for the dead were replaced by new arrivals every day.

"Do you know why we're not using the train today?" Anton surprised Floris as he appeared alongside him. "I hate this walk. It means we'll be carrying back a lot of them in a cart at the end of the day." He looked annoyed at the thought.

"Don't know. Nobody really tells us anything, do they?" Floris shrugged. "Besides, you won't need to carry them, so why do you care?"

"It's a hassle. Too many of them are keeling over on the way back. It slows things down, and it makes me look bad. I've had Mayer on my case a few times now. It's not my fault we're not giving them proper clothing. What am I supposed to do about it?"

Unterscharführer Mayer oversaw their part of the construction of the St. Georgen tunnel system, and Floris had quickly learned life was a lot easier without Mayer's attention.

"Try to stay out of sight, maybe switch places with some of the other guards," Floris suggested. "Besides, aren't you close to finishing the first part of the tunnels?"

"If we don't lose too many men, we should have the first fifty meters reinforced by the end of the week."

"Then try to get yourself a spot overseeing the reinforcement works. You'll be out of the cold, and so will the prisoners. Fewer casualties that way, and you'll only need to keep the Kapos in check. Mayer will be more concerned about the new tunnels."

Anton grunted something as they passed through a small settlement, the road narrowing. It meant they were only fifteen minutes away from the worksite, and Floris' spirits lifted at the thought of a hot drink on arrival. The column slowed down as the prisoners passed the houses. A woman peered out from one of the doors, dressed in the traditional garments for the area. Her dress was dark green and covered by her heavy brown coat, and she carried a piece of bread in her hands. Compassion was written all over her face as she scanned the prisoners. Floris had seen this kind of thing before.

He wouldn't intervene if the recipient wasn't wearing a yellow star. *At least they'll have a bit of extra energy for the day's work.*

The woman looked up and down the procession before taking a step forward. Then she dropped the bread on the snowy ground before rushing back into the warmth of her home. Even before her door slammed shut one of the prisoners on the edge of the procession scooped up the bread, greedily stuffing it in his mouth. Some of the others clawed at what was left in his hands, but he fought them off as best he could while chewing furiously.

"You want to do anything about that?" Anton had also witnessed the situation.

"Not really. I'd like to get to St. Georgen without delay." Floris had only just finished speaking when there was movement ahead. The man with the piece of bread suddenly lost his balance, the half-chewed bread spilling from his mouth as he crashed to the ground. A gap formed as the other prisoners passed the man.

"What the hell?" Anton stepped toward the man, some ten meters away. Floris caught up with him and put a hand on his shoulder, stopping him.

"Wait, let's see what happens first." He nodded toward another group of guards on the other side of the column, recognizing Unterscharführer Mayer among them. "Don't want to draw any unnecessary attention to yourself."

The column had stopped and guards started barking orders. Floris saw the prisoner on the ground, and it was now clear what had happened. The man hadn't tripped over anything, nor had his determination to hold on to his bread caused him to fall. Crouching over the man stood a childlike figure, screaming at him in an unusually high-pitched voice. It took Floris a few seconds to realize this was no child, but an unusually short man. He yelled at the man on the ground, spittle flying. Floris' eyes flashed to the other guards, who looked on with amused faces. As the smaller man kicked out at the downed man's ribs again, Floris noticed the armband identifying him as a Kapo.

"Did you really think you could just pick up and eat that?" the Kapo yelled as he stepped on the man's hand holding the remainder of the bread. With a yelp of pain, the man opened his fingers and the bread rolled away from him. The Kapo picked it up and took a large bite before crouching next to the man. "What's that? You still have something in your mouth?"

In what appeared to be a reflex, the man swallowed the last of the bread. This threw the Kapo into a rage. He closed his hands around the stricken man's throat and pushed down. There was a gargling sound as the much larger, but weakened, man struggled for breath. Floris heard Anton chuckle beside him while the other guards urged the Kapo on.

"Go on then, show him who's boss!"

The Kapo leaned forward, putting his full weight into his murderous act. The man on the ground had stopped struggling, his face turning blue. Floris looked away; he knew how this would end.

Then, to his shock, he heard a deafening gulp. The Kapo relinquished his crushing grasp around the man's throat and now observed the prisoner gasping desperately to recover his breath. Floris scowled; this was at odds with the ruthlessness he'd witnessed from the other Kapos in Gusen. The man would've made an effortless public execution. With Mayer standing close by, no less!

It took the prisoner about half a minute to stop coughing while the other men, prisoners and guards, looked on. As the man on the ground attempted to sit up, the Kapo moved toward him. The prisoner saw the Kapo approach, murder in his eyes. It was clear he wasn't done yet. In one fell swoop he took the man's cap and threw it in a ditch to the side of the road, about two meters from the column.

"Get your cap." There was ice in his voice.

The man's eyes darted between the cap and the Kapo. He looked for support from the other prisoners. It was in vain, as they all kept their eyes averted. Everybody knew what was about to happen next. Some of the guards held their rifles at the ready.

The prisoner struggled to his feet and faced the Kapo. Floris was surprised to see defiance in his eyes. The Kapo took a step toward him, growling. The prisoner held his gaze this time, but took a step away from the column, toward the ditch. The sound of rifles being cocked reverberated in the silence. The prisoner straightened his back as he walked on, but Floris was close enough to spot the trembling hands. The man climbed down into the shallow ditch, crouched, and picked up his cap. He replaced it on his head and paused. He was somewhat sheltered now, and Floris watched the man close his eyes. Then he stood. Before he could turn around, half a dozen rifles exploded into action. At this range, none of the shots missed, and he was dead before his body hit the snow.

Less than a minute later, the procession continued toward the day's labor.

———

Floris was on his way back to the main Mauthausen camp. It was still early, and he'd just finished breakfast, but he was in a hurry. He needed to make the best of his day off. Getting reassigned to the Gusen II camp just when he had placed Christiaan in the administration block had been a huge setback. Gusen II wasn't just a worse place to be for prisoners; the guard quarters weren't on par with his accommodations in Mauthausen. More importantly, if he wanted to obtain any information from Christiaan, he needed to build up a relationship with his estranged brother. That would be hard if he could only see him once every fortnight.

He had spent the entire night brewing a revised plan. It needed to be executed quickly, otherwise he'd have to wait months for Christiaan to open up. However, while lying amid the sound of his snoring friends, the answer came to him in a sudden moment of clarity. It was something he had never done before.

Floris nodded at the guards, who let him pass without incident. The administration building was the first to his left, and even though he'd find his brother there, he needed to prepare for the interrogation first. He needed a space where they wouldn't be disturbed. He turned right, toward the laundry block. Instead of heading inside, he took the stairs, stepping into the deserted changing room and quickly checking the shower room. There was no one there, and he smiled. This would do just fine.

He rushed back up the stairs and crossed to Block 1. It was divided into two parts, and he passed the boarded-up windows of the brothel section with little interest. It was populated by Jewish women brought in from other camps, forced to satisfy the carnal desires of cooperating prisoners. He'd even heard of some guards making use of the brothel. Floris couldn't imagine coupling with a Jewish woman, no matter how long it had been. He had more important things on his mind as he entered the other half of the block, where the administration was housed.

As soon as he stepped into the large room, he was struck by the efficiency of the men behind the desks. They clacked away on their typewriters, pretending not to notice him. Of course, were he to address them, they would jump to attention. Now, however, he preferred to take a stealthier approach. He spotted Christiaan in the back. He hadn't looked up, and Floris was certain his brother hadn't noticed him yet. *All the better.* He navigated through the rows of tables, eyes on Christiaan. His brother was so focused on his task that he didn't notice Floris until he placed a hand on the table. Christiaan looked up, surprise in his eyes.

"Come with me. You're needed in the penal block," Floris said in German. Christiaan frowned and opened his mouth, but Floris shook his head. "Outside. Now."

His brother reluctantly got up and Floris let him pass ahead of him as they walked through the room. He noticed Christiaan nodding at a stocky man, the only clerk to look up as they left the room. *Has Christiaan made a friend?*

They stepped outside, where a slight drizzle had started. Christiaan turned around. "What do you need from me, Floris? Are we really going to the penal block?" He spoke calmly in Dutch.

Even though they were well out of earshot of the guards at the gate, Floris was nervous about being overheard. He took his brother by the arm and pulled him across the road to the laundry block. Christiaan followed without protest, no doubt realizing both of their positions. Floris signaled toward the stairs leading into the basement, and Christiaan hesitated for a moment.

"Come on, I just want to talk. There's no one else there." Floris gave his brother a slight push toward the stairs while he glanced around. The guards at the gate were occupied with something happening on the other side. "Hurry, before someone sees us." Christiaan gave him an odd look but made his way down the stairs.

They entered the changing room and Floris closed the door. The air in the room was damp, the mold on the walls making each breath feel heavier than usual. Floris waved at one of the narrow wooden benches lining the wall. "Have a seat, Chris." His brother reluctantly did as he was told, then looked up at him.

"It was you who got me the job in the administration, wasn't it?"

Floris leaned against the wall. "Yes. Do you like it? Beats carrying boulders up the stairs of the quarry, doesn't it?" He studied his brother, who appeared relatively healthy. He didn't have the gaunt look of many of the walking dead condemned to manual labor. He suppressed a grin; moving his brother to the cushier surroundings of the administration block had proved a shrewd move. *Perhaps he understands how lucky he is? Maybe this won't have to be that hard?*

Lines formed on Christiaan's face. "Why?"

"What do you mean?"

"Cut it out, Flo." Christiaan's voice was strained. "I saw you and Hans in Amsterdam. You were rummaging through my house. And I've heard about what happened between you and Nora." He grimaced and looked away before he regained his composure, a hard look on his face. "You would've turned her in to the Sicherheitsdienst if her friend hadn't stopped you. I don't believe you've saved me out of the goodness of your heart."

Floris cocked his head. This was disappointing. "I hoped you'd

179

show a bit more gratitude after I saved your life. Not once, but twice now. You wouldn't be here if it wasn't for me, you understand that don't you, little brother?" Christiaan's eyes shot fire at the last words, but Floris didn't give him a chance to respond. "But you're right about one thing. Nora was a traitor, working for the resistance. I knew that much for certain. I wasn't so sure about you, though, and you can imagine my surprise when you showed up with those British spies."

"Not as surprised as I was to find my brother working in a concentration camp," Christiaan said, his eyes shifting to Floris' leg. "Where did you pick up that limp? What have you been doing? I thought you had it made in Amsterdam."

Floris flinched at the memory of his previous life. "I could ask you the same thing. In fact, that's what I wanted to talk to you about. Are you a British spy?" He asked the question almost casually, closely observing his brother. To his disappointment, Christiaan's stance remained the same, revealing nothing as he crossed his legs and folded his hands on his knees.

"Does it really matter? I'm here now, barely surviving." The lines on his face softened somewhat. "Look, Flo, I appreciate you moving me to the administration. But I don't trust you. You're a Nazi. I've seen what you've done to people back home, and I don't know what got you here, but you're part of a machine operating the conveyor belt of death. Even if I was a British spy, I'd never admit to it. Not to you or anyone else. Trust me, you're not the first to ask."

Floris was taken aback by his brother's measured response. He'd expected him to deny, to laugh at him, to wither and cringe at the accusation. It would've been a natural response considering the circumstances. Floris held the power of life and death over every prisoner in the camp, and they knew it. Any other prisoner would've flat-out denied being a British spy, knowing even the hint of confirming the accusation would mean a trip to the torture chambers in the penal block. But Christiaan remained composed. Floris felt a tingle of excitement as his instincts and experience as a police officer kicked in. *He's lying. But if I push him now, he'll never admit to what he's done.* Floris studied his brother, who looked almost at ease as he tapped his foot on the cold tiles. *He doesn't fear me.*

Floris clapped his hands and turned to the door. "Let's get you back to work, then." Christiaan appeared surprised as he got up. *Good.* Floris mounted the stairs and waited at the top for his brother to catch up. A group of new arrivals was just passing through the main gate, and Floris hurried away from the laundry block.

When they returned to the administration block, Floris followed his brother inside on a hunch. Christiaan seemed surprised but walked toward the clerks' room. Floris placed a hand on his shoulder before he entered. "I'll be back in a few days. Perhaps your memory was a bit foggy this morning. Why don't you think about your time away from Amsterdam a bit more, and we can chat later." Christiaan looked at him blankly before turning and entering the crowded clerks' room.

Floris stood in the doorway, watching his brother move through the room. As he passed the desk of the stocky clerk, the man looked up anxiously. Christiaan stopped and they exchanged a few words, inaudible to Floris. The man's expression changed to one of surprise, mixed with a bit of fear. Floris smiled and turned away. He knew enough.

CHAPTER TWENTY-SEVEN

L isa awoke to find the camp bustling with activity, men rushing between the tents in a sort of controlled disarray. She rubbed her eyes as she emerged from her tent. Her sleep had been brief due to having worked an additional half shift during the night, replacing one of the nurses too ill to work. There had been a few soldiers that required her help, but mostly they just wanted someone to talk to while they dealt with their pain. Whenever she could, Lisa provided some comfort in addition to medication for their ailments. By the time the lead doctor released her back to her tent at three in the morning, she was completely exhausted.

It was now seven, and she headed toward the canteen. She needed some coffee, and she was keen to know what had everybody on the move. There had been rumors of General Patton being summoned for an important meeting a few days ago, and Lisa felt certain the activity around her had something to do with it.

She joined the short queue and secured a large mug of coffee, toast, and jam. Scanning the tables, she smiled as she spotted Steve sitting by himself.

"Morning, mind if I sit here?" She set her plate, mug, and herself down before he could answer. "What's got everybody so hot and bothered? Did I miss something?"

"Orders to move out came about an hour ago. The armored and mechanized units are getting their tanks and trucks ready. We're finally leaving this place!"

"You think Patton secured some fuel?" Lisa spread a generous layer of jam on her toast and took a large bite, continuing to speak while she chewed. "Are we crossing the river?"

Steve shook his head. "Remember how our scouts reported German troops heading north? And the little resistance on the riverside these past two weeks?" Lisa nodded, slurping while she took a large swig of coffee. Steve seemed unperturbed by her less-than-ladylike table manners. "Turns out Patton's suspicions were correct. They've smashed through our lines in the Ardennes Forest in Belgium, about two hundred kilometers north."

"What does that mean?" General Patton had warned Allied command about the German troop movements for weeks. The men of the Third Army had been anxious to do something about it, laying out their plans to strike against the convoys moving along the river.

"They've broken through our lines with hundreds, some even say thousands, of tanks and several hundred thousand troops. They've got Bastogne surrounded, with our boys from the Hundred and First Airborne the only ones holding the city."

Lisa gasped. "Sounds like we underestimated them."

"We?" Steve snorted in disgust. "If only Eisenhower and the others had listened to Patton, we could've stopped this before it even started."

"So how many of us are heading north?" Lisa finished the last of her toast and wiped her mouth with a napkin.

"The entire Third," Steve said, the hint of a smile on his face. "Including you. We're going to hit the krauts with everything we've got. This is it, Lisa. We're going to race to Bastogne and wipe them out."

"I just hope we make it there in time." Lisa stood. "I better report to the Red Cross tent and see when we're shipping out. I'll see you soon. Take care, Steve."

He gave her a half salute. "You too, Lisa. And don't worry, we're going to get our boys in Bastogne out."

———

Two hours later, Lisa sat in the back of a truck. The convoy was moving forward at a snail's pace because of the conditions; snow and frigid temperatures had made the roads icy and treacherous. Even though everybody was anxious to reach Bastogne, it was still necessary for drivers of tanks and trucks to be cautious.

When Lisa reported to her superior, he'd told her to immediately pack her things. She was also given an extra bag of rations and first-aid supplies for the journey. Even though their intelligence reported little to no German activity on the road north, that could change in an instant. The Red Cross nurses and doctors were spread out across the column, ready to help whenever it was needed.

It felt good to be useful, but it felt even better to know they were finally going to face the enemy head on. The army had been stuck in Saarlouis for too long, and despite the frequent sorties across the river to engage the German patrols, the men had grown restless. It had carried over to Lisa as well, and she had questioned the earlier optimism about a swift liberation. Now, they were on the move again, and she felt a surge of energy in her bones as the truck bundled on.

Lisa eyed some of the soldiers. Most leaned their heads against the tarps, eyes closed as they took advantage of the journey to catch up on some sleep. Even though their time in Saarlouis had been mostly uneventful, what was ahead would surely test their resolve and endurance. On boarding the truck, most of the men had been exhilarated, shouting and whooping their approval at heading out. After weeks of idling in Saarlouis, they would finally see some action.

She thought back to her encounter in the city, now two months ago. Lisa had joined several patrols since, but she had never encountered a German assault like the one in Saarlouis again. She often wondered if the assailants knew they had killed half a dozen of their own men. Lisa preferred to think they didn't, but doubt had nagged at her for weeks after. The young men had been well informed about the army's movements, and she wondered if it had simply been easier for their commanders to take them out to make sure they stayed quiet. She shook her head; surely the Germans wouldn't be that heartless? They would care about their own, just like the men around her did.

The truck stopped, its brakes hissing softly. There were voices outside, shouting to move along. Her mind wandered back to London. How would her colleagues at the Bureau be doing? Would Colonel Somer have moved back to the Netherlands yet? She smiled at the memory of her former boss. He had been adamant that he would move back as soon as the first city was liberated. From what Lisa had heard, most of the south now was, so she imagined him controlling operations only a few hundred kilometers north from her position.

She trusted Somer would do everything he could to make sure information fed to the approaching Allied forces would be reliable. She thought of Christiaan and felt a stab of pain in her heart. Even though she continued to tell herself he was alive, it became harder to believe with every passing day. She shook her head. *I can't do this to myself. There is no way to get into contact with him from here. I need to have faith.* It was perhaps her only regret at leaving London: no longer having access to the intelligence coming in from all over the Continent. Even if Christiaan made contact, Lisa wouldn't know. She steeled herself and looked around the truck once more. All the soldiers had their eyes closed, their heads bobbing along with the cadence of the truck. She was here to free Europe. And the sooner they did, the sooner she'd be able to look for the man she loved.

———

The convoy trudged along the frozen roads for three days, finally arriving in Arlon, 40 kilometers south of Bastogne. As the troops stepped off the trucks, Lisa was glad for the chance to get out and move around for a couple hours. Farther up in the column, General Patton instructed the senior staff. Lisa reported in to her commanding officer, who sent her to one of the supply trucks stationed near the tail end.

She carefully navigated the streets of the city, crowded with military vehicles. Soldiers sat around smoking cigarettes, scooping beans from cans, or simply lounging around and talking. Lisa soon found the supply trucks and refilled her first-aid kit with motion sickness medication. Some of the men had suffered from the skidding and bumping on the way up, and she wanted to make sure they were all rested before they carried on. Bastogne was only a few hours away. When she listened closely, she thought she could hear fighting in the distance.

Returning to the truck, Lisa was surprised to find Steve waiting. She hadn't seen him for three days and she gave him a quick hug. "How has your drive been? You hanging in there?"

"It's taking a bit too long for my liking. We could've been there yesterday if it wasn't for this damn snow," Steve said.

"Don't worry, you'll get your chance to fight the Germans soon enough." Lisa looked around; the soldiers' faces were lined with tension. *They all know.* "What do you think the general will decide?"

Steve looked up at the gray, cloudy skies. "I think he'll want us to go into battle as soon as we get near Bastogne. Quickly get this over with. My CO said he wouldn't be surprised if we ditch the trucks for the last few miles and march."

"Surprise the Germans?"

"Something like that, yes. Although it will be hard to conceal all those tanks rolling along." Steve glanced at a few of the tanks lined up alongside the road. "We'll definitely need those if we want to make a dent in the German lines."

Lisa wanted to answer but there was movement up ahead. Men

were climbing back on board the trucks. Steve whistled through his teeth. "Time to go! See you later, Lisa." Before she could say anything, he'd turned and joined the men hurrying toward the trucks. One of the soldiers in the back of her truck spotted her and held out his hand. She grabbed it, and he pulled her up effortlessly. Five minutes later, the truck was rolling forward. In the distance, the booming of artillery was impossible to miss.

———

The next week was spent in a daze. Steve had been right; the trucks had halted in what appeared to be the middle of nowhere. There, the soldiers had moved out, the tanks continuing forward on the road. Lisa was moved to a new truck where she linked up with her Red Cross colleagues. For the first time since arriving in France she was relieved to stay away from the front lines, to be with the other nurses and doctors. Tens of thousands of soldiers marched past, their faces serious and focused, ready for battle.

Lisa and the rest of the doctors and nurses set up a field hospital a couple kilometers from the front. They were so close that they could feel the ground shaking at times. Soon, the first dead and wounded returned to the camp. The latter quickly filled the beds in Lisa's hospital, and she worked around the clock. At the end of the second day, one of the doctors ordered her to bed for a few hours.

"You can't treat these men properly if you're falling asleep yourself, Lisa. Get some rest."

Unsurprisingly, sleep had come quickly, and she felt refreshed when she returned only five hours later. The snow had finally stopped, and the blue sky lifted her spirits as she crossed the short distance from her sleeping quarters to the hospital.

She entered the hospital and gasped. All cots were filled, with soldiers unable to find a cot now lying in the gangways between. Lisa rushed toward one of the doctors.

"What happened? Where did they all come from suddenly? Why

didn't you call for me?" She heard the annoyance in her voice and held up her hands. "Sorry, I didn't mean to overstep."

He looked at her with a calm, open face. "Don't worry about it. You care. From what some of the men told me, the fighting has intensified. It seems they're closing in on the city."

Lisa felt a flutter in her stomach. "On Bastogne? Already?"

"It appears so." The doctor's voice was steady as he studied a chart. "Why don't you help out on the far side, over there." He pointed at a group of soldiers standing around. Their clothes were dirty. "They all have relatively small injuries, but they'll need treatment. They can find themselves a spot between the beds if you feel they need a rest. Otherwise, if they feel up to it, they can catch one of the trucks outside. They'll take them up to the front."

The first soldier had a gash across his forehead, and Lisa introduced herself while she waved him to a chair. "How many fingers am I holding up?" she said while she reached for a thick roll of gauze.

"Four, ma'am," the soldier answered. She nodded while she studied his wound. It would need to be disinfected first. "Hang on, this will only sting a little." She cleaned the wound while the young man winced but didn't let out a peep. She started rolling the gauze around his head, creating a headband. He held his eyes closed; his jaw clenched. It was important to keep the young men calm.

"Where are you from?" she asked while she tightened the gauze.

"Mississippi, ma'am. Born and raised in Jackson." He winced while Lisa secured the headband, using a generous amount of tape to make sure it would stay in place. "Yourself, if you don't mind me asking, ma'am? You have an interesting accent."

Lisa smiled at his good manners. Most of the American soldiers were overly polite, something she wasn't used to from back home. "Amsterdam."

He looked surprised for a moment, then caught himself. "How did you end up with the US Army?"

"Long story, soldier, and for another time."

"Ma'am, can I return to my unit?" He made a move to get up, and Lisa pushed him back in his chair.

"Absolutely not. You've got a serious head injury. You'll need to stay here for a bit."

He looked confused. "But ma'am, I can't abandon them. They need me there."

"Not today, they don't. We're going to find you a place to lie down."

For a moment, the soldier looked ready to challenge her, then he nodded. "All right, I'll follow you, ma'am." He stood and wobbled on his legs, almost falling over, before Lisa caught him.

"Easy now," she said as she supported him. She saw another soldier get up from his cot, grabbing his field pack and moving toward the exit. She guided her soldier to the cot and eased him down. When he was settled, she asked, "What's your name?"

"James, ma'am, but my friends call me Jim."

"You need to rest. Okay, Jim?"

"When can I go back?"

"A doctor will check on you in a bit, but you won't be going anywhere until tomorrow at the earliest, okay?"

He looked disappointed.

"You feel like you're letting your friends down?"

"Them, but the general also."

"General Patton?" Lisa was only mildly surprised. The general was held in high esteem by practically the entire Third Army.

Jim looked at her intently. "He was right there on the front lines. I was freezing in my foxhole, waiting for the command to push forward, when a jeep roared by. It was going too fast, and the driver lost control and it slid into the ditch next to the road. I remember saying to Murphy in the hole next to me, that driver is an idiot for driving like that, so close to the fighting."

His eyes were a little glassy, and Lisa considered telling him to stop talking, then spotted the determination in Jim's eyes, and said nothing.

"Imagine my surprise when none other than General Patton jumped from the passenger seat. We didn't hesitate and helped push his jeep from the ditch. He was right next to me in the muddy snow, pushing that damn jeep back onto the road." Jim smiled at the memory, then closed his eyes. "We can't lose with someone like him in charge, ma'am. We just can't." His face relaxed, and a few moments later he was snoring softly. Lisa carefully adjusted his blanket and walked back to the group of soldiers waiting for her.

The next day, the news came. The Third Army had smashed through the German lines, breaking the siege of Bastogne, and had linked up with the 101st Airborne inside the city. The German army was on the back foot, and soon on the run. Lisa smiled at Jim's words and realized he was right. With a man like Patton leading them, there was no stopping this army.

CHAPTER TWENTY-EIGHT

Nora slowly lifted her aching head from the uncomfortable bed, and with some effort she managed to slide her feet off the mattress onto the cold floor. She cracked her neck and rubbed her eyes. Through the small window above her, bright light shined in, indicating it had to be at least eight or nine o'clock in the morning. It was hard to keep track of time spent in the cell, and Nora couldn't remember if this was her fourth or fifth night.

She did remember the night she got to the cell. The strong hands that forced her to the ground on the riverbank were those of a cold-eyed German soldier. His patrol had spotted her emerging from the mist. They had taken Nora to their position near the bridge. She only spent a few hours there as they waited for the Sicherheitspolizei to arrive in the morning. They didn't ask her any questions during the car ride, and Nora had wondered where they were taking her. It soon became clear as they reached The Hague and kept driving. Soon, they crossed the dunes, revealing the North Sea glittering in the distance. They had reached Scheveningen. A few turns later, they drove alongside a high wall running parallel to the road. They stopped in front of a heavily guarded gate, where four Sicherheitsdienst guards inspected their credentials. When they continued, Nora noticed the imposing building in front of her. The red-brick walls rose at least four stories high, the barred windows letting in light but restricting its occupant's freedom. It was the notorious *Oranjehotel*, where the country's resistance fighters were imprisoned. She shivered as she was led inside by the two silent guards. They passed through a hallway and she vaguely remembered being processed. Her belongings were taken, and she was given simple, drab, and ill-fitting clothes. The next thing she remembered was being shoved into a tiny cell, the door smashing closed behind her.

There was constant activity outside her cell, including guards silently patrolling and at times agonizing screams and pleading cries for help. She couldn't see what happened outside, but she had an idea about the horrific fate that awaited those who were taken away. The cells around hers fell to silence after their removal; muffled whimpering occasionally could be heard when they were brought back, but two never returned. A cold shudder ran down her spine.

Once or twice a day one of the guards came in to bring her water and something inedible. Her stomach had rejected her first effort at keeping the food down, forcing her to throw up in the small bucket that she also used to relieve herself. It had only made things worse; the smell in her cell was unbearable.

Nora stood and instantly felt woozy, her world spinning. She closed her eyes and rubbed her temples, concentrating on staying upright. *Just stay strong, keep breathing, one day at a time.* The dizziness passed and she opened her eyes, taking a few steps in the confined space. Her cell was tiny, and it took just four steps to reach the door from her bunk. She pricked her ears for sounds in the hallway. It was quiet, although she heard someone shuffle in the cell next door. She hadn't yet dared to reach out to any of the other prisoners, afraid to attract unwanted attention from the guards.

A door opened with a loud clunk. There were multiple footsteps, and Nora strained her ears. *Two, three men?* It seemed too early for her daily rations; there was no such thing as breakfast in the prison.

The prisoners were served food whenever the guards felt like it. It was uncommon to receive anything before midday. *Have I slept for that long?*

The footsteps neared, and Nora stepped away from the door. Keys jingled, and a few seconds later, the bolt in her door was unlocked. It swung open, and two guards stepped inside, making the confined space even smaller. Nora felt as if the air was sucked from the room as one of the men motioned at her.

"Come with us, now." He spoke in German, but even if Nora hadn't understood the language, it would've been clear enough what was expected of her. Cautiously, she took a step forward. This visibly annoyed him, a grimace appearing on his face. "Schnell, schnell! We don't have all day!"

Nora followed her captors out of the small cell, suddenly feeling a sense of relief from being in a more open space. However, this did not last long, as she was quickly ushered toward a door at the end of the hallway. The pit of her stomach churned with fear and a sour taste rose in the back of her throat.

The men guided Nora down four flights of stairs, into the basement of the building, the air getting colder with each step. The ground beneath her bare feet was dusty and dirty. The walls of the basement were uneven, eaten away by years of humidity. The cobblestone walls made the area feel medieval. Nora's heart hammered in her chest. The guards appeared unconcerned as they stomped on in their heavy black boots. They passed through a brick archway, leading to another thick door that opened into a small room with a concrete floor. The ceiling was low, and Nora had to duck to avoid hitting her head on one of the pipes running across from corner to corner.

The air was as musty—foul, even—as in the hallway, but it was a lot brighter inside the room. A man sat at a steel table that looked both out of place and too big for the space. He was studying a thin file on the table and glanced up momentarily to wave Nora to the single chair opposite him. "Sit." To Nora's surprise, the man addressed her in her native language.

The wooden chair creaked, and Nora found herself leaning forward to correct the imbalance as it gravitated backward. Or was the ground uneven? It didn't matter; she was no doubt placed in this uncomfortable position on purpose. The door behind her closed softly, the guards' footsteps fading in the hallway. Nora placed her hands in her lap and studied the man across the table. His hair was neatly combed back, exposing a significant receding hairline. His eyes scanned the words on the page in front of him, and Nora followed his gaze. The lines were neatly typed out, and it looked like some sort of identification document, with a space for a passport-sized photograph in the top left corner. The space was empty. The man looked up and caught her gaze, and Nora looked away at the wall behind him.

"Well, well." He chuckled and spoke in a measured tone that immediately unnerved her. "Interested in what's in your file, miss?"

Miss? He hadn't addressed her by name. She felt a bit of confidence returning and shifted her attention from the wall to meet his eyes but said nothing.

The man leaned back and ran a hand through his hair. He looked at ease and patient, appearing to have all the time in the world. "How has your stay in the Oranjehotel been so far? I expect the guards have taken good care of you?" His tone was mocking, and his dark brown eyes locked onto hers. *How much does he know?*

"I'm not sure why I was brought here," she started, immediately regretting it. Her voice was too high pitched, her nerves filtering through. The man's expression remained unchanged. "I don't even know how long I've been here. It feels like a big mistake."

The man's eyes narrowed as he leaned forward, placing his hands on the table between them. "You think you're here by mistake? Well, let me disabuse you of that notion. You were found stalking near the river at night, without papers. You are aware of the curfew, right? And I'm sure you know the area you were found in is right across from where the Canadian and American forces are stationed?" Nora didn't answer, and he leaned farther across the table. "What were you doing there in the middle of the night?"

Nora gripped her shaking hands tighter, hoping the man wouldn't notice. His eyes shifted quickly, missing nothing. *Shit.* She swallowed and forced herself to look him in the eye. "I was lost." It was all she could come up with, and she was aware of how pathetic it sounded.

"Lost? At three in the morning?" He stood abruptly. "Hardly." His voice remained frustratingly composed, as if he were talking to a child. "I'll tell you what I think, because it's quite plausible, from the way I look at it." He moved around the table and sat on the edge, the toes of his shoes almost touching her knees. "I'd say you were dropped from the other side somehow. You were nowhere near a bridge, and the nearest town is a few kilometers away. We checked with the nearby farmers, and none of them were missing someone fitting your description. So, you were either very, very lost, which I find quite unlikely. Or"—he moved a strand of hair from his forehead —"you were sent by our *friends* across the river. Personally, I subscribe to the latter theory. And that's why it's no mistake you're here." His leg dangled casually on the side of the table.

Nora looked at him blankly, not sure how to respond. She felt flushed, the back of her neck burning. Her mind raced as she racked her brain for a plausible explanation. If only she'd made it to one of the farmhouses. The farmers would've let her stay the night in their barns. But as she eyed the man on the table, she knew she had no chance. There was only one thing left to do.

"I wasn't dropped from the other side of the river. I was simply lost," Nora said, trying to sound more confident than she felt. A thought struck. "It's actually a bit embarrassing." She tried to sound as coy as possible.

The man's eyebrows shot up. "What's that?" The lack of emotion didn't match his curious expression.

"Well, I tend to have bouts of sleepwalking. This wasn't the first time I woke up outside. It's happened before." The man sighed, but Nora persisted. "The patrol finding me was the first thing I remember after going to bed that night. I remember going to sleep and then waking up outside, getting strangled by one of the German soldiers." There was a tremble in her voice, not because of the memory, but because she feared the man across from her would see through her lie. "After that, everything went so fast, and I was scared to speak to them."

The man stood and crossed back to his side of the table. He didn't say a word as he sat down in his comfortable chair, his eyes distant. *Is he buying it?* Nora felt a flutter of hope as she tried to read his face. He scratched his chin before his eyes returned to focus. She held her breath as he opened his mouth.

"Bullshit." Her heart dropped, but she forced herself to hold his gaze. "That's the worst lie I've heard in a while, and I talk to a lot of people." He tapped his fingers on the file in front of him. "According to the report from the patrol, you were present and conscious when they encountered you. And if you were sleepwalking, where did you come from? Nobody in the vicinity reported a woman missing. You're lying."

His words hit Nora like a punch to the gut, the energy draining from her body. The gravity of the situation started to dawn on her. This prison, the Oranjehotel, was reserved for suspected resistance fighters. That meant they must consider her one. She almost chuckled at the irony; she'd operated under Floris' nose for more than a year, but she got caught somewhere in the middle of nowhere when she wasn't connected to the resistance anymore.

"I'm going to give you one last chance to come clean on your own. Tell me your story, tell me who sent you, and there might be something we can arrange." His eyes were almost friendly as he placed his hands palms up on the table. *Don't buy it, Nora.* "Or, you can say nothing, and we'll extract the truth from you in other ways. Your choice." He leaned back in his chair and crossed his legs, tapping the tips of his fingers against each other.

Nora considered her situation. There was no one in the Oranje-hotel who knew her identity. And no one would know if she kept her mouth shut. If she confessed now, she knew she'd only hasten her sentence, which was almost certainly death. She thought about Somer and the soldiers she'd met before her crossing. They all seemed very confident of breaking through the German defenses sooner rather than later. They might already be on their way. *I have nothing to lose, but everything to gain by dragging this out.* She swallowed hard as she thought of the *other ways* her captors had to make her talk. *So be it. It's my only chance.* Her eyes stung, and she squeezed them, blinking the tears away before the man across from her could notice. She looked at him, clenched her jaw, and shook her head. *No more talking.*

"All right, then. So, you choose the hard way. That's all the same to me. Everybody talks in the end." He slowly rose and walked past her, opening the door. "Guards!" The door farther down the hallway immediately opened and Nora heard footsteps approaching. She closed her eyes for a moment and collected herself. Her entire body was shaking, but she somehow found a way to get up from the chair on her own. She turned toward the door, where the guards stood in the opening. The other man leaned against the doorpost.

"Take her back to her cell," he instructed the guards, who walked in, the taller one roughly grabbing her elbow. "We'll be seeing much more of each other soon, miss."

His vicious smile was filled with anticipation, chilling Nora's blood.

———

Nora was back in her cell ten minutes later. The door slammed and she was alone again. She wrapped her arms around her chest as she sat on her bed, still shivering. The man's final words had rocked her, and the walk from the basement had given her time to consider what would happen next. The guards had taken a different route back, and she'd heard cries of anguish from behind the closed doors they passed. That had been no coincidence, and it had worked. Nora had never been this terrified.

She sat in a haze and didn't hear the door open at first. It was the light draft against her legs that alerted her to the slender woman standing in the doorway. Nora's surprise must've shown, for the woman held up her hands, revealing a large hunk of bread in one.

"Sorry, I didn't mean to scare you." She softly closed the door and approached Nora, the hand holding the bread outstretched. "Please take this. You're going to need it."

Nora reluctantly took the bread and inspected it before taking a cautious bite.

"It's good bread, you can eat it. Trust me." The woman knelt next to her and produced a flask of water. "Here, drink. They don't give you half enough water in here."

The expression on the woman's face was soft and familiar, and Nora did as she was told. She drank greedily, the cold water invigorating her. "Who are you?" she managed as she wiped her mouth with the back of her sleeve.

"A friend, dear. I came to warn you."

Nora sat up, looking into the woman's bright eyes. "For what?"

"When they come for you, you need to tell them something. It doesn't have to be the truth, or the whole truth. Just think of something that is at least slightly plausible. If you don't give them anything, they will kill you." Her eyes turned sad. "Trust me, I've seen it many times before."

"But when will it be enough? Won't they keep going until I tell them what they want to hear?" The words tumbled out of her mouth before she realized. *I don't even know this woman. What am I doing?*

"It doesn't matter. I'm sure you can come up with something that they might consider interesting but is no longer relevant. Maybe something from your past?" The woman looked at her keenly, as if looking into her soul. "Give them the impression that they're making progress. Just don't admit to the big stuff."

Nora slowly nodded. The woman placed a hand against her cheek, then rose and pointed at the bread. "I'll look after you. Just stay alive long enough to make it out of here, okay?"

"Who are you?" Nora repeated. It was the only thing she wanted to know.

The woman shook her head as she made for the door. "Eat. Rest. You'll need your strength when they come for you." She slipped through the narrow opening and closed the door, leaving Nora confused, exhausted, and utterly alone.

CHAPTER TWENTY-NINE

C hristiaan stood looking at the back of the man in front of him. The wind had free rein on the thoroughfare, and he shuffled on his feet, his teeth chattering. The sun had set a few hours ago. The bright lights of the Appellplatz illuminated every movement. Evening roll call had lasted longer than usual, and even though Christiaan didn't know exactly how long they'd stood there, he knew something was up.

Bachmayer had departed once the counting was done, but now the Hauptsturmführer re-emerged from behind the prison block with four of his subordinates. Christiaan studied the officer's face, trying to discern any hint of anger or annoyance—and finding both. Instinctively, he turned his head slightly toward Petr and caught a nearly imperceptible nod from his companion. *He's seen it, too.* Fear flashed through him as he remembered the last special roll call at this site and the execution of the clerks. He glanced back at Petr again; his friend's features remained serene, and that gave Christiaan some solace. Maybe this time it wasn't about them?

His answer came a few moments later. The camp's main gate opened, the creaking of the hinges sounding especially ominous in the quiet of the surroundings. Christiaan resisted the urge to turn and watch, but he didn't need to. The sound of barking dogs and guards yelling was enough—new prisoners. *But why are we waiting for them?* There was movement in the corner of Christiaan's eyes as the sound of the incoming transport increased.

The head of the column came into view, and Christiaan was surprised by the show of force. Normal escorts from the train station were accompanied by a reasonable number of guards. A quick count showed about a hundred prisoners, with nearly as many guards, most wielding MP40 submachine guns. It was excessive, especially considering the state of the men they were beating and kicking toward the center of the Appellplatz. The men looked pitiful, their clothing ripped, their faces bloodied. Half the number of guards would've sufficed. The dogs strained on their leashes, exposing their fangs. Their handlers clearly enjoyed the terror their charges instilled, allowing the dogs to nip at the slower prisoners.

The new arrivals were soon gathered in front of the rest of the prisoners. Crowding together, they were silent. Those who had the strength and courage to look up from the ground eyed the mass of shaven-headed prisoners with curiosity, but without surprise. For a few seconds, nothing happened, both sets of prisoners staring at each other. Then, Bachmayer moved in, his voice booming across the Appellplatz.

"You can all see what these are, can't you? The Red commissars—communists. Look at them, those weaklings!" There was hatred in his voice, and Christiaan was close enough to see the thunderous, murderous fury in his eyes.

As if on cue, a few of the men in the group of Russians collapsed to the ground. There were no wails, no grunts, as their legs gave out. Only the dull thud of their bodies hitting the ground. Bachmayer didn't hesitate as he called out, "To the crematorium with those dogs, immediately!" Several of the guards surrounding the Russian prisoners raised their guns, while a few others waded into the crowd to drag four motionless bodies out. While three of them had their eyes closed and appeared at the very least unconscious, one had his eyes open, terror etched on his face as he disappeared behind the prison block. Christiaan closed his eyes for a moment and prayed one of the guards would be merciful enough to shoot him before dispatching him into the ovens.

At the front, Bachmayer mumbled something, and Christiaan thought he caught the Hauptsturmführer mention "too many of them." An instant later, he waded into the group of prisoners and pointed out another six men. The guards didn't need to be told what to do next, but Bachmayer removed all doubt: "Them, too. Crematorium." The ominous words echoed across the Appellplatz, and even if they didn't understand his words, the meaning was clear enough for the terrified men being hauled off. Despite their impending death, they went silently. These weren't ordinary prisoners.

Bachmayer waited for the men to disappear behind the prison block, then clasped his hands behind his back and addressed the remaining Russians. "Not so brave anymore, are we?" he said, and a prisoner standing alongside him translated to Russian. The faces of the men in the group remained stoic, despite having seen their comrades hauled off to death moments earlier. Some even looked up defiantly, meeting Bachmayer's gaze. "How many of you would now still openly declare yourself a commissar and communist?" There was a delay as the prisoner translated, and Bachmayer looked especially pleased with himself. The prisoners around Christiaan stood quietly as the translator finished. Most of them had understood Bachmayer's original words, and they all knew there was no correct response to the Hauptsturmführer's question. Silence was the only option. That, and prayers that they would not end up in the crematorium themselves.

To Christiaan's horror and surprise, there was movement in the middle of the column of Russians. A man struggled forward; his army uniform was reduced to bloodied rags covering only a fraction of his body. His face was bruised black and blue, an angry-looking cut slashed across his left cheek. Christiaan could almost feel it pulsating on his own face as the man reached Bachmayer. In a voice stronger than expected, he spoke quickly, in words Christiaan did not understand. The message, however, was clear. When he stopped talking, the interpreter was visibly shaken. Christiaan quickly looked to Petr, whose face betrayed fascination and respect. The interpreter composed himself and relayed the Russian's message in a measured tone.

"I, Morozov, Alexander Dimitrovich, am a commissar and communist. I was a communist, am a communist, and will forever remain one." In an instant, Bachmayer's expression changed. He still looked gleeful, but another emotion became visible: hatred. Before he could respond, another man stepped from the crowd.

"My name is Ponoramev, also communist and commissar." He stood next to Morozov. There was more movement in the ranks as two more men joined them, then another six. Bachmayer's face went red from fury, and he undid the whip on his belt. He lashed out at the Russians who'd dared to defy him so publicly. They shrank back but held their ground.

After a dozen lashes, Bachmayer appeared to catch himself, and stopped. His face was flushed, and Christiaan thought he detected a slight frothing around the mouth. This was not a good look for one of the most powerful men in the camp, and the Hauptsturmführer appeared to realize it as well. As he put the whip away, the man called Morozov yelled something in Russian. The interpreter duly translated. "Kill me, you fascist pig! Your journey to hell will start soon enough!"

With visible restraint, Bachmayer eyed Morozov, then turned to the translator. "Tell him he'll be the last to die. He'll get to watch his comrades die, and by the end, he'll be begging to be put down like the dog he is." He waved his hand dismissively and turned his back to the group as he walked from the Russian prisoners.

When the interpreter finished, Bachmayer turned back one more time. He looked thoughtfully at the group of ten directly in front of him. "Actually, why don't we give them a nice night instead. Have them strip, and make sure they receive showers every half an hour. Let's see how strong they are." The interpreter looked unsure, but Bachmayer shook his head at him. "The rest will be put in Block 20 for now."

The assembled prisoners were forced to wait as the main group of Russians was marched off. At the same time, the ten defiant Russians were told to strip. When they all refused, the guards tore off their clothes, until the men stood naked in the cold. They were quickly tied up to chains lining walls of the prison block. Christiaan looked at the shivering men and pitied them. His own clothes at least offered some protection from the cold. These naked, weakened men had no chance of surviving the freezing night.

Five guards appeared from the laundry block, each carrying two steaming buckets. Bachmayer instructed them to place them on the ground in front of the Russians. They had retained their composure until this point, but realization appeared on the faces of the bound men. The buckets meant death. For a few seconds, Christiaan considered the possibility that Bachmayer was bluffing, but then the soldiers picked up the buckets, and the first five Russians were doused with water. The men screamed in agony. The water was boiling hot, scalding the men's freezing bodies crimson red. Seconds later, the other five were subjected to the same torture. Christiaan breathed out, aghast, his breath appearing in a vapor cloud in front of him.

"That's enough for now," Bachmayer said, loud enough for everyone in the Appellplatz to hear. "Back to your blocks. This roll call is over."

The assembled prisoners scattered to their dwellings. Christiaan looked at the ten naked Russians at the front. Their bodies were oddly shiny in the floodlights of the night, contrasting sharply with the bluish hue of their faces. It took him a second to realize what he was looking at, then he turned away in horror. A thin layer of ice had formed on the men's bodies.

Christiaan woke up with a sick feeling in the pit of his stomach. He'd gone to sleep with the image of the ten freezing Russians etched in his mind. He'd fallen asleep quickly enough—his body and mind were exhausted, and no amount of horror could stop that—but woke up feeling a strong sense of dread. The block was more quiet than usual as they prepared to head out for roll call.

When they arrived, Christiaan could hardly believe his eyes. He'd witnessed plenty of dreadful things in the camp, but the sight that greeted him that morning took it to another level. The ten Russian soldiers stood in the same place, their hands still tied behind their backs. Their faces were turned downward, toward an invisible adversary trampling over their bodies. Every hair on their heads was frosted white with icicles, and ice had already formed around their extremities. Christiaan wanted to look away, but snowflakes falling on his face and a gust of cold wind drew his eyes back to the macabre sight as he filed into position among the rest of the prisoners. The water buckets lay carelessly tossed around the frozen bodies as mute testimony to this evil.

The Appellplatz filled in silence, the prisoners paying their respects to the brave but foolish Russian sculptures. The guards moved in and started their prisoner counts without acknowledging the dead Russians. Another day at Mauthausen had begun.

An hour later, Christiaan finished processing the names of the Russians, and an SS officer had signed off on the sheet. He looked at their names and noted the causes of death. Collapsed during work duty, stopped while trying to escape, killed by another prisoner. He shook his head. They were laughably transparent to anyone vaguely familiar with the workings of the camp. But what did it really matter? In a few weeks, none of the men present during roll call that morning would be left to contradict the words on paper.

Not for the first time, he questioned his own future. Christiaan knew enough to be a threat to the men running the camp if they were ever freed. And the talk among the new arrivals was that the Russians were making steady progress in the east, while the Americans, British, and Canadians had crossed into Germany recently. While Christiaan was encouraged by their progress, he also knew the threat to his life increased with every kilometer they gained on Mauthausen.

"Did you get that document on the Russians signed off yet?" Christiaan was surprised to find Petr at his desk. He nodded and tapped on a single sheet of paper. Petr jerked his head to the door. "Come, I'll help you file it."

Christiaan followed his friend out of the room. Once they reached the hallway, Petr turned around and took the piece of paper from Christiaan.

"Thanks, I'll take it from here. You can just return to your desk." A smile played on his friend's lips before Petr turned toward the front door of the block.

Christiaan grabbed Petr by the shoulder and said in a low but persistent voice, "Where are you taking those papers? I want to know what you're up to."

Petr's smile increased, his eyes twinkling. "Are you sure? Do you want to be an accomplice?"

"I'm already an accomplice." Christiaan's tone was harsher than he intended, but he pushed on regardless. "We're helping the Nazis get away with murder. Did you see what I had to list as causes of death of those men who were frozen to death last night?"

"I know." Petr didn't even look at the piece of paper. He didn't have to.

"This is what you were talking about the other day, wasn't it? Information is power, that's what you said. What are you doing with these papers, Petr? Tell me."

"Are you sure?"

Christiaan felt frustration bubbling over, and he tore the paper from his friend's grasp. He pointed at the top of the form. "You see that prisoner number? That's mine."

"Technically, it's Max Oswald's." Petr's voice broke a little.

"As far as the camp administration is concerned, I'm Max Oswald." Christiaan pointed at the prisoner number on his chest. "And that means if you get caught, it won't take a genius to figure out I was involved. You filed most of my papers. Tell me."

Petr looked at him for a few seconds, then his eyes narrowed. "You're right. Come, I'll show you. But give me the piece of paper." Christiaan did as he asked, and Petr folded it and slid it down the side of his pants. He confidently walked toward the exit, and Christiaan followed him somewhat apprehensively.

"Can we just walk out of the building?"

"We won't go far. It's just around the corner," Petr said as he turned to the front door. As he did, he bumped into someone walking in. Petr stumbled backward, and Christiaan only just managed to catch him. The Czech immediately took off his cap and bowed, apologizing profusely as a guard walked in. Christiaan did the same, taking off his cap, inclining his head, his eyes on the man's boots.

"You idiot! Imbecile, watch where you're going!" Christiaan's heart froze at the guard's curses. It wasn't so much the abuse, which was to be expected. It was the voice. Christiaan would recognize it from millions. It was Floris.

Christiaan looked up, and to his horror, there was little surprise in his brother's eyes. *He's here for me.*

Floris clasped his hands and looked satisfied. "Well, well, just the man I was looking for." He spoke in Dutch, and Christiaan saw the confusion on Petr's face. "You made a friend in here, didn't you? Interesting." He feigned nonchalance. "So where were you headed? Last I heard, you're supposed to stay inside the clerks' room, and you're only allowed to leave when escorted by a guard."

The words came through with a delay, and Christiaan struggled for a plausible response. His brother's mouth kept moving, but the words didn't register. *I need to think of something, quickly.* It didn't matter, his mind was drawing a blank. He saw his brother's attention shift to Petr, addressing him in German.

"What's that you have over there?" The words still sounded far away, but when Christiaan followed his brother's gaze, he was pulled back to full consciousness in a heartbeat. The list of Russians was protruding from Petr's pants. The collision with Floris must've moved it. Christiaan was helpless as Floris took the piece of paper, his eyes quickly scanning the lines. Hoping against hope, Christiaan prayed his brother wouldn't make the connection. That hope evaporated seconds later, when a sinister smile appeared on Floris' face.

"This doesn't look like a document that should be taken from this building," he started, his eyes moving between Petr and Christiaan. "Unless it's an officer who needs it. But it looks a lot like you were trying to take it somewhere else." His eyes homed in on Petr. "Where were you taking this? And to whom?"

Christiaan glanced at Petr, who made no move to speak. He thought of the men who'd accompanied him to Mauthausen. None had admitted to being spies, despite the Nazis' persuasive efforts in the Haaren, Assen, and Rawicz prisons. Christiaan could still feel the cold metal clasps on his body before the agonizing force of electricity ripped through his entire body.

"So, you're not going to tell me?" Floris had stepped closer to Petr, eyeballing him. Petr didn't respond. Floris cocked his head, something Christiaan had seen him do so many times before. It meant something in his mind had clicked. In this case, it couldn't be anything good. He turned to Christiaan and switched to Dutch. "You know, I don't really care about this piece of paper. Whatever you're doing here is of little relevance to me."

Christiaan frowned. *Where is he going with this?*

"I can forget I caught you and your new best friend, if you tell me about your work for the British intelligence."

The reality of the situation struck Christiaan like a hammer. His brother had planned this. That he caught them trying to smuggle a document out of the building was merely a bonus to him. He racked his brain, wondering how Floris knew about his friendship with Petr. It didn't matter. He looked at his brother, then at Petr.

"How do I know you'll keep your word?"

Floris let out a mocking laugh. "You don't. But here's the thing. You have no choice but to tell me everything you know, if you care even a little bit about your friend's life. Or your own, for that matter. If you don't, I'll make sure he's hauled off to the penal block for attempting to smuggle documents from the clerk's office. And while he's there, I'll make sure word filters through that you were responsible."

"You'll make me out to be a traitor?" Christiaan's throat constricted. It was a death sentence. He wouldn't survive a day in the block once the word was out.

Floris nodded. "Rather fitting, don't you think?" His voice had turned to ice. There was no doubt he would carry out the threat. *He's desperate, but why?*

"Okay. I'll tell you everything I know, but only if you answer one question of mine first."

"Fine, I'll play along." Despite his efforts at keeping a neutral face, Floris' voice was slightly higher pitched, betraying his excitement.

"What do you gain from proving I'm a spy? At best, you'll confirm something to the camp leadership that they already knew, and I get killed. Is that what you're going for?"

Floris gave him an amused look, one Christiaan recognized from when they were younger. "Little brother, you really don't understand, do you? I'm not going to tell anyone in the camp." He shook his head, the smile on his face widening. "This is not about Mauthausen. It's about something much more important. You're my ticket home, Chris."

CHAPTER THIRTY

A week later, Floris stood near the gate to Block 20, the Russian block. The sun was high in the sky, and he enjoyed the warmth of its rays on his face. Things were looking up. After catching his brother and the Czech clerk, Christiaan had finally seen sense. They'd met a few times that week, and Christiaan had related his journey since leaving Amsterdam more than two years ago. Floris had listened with amazement, and there were times when he thought his brother was leading him on, only for Christiaan to share certain details that Floris knew he couldn't possibly make up. He licked his lips at the amount of information his brother possessed; it was even better than he'd expected.

He had to admit some of the things Christiaan shared had annoyed him. He was disappointed his brother had caught him when he searched his home in Amsterdam. His life would've been so different if Christiaan hadn't run away the next day. Neither would have ended up in Mauthausen. Then he remembered what had happened in the crèche's yard that fateful night when Nora had betrayed him. He shook his head; it wasn't just what Christiaan had or hadn't done. Nora had played her part in his journey as well, perhaps even more so. Still, his mind wandered as he considered what catching Christiaan would've meant for his chances of uncovering Amsterdam's resistance network. Maybe he would never have given Nora's goons a chance to overpower him that night.

Floris' thoughts returned to the present. There was no sense in dwelling in the past. What mattered was what he knew about his little brother. He really was involved with the British intelligence agency and had been sent back to report on the German positions as the Brits and Americans prepared their attack on the Reich. Floris was aware of the advancing Allied armies from the west, as well as the Russians coming from the east. He had put Christiaan's story and the timeline of their invasion on the beaches of Normandy together, and it made sense. Well, Christiaan wouldn't be reporting back any positions any time soon.

Floris promised Christiaan he would keep him alive for as long as they both were in the camp, while making sure he felt no such loyalty toward Christiaan's Czech friend if his brother lied about his past. In addition, he promised he'd take Christiaan back to Amsterdam. He didn't tell him the true purpose of taking him back. He would find out soon enough.

Now, after a week of talking, Floris was confident Christiaan had plenty more valuable intelligence to extract. He hadn't rushed or pushed his brother, looking to build some degree of trust. In Mauthausen, even the strongest prisoners eventually broke, and Floris had time. Besides, he knew the true value was in getting Christiaan on a train home with him, to the interrogation chambers of the Sicherheitsdienst headquarters. There, he would watch from the sidelines while the experts extracted every bit of information from his brother.

It presented Floris with the next challenge. He needed to report back to Amsterdam, to warn them of the growing spy network, and secure their passage back home. In truth, there was no guarantee he'd be recalled to Amsterdam. The chances of being allowed to escort Christiaan back were even slimmer, but he'd cross that bridge when he got there. *In the worst case, I can get every last bit of information from him before I leave, and he can fend for himself.* In his heart, he knew it would be Christiaan's death sentence. He felt oddly detached from his brother's fate as he thought of returning to the *Bureau Joodsche Zaken*—the Bureau of Jewish Affairs—a returning hero, striking the final crippling blow to the resistance network in Amsterdam, and perhaps even beyond. His biggest challenge was reaching someone back home. He could think of only one person: Hans. But to reach his friend at the Bureau, he needed to send a telegram. And that would be possible only if he curried favor with the leadership. Personal telegrams from guards were only very rarely approved, and it was why Floris had volunteered to guard the prisoners in Block 20. *I'll send a regular letter later today as well.*

His thoughts were interrupted by a voice close by. Floris spun around and noticed a thin man wearing a stained and tattered Red Army uniform gazing at him through the steel strands. The stranger's eyes held curiosity and suspicion, and Floris shook his head in reply. "What did you say?"

The man repeated his garbled message in Russian, a language Floris didn't understand. Annoyed at the interruption, he shooed the man away, waving the butt of his gun at him. "Piss off, communist bastard! Run off, before I bash your face in."

The man mumbled something as he stalked off, and Floris considered stepping into the enclosure to teach the vermin a lesson. The Russians and Jews deserved all the pain and anguish that came their way in Mauthausen. He scanned the men in the enclosure with satisfaction. These were the same men that caused so much trouble on the eastern front. He unconsciously rubbed his limp leg at the memory. Hiding behind their T-34 tanks, the Russians were invincible. *Now look at them, locked up like animals, starving and pitiful, begging for scraps.*

The wiry man had moved along the barbed wire, trying his luck with another guard. The man barked at him much in the same way Floris had, and Floris smiled. *Scum won't get anything from us.* He remembered with glee the image of the ten Russians who'd dared speak up against Bachmayer in front of the entire camp population. Seeing their frozen bodies in the morning had warmed Floris' heart as he remembered the many nights he'd spent almost freezing to death on the eastern front. *They had it coming.*

The slender Russian was having a chat with one of the guards, stationed about thirty meters away. Floris frowned and focused his attention on the men talking through the barbed wire. The Russian talked animatedly, and the SS guard was nodding, prodding him along. *What's this about?* The Russian appeared hurried, his head scanning his surroundings before the guard wagged a finger at him. The man jumped up as if bitten by a snake. He looked indignant and scared at the same time, but he bobbed his head up and down furiously, his eyes wide. The guard held his gaze for a few seconds, then turned and signaled to another guard. The Russian stalked away, a look of disappointment now on his face, his shoulders slumped. Yet Floris felt something wasn't quite right, and after the guards conferred for a minute, the one who'd spoken to the prisoner hurried off. Floris' interest was piqued. What had he just witnessed?

———

Floris finished his shift and headed for his quarters. He hadn't seen the other guard return, and he wondered what had caused the man to disappear like that. Perhaps he'd find him at dinner and satisfy his curiosity.

He entered the mess hall and collected his tray. Scanning the room, there was no sign of the man, but Anton waved from a table in the back. Floris smiled, pleased to see his best friend. They had both been moved from Gusen to Mauthausen two weeks ago. It had been a welcome transfer, and Floris was glad he didn't spend half his day marching from Gusen to St. Georgen and back. And he certainly didn't miss his time in the dark, dust-filled tunnels.

Anton's plate was half-empty, and Floris sat across from him with a sigh.

"Tough day?" his friend asked, scooping a large spoonful of potatoes. The prisoners might be starving, but the guards always had plenty to eat, and Floris took a quick bite of his pork chops before answering. The juicy, salty meat invigorated him.

"Spent the whole day standing guard at Block 20. Not very exciting—most of them were too tired to stray far from their bunks in these temperatures. You?" He cut a larger piece of meat and stuffed it into his mouth, chewing furiously.

"Quarry duty. Lots of parachutists." Anton reported the deaths of the men pushed off the top of the stairs with indifference. "Mostly Jews from Auschwitz, I believe. Some of the other guards said these were the last transports. Apparently, the camp command was preparing to abandon the camp."

"Russians?"

"Yes. I tried to talk to some of the prisoners, but they were all Hungarian, and I didn't find any that spoke German. Or maybe they pretended they didn't. Either way, only a few of them survived." He scraped his plate as he collected the last bits of mashed potatoes and peas.

"Brouwer?"

Floris looked up, not recognizing the guard standing next to the table. The man didn't wait for an answer. "You're to report to Bachmayer's office."

Floris looked at him in surprise, his fork halfway between his plate and his mouth. "Now?"

The man rolled his eyes. "Yes. Come with me."

———

The camp was quiet when Floris followed the other guards along the main thoroughfare. There were at least a hundred of them. Most carried sidearms, but a number had their MP40 submachine guns out. Coming at the rear of the group were about thirty Kapos, carrying their leather-tipped truncheons. Evening roll call had finished an hour ago, and all prisoners were confined to their blocks. If any dared venture outside now, they would be shocked by the force on display.

The group soon reached the gates of the quarantine camp, where four guards hurriedly opened the gates, allowing Floris' party to silently approach Block 20, all the way in the back.

Floris had been excited when he heard of the night's plan. It turned out the Russian approaching him earlier wanted to share news about a planned uprising in Block 20. Even though he was pleased the man had approached them—and found a guard that understood him—he wondered what had happened for the man to turn on his fellow prisoners. Did he believe he had a better chance at survival by ratting them out? As the darkened block came into view, Floris gripped the pistol in his right hand tighter and felt for his baton with his left hand. Adrenaline was coursing through his veins as the leader of their assault moved toward the door of the block. He signaled for the men to ready their arms. It was an unnecessary order; they were all ready.

The assault leader opened the door and stormed inside. The other men pursued, and they were met with surprised shrieks. Floris was in the middle of the group and pushed forward, impatient to get inside. The guards yelled at the prisoners.

"Get down, everybody on the floor, hands behind your heads. Do it now, or we will shoot!"

When Floris finally rushed through the door, he was surprised by the masses of people on the ground. The first guards reached the back, their pistols raised at a number of prisoners who hadn't climbed down from their bunks. They were speaking in Russian, and it was clear the guards at the front didn't understand them, waving their guns to get the men down.

Suddenly, one of the men on the floor reached for one of the guards' guns. The guard lost his balance, his pistol clattering on the floor. Floris felt his heart skip a beat as the scene played out in slow motion. The guards were distracted as their attention was shifted to their falling comrade. One of the men on the ground reached for the pistol on the ground, and two guards immediately swung toward him, their guns pointed at his chest. It was then when four of the men on the top bunks jumped down, launching themselves at the nearest guards. Floris watched in horror as two guards lost their balance, the Russians overpowering them. Despite this, they did not let go of their guns. The prisoner holding the gun made the mortal mistake of lifting it ever so slightly. Two MP40s exploded into action, the sound deafening in the confined quarters. It brought the rest of the guards back to their senses, and more shots and grunts of pain followed. Floris moved toward the back, where a spray of bodies now lay tangled on the floor. The scent of blood and gunpowder hung in the air, and when the shooting stopped, five prisoners lay motionless on the floor. Blood poured from the countless holes in their bodies, and small pools of blood were forming around them. Floris quickly checked on his fellow guards. Apart from a few bruises, they seemed unhurt.

Two prisoners still sat on the top bunks, looking aghast at the scene below. The assault leader rose to his feet and wiped his bloody nose. He looked at the men atop the bunks and raised his gun at them. With an air of complete indifference, he pulled the trigger twice, killing each man with a single shot to the forehead.

It was now deathly silent in the block. All prisoners—dead and alive—lay motionless on the floor. Moving to the front of the room, the assault leader pulled out a list of numbers. Slowly, he started calling them out, and men reluctantly got up and reported to him. After confirming their prisoner numbers, they were taken outside, where the other half of the guards stood waiting.

———

They reached the penal block fifteen minutes later. The guards had split up, with half the group keeping an eye on the prisoners in Block 20, while the other fifty escorted the twenty-five Russians.

The short walk across the main thoroughfare was done in silence. Instead of taking the men to the cells on the ground level of the building, the squad leader opened a heavy iron door leading into the basement. Floris had never been here before, but he knew what happened down there.

"We'll start with the first ten. The rest of you wait out here in the courtyard. I'll let you know when you can bring in the next batch," the squad leader said. Floris stood at the front, and the squad leader signaled for him to enter with his prisoner.

Floris pushed the Russian down the short flight of steps. The man almost banged his head against the low ceiling, but Floris didn't care, ducking and prodding him along with the tip of his pistol. He wasn't taking any chances.

The first thing he noticed was the intense heat coming from a single, red-brick oven directly to his right. A stoker was adding coals to the fire. They were in the camp's crematorium. A narrow passageway ran next to the oven, providing access to a cramped room. More men followed, and the squad leader directed them to the oven's door and the room in the back.

Floris stood behind his prisoner, and he could see the man shaking, despite his efforts to keep a brave face. As the Russians stood just a meter or two from the bellowing fires in the oven, cracks appeared in their tough exterior. It was the signal the squad leader was waiting for.

"Did you really think you would get away with an uprising in the block? Did you think we wouldn't find out?" he bellowed at the ten Russians, now neatly lined up. The guard that had spoken to the Russian informant appeared next to the squad leader and translated.

"Would anyone like to speak? Tell me whose idea this was, and we might spare your lives. This is your only chance."

Floris studied the faces of the Russians as the message was translated. His prisoner's shaking intensified, and he could hear the man's teeth chattering. Perhaps he would break? Floris nudged him forward, poking the barrel of his gun in the small of his back. He felt the man tighten his muscles as he pushed back defiantly. Floris felt a surge of anger at his insolence and shoved the man forward.

The Russian stood alone between his comrades and the squad leader. The latter eyed him suspiciously. "Did you want to tell me something?" The intense heat of the room was reflected in the man's voice.

The Russian's eyes bulged as he turned back to the other prisoners, who witnessed the spectacle without any apparent emotion. *They've already decided they won't speak.* He turned back to the squad leader and with an effort, squared his shoulders and shook his head. *"Nyet."*

No translation was necessary, and for a few seconds, nothing happened as the squad leader considered his response. From the man's calm demeanor, Floris knew the squad leader had planned for this. He hadn't expected anything less.

With a flick of the wrist, the squad leader signaled to four guards. "Tie him up. Hands behind his back." They grabbed the Russian, who didn't resist. The squad leader then spoke to the stoker, who stood silently by the side of the oven. "Is it at temperature? Hot enough?"

"Yes, sir. I cleaned it earlier this morning. It won't get any hotter than this."

"Very well. Open the door."

The stoker did as he was told, and the heat coming from the oven nearly scorched Floris' eyebrows. He turned his face away, as did the other men in the room. The stoker looked pleased. The squad leader turned to the four guards surrounding the bound Russian. "Lift him into the oven, feet first."

The guards didn't immediately respond, blinking as they processed the order. The Russian responded quite differently, his eyes bulging in terror as he tried to take a few steps away from the oven. He was no longer hiding his fear, his entire body shaking. The guards responded to the order and grabbed the bound man. He struggled and kicked, but the four men were too strong and held his legs in place as they lifted him toward the roaring flames.

Floris watched in fascination. His eyes shot between the man suspended in the air, heading toward his fiery death, and his comrades. Two looked at the floor, but Floris was impressed to see most of them following their comrade's fate. They looked shaken, for they knew they would be next. *Perhaps they think the squad leader is bluffing?*

That hope was squashed a few seconds later. Closer and closer the guards pushed the man to the mouth of the oven. The man's shoes slowly became engulfed in flames, and he screamed in agony as the heat singed his skin. The smell of burning flesh filled the room until finally, the last thing Floris saw was the man's face twisted in pain as his body disappeared into the flames. When the stoker closed the oven door, there were no more screams—only an eerie silence that settled over the room like a thick fog.

Floris felt his heart beating fast, adrenaline shooting through his veins. He looked at the faces of the remaining Russians. Without exception, they had gone pale as sheets. Surprising himself, Floris felt a tingle of excitement at the thought of witnessing at least nine more executions. Drinking in the fear on the terrified faces, he realized why this felt so good. These men had inflicted unbelievable anguish on him in the east. They were the reason he was in this hellhole. As the next man was pushed forward, wailing as he was tied up, Floris grinned. This was payback.

CHAPTER THIRTY-ONE

The atmosphere in the clerks' room was gloomy the entire morning. News of the previous night's raid on Block 20 had spread through the camp, and the prisoners behind their desks in the administration block were the first to hear what had happened. Not least of all, Christiaan, who was tasked with updating the prisoner lists after morning roll call. He was used to the lists of names every morning, as plenty of men closed their eyes for the last time each night. But when he scanned the names of the deceased from Block 20, he felt an unusual heaviness. He didn't know what had happened to these men, but he knew their deaths had not been natural, if that word could be used for any death in Mauthausen.

It took him fifteen minutes to process the list. After double-checking the details, he stood and moved to the SS officer sitting in the front. It was unusual for an officer to be in the room, but Christiaan had been told to prioritize Block 20's list and hand the finalized list to the man as soon as he finished.

"Sir, here's the list you requested." Christiaan held out the single sheet as he kept his gaze on the paper.

The SS man took it without a word, holding up his free hand

before his eyes scanned the lines of names and numbers. Christiaan waited, standing awkwardly, aware of the other clerks' eyes on him. He assured himself he'd processed the list without any mistakes.

"Very well," the SS man said as he reached for a pen and signed at the bottom of the list. Then, to Christiaan's surprise, he folded the paper neatly and placed it in the inside pocket of his jacket. "Carry on." The man stood and turned toward the door.

"Don't you want me to file the paper with the others, sir?" The words came before he had a chance to catch himself.

The officer turned around and gave Christiaan a curious look. "Are you questioning me, prisoner?" He took a step forward, frowning. Some of the clacking of the typewriters behind Christiaan paused. "I'll take care of these papers. You just do as you're told, you hear me?"

Christiaan felt himself flush and held up the palms of his hands, inclining his head slightly. "Apologies, sir, of course not. You know best. I'm sorry again, sir."

The officer's face changed, and the man smirked at him. "Don't ask too many questions. Just follow orders." With those words, he turned on his heel and left the clerks' room. The sound of typewriters clacking returned, and Christiaan wondered if his fellow clerks had paused to listen, or if he'd simply blocked out all sound. It didn't matter. He shouldn't draw attention to himself like that. Especially when it came to the filing of papers. He walked back to his seat and caught Petr looking at him with alarm. He slowed down.

"We need to talk. Now," Petr said in a low voice. "Meet me in the filing room."

———

Petr leaned against one of the filing cabinets while Christiaan stood in the doorway. He kept an eye on the empty hallway. His head was spinning from what Petr had just told him. "They tortured them and burned them alive? Who told you this?"

"One of the men in my block knows some of the men working in the crematorium in the penal block. They were told to report late in the evening, which was unusual. They came back early in the morning, just before roll call. They were pretty shaken up by what they'd witnessed. Apparently, the SS interrogated the Russians throughout the night and made the others watch the torture and executions." Petr's voice was shaky, and he gripped his fingers around the edges of the filing cabinets as he spoke. Christiaan had never seen his friend this rattled.

"Do you know why they were taken from the block?"

Petr opened his mouth, then appeared to think of something. He crossed the room and scanned the hallway. "I don't know. Maybe they wanted to extract information from them. The war's not going well for the Nazis, so perhaps they thought these soldiers could tell them more about what was happening on the eastern front." He checked the hallway again, and Christiaan followed his eyes. It was quiet, only the clacking of the typewriters audible from the clerks' room on the far side. "But it gets worse, Chris. Your brother was one of the guards involved." Fear was etched in Petr's eyes.

Floris' involvement didn't shock Christiaan. "He's a guard, Petr. He's bound to be involved in all sorts of horrible things. It's not much different from him working the stairs at the quarry." He spoke slowly, hoping it would calm his friend.

It didn't work. Petr shook his head. "I don't trust your brother. Ever since he caught us, I've had trouble sleeping. I keep thinking he'll storm into my block and take me to a cell. Or worse, like what he did to those Russians last night."

"You're not a Russian soldier, Petr. You're nowhere near as interesting." He placed a hand on his friend's shoulder and felt him shaking. "I understand you don't trust him, but you trust me, don't you?"

"Of course. You're my only friend in the camp."

"Exactly. Look, my brother is only interested in one thing. Getting away from Mauthausen and back to Amsterdam. I told you he used to be quite a big shot in the police department. He believes I have enough information to have him pulled from his exile."

"Do you?" There was hope in the Czech's eyes. "Can you get him back to Amsterdam?"

"I believe so. But I need to play my cards right."

Floris' plan had become clear very quickly. In Mauthausen, he was but a mere guard, whereas in Amsterdam he was used to status and power. Floris hadn't said it in as many words, but his chances of climbing the ranks in Mauthausen were close to zero.

"So, I won't be safe until you and Floris are on a train to Amsterdam," Petr said, his eyes calculating. "And even then, he could break his promise."

Christiaan was surprised by Petr's sudden pessimism. Their lives were always at risk, with or without Floris. Something else was going on. "Where is this coming from? Did you know any of the men that were killed last night?"

Petr shook his head resolutely. "No, no. It's nothing like that. And I know we could be killed at any time. But none of the guards paid me any extra attention. Not before your brother caught us with the document."

"It's not about the document," Christiaan said, struggling to keep his calm. "He knows we're friends, and he's using that to get me to cooperate. Listen to me when I say I will do everything I can to keep Floris away from you." An idea formed in his head. He was only useful to Floris alive. "I'll tell him I'll kill myself if anything happens to you. He'll have nothing."

Tears formed in Petr's eyes. "You would do that for me?"

"There's no other way. We either do this together or not at all." As Christiaan spoke the words, he prayed he'd never have to follow through. But he was certain his threat would keep Floris from Petr.

———

Floris and Anton walked from the mess hall to the main gate. They were assigned patrol duty for the evening. Floris had raised his hand when one of the commanding officers came in during dinner looking for volunteers. A number of the previously assigned guards had fallen ill during evening roll call. Even though Floris would've preferred to be in his barracks on this cold February night, he knew he'd create a lot of goodwill by volunteering. Anton hadn't hesitated and agreed to spend the evening walking beside him. Floris glanced at his friend and was grateful to have met him in Sennheim.

"Can you believe it's been a year and a half since we finished our training?" Floris said as they walked through the imposing gate. The medieval-style towers with turrets never failed to impress; Floris felt as if he entered a castle every time. "And look where we are now."

"I'll be honest with you, Flo. This certainly beats fighting on the eastern front." Anton nodded at the two guards, who grunted something in response behind the heavy scarfs wrapped around their faces. Floris took a deep breath of the fresh air and savored the silence of the camp's thoroughfare. During the day, it was almost impossible to find a moment of silence as prisoner work details went about everywhere he looked. Now, with evening roll call finished hours ago, the prisoners were confined to their blocks. They were strictly forbidden from going outside, and even though most adhered to this rule, there were always one or two hardheaded men who decided they needed some fresh air. Floris rubbed his hands in anticipation at dishing out their punishment.

They passed Block 1, where faint light could be seen behind the barred windows. The camp's brothel appeared busy this evening, and Floris increased his pace. He didn't want to think about the risible things going on in there. The next few large windows were unobstructed, but the large room inside was dark. This was the camp's administration, and Floris couldn't help but smile. He'd spoken with Christiaan a few days earlier, and his brother appeared concerned for his Czech friend. He even went as far as to say he'd kill himself if Floris did anything to harm the Czech. Floris had played along, reassuring his brother no harm would befall his friend if Christiaan cooperated. Floris didn't care if the Czech lived or died. He was a means to an end, and that was keeping Christiaan in line and securing their passage home. So far, things were moving along nicely. Tonight's extra shift would surely put him in a good light with the commanding officer. *I should pay him a visit tomorrow and see if I might be allowed to send a telegram.* Floris was confident he'd be on a train home soon.

"Seems especially quiet today. We should have an easy night," Anton said, interrupting his thoughts.

"Let's make sure it stays that way. Why don't we have a look around these blocks?" Floris pointed at the first rows of barracks off the main thoroughfare. They walked on, and Floris glanced at his best friend. He'd been thinking about ways to get him on the train home again, but he hadn't come up with anything. Alas, he hadn't told Anton about his plan yet, and he felt a pang of guilt. *I'll find a way. First, I need to get in contact with Hans and get the information to him. I'll worry about getting Anton on the train later.* He was convinced the brass in Amsterdam would jump at the chance of getting Floris and his brother back. *I'll be in a good bargaining position.*

"Hey Flo, what was it like going into Block 20 and taking those Russians to the crematorium?" Anton's voice cut through the night air, his inquisitive eyes looking at Floris with interest. "I know we fought the bastards on the front, but this must've been very different."

Floris' mind went back to the events of only a few nights ago. Anton had asked about it before, but they had been interrupted. "It wasn't anything like the front lines, but it was clear these were the same men. It wouldn't even surprise me if we'd fought some of these bastards. They were tough, but we broke them in the end." The excitement of the night's events returned with a tingling sensation in his stomach.

"Did any of them admit to planning an uprising?"

Floris grimaced. It was the only stain on the night. "No. None of them talked. They were determined, I'll give 'em that. Not even after we started pulling out fingernails and teeth before throwing them in the fire." Floris had watched with fascination as the camp's torturers carried out their tasks. He couldn't imagine holding out the way the Russians did if the roles had been reversed. They reached the barbed-wire fence, the soft humming confirming the deadly current running through. Floris and Anton turned back toward the main thoroughfare.

"Do you think they were planning something? I mean, you saw them. Did it look like they were hiding anything?"

Floris had asked himself that question many times in the past days. "I really couldn't tell. Apart from their cries of pain, they said nothing. Their faces betrayed no knowledge of anything we asked, no trace of deceit. To be honest, once we reached the last men, they were so delirious that there was no sense in asking them anything. They went straight into the ovens."

They walked on in silence for a few minutes before they returned to the Appellplatz. The silence was abruptly interrupted by what sounded like shouts farther ahead. Floris turned to Anton. "Did you hear that?"

"Sounds like it's coming from the quarantine blocks."

The quarantine blocks were located opposite the penal block, about halfway down the camp's main thoroughfare. They were separated from the main camp by three-meter-high walls. Beyond it was another, separately walled-off section where Block 20 was located. Floris had a sense of foreboding as they increased their pace, heading straight for the closed gate of the quarantine area.

They were not alone. The noise had attracted the attention of the other guards on patrol, as well as those in the watchtowers on the camp's perimeter. The sound of voices increased with every step, and Floris felt for the pistol hanging on his hip. It was there, and he felt safer.

By the time they reached the closed gate of the quarantine camp, more than twenty guards had gathered, including a more senior Untersturmführer. The man immediately took charge.

"Take out your pistols and prepare to shoot on sight. I don't know what's going on in there, but we're going to make sure it ends now," he said, unholstering his own gun and nodding at the guards to open the gate. Floris swallowed hard. The sounds on the other side of the wall had grown louder, with multiple voices screaming and yelling in several languages. He looked at the men around him, their tense faces betraying their anxiety.

They stepped inside the quarantine camp where everything was silent. They walked past the barracks, but none of the prisoners had moved from their blocks. Even though they must've heard the commotion outside, they had made the wise decision not to get involved. It meant the noise could only come from one place: Block 20.

Before they reached the gate, gunshots rang out. Floris instinctively ducked, but immediately realized no one was firing at them. *The shots must be coming from the guard towers.*

The Untersturmführer surged forward, leading his men toward the gate a few meters ahead. Dozens of voices could be heard. Some were talking, others shouted what sounded like angry curses, while a few spoke in calm, measured tones. Even though Floris couldn't understand the words, he recognized orders, delivered in a clear, measured military tone.

Floris was among the first to reach the gate. What he saw made his heart stop. The yard of Block 20 swarmed with men carrying stones, pieces of coal, and makeshift weapons. There had to be at least four hundred men crowding around. They focused on the other side of the yard, where a number scaled the wall. There were no more shots from the guard tower, and it soon became clear why. A group of prisoners had stormed the tower and overpowered the guards. Their bodies lay on the ground, strewn with those of the Russians they had downed as they defended their position. Floris felt sick as he watched more Russians storming toward the wall.

All eyes were on the Untersturmführer, who looked overwhelmed. He turned back and found twenty pairs of eyes looking at him. The man was in an impossible situation. He couldn't let these prisoners escape, but their force was too small to stop them. At that moment, the camp's siren started blaring, its piercing drone momentarily startling the prisoners on the other side of the gate. A few of them turned back instinctively and spotted Floris' party behind the gate. *Oh shit.*

While most prisoners were concerned with climbing the wall on the far side, the appearance of the guards drew the attention of a group of about fifty men. Even with the distance between them, Floris could see the hate in their eyes. They hadn't forgotten what had happened to their comrades a few nights ago. Floris gripped his pistol tighter. Would the Untersturmführer snap out of his stupor and make a call, or would the Russians force his hand?

Time slowed as he looked at the men around him. Most were younger than him, and he was certain very few had fired a gun in anger before. These weren't battle-hardened soldiers. These were young men recruited straight from the Hitler Youth. And now they faced a mob of enraged, experienced Russian soldiers with little to lose. He closed his eyes for a moment, until he heard an animallike roar from the yard. The group of fifty had swelled to over a hundred, and they stamped toward the gate, the ground shaking, angry voices shouting curses.

Floris knew the gate wouldn't hold for long, and his first instinct was to run. But the Untersturmführer had other plans.

"Hold the line, everybody fire at will once they get close enough," he snapped at the men, raising his pistol at the oncoming Russians.

Is he mad? Fear gripped Floris' throat as he looked to Anton. His friend appeared remarkably calm, his trained hands calmly pointing the gun at the oncoming soldiers. Floris could sense the fear of the men around him as twenty stood against a hundred.

The first shots were fired. Nothing happened as the untrained guards wasted their bullets, a few pistols even flying from their grips.

The Russians poured forward and were now only ten meters from the gate. A few launched stones at the group of guards, and some of the projectiles flew through the bars. Floris ducked in time, but the guard next to him was less fortunate. A stone the size of a tennis ball impacted squarely against his forehead. The man dropped to the ground without another sound, his eyes blank.

"Fire at will!" the Untersturmführer yelled while squeezing the trigger of his own pistol. He managed to down three Russians before his pistol clicked. Floris did the same, downing an impressive four from five shots. It did little to stop the wave of prisoners and they crashed against the gate. The Untersturmführer finally saw sense and called the retreat.

"Run, you bastards!" the Untersturmführer yelled. The guards turned and made for the larger gate some fifty meters away. Floris could see a machine gun nest had hastily been set up to stop the Russians from pouring into the main camp. They wouldn't start shooting until Floris and the others reached safety, but there was no time to lose.

Behind him, the gate was unhinged by the fury of dozens of Russians pulling and beating at it. With a mighty crash, the gate door was pulled from its hinges and crashed onto the ground. Floris turned around to see the first Russians make their way through the opening. In front of him, the younger guards sprinted toward the safety of the machine gun. Floris found himself lagging as his bum leg slowed him down. He was halfway to safety when he looked back and knew he wouldn't make it. The Russians were closing in too fast. Dread overcame him, and he gritted his teeth, trying to ignore the pain. It was impossible, and tears of frustration formed in his eyes. *Not like this. This is not how it ends.*

Then he felt strong arms lift him up. It was Anton, who had come back for him. He felt relief as his friend slung him over his shoulder. As he did, however, Floris saw the Russians were now less than fifteen meters away and gaining quickly. Anton wouldn't make it in time like this. They would both die. *I can't let that happen.*

"Anton, let me go. We won't make it together," he said rapidly. "Let me go, save yourself."

"I can't, Flo. You saved my life, let me do the same."

"You can't save me anymore. Run, you stubborn fool. Save yourself." With a mighty effort, Floris rolled from Anton's shoulder, making it impossible for his friend to hold onto him. Floris landed roughly on the cold hard ground. Anton stopped and looked at him in confusion. Floris shook his head resolutely and raised his gun. "Get out of here, before they kill us both."

Anton hesitated only for a moment, then understanding appeared on his face. "Farewell, brother. It was an honor." Floris watched his friend sprint off and smiled. Then he turned around to see the horde of Russians approaching, less than a few meters away. He pressed the pistol against his temple, the sensation of the cold steel sending a shiver down his spine. *You won't take me alive.* He closed his eyes and squeezed the trigger.

CHAPTER THIRTY-TWO

A few hundred meters away, Christiaan sat upright in his bunk. The room was dark, but everyone in the block was awake as the siren howled outside. They spoke in hushed, uncertain voices, wondering what the noises meant. The clatter of the mounted machine guns atop the guard towers echoed into his room. *An escape?* Heavy boots stomped by, followed with frantic voices yelling orders in German. It sounded like a large contingent of guards had been mobilized. Something big was happening, and Christiaan felt a spark of hope. Was this another attempt at a prisoner uprising he didn't know about? He thought back to the previous days in the administration. Apart from the murder of the Russians in Block 20, nothing had been out of the ordinary.

He tried to make out the direction of the gunfire. It was almost impossible; between the shouting, the constant machine gun fire and the voices of the men in his block, things appeared to be happening all around the camp.

There were suddenly heavy footsteps just outside his block. One man issued what sounded like orders—Christiaan couldn't quite make out the words—as the others responded in short affirmations.

A few seconds later, the door to their block burst open. Two SS guards stormed in. The room instantly went silent. The first thing Christiaan noticed were the MP40 submachine guns in their hands. This was unusual, for the guards normally only carried a sidearm in addition to their batons. They certainly never entered the blocks wielding MP40s. He shrank back in his bunk while the taller of them shouted instructions, his face flushed, deep lines running across his forehead.

"Everybody stay in your bunks, and don't even think about going outside. Any prisoner found outside will be shot without warning. Don't exit the block until we tell you to."

Before anyone could respond, he turned and left almost as quickly as he'd come. The door had only just shut when a loud burst of gunfire erupted outside. There were muffled screams, then silence. Christiaan eyed the single glass window only a meter from his bunk. He lay on his back, deciding it was the smartest thing he could do. They'd surely find out what had happened tomorrow morning.

———

The shooting ended a few hours later. Christiaan had been unable to sleep as he listened to what was going on outside. The fighting was far away, and apart from the SS troopers passing their block on their way toward the gunfire, it had remained relatively quiet in their area. Few of the men in the block had slept, many staying up and gossiping. The truth was, nobody really knew, but something had rattled the SS, and that was enough for these men.

The morning light came, and it was deathly quiet outside. They would normally be on their way to their work details by now, if morning roll call hadn't sprung any surprises. Christiaan sat in his bunk, confident the risk of stray bullets flying through the window by his bunk had passed. During the night, there had been plenty of nearby gunshots, and he'd heard the sound of splintering glass plenty of times. He was grateful he'd come through the night unscathed. With every minute that passed, though, he worried what he'd find out once they were finally let out of their blocks.

He didn't have to wait much longer. Fifteen minutes later, the door to their block opened. Two SS guards—now wearing their usual equipment, sans MP40s—ordered them to report for roll call in ten minutes. The block came to life as the men rushed to the latrines. Christiaan splashed some cold water on his face and made his way outside.

It felt good to feel the crisp February morning air on his face and to see the sun slowly climbing in the distance.

He turned onto the camp's main thoroughfare that doubled as roll call area. What he saw made his breath pause. Bodies were strewn across the sides of the road. He slowly walked to his usual spot, taking in the surreal surroundings. As he gazed farther down the thoroughfare, the number of bodies increased, some piled atop each other. The other prisoners looked on with expressions of shock and horror. These men were used to death being ever-present, each day of their lives, but this was another level. Christiaan tried to count the bodies, but he stopped once his gaze reached the gate of the quarantine blocks. There was a pile of dozens of bodies reaching a few meters high. SS troopers wielding their submachine guns stood by, their faces relaxed but their eyes alert as they followed the prisoners lining up for roll call.

As Christiaan reached his place in line, he felt nauseous and took a deep, calming breath. He focused his eyes on the ground while he heard the other prisoners shuffle to their places. *What had happened last night?*

———

Roll call finished quicker than ever before. It was clear the SS were keen to get the prisoners to work. Bachmayer even made an appearance, walking along the lines, inspecting his charges. He was no doubt calculating the loss of productivity from last night's events.

They were told nothing about what had happened, and Christiaan found himself walking toward the administration in a slight daze. He tried to avoid looking at the bodies, but it was impossible. The dead were riddled with bullet holes, a number of them also sporting dark black-and-blue bruises on their faces and arms. Christiaan couldn't help but notice all of them wore the red patches of political prisoners, with the letter *R*. They were all Russian prisoners. It wasn't difficult to put the pieces together. Something had happened in Block 20. Something significant.

He felt a presence next to him and found Petr alongside him. His friend's face was troubled, but Christiaan was pleased to see him, nonetheless. Christiaan had worried about him during the night when it was unclear what was happening.

"Are you all right? Do you know what happened?" Christiaan asked as they followed the stream of prisoners headed for the main gate, where most of the work details gathered.

"I'm fine. Hardly slept, though, but I suppose few did." Petr grinned at him, but Christiaan instantly saw it was insincere. Petr's eyes were sad, worried even. "I overheard some of the guards standing nearby at roll call. They said the Russians in Block 20 rose up, attacking one of the guard towers with more than five hundred men."

"So they actually went ahead with it, after all." Christiaan admired their tenacity and bravery. "Even after seeing what happened to their comrades a week earlier. I suppose the warning didn't really help."

"More like it fanned the flames of their resistance. They realized they could easily be next and decided to go down fighting." Petr spoke with remarkable confidence, as if he had been there, fighting alongside the Russians. "If I understood correctly, hundreds escaped after they took the guard tower."

"How? The fences are electrified."

Petr shrugged. "They must've short-circuited them somehow. Wet blankets, maybe? That should do the trick."

Again, Christiaan was impressed. "Did they have any weapons? Guns? You don't just knock down those guard towers." The towers were equipped with machine guns and rose five meters high.

"I'm sure quite a few of them lost their lives, but it's impossible to stop hundreds of determined men."

They reached the administration building and stood outside for a moment. There were no guards around, and Christiaan enjoyed a moment of rest. His head was heavy, and he sighed at the idea of processing the deaths of the men scattered around the camp. At that moment, a group of prisoners pulling a large cart passed in the direction of the quarantine blocks.

"Just imagine having to collect all the bodies today. I don't envy them," Petr said, and Christiaan chided himself for his earlier thoughts. He had it easy, compiling a list of the deceased, then filing it in a large cabinet where nobody would ever care to look again. Like the men never existed.

"The good news is that plenty of Russians escaped," Petr said, a genuine smile on his face now. "They might just make it out and reach their compatriots. I'm told they're making good progress in the east."

Christiaan had heard the same, but his friend was stretching the truth a bit. They were still hundreds of kilometers from Mauthausen, with plenty of German resistance. He looked to the packed snow surrounding the buildings and questioned the escaped prisoners chances. Outside Mauthausen's walls the vast countryside was covered in deep snow. He wanted to tell Petr that it would be difficult to traverse with the right gear, and nigh impossible for the exhausted, poorly equipped prisoners trying to make their way through a foreign, hostile land.

"Come, let's go inside. There will be plenty of work waiting," Christiaan said instead, taking a step inside. As he sat at his desk, organizing the large pile of papers he found there, his thoughts wandered. He was impressed by the boldness of the Russian escape. While he—like every other prisoner—had considered the thought of escaping many times, he knew the odds of survival were minimal. There was nowhere to go, and his ragged prisoner clothes would make him instantly recognizable as an escapee. From what he'd heard from other prisoners, the local population was hostile at best, and Christiaan didn't want to take the chance of being turned in or worse.

———

The day crept by, and Christiaan's head became heavier with every stroke on the keys of his typewriter. He tried to ignore his exhaustion, and when he felt like closing his eyes, he got up to make the short journey to the filing room. It was the best he could do to not fall asleep.

He had just returned to his seat when he heard the familiar sound of boots stomping in the hallway. His muscles tightened as he focused his eyes on the sheet of paper in the typewriter in front of him. Christiaan pretended to be hard at work but glanced at the doorway as the boots rapidly approached.

Four guards stormed in, and it was clear this wasn't a regular visit. The man leading the group scanned the room as if searching for someone. Christiaan looked away, his focus now completely on the typewriter. Yet, he could feel the man's stare resting on him for an instant longer than normal. The hairs on the back of his neck stood up as he took a deep breath, trying to compose himself. *Don't give them any reason to come talk to you.*

"You!" The man's deep voice boomed through the confined space, and the sound of fifteen or so typewriters died away instantly. Christiaan had no choice but to look up and meet the man's gaze as well. To his relief, the man wasn't pointing at him.

His relief was short lived.

"Come with me, right now."

The guards barged through the room, heading straight for Petr.

The Czech barely had a chance to rise from his chair before he was roughly manhandled from the room without another word.

———

Christiaan finished his day much like he'd started it: in a daze. He ate his meager dinner of tasteless soup and a tiny piece of bread alone, chewing automatically. His mind was preoccupied by the fate of his friend. When he climbed into his bunk and the call for lights out rang out, he was one of the few men unable to catch sleep. As the exhausted prisoners around him drifted off to escape their reality for a few hours, Christiaan's mind would give him no respite.

There had been no mistake in Petr's arrest, of that Christiaan was certain. The guards who came for him knew exactly whom they were looking for, homing in on him from the second they walked in. Worst of all, Christiaan hadn't even been that surprised to see them come for his friend. Petr seemed especially well informed about what had happened in Block 20 the night prior. And Petr had been overly worried about Floris' threats after finding out about their document smuggling. Christiaan was suddenly wide awake. Had Floris sold them out? Had he overplayed his hand by tying his future to that of Petr? Was this Floris' way of calling his bluff?

Christiaan lay in the darkness while he considered the possibility that Floris was involved. If he was, Petr would be in the penal block, perhaps already under interrogation. Christiaan broke into a cold sweat at the thought of his friend being questioned. There was no doubt he would hold out for as long as possible, but everybody spoke in the end. Well, everyone except the Russians.

Christiaan shook his head, then realized if Floris had been responsible for Petr's arrest, and if he'd wanted to send a message to his brother, he would've been part of the group storming into the administration block. He wouldn't have passed up the opportunity to intimidate Christiaan and take credit for the arrest. Something else was going on with Petr, but Christiaan's mind was blank.

He closed his eyes for a moment, trying to block out the thoughts of his friend getting tortured, but it was impossible. Then, just as his visions became clouded and he felt sleep overpowering him, his mind threw him a final curveball. What if Petr mentioned his involvement in the smuggling of the paperwork?

————

"If you don't get out of bed now, I'll make sure you never get up again!"

Christiaan didn't remember falling asleep, but the snarling voice awoke him with a start. He jumped from his bunk fully clothed. All around him men rushed by, to the latrines and then roll call. "I apologize, sir, it won't happen again, sir." Christiaan held his cap in his hand while he bowed at the Kapo.

The man couldn't resist slapping Christiaan in the face twice, the blows landing viciously, stars clouding his vision. Christiaan just about managed to stay upright while he clenched his jaw. The Kapo mumbled something before stalking off to find his next victim.

Christiaan held on to the side of the bunk bed for a few seconds while the dancing stars disappeared. He felt woozy and tired but composed himself and joined the other prisoners as they headed for roll call.

Unlike the previous day, this was a regular day at Mauthausen, starting at four. It was freezing, with some light snow fluttering from the dark heavens. The snow on the ground crunched under his feet, and he thought how nice a start of the day it would be if he were anywhere else in the world. He hoped roll call would pass quickly and he could make his way to the shelter and relative warmth of the clerks' room.

He arrived to find most men already in place. Christiaan quickly found his spot in line, barely in time to see Bachmayer appear on a platform at the front. Christiaan swallowed hard as he noticed the gallows behind the commander were readied with ten ropes.

Bachmayer grabbed a microphone, and his voice was instantly amplified across the thoroughfare. "I'm going to keep this brief, for I've heard the weather will only get worse. But this needs to be done." He snapped his fingers in his customary way, and the door to the penal block opened. The Hauptsturmführer had a certain macabre flair when it came to executions, timing his words and actions perfectly. Christiaan kept his eyes fixed on the prisoners as they were pushed toward the gallows. When the last of the ten appeared, Christiaan felt as if his heart were being crushed. It was Petr.

His face was almost unrecognizable. The area around his eyes was swollen, reducing them to dark, thin slits. His face was caked in dried blood, his lips cut and his cheeks a dark shade of blue. He walked with a limp, and the guards needed to lift him atop the gallows.

Bachmayer's voice droned on in the distance, but Christiaan didn't hear him. His eyes were fixed on Petr's, hoping he would look up, so he wouldn't be alone in his final moments. It wasn't to be. He kept his gaze on the wooden floor of the gallows while he was lifted onto a stool and the noose fastened around his neck. *Look up, Petr, damn it. Look at me.* Christiaan's eyes stung, a hot tear escaping but freezing before it could make it to the bottom of his face. *I'm here with you. Look at me!*

"And because these men assisted the communist scum's escape from Block 20, they will pay the ultimate price!" Bachmayer spoke his final words and stepped away from the microphone, turning around to the condemned. It would be mere seconds until the stools were kicked from under their feet. Minutes until the life was choked from them, the light forever dimmed.

In a move that drew surprised gasps from the crowd, Bachmayer kicked the first stool himself, the rope snapping tight, the prisoner's feet searching in vain for a foothold. His death struggle carried through the entire roll call area as he choked and swung on the rope.

It took less than a minute for his head to drop, his body swinging limply in the snow.

Bachmayer continued, walking down the line, systematically kicking stools. Petr was at the end of the line, and Christiaan kept his eyes on his friend's face. Bachmayer was only three executions away from him when he finally looked up. Despite the immense crowd, his eyes found Christiaan's.

Christiaan narrowed his eyes, mustering all his strength, hoping it would somehow carry to his friend. He didn't want Petr to leave this world carrying Christiaan's pain as well. He needed to be Petr's beacon.

Recognition appeared in Petr's battered eyes. His mouth turned into a pained smile, revealing shattered teeth. Bachmayer kicked the stool of the man next to him. Christiaan held his friend's gaze. Then, as Bachmayer moved toward Petr, his friend gave him an almost imperceptible nod. Christiaan returned the gesture, clenching his hands into fists beside his shaking body.

Bachmayer stepped between them and kicked the final stool. He stepped to the side, admiring his murderous handiwork. Within seconds, Petr's face turned red, his body convulsing in the death struggle. Christiaan's eyes never left his friend's. When his face turned an unnatural shade of blue, his panicked eyes met Christiaan's one last time. Then, he relaxed, and Christiaan saw his best and only friend's soul leave his tortured body.

CHAPTER THIRTY-THREE

Nora opened her eyes to the usual pitch-blackness. Her head was throbbing, just like it had been for weeks—or was it months? Days blended into nights in the shadowy cell. She'd grown accustomed to the darkness.

She licked her cracked lips, her parched throat aching as she swallowed. It did nothing to quench the raging thirst that tortured her. The guards had stopped bringing her regular meals after her first week, ever since she'd spoken to the Dutch interrogator in the room upstairs. Nora had no idea how long it had been since she'd first met him, but she'd been dragged from her cell many times since. She felt the tips of her fingers, the raw flesh where her fingernails used to be sending a sharp pain up her arm.

The woman that brought her water and bread after her first interrogation had shown up twice more, then disappeared. Perhaps the guards had found out about her acts of kindness? Nora had worried about her for a few nights, but she soon found she needed to focus her energy on herself instead.

She closed her eyes as she tried to block out another wave of pain in her head. It didn't help, and she took a few deep breaths as the pain slowly subsided. The interrogator had carried out his threats, but Nora hadn't cracked. Not yet anyway. With every trip to the man's room, she felt her resolve wane. She wasn't sure how much longer she would be able to resist. She had done as the mysterious woman who'd visited her cell had instructed. She'd given the man little pieces of information, and that had worked at first. After a while, however, his stance had changed. He'd seemed unsurprised by her admissions, insisting she was useless to him if she didn't tell him something he didn't know yet. Nora had almost panicked and told him about her true mission, but she realized just in time her mind was likely playing tricks on her. She was repeating what she'd told him before. It frightened her to think she wasn't in complete control of her thoughts anymore, but she wasn't surprised. Her captors were wearing her down. She swallowed hard. *I have to be strong; it can't be much longer now.*

The thought that the liberating forces must be making their way north was the only thing that kept Nora going. When she was brought back to her cell after the first meeting with her interrogator, she had despaired, fearing she would die within the next days. She had fallen into a fitful sleep, but when she awoke, she saw things more clearly. Somer would know something had happened to her when she didn't report back after crossing the river. She hoped her disappearance would at least give them some indication of German activity on the occupied northern riverbank. And the Americans wouldn't camp out on the riverbank indefinitely, surely? Nora hoped the liberating army had found a way across the river. Somer had made it clear the river crossing was the largest obstacle to the liberation of the north. *They will be here soon enough.*

They would have to be. With every passing day, Nora felt her strength withering away. This morning her headache was more severe, flashes of pain radiating from the sides of her forehead. By not feeding her, and barely providing enough water, her captors were slowly chipping away at her resolve.

Nora shifted on the hard bunk, the muscles in her back

protesting as she tried to sit up. A cramp shot up her leg, and she couldn't suppress a desperate moan as she tried to stretch it, gritting her teeth at the effort. The cramp in her calf subsided after a few seconds, but a bead of sweat trickled down her brow. Panic gripped her as she wiped it away and felt her forehead. She was burning up. *No, not now.*

She considered her options as she felt the fever spread from her head to the rest of the body. Her muscles ached, her stomach turned, and she only just managed to suppress the wave of nausea rising in the back of her throat. Despite the darkness, her eyes felt heavy, and a few specks danced around her vision, increasing her discomfort. Reluctantly, Nora lay back down and closed her eyes. There was nothing she could do but rest and pray her broken body would find the strength to heal itself.

———

She opened her eyes and didn't know if she'd slept for hours or a few minutes. Her head was still heavy, but something in the cell was different. Light filtered in from under the door to the hallway, diluting the darkness for the first time in days.

There were voices in the hallway, and with an effort, Nora forced herself to sit up. She could feel her heart rate increase, as it did every time they came for her. She held her palm against her forehead. Still sweating, but not as fiery as before, and Nora breathed a silent prayer of relief.

A moment later the door swung open. The light from the hallway blinded her—a crippling pain shooting through her head—and she turned her face away, closing her eyes. It was dangerous, for the guards might take it as a slight when she didn't acknowledge them. At this point, she didn't care. They were coming for her, and they would take her to the interrogator, her tormentor. In her current state, she knew she wouldn't be able to hold out under his questioning and torture.

"Please get up from the bed." The voice was calm, soft—almost soothing. Nora opened her eyes and looked up to find a single guard next to her bunk. She didn't recognize him, which meant he was new, or her exhausted mind hadn't registered his face before. It didn't matter, for he held out a hand, repeating his instructions. It was then that Nora realized he was speaking in Dutch. He was only the second person—after her interrogator—in the prison to address her in her mother tongue.

"Can you stand up?"

Nora moved her legs to the side of the bed, slipping her feet into the dirty shoes she'd been allowed to keep. She tried to get up by herself, but the effort was too much. The guard grabbed her by her wrists and helped her to her feet. His touch was surprisingly gentle, and Nora nodded her thanks as she found her balance.

"Follow me." The guard stepped into the hallway, turning and waiting for her. Nora did as she was told and followed him through the hallway, the bright ceiling lights stabbing at her brain as she struggled to keep up with the guard.

Ignoring the pain and her blurred vision, Nora's mind was racing. Her fever had dropped, but every step felt as if lifting a leaden leg. She was in no state to survive another interrogation. A sense of despair filled her; she was doomed. There was only one thing she could do. *Keep my mouth closed for as long as possible.* Her eyes went to her bloodied fingers and fear constricted her throat. *Be strong, Nora.*

The guard reached the top of the stairs well before her. When she reached the top, she automatically turned toward the interrogation room.

"Hold on, we're going this way," the guard said as he opened a door in the opposite direction. Confused, Nora followed him into a long hallway with narrow doors on either side. Each door had a small, barred window, and Nora was surprised to hear hushed voices coming from the other side of the doors as they walked down the corridor. The guard stopped at one of the doors in the back and produced a set of keys. He opened it and signaled for her to step inside.

Reluctantly, Nora crossed the threshold to find three women sitting on their bunks. Their faces revealed shock and surprise as Nora met their eyes. Behind her, the door closed with a thud, the lock clicking into place. The women remained silent as the guard jangled the keys before his footsteps retreated in the hallway.

Nora took a moment to inspect her new surroundings. Apart from the three other prisoners, this cell felt more spacious, and most importantly, there was a window allowing daylight to filter through. It was the opposite of her solitary cell in the basement.

"What happened to you?" One of the women rose from her bunk and approached Nora. Her face was lined with worry, her dark brown eyes inspecting Nora. "Can you talk? Are you all right?"

Nora blinked hard, the woman's words of concern the first she'd heard in a long time. Slowly, she nodded and opened her mouth. "Yes. Sorry." The words came out as a croak, and she tried clearing her throat, but it was too dry, and she burst into a coughing fit instead. Her head felt as if it would explode, her vision blurring as she doubled over. She heard the woman say something she couldn't understand, but a moment later the woman held out a small cup.

"Here, drink something, you poor thing." The woman's voice was soothing.

Nora drained the cup in one swig, and she took a deep breath as the coughing subsided. The water revived her as it made its way down her throat. She gratefully accepted another cup, which she drank only marginally slower. The fog in her brain cleared somewhat, and she focused on the woman in front of her.

"Thank you," she said in a soft voice. "I can't remember the last time I've had anything to drink."

"By the looks of you, it's been a while," the woman said, her eyes now on Nora's fingertips. She recoiled, but her voice remained steady. "What happened to you?" She met Nora's eyes again, her own gaze steady and determined.

"I'm not sure; the past few weeks have been a bit of a blur," Nora said, almost apologetically. She eyed the other women, who looked remarkably healthy. There were no signs of any abuse or torture, their faces clear of any marks or bruises. "What's the date?"

"Fifth of March," one of the women on the bed said, also standing up. "When did you arrive?"

Nora's knees trembled as the woman's words sank in. She had crossed the river in early January. *Have I really been in the basement for almost two months?* She felt lightheaded and leaned against the wall. She closed her eyes and shook her head. "I can't believe it."

The woman who gave her water moved closer, putting a hand on her arm. "Why don't you lie down? They should be here with our breakfast soon. We'll save you some of ours. You need it more than we do."

Nora looked up. The expression of concern was genuine. She felt a trace of hope and allowed the woman to guide her to one of the bunks. As the other women helped to gently lower her down, a thought struck. "What are you in for?"

"Food coupons," the woman with the brown eyes said. "We were caught with a pram full of them." She looked at Nora sternly, and it was then when Nora noticed the woman was about the same age as her. "Now rest. There will be plenty of time to get to know each other in the next few days." She placed a hand on Nora's forehead and flinched. She turned to one of the other women. "More water."

Nora closed her eyes and felt a soothing, cold sensation on her forehead before drifting off.

———

Nora opened her eyes at the touch of a hand shaking her shoulder. She looked into the brown eyes of the woman who'd seen to her earlier.

"Wake up, they're coming."

Confused, Nora sat up, the urgency in the woman's voice jolting her into action. "Who?"

The woman pulled Nora to her feet, shaking her head. "The guards. They started with the cells at the front."

Nora slipped into her shoes, her mind fully alert at the sounds in the hallway. Men shouted commands in Dutch and German, and this was followed by an occasional yelp of pain or fear in reply. The cell door next to theirs was opened, and Nora could hear the shuffling of its occupants' feet in the hallway a few moments later. The woman with the brown eyes handed Nora a small stack of clothes.

"Here, put those on. You'll never know where they'll take us, but you can't go anywhere in those rags."

Nora looked at the other women in her cell. They each wore two sweaters, as well as a thick jacket. She looked at what she was wearing and understood. Her pants were full of holes, and her ratty sweater was torn in multiple places. She changed into the simple woolen sweater the woman with the brown eyes had given her and barely had time to change her pants before the door to their cell opened. Two guards stepped inside, each wielding a baton. The tallest looked at the women and smiled.

"I see you're prepared for the journey." He sounded amused, a mocking smile on his face. "Take anything you can carry in a small backpack. You have one minute."

The other women picked up small bags they had evidently prepared beforehand. Nora looked around awkwardly. She had nothing but the clothes she had just been given. The woman with the brown eyes took a step toward her and placed a small bag in her hands. Nora looked at her in surprise, but the woman's eyes narrowed, and she gave her a small nod. "Stay with me," she whispered. "Later."

Nora took the bag gratefully, glancing inside. There was a small piece of bread, cheese, and what looked like a piece of chocolate. She could hardly believe it and had to control herself not to reach inside

247

immediately. Her mouth watered at the thought of the sweet taste of chocolate. How had the women obtained this in their cell?

She didn't get a chance to ask, for the guards indicated they needed to move out of the cell. Nora's body protested, pins and needles biting into her calves, her feet hurting at every step as they followed the guards through the hallway. Nora made sure she kept close to her cell mates. The hallway was crowded but orderly as the cells emptied. They reached the stairway, the same one she'd come up the day before, and climbed two flights. A gentle breeze flowed through an open door at the top. Stepping through, Nora found herself outside in a large courtyard. The sensation of being outside after spending months inside the prison's basement was overwhelming, and Nora took a deep breath. The fresh air stung her throat, but in a good way. Her eyes watered, and she wasn't sure if it was because of the emotions welling up inside, or the cold air.

"Come on, keep moving! We have a train to catch!" A burly guard pushed her forward, and Nora was back in the present. A small gap had formed between her and her cell mates, and she hurried to catch up. She looked around and now saw the scores of open-bed cargo trucks parked a little farther ahead. There were at least twenty, and more than half were filled with prisoners lining the sides of the cargo areas. Nora boarded her truck, making sure to find a seat next to the woman who'd looked after her so far.

They sat in silence while they waited for the stream of prisoners coming from all sides of the prison to board. Nora looked around and caught the high walls surrounding her on all sides. She vaguely remembered arriving here in the darkness. *Was that really two months ago?* The walls had looked more imposing back then, but perhaps the darkness had something to do with that.

Two guards climbed aboard, and the driver started the engine. The truck came to life, shaking the simple wooden benches the prisoners sat on. Nora's was among the first to pass through the large gate out of the prison and into the relative freedom of the streets. The guards kept their hands on their holstered sidearms, making it clear any thoughts of escaping would be futile. Nora didn't even consider it: she was still winded from the walk from her cell. Utterly exhausted, she almost didn't care where they were taken next. She needed to keep her wits about her. Most importantly, she needed to stay close to the woman next to her.

The procession of trucks soon pulled away from the seaside town of Scheveningen, and they reached The Hague ten minutes later. Nobody spoke, but they were all wondering where they were headed.

The trucks stopped some fifteen minutes later, at a small station called Den Haag Staatsspoor. A large concentration of SS guards wielding rifles lined the area near the station's entrance. The guards sitting in the back opened the tailgate and jumped out.

"Get out! Hurry up, come on, come on!" they shouted, and the prisoners quickly climbed down. A young man in front of Nora jumped out and turned around to offer her his hand. As she reached for it, the man was roughly pulled away by one of the guards. Nora almost slipped but caught herself just in time. She landed awkwardly on the street, grazing her knee. She suppressed a cry of pain, but tears sprang to her eyes. She looked up to see the young man roughly pushed toward the station's entrance. Nora pushed herself to her feet, then felt a pair of hands helping her from either side.

"Let's not draw any attention to ourselves," said the woman with the brown eyes as she took Nora's arm.

They followed the stream of prisoners toward the station. Stone-faced SS guards formed a cordon, and Nora spotted some curious bystanders on the other side. Some looked on with pity on their faces, while others looked almost gleeful. She turned her attention to the street directly in front of her, keeping her head down. *I don't need to see them.*

Inside, the station had been cleared out and guards urged them on, telling them they had no time to lose. They walked through the small station hall to the only occupied track. There, a train with a dozen boxcars stood waiting. Nora felt her throat constrict at the sight. Her mind only briefly considered the thought of the train not being intended for them when she noticed other prisoners boarding the cars at the end. She was herded in the same direction. Less than thirty seconds later, she stood in the back of one of the boxcars. More people piled inside, and she felt herself getting squeezed more and more toward the walls. When it seemed like the car couldn't possibly fit any more people, a last person was pushed inside by the guards. Seemingly content, they slid the door closed, and the lock fell into place.

Nora could hardly breathe or move. She felt herself shivering, despite the heat radiating from the bodies pressing against her. She clutched her small bag tighter.

The train finally started moving an hour later. No one had told them where they were headed, but Nora knew these trains were all headed in the same direction. East, to the concentration camps she'd saved so many children from.

CHAPTER THIRTY-FOUR

L isa walked along the main path running the length of the camp. Tents were pitched with military precision all around, making it easy to navigate. She could hear the fighting in the distance, the thunder of German and American artillery targeting each other's troops on opposite sides of the river.

After the Third Army's decisive victory at Bastogne in December, Lisa was certain the Germans would be defeated and pushed back east soon. She, along with many of the troops around her, felt they had turned the tide of the battle, maybe even the war. The battle in the Ardennes area lasted for another month before the Germans finally retreated. Lisa was somewhat surprised the Third Army wouldn't pursue them, but turned south instead, back to Saarlouis.

The German defenses on the Saar River were still holding strong, and the front lines around it hardly moved in the month and a half that Lisa had been stationed here. At times Lisa felt frustrated at their lack of progress, but she knew General Patton was working on a plan to breach the Germans' defensive positions along the river.

"Hey, Lisa, wait up!" A familiar voice sounded behind her. She turned around to find Steve running to catch up, carrying a stack of envelopes.

"Did you get mail from back home?" Lisa smiled. Letters from across the Atlantic raised the men's morale like nothing else, and she was always pleased to hear the stories of what happened far away in America. Judging from the stories of the men around her, the United States was a place where anything was possible, where many had looked in horror at what was going on in Europe and wanted to help. She was grateful for their sacrifices. It couldn't be easy being so far away from home, fighting in an alien land against people who don't speak your language, or wanted to kill you. Or both.

It reminded Lisa of her own situation. Even though she wasn't nearly as far away from home as Steve or the others, she might as well be. She wondered how the liberation was going. Last she heard the American and Canadian troops were stuck in the southern part of the country, the combination of the rivers and an organized enemy proving impenetrable so far. Lisa shrugged. She'd been with the Third Army long enough to believe the American, British, and Canadian generals would soon find a way to breach the German defenses in her home country as well. If they hadn't already, by now.

Steve appeared alongside her, breathing heavily, eyes sparkling. He held up one of the envelopes. It was already open. "I'm going to be an uncle!" The excitement in his voice was contagious, and Lisa felt her heart swell. She threw her arms around him, and they jumped up and down in the middle of the camp a few times.

"That's fantastic news, Steve! I'm so happy for you!"

"My younger brother just finished his training in the air force last month, and he's set to ship out this week. Apparently, they found time to make sure Janey will be busy." Steve grinned. "I can't wait to meet the little guy or girl!"

Steve's joy made Lisa forget her worries, and they walked down the main path, greeting acquaintances on the way.

"Any news from home for you?" Steve asked, returning her thoughts to the Netherlands.

"Not really. Last thing I heard not much had changed. But that's over a month ago. I'm sure they're doing everything they can to push north."

"Of course. And didn't you say there's a strong resistance in your country? They should be able to help, right?"

Lisa furrowed her brow, her mouth involuntarily twitching. "I'm not so sure, to be honest. When I was back home, the resistance was strong; hiding people, even smuggling them out of the country. I've been here for nine months, home feels a long time ago." She thought back to the journey she'd taken with Christiaan, which now seemed a lifetime ago. The thought of the man she loved caused a wave of agony to surge through Lisa. It was getting more difficult to imagine he was still out there somewhere. She steeled herself and continued. "But when Christiaan was sent to contact them, I got the impression the Nazis had curtailed the resistance efforts quite well. It sounded like they were weakened. It felt like Christiaan needed to revive them." If anyone was able to do that, it was Christiaan.

"I'm sure we'll find a way to break the German defenses in the Netherlands soon enough, Lisa. And who knows, maybe Christiaan is lying low, waiting for the right opportunity to strike? To rise up with the resistance he's organized? Wasn't that his mission?"

Steve's face showed a lot of compassion, but also belief. It was an American trait Lisa admired but hadn't quite picked up yet. *They're so convinced of their success.* The Americans had a firm conviction that their strength of will could make their goals a reality—a confidence exemplified by General Patton and his Third Army. If they held enough faith, they created their own luck. Who else would've been able to move an entire army north within a week, and then defeat a German force vastly outnumbering them? She vowed to try and think a bit more like Steve and his compatriots.

"You're right. I need to have a bit of faith." She forced a smile and pointed at the canteen tent in the distance. "Do you have time for a coffee? I want to hear all about your news from back home."

Steve nodded. "Absolutely."

———

Lisa returned to the Red Cross tent half an hour later. She wasn't on duty this morning, but she liked to check in on her colleagues and see if they needed help. Things could quickly change, and it wouldn't be the first time an extra pair of hands was much appreciated. She was pleased to see less than a quarter of the beds occupied. Judging from recent occupancy in the tent, the battle was going well. Then again, one or two well-aimed artillery shells could change the situation instantly.

One of the doctors passed by, greeting her at first, then stopping and turning back, looking surprised. "Did you get the summons from battle command?"

Lisa raised her eyebrows. "No, what do you mean?"

"There was a corporal here about an hour ago. He was looking for you, said it was urgent. I told him you were off and sent him to your tent. I guess you didn't run into him, then."

"You're sure he was from battle command?"

The doctor nodded. "Oh yeah, that's for sure. He was carrying some important-looking papers. Best go and report to see what they have to say. Probably another important mission." He winked at her, easing Lisa's anxiety somewhat. All her Red Cross colleagues knew she wasn't just a nurse. Even the doctors treated her with an unusual level of respect.

She headed for the large congregation of tents in the middle of the camp. It wasn't her first visit to battle command, but it usually meant venturing on a mission outside the camp. It was exhilarating yet terrifying.

Two soldiers stood at the entrance, and Lisa presented her name and credentials. They let her through after a quick glance at a sheet of paper. Inside was a hive of activity, with military clerks shuffling papers and busying themselves, all doing their best to look important. She approached one near the entrance. He nodded and directed her to a somewhat quieter area in the back.

"The captain will be with you shortly; he's just finishing something up," the young man said. "Make yourself comfortable." He pointed at a jug of water in the corner and disappeared.

Lisa sat and listened to the voices around her. Most spoke in reserved tones, but the sheer number of people clacking away on typewriters and conversing in the restricted space meant the cacophony was almost overpowering to Lisa's senses. She stood and poured herself some water, closing her eyes as she took a sip. Her mind wandered to what would be required from her this time. The last time she was summoned to question several German POWs in a nearby village—Lisa had become used to speaking with the enemy. Most of the men were much like those she'd encountered in Saarlouis on her first trip outside the camp. Generally younger than her, frightened about what would happen to them, and eager to please. It helped that Lisa spoke their language almost fluently, and that she was a woman. Most opened up to her quickly, and while her allegiance was firmly with the American army, she was pleased to assure the German soldiers they would be treated fairly in captivity. Some shared horror stories of what they'd heard happened to German soldiers captured by the Soviets. Lisa had initially dismissed them as fabrications, until her American friends in the camp confirmed they'd heard the same.

"Miss Abrahams?" Lisa had been so caught up in her thoughts she hadn't heard the tall man wearing a captain's uniform enter. She stood but didn't salute him. As a nurse she wasn't required to do so, and he gently waved her back to her chair. "At ease, please."

The man sat across from her. Apart from being tall, he was also well built, his broad shoulders stretching his uniform. He appeared in his midtwenties, making him relatively young for his rank. He placed a large folder on the desk but didn't open it. Instead, he placed his hands on the table and looked at Lisa.

"My name is Captain Hanson. I'll keep this short because I know your time is valuable." He smiled, flashing perfect teeth. "I looked at your file earlier, and I know you've been involved in many important missions. For a nurse, you've been quite busy outside the hospital tent." His eyes were sparkling, and it wasn't hard to catch the admiration in his voice. "You're experienced, Miss Abrahams. You've been with us for a little under a year now?"

"Nine months, yes."

He waved his hand. "Practically a veteran, then. You must've noticed the new arrivals this past week, right?" Lisa nodded. A lot of new faces had reported to the camp. "Those boys are the Sixty-fifth Infantry, and they're fresh off the boat. Literally. They arrived at Le Havre a few weeks ago."

"Yes, sir." Lisa wasn't sure where Hanson was going.

"They've been trained, they know how to fight, and I'm glad they're here. There's just one thing. Most of them don't have a clue about the area, the people, or the language." He leaned forward and looked at her intently. "Yet, we'll be sending them out on patrols and into action soon enough. We're merging some of the experienced soldiers into their units."

Lisa caught herself nervously tapping her foot. She crossed her legs and placed her hands on her knees. The move wasn't lost on the experienced captain, who gave her a reassuring smile.

"Miss Abrahams, we'd like to move you to one of the new squadrons. Above everything else, they'll need your language skills. We've encountered more and more Germans crossing the river to surrender. It's imperative we reach them before their countrymen do. There are reports of kill squads operating between the lines, seeking out deserters. We need to get to them first and talk to them while their intel is still fresh. The general believes it could give us a crucial edge in breaking through the *Westwall*."

Lisa felt her adrenaline levels rise at the thought of playing a part in breaking through Hitler's line of defensive fortifications running north to south between Germany and the Netherlands, Belgium, Luxembourg, and France. It had proved impregnable so far, but if Patton saw a chance to smash through it, Lisa was excited to play her part.

"I'd be honored, sir. What do you need from me?"

Hanson leaned back in his chair and folded his hands. "Glad to hear it, Abrahams. For now, you'll return to your duties as nurse. We'll call for you when we need you, but know you'll likely be involved in many more missions outside the camp."

Lisa felt herself shaking but retained her composure. "I'll be ready, sir."

———

Lisa didn't have to wait long. Two days after meeting with Hanson, she was called up and placed with the 261st Regiment of the 65th Infantry Division. There were five thousand soldiers in the regiment, but Lisa met with a much smaller squad in the early hours of a rainy morning. To her surprise, Steve was part of the dozen men waiting to set out. He had been chosen to help the new soldiers get acquainted with their surroundings.

The rain was coming down hard and the small squad set out at a brisk pace. Unencumbered by the heavy equipment most of the soldiers wore, Lisa had no trouble keeping up. Their mission was straightforward, and Lisa was pleased she would play a large part in it. One of the civilian resistance groups operating on the French-German border had contacted the Americans, indicating they had valuable information about recent German troop movements and fortifications. Battle command had interacted with the group in the past and deemed them trustworthy. The group had asked to meet in the small village of Berus, a short trek southeast of the camp.

Lisa was impressed with the discipline shown by her companions. They had decided to be quiet during their passage to Berus, only speaking if they encountered difficulties. The front lines were located to the east, close to the river, and they didn't anticipate much trouble. It made sense that the resistance group requested a meeting in this relatively protected area. Nevertheless, the men remained watchful and vigilant, keeping an eye on the surroundings.

It took them forty-five minutes passing by abandoned farms before reaching Berus. The town was even smaller than Lisa had expected. The rain muffled all other sounds around them, and the squad slowed down and split to both sides of the road as they approached the first houses. Lisa walked in the back and didn't have a weapon, but kept her eyes peeled. Her gaze swept over the small homes, doors and windows boarded up tightly with wooden planks. The inhabitants had first experienced the fighting and violence of the initial German invasion, and now the war had returned in earnest as the Germans fought tooth and nail to keep their foothold along the river. As a result, many of the inhabitants had fled the area. Lisa hoped these people could soon return to their homes.

They reached the center of the village a few minutes later. One of the men in the front held up a fist and crouched down. The rest followed his order to stay in place, as did Lisa. A sliver of fear crept into the back of her mind. Had he spotted something?

Lisa looked ahead and could only make out the bell tower of the local church. After a minute, the man at the front rose again and, hugging the wall of the building next to him, peeked around the corner. His shoulders sagged, then he lowered his gun.

"All clear. But I fear we won't be talking to anyone today." He sounded disappointed, a little sad. "Move out into the square."

Lisa was the last to turn the corner, but from the faces of the men ahead of her, she knew something was wrong. Nevertheless, she gasped in horror when she saw the scene on the far side of the square.

Five bodies hung from ropes tied to the exposed roof beams. The men's faces were blackish and blue with bulging eyes. They had been tortured before they were unceremoniously strung up in the middle of the village. Next to the bodies was a handmade sign painted in crude black strokes on rough wood. It read, in German, "These traitors have nothing left to say."

The first soldiers reached the men, and one of them looked down at something on the ground. His gaze then went back up to the faces of the men, and he doubled over, emptying the contents of his stomach on the wet ground. Another soldier called out in disgust, "The bastards cut out their tongues!"

Lisa stopped in her tracks. She knew there was nothing she could do for the dead men. She had no desire to see the horror the Germans had inflicted on them from close up. The soldiers proceeded to cut down the bodies, and Lisa looked for some shelter from the rain, which only seemed to grow in intensity. She was looking forward to heading back to camp.

She turned away from the square but, as she did, thought she caught movement at the top of the bell tower. *No, it's impossible.* For a second, she thought it might be villagers hiding from the soldiers, but then she saw the familiar shape of a muzzle pointing down onto the square. She opened her mouth, but it was too late. Muffled only slightly by the rain, the rattle of machine gun fire tore through the sky.

"No!" She raised her hands before her eyes as the first bullets struck. Two soldiers went down, blood splattering on the wet ground. Stray bullets found their marks in the bodies of the hung men, the impact producing dull thuds.

To their credit, the American soldiers responded decisively. Two immediately returned fire, momentarily giving them a reprieve. The others dragged the two injured soldiers to the safety of one of the nearby houses. A soldier had already smashed open the door, and they quickly poured inside.

Strong hands grabbed Lisa and pulled her into a nearby building. It was only just in time, for the machine gunner opened fire again, this time in her direction. Wood splinters flew all around as she was pushed to the ground. Bullets zipped by overhead as the windows were blown out, destroying kitchen cabinets and their contents on the far wall. Glasses exploded and plates crashed to the floor, and Lisa covered her head with her arms, clenching her jaw as she waited for shards of glass to cut into her.

"Stay down! Keep your head down!" a voice shouted. More

bullets whizzed by, then things became quiet. Lisa risked a quick peek. The living room was destroyed. Windows were shattered, but thick concrete walls had protected them from certain death. *If this had been a wooden home.* Lisa was with three soldiers she didn't know. *Where is Steve? He must be on the other side.* Fear gripped her as she replayed the scene of a minute earlier. Was Steve hit by the initial barrage? She had been so shocked she hadn't seen who was hit. It could easily have been her friend, for he was near the front of the squad.

"Are you okay?" the soldier next to her asked, his eyes full of concern. "Were you hit?"

She checked herself, feeling no pain or blood. "I'm all right."

None of the soldiers in the house were hurt, but they were stuck. There was no back door, only a side door opening into the street they came from. Both the front and side door would expose them to the machine gunner perched in the bell tower.

"What can we do, sarge?" One of the soldiers looked to the man who had pulled Lisa into the building earlier. Lisa turned to him in surprise. *This young man is a sergeant?*

From his calculating eyes, it was clear the sergeant was considering his possibilities. The squad wasn't equipped to take out a machine gun position in an elevated location more than fifty meters away, even Lisa could see that. They hadn't expected an ambush.

"As far as we know, they only have one gun up there," the man started, looking at the two other soldiers. "That means they won't be able to cover both of our positions at the same time. They also know this, so I wouldn't be surprised if the bastards already sent soldiers across the square to attack us from close by. That's what I would do if I had them pinned down like this." He scowled, but Lisa was impressed with his quick thinking. It made sense. "Drop a few grenades into the buildings and we're toast."

The other soldiers flinched, but quickly recovered, nodding. "Jackson has a comms kit, sir. Can we call in reinforcements?"

The sergeant shook his head. "They'll never make it in time. We're on our own."

"What about air support?" Lisa spoke before she realized it. She clasped her hand in front of her mouth, feeling her cheeks burn. "Apologies, sir."

The sergeant looked at her curiously, then a smile formed. "Might be worth a shot. But they probably wouldn't be here in time, either. We'll need to prepare for the worst, but let's see if Jackson can reach battle command."

The sergeant moved to the window and risked a quick peek. Lisa closed her eyes, bracing herself for the inevitable burst of machine gun fire. All remained quiet, and she opened her eyes when she heard his strong voice boom across the square.

"Jackson, can you call in the birds to sing?"

Lisa flinched at the man's boldness. Even though most German soldiers hardly spoke English, the sergeant's words would be easy to decipher for one that did. *Or am I overestimating the enemy?* The response from the other house, some thirty meters away, was swift and short.

"Roger, sir. Contacting keeper."

Lisa wondered if this was standard procedure, the men speaking in code, or if they were improvising. She didn't dare ask, and she held her breath while they waited for Jackson's response. The sergeant turned back to Lisa and the soldiers.

"Listen, even if we do get birds, we'll need to get out of here." His eyes went to the side door. "That's our best bet right there. I'll provide cover fire from the window facing the square, and the three of you run like hell and don't look back." The soldiers nodded, and Lisa swallowed hard.

"Sir, birds in ten."

The words sounded magical, and the faces of the soldiers in the room lit up. Lisa felt hopeful. *Maybe we don't have to make a run for it? She was terrified of being ripped to pieces by the machine gun, even with the covering fire.*

Her answer came moments later. A loud whooshing sound cut through the silence on the square, followed by a deafening explosion shaking the ground. The sergeant looked out the window again; waiting for the airplanes to arrive wasn't an option.

"Shit, they're using *Panzerfausts* from the bell tower!" For the first time, there was a hint of panic and fear in the man's voice. "They only barely missed the others, but we can't stay here a second longer!" He turned around. "Get ready to move! When you open the door, run like hell!" In the same movement, he yelled instructions to the men in the other building. "Two men, provide covering fire. Everyone else, make for the red farm we passed on the way in. Start firing when I do. Understood?"

"Roger!" The reply was instant.

Another whoosh from the bell tower. Everybody in the building pushed themselves harder into the relative safety of the floor. Lisa prayed the rocket-propelled grenade would again miss its mark. There was a loud explosion and the distinct sound of wood cracking. Seconds later, the sound she'd dreaded hearing. A man cried out in pain from across from the square—Steve. Her world slowed down as she heard only her friend's cries of anguish.

Around her, the soldiers sprang into action. They moved in a haze, and Lisa heard the voice of the sergeant as if she were under-water. All she could hear was Steve, thirty meters away, his cries getting louder and more urgent.

"Are you ready?" The sergeant's voice cut through her thoughts, bringing her back to her own pressing reality. "You need to run!" He was positioned underneath the window, his gun at the ready. Lisa looked at the other two soldiers, who crouched near the side door, ready to bolt.

"But, what about the others? What about Steve? They were hit!"

The sergeant gave her an annoyed, impatient look, and spoke quickly. "They will make their way out, but this only works if we all run at the same time! If we stay here, we'll all die! We must move, now!"

Lisa felt helpless, but she knew there was nothing she could do for Steve now. There was no way she could make it to him, and she needed to trust the other soldiers to bring him along, if he was still alive. She swallowed hard and moved in a crouch toward the side door.

"On three!" the sergeant said. "One."

Lisa gritted her teeth. *I can do this. And the airplanes are only a few minutes out. We'll come back for Steve.*

"Two."

She clenched her hands into fists and looked at the two men opposite her. One gave her a quick nod of encouragement while he reached for the door handle.

"Three. Go! Go! Go!"

The sergeant slung his semiautomatic weapon over the windowsill and aimed it at the bell tower. The soldier swung the door open just as the sergeant's gun exploded into life. The soldiers jumped out of the house, Lisa only a few steps behind. More gunfire erupted in the square behind her, but she didn't look back. She expected to be struck down at any moment as the gunner in the bell tower would surely spot them. She focused on the men in front of her, her lungs burning as they increased the distance between them and the square.

Then, out of nowhere, two fighter planes appeared in the sky ahead of them. They shot over them at low altitude, and Lisa could almost feel the force of the propellers. A few seconds later, their imperious machine guns opened fire on the bell tower. Lisa couldn't resist looking back, and she stopped running, breathing hard as she watched the top of the bell tower collapse onto itself. It was a glorious sight, and Lisa couldn't help but smile as the incessant rattle of the machine gun stopped.

The Mustangs were already banking and preparing for a second run on the village when the sergeant appeared from the side door. He quickly glanced back to the square, which appeared deserted, before sprinting toward them. Behind him, the Mustangs reappeared. The first released another torrent of bullets near the bell tower, and Lisa realized they had spotted German troops. The second plane seemed to slow down a little, then released something from underneath its wing. It quickly pulled up, and as it did, a massive explosion flattened the buildings behind it. Lisa could feel the fierce heat emanating from the ferocious blaze. She was in awe of the display of the two pilots, who had taken out the German fortification in a matter of seconds. They passed by once more and tipped their wings at them before disappearing as quickly as they had come.

The sergeant reached them, winded but content. "Let's keep moving. I saw the others make their way out as well, along with a couple of wounded."

———

Lisa's group was the first to reach the farm. The soldiers took positions facing the village, just in case the Germans had any illusions of pursuit. Lisa's doubted they would be foolish enough to attack the Americans after that display of force.

She sat inside while they waited for the others. It felt as if it was taking too long for them to cross the distance, even if they were carrying wounded. Lisa stood and was pacing the small living room when she heard voices outside. She looked through the window and saw the rest of their squad arrive. Or what was left of them.

Her throat went dry when she scanned the faces. A few of them looked pale, shaken, and even distraught. She didn't see Steve. Her heart was beating hard, her throat now constricting. *Where is he?*

Lisa could no longer control herself and stepped outside. The men turned to her, and as soon as they saw her, she knew Steve hadn't made it. Lisa walked toward them, shaking her head.

"Where is he?" Her voice was croaking and unnatural.

The sergeant stepped forward, a heavy look on his face. "I'm so sorry, Lisa. He didn't make it. He stayed behind so the others could run."

The words hardly registered as Lisa felt her knees buckle, her vision clouded by tears. The world started spinning as she tried to control the heaving of her chest. "No. It can't be," she managed through sobs. Finally, her legs gave way, and she lost her balance. The last thing she remembered were strong hands catching her before she could hit the muddy, rain-soaked ground.

Part Three

RAVENSBRÜCK CONCENTRATION CAMP, GERMANY, 25 MARCH 1945

CHAPTER THIRTY-FIVE

For a few hours in the very early morning, the block was quiet. The first hours after lights out, women tossed and turned, the fortunate ones finding sleep sooner rather than later. Some cried softly, cursing their lives, while still others snored, blissfully unaware of their surroundings for a few hours. In the deep of night, a couple hours before the camp sirens wailed the inevitable call to wake up, most women in Ravensbrück's barracks were finally asleep.

It was around three in the morning, and Nora lay awake in her bunk, listening to the soft snoring of Sophie next to her. She owed her life to Sophie, for if she hadn't handed her those warm clothes and the bag of supplies in their prison cell in Scheveningen, Nora would've succumbed to the freezing conditions in their boxcar. They had traveled for three days and three nights before their train pulled into the small station near Ravensbrück's concentration camp in the north of Germany.

They had stopped many times along the way, sometimes at small stations, but more often on a sidetrack in the middle of a snow-covered field. There, they waited for the freight trains transporting important war materiel before continuing their journey. Not once had the doors been opened. The single bucket of drinking water was empty before the train left the Netherlands, and never refilled. Once, when they stopped at a small station on the second day, the prisoners in the boxcar ahead of them had begged for water. The guards had responded by taking buckets of water from the station and drenching the occupants of the car with it. After that, no one had asked for water. On arrival, the frozen bodies of the women in that car had tumbled out when the doors were opened.

In Nora's car, only half of the seventy women had survived the journey. When the door opened in the early morning and they were greeted by abusive guards yelling conflicting commands at them, Nora had jumped out as quickly as she could. The stench in the boxcar had been nauseating, and she had only survived because she'd somehow found a spot with a bit of fresh air coming in through the broken wall. She and Sophie had taken turns breathing in the cold air while the number of corpses around them increased. Not knowing where they were going, or how long the journey would take, Nora had rationed her food as best she could, but it had been almost a full day and night without food when they arrived.

They were put through an exhausting and excruciatingly long registration process. When she was finally given her camp uniform at noon, she was sent straight to one of the sewing workshops. It was through sheer willpower that she hadn't collapsed on the job. By the time she received her weak portion of watery porridge in the evening, it tasted like the best meal in the world.

Sophie stirred in her sleep, turning around, and placing a hand on Nora's neck. She gently took her friend's arm and moved it beside her. Sophie mumbled something, then sighed and continued snoring. Nora looked at the window next to her bunk. The thin, dingy curtains did little to block the glare of the bright searchlights outside. She was convinced the SS kept the lights on during the night partly to keep an eye on what was going on, but more so to torture the prisoners, making it harder to sleep. In Nora's case, it worked, although the lights weren't the primary reason for her sleepless nights.

She worried about her survival chances in Ravensbrück. So far, she'd been able to blend into the population quite well. When she arrived and noticed the camp was run by female guards, she felt optimistic. That had been quashed only minutes later, when she saw one of the guards beat an older woman to death for misunderstanding an order. The viciousness with which the guard—an attractive blond in her early twenties—assaulted the older woman had shocked Nora. And it wasn't an exception. Over the next hours, Nora witnessed at least half a dozen more deaths. Nora decided she needed to be invisible. In the daytime, she did what she was told in the sewing workshop, and at night, she disappeared into her barracks as soon as she could.

She also kept her distance from most other prisoners. Instead, she spent her time with Sophie and her two former cell mates from Scheveningen, Bregje and Elise. Even though the latter two were assigned to a different block, they still found ways to meet after work. They worked in the camp's kitchen, and occasionally smuggled out additional vegetables, which they shared with Nora and Sophie. It was dangerous, but the women assured them they had the right connections to make it work. Nora was grateful; any extra rations meant the difference between life and death.

The camp siren screeched into life outside, indicating it was four in the morning. Nora sighed as the women around her awoke with a start. Within a minute or two the block elder and Kapo would storm into the room, using their batons to wake anyone who dared to steal a couple minutes extra sleep. They would be loud, and they would harass the women into getting dressed and ready for roll call. Sophie looked at her, bleary eyed.

"Is it morning already?"

Nora nodded and prepared to climb out of her bunk. The priceless hours of rest were over. Another day in hell awaited.

———

Nora and Sophie stood next to each other at roll call. An icy wind blew across the depressing open area between the barracks as endless rows of women shivered and shook as they waited for the guards to finalize their counts. The ordeal started over two hours ago, but the guards had found something they didn't like, now recounting the prisoners for the fifth time. Nora kept her eyes on the ground and only glanced up when she was certain there were no nearby guards. More than a few women had already collapsed from exhaustion and were mercilessly beaten to death. Their bodies lay scattered across the Appellplatz, to be disposed of like garbage.

Fifteen minutes later, it appeared the guards were finally content with their count. It was impossible to know what had upset them during the first four counts, but Nora had long since abandoned understanding the logic of the camp regulations.

"Listen up." Even without looking, Nora recognized the harsh voice of *Chef Oberaufseherin* Luise Brunner. Having climbed the ranks from regular guard to become the most senior female guard of the camp, she continued to carry out her duties with zeal. Brunner often insisted on inflicting the first blows in the daily murders during roll call. Once a woman was beaten to the ground by Brunner, she let the regular guards finish the job. She struck terror in every single woman's heart.

"This took much longer than I had hoped, and as a result you'll all receive half rations this evening. I do hope tonight's roll call is carried out properly, or we might take that half as well." Despite this terrible announcement, the women in the roll call area knew better than to react in any way, and it remained deathly quiet. Brunner wasn't done yet. "The women in Block 14 won't need to report for work today. Instead, you'll return to your block and gather your belongings. You'll be ready to leave in an hour." Brunner stepped away without another word, and the other guards immediately started yelling at the women to move and report for their jobs.

Instead of following the other women to their workshop, Nora and Sophie returned to their block.

"What do you think this means?" Sophie said softly, her voice quivering. "Are they really putting us on another transport?"

Nora felt sick. There had been transports leaving the camp almost every day, and the rumors about their destinations weren't encouraging. Despite her fear, she tried to put on a brave face. "I'm sure they just want us working somewhere else. Or they might be concerned about the Americans and Brits making their way here sooner than expected?"

Nora continued to hold on to the hope that the Allied invasion continued its momentum. Some prisoners said they had been transported from Auschwitz-Birkenau a few months ago because the Soviets were advancing so quickly from the east.

They entered the barracks and gathered their few belongings. Nora sat on her bunk, holding her small bag. From what she knew, they were in northern Germany, quite close to Denmark. If the Americans were coming from the west, and Soviets from the east, there was only one direction they could realistically be taken. South. But what was south?

CHAPTER THIRTY-SIX

I t was unusually quiet in the clerks' room; only the sound of the clacking typewriters and the occasional clerk shuffling by disturbing the hush. Christiaan was quite content with that. The pile of papers on his left appeared to grow every hour, as SS guards came in carrying more stacks. When he took a minute to look around, the situation was much the same for the other clerks. It had been like this for a few weeks now, and it was impossible to miss the dramatic increase of prisoners dwelling around Mauthausen and its subcamps. Scores of emaciated prisoners arrived from camps in the east every day. Most of them were hardly able to stand for longer than an hour, and many perished within a few days. There wasn't enough room to house them in the barracks in the main camp, which meant most were assigned to the newly constructed tent camp, which sounded nicer than it was. The hastily erected tents left much to be desired, and the mortality rate in this section was atrocious. Christiaan saw the numbers pass his desk every morning.

Other new arrivals were placed in the *Sanitätslager*, what was supposed to pass for an infirmary. Its name had always been a mockery of what it was; prisoners were sent there to die. There was no real medical attention, and even though the poor prisoner nurses did their best to make their patients as comfortable as possible, most patients left the hospital horizontally.

Christiaan finished typing up another sheet, the neat rows filled with names and numbers. He prepared a fresh sheet of paper in his typewriter and was about to start typing when a familiar voice sounded to his side.

"Prisoner, come with me." It was Floris' friend Anton. He had a neutral expression on his face, but Christiaan knew there was nothing neutral about the man's intentions. It had been Anton who'd informed him of his brother's death two months ago. Christiaan had felt something resembling loss at the news, a brief sense of grief, despite their differences. Floris chose his own path a long time ago, siding with the Nazis, sending all those innocent people to their deaths, and it had brought him to Mauthausen. In a way, it was ironic that his brother, a guard, died before he did.

Reluctantly, he got up and followed Anton out of the room and into the fresh April air outside. It was a beautiful day, the sun high in the clear blue sky. In any other place, it would be enough to lift a man's spirits. For Christiaan, the pile of bodies less than twenty meters down the road was enough to keep his optimism in check.

"Come, walk with me," Anton said as he headed in the opposite direction, through the main gate, toward the SS quarters. Christiaan frowned but had no choice but to follow. He would need to find a way to explain his absence from the clerks' room later.

"So, have you considered my proposal?" Anton kicked a small stone down the road as they left the main camp behind. The barracks of the SS guards lined the road, but there were few of them around. Anton appeared confident enough to speak freely. "I can keep you alive until the Americans or Russians arrive, and you vouch for me when they get here."

Christiaan didn't immediately respond, keeping his eyes on the road. The quarry was only a hundred meters ahead, and the sound of clattering of pickaxes greeted them. He remembered his time down there. *I would've been dead if Floris hadn't intervened.*

He glanced at Anton. He had been surprised when his brother's friend approached him with extra rations about a month ago. Christiaan hadn't interacted much with him before, only remembering the man hovering around Floris most of the time. He'd never seen him abuse a prisoner, but Christiaan also knew that meant nothing. Anton and Floris had worked in Gusen II, and he'd heard prisoner abuse was even more widespread there than in the main camp. The mortality numbers alone were enough proof to know something very sinister was going on in Gusen II. He didn't trust Anton, but the guard had persisted in bringing him food, and Christiaan felt stronger this past month than he had in the entire previous year. That alone was enough to keep him talking to Anton. *I must survive somehow.*

A few days ago, Anton had suggested a pact. By doing so, he confirmed the rumors about the Americans and Russians making good progress in their liberation of the Continent. It wasn't just Anton, though. Many of the guards had changed their behavior toward the prisoners. They had become less brutal, some even downright friendly. Christiaan and the other clerks were left alone for most of the day, and some of the guards even asked if they needed anything. It was confusing, because Christiaan had no illusion they wouldn't be among the first to be killed once the Allied forces approached. They knew too much. Yet here Anton was, offering to keep him alive.

"You can't guarantee that I won't be killed by one of your colleagues."

Anton stopped and shook his head. "I can't. But I'm your best chance regardless. I'm providing you with food, and I can warn you when they come for you. I promise I'll do anything I can to keep you alive. If you're dead when the Americans arrive, there will be no one to vouch for me."

Christiaan was surprised to see genuine fear in the guard's eyes.

The Americans must be closer than I thought. He considered Anton's words and his end of the bargain. If he was still alive when the Americans arrived, would he be able to save Anton? And would he want to? He was still a camp guard. An SS Nazi. Christiaan decided it didn't matter. As long as Anton kept his side of the bargain, he would have additional rations, and he would know when the guards came to kill him. He could act on that and decide on helping Anton later. He turned and looked around, then held out his hand.

"Deal. We keep each other alive."

There was evident relief on Anton's face as he firmly gripped and shook Christiaan's hand.

———

Upon returning to the clerks' room, Christiaan was surprised to find it deserted, but for two SS guards going through some of the papers. They heard him come in and turned around. Christiaan immediately recognized them; they were part of the detail that made sure the clerks stayed in line.

"What are you still doing here?" Wolff asked with a distinctly Austrian accent. He was one of the few Austrian guards Christiaan had encountered in Mauthausen. "Did you forget something?"

Christiaan's confusion must've shown, for the other guard, a young man named Groß, stepped toward him impatiently. "You weren't here when we told the others, were you?" When Christiaan didn't immediately answer, his tone became hostile. "Where were you? Skipping work?"

"No, sir, absolutely not. I was told to deliver some documents to the Kommandant's office." Christiaan didn't know what else to say. He could hardly say he was solidifying his pact with Anton. To his relief, Wolff appeared to believe him as he stepped in front of the junior guard.

"All right then, that's fine. You'll need to hurry, then."

"What's happening, sir?"

"You're leaving the camp."

Christiaan wasn't sure he heard the man correctly. "Sir?" *Leave Mauthausen?* He felt a trickle of sweat run down his spine.

"You have thirty minutes to get your things and report to the main gate. You're being moved. Better get going." Wolff turned around, returning his attention to a stack of papers on one of the desks. It was clear the conversation was over, and Christiaan looked at his small desk one more time before leaving the room he'd spent the past five months in. Despite the horrors of the camp, his time in the clerks' room had given him a sense of normality. It was a place he went every day, almost as if going to a regular office job.

He stepped onto the main thoroughfare, the bright sunlight momentarily blinding him. Anton's offer had come too late. Wherever he was taken, it was certainly not going to be better. He passed the corpses in the middle of the Appellplatz, and a terrible thought struck. What if they were taking him to his death? Would he be gassed in the nearby Hartheim Castle? Or shot in the woods? Suddenly, all the names he'd so mechanically—carelessly, even—marked as deceased over the past months flooded back into his mind. He felt faint as he considered the terrible reality. It was happening. The camp leadership had finally decided the clerks knew too much.

———

Less than half an hour later Christiaan reported to the main gate. It hadn't taken long to collect his belongings. Carrying nothing but a small satchel and the clothes on his back, he joined a group of clerks sitting on a bench made of mismatched pieces of granite. He looked around and counted at least two hundred other prisoners crowding around. He was encouraged to find it wasn't just his colleagues from the clerks' room. The men spoke in soft voices under the watchful eye of a dozen SS troopers. *Not too many guards for such a large group.* That was odd. Christiaan turned to one of the clerks, Mattias.

"Did they tell you where they're taking us?"

Mattias was a gentile Pole who had ended up on a transport from Warsaw. It was rumored he had taken part in the city's uprising, but he never confirmed this. Christiaan found him easy to get along with, and after Petr was executed, he'd spent more time working with the young Pole.

"They did. KZ Gunskirchen, apparently. You were away when they came in, weren't you? With that same Dutch guard, right?"

He doesn't miss a beat. "Gunskirchen? I thought that was reserved for the Hungarian Jews?" The camp had only recently went into operation, and most of the Hungarians Jews arriving at Mauthausen were sent there. Little was known about the purpose of Gunskirchen, but Christiaan couldn't imagine a need for clerks. His worries further increased when he saw another group of armed SS guards appear from the gate. Their escort more than doubled to some thirty guards.

It didn't take long for the procession to start moving. Christiaan walked in the back, and as they turned left at the end of the road, he looked back one last time. The towering granite walls of Mauthausen loomed up like a medieval castle. Behind him, the sounds of the quarry faded. They walked on, and the Sanitätslager loomed up in the meadow to his right. From his vantage point, he could see the people crowding together in the barbed-wire enclosure. Even though Christiaan had an idea of the number of prisoners assigned to the section, seeing it firsthand still shocked him. People piled out of the barracks, women carrying children, men jostling for space as they stared at the procession moving by on the elevated road. Christiaan looked away, almost feeling guilty for the relative comfort of his position in the clerks' room.

He quickly dismissed the thought as he took another dust-filled breath. He was no longer a clerk. He was just another prisoner on his way to a new, unknown hell. In a few hours, he might very well be dead. The thought exhausted him, and as they made their way down the hill his shoes suddenly felt filled with lead. He struggled to lift his feet, the muscles in his legs and back aching. All he wanted was to sit down. Small specks blurred his vision. He closed his eyes for a moment and stopped walking. He was vaguely aware of the voices around him, urging him to keep moving. He didn't hear them as he stood and took a moment of relief.

A loud bang brought him back to his senses. He opened his eyes in alarm and felt a hand push him forward.

"Don't want to end up like him, do you?" It was Mattias, his eyes on a man to the side of the road. There was a neat little hole in the back of his neck, blood trickling out as he lay face down in the grass. A guard holstered his pistol and returned to his position to the side of the procession of prisoners.

Christiaan summoned every bit of his remaining strength and felt the fire in his veins burn. He cast away the fatigue that had been weighing him down and recalled the dire rules of his previous journey up this same path just months before. Veering from the road meant death. With a renewed determination, Christiaan declared he would not meet such a fate today.

CHAPTER THIRTY-SEVEN

The train stopped abruptly, its brakes creaking. Nora didn't respond as she sat slouched in the corner of the boxcar, not bothering to get up. She'd lost count of the number of times the train had stopped in the past three days. It had felt much like the journey from The Hague to Ravensbrück, although the temperatures were much more agreeable this time. Everything else had been the same; no water, no sanitary stops, and no indication of how much longer the journey would be.

Two of the other women rose and peered through the cracks in the boxcar.

"Hey, we're at a train station. This place looks quite nice," one of them said.

Nora listened to the women but remained in her spot. She felt drained, her energy sapped from the journey. Wherever they were headed, she was certain she'd need to conserve her strength.

"How are you feeling?" Sophie's soft voice was by her side, and Nora smiled at her friend.

Nora licked her cracked lips. "Tired. So tired. And thirsty. You?"

"Surely it can't be much longer," Sophie said, not answering her question. From the looks of her, her friend was quite the worse for wear herself. There were heavy bags under her eyes, her cheeks red from exhaustion. Nora hadn't seen Sophie sleep but for a few hours the previous night.

Nora heard the loud clang of metal. The doors to the boxcar were being opened from the outside.

"Looks like we've arrived," Sophie said, just before their door was opened, sunlight streaming into their previously dark surroundings.

A group of SS guards yelled for the women to get out. Numbly, Nora and Sophie joined the other women in getting off the train, squinting in the bright sunlight. Some of them looked around with curiosity at their new surroundings, a small town nestled among rolling hills, but Nora could only focus on putting one foot in front of the other.

As they followed their guards along a cobblestone road into town, Nora took in details that would normally have gone unnoticed: a farmer flying a kite near his barn; a child walking toward school; an old man sitting alone on his porch, watching as they passed by. Life in this little town with colorful houses carried on as usual. There was no sign of the war here.

The guards led the women through town and up a steep hill. Each step was a struggle. The air was thin, and the sun beat down fiercely on their backs. Nora was breathing hard, but the SS guards harassed and hurried them on. She felt her chest tighten with every breath. Her head weighed heavily against her shoulders, but she gritted her teeth and forced herself to keep climbing.

They made a few more turns, the road becoming steeper, and Nora noticed something peculiar along the sides of the road: corpses. Men wearing tattered clothes with bullet holes in the backs of their necks. She felt her stomach lurch and looked away. At that moment, there was the unmistakable sound of a gunshot behind her. She turned around to see a guard leaning over the motionless body of a young woman. His expression was hard, his eyes gazing around. He seemed a little unfocused, and his boots crunched on the rocky road as he stepped over the woman's body and moved on.

"Keep going, Nora. Don't give them a chance to single you out." Sophie's voice was firm as she walked beside her.

Another shot rang out, startling Nora. They walked on for another ten minutes, with at least the same number of gunshots. The number of male corpses strewn alongside the road thinned as they made it farther up. It became clear these men had been headed in the opposite direction. *Where are we going?*

She didn't have to wait long for her answer. The road made a wide turn and opened up into a large meadow on either side. The air up here was fresh, and Nora took a deep breath. It helped to clear her head and revitalize her for what she hoped was the final stretch of their ascent. Even though she couldn't see the top of the hill, the sound of many voices and the clanking of hammers—or was it something else—drifted down from above.

"Do you hear that? We must be close to something." Sophie had also heard, a sliver of hope in her voice. "Sounds like people working?" She raised an eyebrow.

Another gunshot. Nora kept her gaze fixed on the road ahead, which was sloping up steeply for another hundred meters. She leaned forward, straining as she focused on putting one foot in front of another. *You're almost there, surely. Keep going.* She was so caught up in her own climb that she almost forgot about Sophie. She turned back to see her friend a few paces back, struggling to keep up. One of the guards was already eyeing Sophie from the side of the column. Nora didn't hesitate and took a few steps toward her. Her friend looked up, her striking brown eyes betraying her exhaustion. Nora held out her hand. "Come on, Sofe. You must make it up. We're almost there."

Sophie tightly gripped her wrist, and Nora pulled her friend along, clenching her teeth. She ignored her burning, protesting muscles. This woman had saved her life. Dragging her up the final part of the hill was the least she could do.

When they finally cleared the hill, Nora rested her hands on her knees for a moment, breathing hard. To her surprise, there was no protest from the guards, and she saw all the women in their group were in the same condition. Their faces and clothes were drenched in sweat, some of them wheezing from the effort. Nora heard Sophie's ragged breath next to her and glanced at her friend. She worried about her. The train journey had taken its toll on Sophie; she hadn't seen her in such bad shape before. *I'll need to look out for her.*

It was only then that she saw the monstrosity rising up ahead of them. Dark-gray walls, completely out of place in the lush green of the surrounding meadow. At regular intervals guard towers rose, and Nora could see men wielding rifles looking down. It was hard to tell from a distance, but it appeared one or two had their rifles trained on their group. To their left, a small camp was constructed, the people crowded behind the barbed wire looking up curiously. Some shouted unintelligible words in languages Nora didn't understand. Nora's gaze returned to the building in front of them. It resembled a castle, but it didn't have the sophisticated architecture of the medieval castles she remembered from her history books. This castle was built recently; the large bricks of its wall held in place by layers of concrete. *What is this place?*

"That's enough rest!" A harsh voice at the front of their procession interrupted her thoughts. The guard pointed ahead at the castle. "We're almost there, and we need to get you processed and ready to work. Can't have you standing around like this." He turned and headed up the road, the other guards following and prodding the women on with their batons.

Nora walked on in silence, keeping her eyes on the building that only grew more terrifying as they neared its ten-meter-high walls. She overheard one of the women behind her ask the guards where they were. She was greeted with a derisory snort before the guard said, "You've arrived in a special corner of hell. This is Mauthausen."

Nora had never heard of the camp before, but the confident, matter-of-fact way the guard added the next words made her blood freeze.

"You'll be lucky to survive more than a week."

CHAPTER THIRTY-EIGHT

As Christiaan's group arrived at the intersection, they noticed a large crowd coming toward them. There were more than a few thousand men, women, and children walking along, escorted by German soldiers wearing Wehrmacht uniforms. The soldiers halted the crowd to let Christiaan's group pass first. These people—soldiers included—were trying to escape the war in the east and make their way back to Germany.

Christiaan couldn't help but notice the tired, haggard expressions of the refugees looking on. The soldiers escorting them seemed just as worn out. Christiaan was one of the last to enter the intersection and he sensed the impatience radiating from those waiting. The Wehrmacht soldiers yelled for the people near the front to be patient, but it was of no use. They surged forward, and out of nowhere, Christiaan found himself swept away from his own group. The crowd had become a force of its own, pushing him along. He knew it was futile to resist the flow of people heading north, so he let himself be swept along. He kept his head low; it wouldn't be long before an SS guard noticed that he was gone, and then relentless hands would latch on to his shoulders and most likely shoot him for his attempted escape. Or maybe a Wehrmacht soldier would take notice.

When nothing happened after ten seconds, and none of the people around him appeared to take notice or alerted one of the guards, he dared a quick peek back to the intersection. He was surprised to see it a good fifty meters behind him. The group of Mauthausen prisoners continued eastward, none of the guards even glancing back in his direction. They were focused on harrying the prisoners forward. A gunshot confirmed another poor soul hadn't been able to keep up.

Christiaan matched his pace to that of the people beside him. He looked around and realized he had a major problem. The refugees had been so focused on crossing the intersection that they didn't take notice of him. But his camp uniform would soon become obvious. He needed to blend in, quickly. He looked to his left, where a tall Wehrmacht soldier marched alongside a young woman. They were chatting amiably, but Christiaan knew if the man noticed him, it would all be over.

Then he noticed something on the ground ahead of him. At first, he thought his eyes must be deceiving him, but as he neared the pile of fabric, he almost jumped in relief. In the middle of the road lay a large raincoat. Whether someone thought they didn't need it anymore in the warm spring weather, or accidentally dropped it didn't matter. Christiaan picked it up and wrapped it around his body in one fell swoop. He instantly felt less conspicuous, now part of the herd of refugees.

He moved along with the group in a daze, not quite believing what was happening. Only a few minutes ago he was walking toward certain death, and suddenly he was free. Or was he? Christiaan had nowhere to go. He didn't know where these people were headed, or where they were from. If anyone started asking him questions, he would have no answers. And how long would they need to march? His stomach grumbled, making him aware of his hunger. He had nothing to eat or drink and was horribly ill-prepared for the long march these people surely had ahead of them. He was already feeling winded.

The road narrowed and the group slowed down as they passed a row of houses on either side. The push of people forced him to the side of the road, and he was surprised to see the door to one of the houses ajar. He stopped and leaned against it. It gave way, and Christiaan quickly slipped inside, closing the door, shutting out the sound of hundreds of feet shuffling by. Having been used to constant noise around him, day and night, in Mauthausen, the silence of the house was deafening. Christiaan stood near the door for a few seconds, taking in this odd sensation.

The room was paneled from the floor to the ceiling in cedar. Large beams dominated the space, while a wooden counter mounted on strong legs was the proud centerpiece of the kitchen. The house looked very homey, and Christiaan cautiously took a few more steps inside. He worried about how he would be received by the people living here. From what he'd seen in the village on arrival in Mauthausen, the local population appeared—at best—indifferent to the plight of the prisoners. However, when the Russian prisoners escaped in February, the locals had been zealous in their attempts to hunt down the escapees. Christiaan had seen the state in which some of the bodies of the Russians who had fallen into the hands of the farmers had been returned. He shivered at the thought of the occupants in this house doing the same to him. Despite his fears, he continued toward the open door leading into the back garden. He stepped outside to find an elderly woman hanging laundry out to dry. She let out a shriek as she saw him, dropping the garment on the grass.

Christiaan quickly held up his hands. "I'm sorry, I didn't mean to scare you," he said in German. "I was lost outside, and your door was open. I'm sorry. I mean you no harm."

The woman put a hand on her chest and exhaled loudly before picking up the garment and securing it on the washing line. Then she turned to Christiaan. "You look hungry. Do you want something to eat?"

Christiaan was stunned. "I would like that very much, thank you."

The woman nodded and slowly approached. Her eyes ran over his body, and Christiaan checked his clothes. His raincoat had slipped open, revealing his uniform. He looked back at the woman, who pretended not to notice. "Come in, I'll fix you something nice." She disappeared inside and Christiaan did as he was told.

Fifteen minutes later he had wolfed down a large plate of cheese and noodles. It was the best meal he'd had in over a year, and his stomach almost hurt. She handed him a glass of cold milk and he gulped it down in one go. The woman gave him a modest smile and refilled his glass.

"You can stay in the garden for a few minutes, but then you need to go, okay?" Her voice was stern, and Christiaan got the point. Despite her kindness in feeding him, she had noticed his uniform, which put her in more danger with every minute he spent inside the house.

"Thank you so much." Christiaan got up and stepped into the garden. The sun was still high in the sky, and he took off his shoes, the soft grass caressing his feet. He slipped the raincoat off and closed his eyes as he eased his way down into the grass. The earthy aroma of the soil and the warm rays of the sun relaxed him. With his stomach full, he forgot about his worries for a few moments as he took in deep breaths.

He was interrupted by the soft but urgent sound of the woman clearing her throat. He opened his eyes to find her standing next to him.

"You must leave." She sounded apprehensive, slightly nervous, her eyes resting on his exposed prisoner identification a little longer than she probably intended.

He sat up. "I will leave right away. Thank you so much for the meal."

The woman grunted something before heading to the shed next to her home. A light breeze made the grass move, tickling the soles of his feet. He enjoyed the sensation for another minute before the sun disappeared behind a small cloud. As he got up, an uncomfortable feeling took hold of him. Someone was watching him. He slowly turned around and his heart dropped. Standing by the back door were two young SS troopers.

CHAPTER THIRTY-NINE

The registration took more than half the afternoon. After entering through the imposing gates, Nora and the other arrivals from Ravensbrück were first kept waiting in the middle of a broad street. It was flanked by barracks on both sides, and guards came and went between the buildings while ignoring the new prisoners. Nora worried a few times that she might faint, but she managed to stay on her feet. She had no doubt the penalty for collapsing within the camp was the same as she'd seen on the walk up.

When they were finally called, they were forced down narrow stairs and subjected to an ice-cold shower. Even though the guards' purpose was obviously to humiliate and torture them, the cold water had the opposite effect on her. She opened her mouth and drank greedily, quenching a thirst that had tormented her from the moment they boarded the train in Ravensbrück. She hardly felt the cold water on her body, and when it stopped flowing, she felt reborn. The same couldn't be said of Sophie, who stood hunched over in a corner, her teeth chattering so hard Nora could almost hear it from across the room. She guided her friend back to the changing room, where she helped her dress in her new prisoners' uniform. The ragged clothes gave off a pungent odor, and it was clear they hadn't been washed after their previous owners were relieved of them. A shiver ran down Nora's back, realizing there was only one reason prisoners wouldn't require their clothing anymore.

After their shower, things didn't move along much quicker. They queued outside, where three clerks oversaw collecting their details. It took an eternity before a clerk pointed Nora toward a large group waiting next to the gate. "You're in the Sanitätslager. Good luck." He spoke without emotion, but Nora could see pity in the man's eyes. His facial features were sharp and angular, with visible cheekbones that were almost painfully jutting through his pale skin. Nora wondered how long he'd been in the camp, but she didn't get a chance to speak more, as a guard nudged her away from the table, making room for the next prisoner in line.

Nora walked toward the group while keeping an eye on Sophie, who was a few spots behind her in the queue. When Sophie was directed to the same group, a wave of relief washed over her. Sophie struggled toward her, her feet dragging. Nora stepped in her direction and took her hand.

"Come, stay with me. We'll make it together." Sophie's hands felt cold and Nora frowned. The temperature was comfortable, especially with the sunshine warming them from the cloudless sky. *Sophie's getting sick.* She placed the back of her hand on Sophie's forehead. She was burning up. *I need to get her to a bed soon.* Nora looked around, spotting a young guard loitering near the gate, looking bored. She considered her chances. Would the man help her, or would asking for help mean instant death for Sophie? She looked back at her friend, whose normally vibrant eyes looked hollow, beads of sweat forming on her forehead. *I have to do something, or she'll be dead anyway.* Frustration boiled up inside her and she took a step from the group. She was a few paces from the guard when someone gently took her arm. Nora's first instinct was to pull it free, but the grip was light yet forceful enough that she turned to see who it was.

She was surprised to look into the face of the clerk who'd processed her earlier.

"Don't expect any kindness from them." He spoke calmly as he gently pulled her back toward the group.

"You don't understand," Nora said, her frustration mounting. "My friend will die if she doesn't get any help."

The man looked at her stoically, but his eyes betrayed sadness. "You won't get any help from the guards. He'll shoot your friend on the spot if she's lucky. More likely, she'll be dragged to the crematorium over there." He pointed to a building halfway down the main road. "And she'll be beaten to death before her body is burned. They don't like to waste bullets."

Nora glanced at the tall building with its barred windows, Sophie beside her, and then at the guard at the entrance gate. He was talking and laughing with one of his colleagues. Nora realized the clerk was right. Was she mad? She knew better than to put her trust in a concentration camp guard. Abashed, she turned back to the man, shaking her head.

"I don't know what I was thinking. I'm just so tired from our journey, and my friend has a raging fever. I got desperate."

"It's understandable. We've all been there. This is a place without hope, but you can't trust anyone, least of all the guards," the man said in a soft voice. He had released his grip on Nora's arm, and his own arms hung by his sides.

Nora looked up at him. "You didn't have to intervene. Why did you?"

"I was just in the right place at the right time, I suppose." His mouth twisted into a sad smile. "No sense in you throwing your friend's life away like that. Or your own, for that matter. First rule of Mauthausen: don't speak unless spoken to."

"It was like that in Ravensbrück as well." Nora felt herself shrink even more. She had almost gotten herself killed within hours of arriving.

"Don't blame yourself too much. That trip must've taken a few days, and the journey from the train station is grueling." The man spoke sympathetically. "When you arrive at the Sanitätslager, you'll need to be patient. The place will be overcrowded, and you might not be able to sleep in a bunk for the first night." A shadow passed over his face. "The conditions there are among the worst in Mauthausen, and you'll be with many diseased prisoners."

"But it's the infirmary, isn't it?"

"Only in name, I'm afraid. Ever since Mauthausen became the destination for prisoners evacuated from the camps farther east, the SS have struggled to accommodate the new arrivals. The infirmary camp is just another place where people are crammed into barracks, whether they are healthy, sick, or close to death. Be careful there and keep a good eye on who's bunking around you. If you suspect they're sick, it's better to sleep on the floor, far away from them."

Nora was horrified by the man's words, but she appreciated the warning. "What about my friend? Is there anything I can do for her?"

"If it really is just a fever, try to keep her in her bunk. As I said, the sick used to be taken to the infirmary, but now the sick are just kept with the healthy prisoners. If you can convince your block elder she's sick, she'll be exempt from work, for now. Make sure she has something to drink. Water is rare everywhere, and there is no medication for the prisoners. I'm sorry."

A shrill whistle near the gate demanded the attention of the prisoners gathered.

"Good luck. I'll pray for you and your friend to beat the odds of this place." The clerk slipped away while one of the guards started yelling commands. A few minutes later, they were once again marching through the camp's gates, back in the direction they came from. The infirmary camp appeared below to her right, and she looked at the hive of activity within its barbed-wire enclosure. She was unable to make out individual faces in the sea of prisoners idling around the barracks and barbed wire. Sophie let out a tired moan, and Nora encouraged her friend on. "We're almost there. Keep your chin up, Sofe."

Nora felt the tears welling in her eyes at the thought of ending up alone in this monstrous camp. The words of the clerk echoed in her mind. *I can't lose Sofe.*

As she followed the sloping path, the faces of the people in the camp became clearer. They were pale, ghostlike, their cheeks sunken and eyes bulging from their sockets from chronic hunger. Men stood bare chested, with ribs protruding, as if they had too little skin to stretch over their bones. Women carried children on their bony hips with blank expressions on their faces and hollow eyes that did not register any emotion. Nora's heart ached for these people, yet she realized that the same thing was about to happen to her. She was about to become one of them.

CHAPTER FORTY

The most terrifying thing was the silence. The SS troopers had told Christiaan to follow them from the garden. When he didn't move quickly enough, they manhandled him outside into the now deserted street. Christiaan wondered whether he would've been better off staying with the masses of refugees. He sighed; it was too late to consider that now.

He had been surprised when the troopers made for the direction the refugees had gone. Were they not taking him back to Mauthausen? Knowing better than to open his mouth, he had followed them meekly. The guards had only exchanged a few quick words with each other, and they spoke in a dialect Christiaan couldn't make out.

From that point onward, there had been only one thought going through Christiaan's mind: When would they kill him? He was obviously an escaped prisoner, and there was only one penalty for his crime. Were the men simply looking for a quiet place to end his life? They didn't need to. Nobody would bat an eye at two SS troopers executing an escaped prisoner. It wouldn't have been the first time.

After about fifteen minutes, they entered a settlement, the

houses painted in yellow, green, and pink, much like those he'd seen on his arrival in Mauthausen.

The sun was still out, and people sat around on benches on what appeared to be the town's main square. Christiaan immediately felt out of place in his prisoners' uniform. An imposing belfry rose in the middle of the square, and a couple of children raced around the square, crowing in delight as they tried to catch each other. Christiaan couldn't help but smile at the scene, despite his situation. He caught disapproving looks from two well-dressed gentlemen sitting on a wooden bench.

The troopers headed for an imposing building in the northeast corner of the square. Its large sign indicated this belonged to the *Gendarmerie*. This was the paramilitary organization in charge of keeping public order and safety. Christiaan had seen them around the camp a few times. They had taken over the role of the police after Austria joined the Third Reich. He sighed as he followed the troopers inside; there would be another lengthy interrogation before they'd return him to Mauthausen.

They stepped inside a well-lit room, albeit smaller than Christiaan had expected. A well-built man wearing the green uniform of the *Ordungspolizei* stood from behind his desk and saluted the troopers. They returned the gesture, and one of the men spoke.

"We found this prisoner in the back of someone's garden just outside town. He couldn't explain why he was there."

The *gendarme* sat back down, eyeing the men with interest, but saying nothing. The atmosphere in the room felt off, and Christiaan noticed the troopers glancing nervously at one another. *They don't know what to do next.*

"Was he hiding?" The man drummed his fingers on the desk, shooting a quick look at Christiaan before returning his focus to the troopers. The one who'd presented Christiaan shook his head.

"Not really. He lay in the grass. We were alerted to his presence by the neighbors. They thought it odd to have a man in prisoner clothing in the next-door garden."

"Hmm. Did you report the address where you found him to anyone else?"

"No, sir. We thought it best to come straight to you."

The gendarme cracked a smile. "You thought correctly." He stood and waved at the door. "I'll handle this."

The troopers looked confused. "Sir? Don't you want us to take him back to the camp?"

"Not right now. I'll call for you when you're needed. I'll handle the prisoner." The man's voice was firm, as if giving an order.

The troopers hesitated for another second, then saluted and exited. The gendarme focused on Christiaan's prisoner badge.

"I see you're German, so I'm sure you understood all of that." The man spoke in a calm voice that felt almost alien to Christiaan. For the past nine months, any person in a position of authority had either yelled, threatened, or used a combination of both when interacting with him. The man opposite him looked relaxed—curious, even—as he leaned forward in his chair, hands on the desk.

"I did, sir."

He waved at one of the chairs. "Why don't you take a seat? I'm curious to hear how you ended up in the garden of a house in Enns. And before you answer, understand I'm not a member of the SS. I don't have a lot of patience for those boys that brought you in. You were smart not to tell them anything."

Christiaan sat and considered his response. It was clear as day that he was an escaped prisoner from Mauthausen. There was no reason to lie to this man; the worst he could do was send him back to the camp, where he would surely be made an example of at roll call. What worried Christiaan was his identity theft. His German was good enough to pass casual inspection, and he'd managed to do so in the camp, but he wasn't sure if he could tell the entire story without tripping over some words. *I might as well tell him the truth.* He took a deep breath.

"The first thing I should tell you is that I'm not really German." He spoke the words, holding his breath as he gauged the official's reaction. The man's face remained impassive for a few seconds, then spread into a smile.

"I know. I could tell from the first words you uttered. I was just curious to see if you would tell me." Christiaan breathed a sigh of relief as the man continued. "Look. Let me make myself very clear. I'm not the SS. I know what's going on in that camp, and it disgusts me." The man caught Christiaan's shock and smiled again. "I don't think you'll share my views with anyone. And even if you did, they'd never believe your word over mine. But that's not the point. I want you to speak freely. Tell me what happened. How did you escape Mauthausen? Because that's what you did, wasn't it?"

Christiaan could only nod, momentarily stunned by the man's candid words. Was he sincere, or was this a trick? He looked at the man again and decided it wasn't a trap. Even if it was, it didn't matter. He would end up back in Mauthausen either way.

"Okay, I'll tell you. This morning, I was assigned to a transport bound for KZ Gunskirchen. We were to walk, accompanied by an escort of SS guards." Christiaan proceeded to tell the man what had happened, leaving out none of the details. It felt good to share his story, and he saw admiration in the eyes of the gendarme when he told him of how he'd gone along with the stream of refugees.

"And none of the Wehrmacht soldiers noticed you?"

"There were hundreds of people clamoring to make it north. The soldiers were just part of the masses of people trying to make it out. They seemed as tired and stressed as any of the refugees."

The gendarme looked thoughtful. "They're getting pushed back on all sides. The war won't last much longer." Christiaan felt a surge of hope at the words. It was replaced by an intense sadness at the realization that he was unlikely to witness the liberation.

"And what happened next? How did you end up in that back garden?"

Christiaan continued his story, finishing with his escort to the gendarmerie. "I was certain those troopers were going to shoot me somewhere along the way, and I couldn't believe it when you dismissed them."

The man leaned back in his chair and nodded. "That's quite a story, young man. In a way, I'm sorry you got caught, although I think you were fortunate to be brought to me. Many people in this region would've reacted quite differently to finding an escaped prisoner in their home. It could've ended far worse."

Christiaan didn't say anything, bowing his head instead. He knew the officer only had one option, and that was to return him to Mauthausen. The man stood abruptly and walked to Christiaan's side of the desk.

"Come with me. It's already quite late, and I'm not taking you back to the camp in the darkness. Wouldn't want those guards in the watchtowers to mistake me for something I'm not. You'll stay here tonight. I have cells that I never use. Come."

Christiaan could hardly believe his ears. He wasn't returning to the camp today? He followed the man down a narrow corridor, where he was directed into the first cell. It was cramped, but Christiaan didn't care. There was a bunk with a blanket and a flat pillow. He stepped inside and turned to the gendarme. "Thank you."

"I'm hardly doing you a favor. I'll be back in a bit; let me get you some water and bread. You must be hungry." He closed and locked the door. Christiaan sat on the bunk while the gendarme's footsteps receded. He ran his fingers over the rough fabric of the blanket. It was by no means luxurious, but Christiaan didn't complain. He had a cell of his own, a little bit of privacy, for the first time in a year and a half. Although he was only here for a night, it meant he would have the opportunity to get some rest, even if he was to die in the next few days. He closed his eyes and drank in the silence.

It gave him a moment to reflect. He thought of his promise to Lisa and cursed his luck. It was clear the war would soon be over. Everyone in the camp knew it, as did the soldiers fleeing the front that afternoon, and the gendarme had outright said so. Yet, when

Christiaan returned to the camp tomorrow, he knew his life was forfeit.

The thought of never again setting eyes on Lisa filled him with grief. Throughout his journey from London, he'd faced many moments of peril: the Gestapo's interrogations in Amsterdam, the endless torment at the Rawicz prison, and his near-death experiences on the Stairs of Death in the quarry. But this felt like the worst blow; to survive so much only for hope to be dashed at the very end.

There was a grating sound at the door. The lock clicked an instant later, the door opening to reveal the gendarme carrying a tall pitcher of water. Christiaan was shocked at what was in his other hand. The sweet, tangy smell from the full plate of scrambled eggs wafted in, making his mouth water. The gendarme set it down on a small table in the corner of the cell. "Eat up. I know they don't feed you anything up there. Regain some strength."

Christiaan approached the steaming plate as the gendarme left and closed the door behind him. Carefully picking up his fork, he took a bite of the warm, fluffy eggs. The taste was overwhelming, and a tear rolled down his cheek. He devoured the plate within minutes and lay down on his bunk. For the first time in over a year, Christiaan Brouwer went to bed with a full stomach.

He was awoken the next morning by the gendarme. The man put a plate of fresh bread, a boiled egg, and a hunk of cheese on the small table. There was even a large portion of real butter, and Christiaan couldn't believe it. The man let him finish his breakfast in peace before returning half an hour later.

"The SS are here to bring you back to the camp," he stated solemnly. "I hope you managed to rest up last night."

Christiaan stood and held out his hand. "You've shown me kindness I haven't experienced in almost two years. Whatever happens next, I thank you."

The man shook his hand, a slightly uncomfortable look on his face. "I only did what I'd hope someone would do if I were in your shoes." He stepped out of the cell and waited for Christiaan to follow.

The same troopers stood waiting in the entrance area. Christiaan felt a stab of fear at the thought of what they would do to him on the way back. It was a long walk, and they could yet decide to kill him on the way. Nobody would know or care.

"I'm handing the prisoner back to you for safe transfer to Mauthausen," the gendarme said in a heavy voice, handing a piece of paper to one of the men. "I'll be checking with the camp administration to make sure he arrived alive and in one piece. Is that clear?" He raised his voice at the last words.

The troopers saluted. "Yes, sir."

He returned the salute, then waved them off. "Very well."

The SS men turned toward the door, and Christiaan gave the man a final, grateful look before stepping out into the deserted square.

"What are you waiting for?" one of the troopers barked at him, a snarl on his face. "We've got quite a hike ahead of us, thanks to you."

Resigned, Christiaan fell in line between the troopers. Considering what awaited him back in the camp, he wondered whether it would be better to have it done with on the way up. A bullet in the back of the neck would be a swift, painless death. He instantly felt disgusted by his thought. *I'm no coward. I'll take whatever punishment awaits me.*

———

Mauthausen's towering walls rose up two hours later. Christiaan was sweating, but the food and night's rest had invigorated him, and he hadn't slowed the well-trained troopers down too much.

They led the way to the main gate, where Christiaan spotted four guards on duty. A knot formed in his stomach, and he felt nauseous as they reached the stern-looking men.

"Returning this prisoner from Enns," one of his escorts reported, handing a piece of paper to the most senior guard. The man scanned the words on the paper bearing the official seal of the gendarmerie and looked at Christiaan, his eyes going to his prisoner identification number.

"Very well."

Christiaan felt his throat go dry. Surely the guard would now send him to the penal block. He'd never been inside the building, but he'd heard the stories of the torturous activities in the basement. Would his body end up strung up in front of the assembled prisoners at roll call? He swallowed hard as he waited for the guard to pass the verdict.

"You're assigned to your old block, prisoner. I doubt your old bunk is still available, but I'm sure you'll manage." The guard flicked his wrist in the direction of the main thoroughfare and turned away.

Christiaan couldn't believe it, and judging from their perplexed faces, nor could the troopers standing on either side of him. He decided not to push his luck and quickly entered the camp, all the while expecting the guards to realize their mistake and call him back.

When he passed the administration block and turned left toward his block, he finally released the breath he didn't realize he was holding. Whatever strings the gendarme had pulled, they appeared to have saved his life. Now he needed to survive long enough to witness the downfall of his tormentors.

CHAPTER FORTY-ONE

L isa lay tossing and turning in her sleeping bag, waiting for sleep to take her. Most of the soldiers around her snored deeply, and she envied their ability to catch some rest at any moment. She was tired, but her mind had other plans, constantly tormenting her. As on many nights, the events of the day Steve died in the German ambush replayed in her mind. Reinforcements arrived half an hour after Lisa's group had made it to safety. The soldiers had returned to the village, finding the Germans had fled. They found Steve's body near the window of one of the buildings, his cold fingers still clutching the gun. He'd held his position until the very end, ensuring the others could escape.

The squad joined the assault on the Westwall the next day, and a week later, the Third Army succeeded in smashing through the German fortifications. Their advance across central Germany was swift as they traversed the flat, open countryside. On the way, they encountered some resistance in the towns and cities they passed, but the combination of tanks, air support, and well-drilled infantry divisions meant they made good progress.

Patton had ordered his army to split up as he envisioned entrapping the German forces in a pincer movement, surrounding them on three sides before closing the trap. As a result, Lisa's 65th Infantry Division and the Sixth Armored Division had arrived in a town called Struth two days ago. Here, they awaited further instructions. Lisa and the two squads she'd been traveling with since they left Saarlouis four weeks ago had found shelter in a number of farmhouses and barns on the west side of town. She felt safe with the men, and she proved her value many times when they needed to interact with the local population, always on hand to provide translations in either German or French. Still, the loss of Steve weighed heavily on her heart.

She turned to her side, hoping it would help her catch a few hours of sleep. Then she heard something outside and opened her eyes. It sounded like the puttering of engines in the distance. The mechanics had worked on the tanks for most of the day, but they had stopped when darkness fell. Lisa frowned; it was highly unlikely any of them would be tweaking the engines in the middle of the night. She sat up and listened closely. Those were unmistakably engines, the sound increasing.

Things suddenly moved very quickly. There was an urgent shout from outside, and Lisa knew what was happening even before the not-so-distant thunder of a cannon. Less than a second later, a nearby explosion shook the windows of the farmhouse. The men around her rose almost as one, instantly awake and alert.

"We're under attack!" Lisa recognized the voice of Andrews, one of the two squad leaders. "Prepare to move out. To the living room!"

The men sprang into action, grabbing their rifles and machine guns. Lisa did the same, grabbing her first-aid bag. They all slept in their uniforms, so it took less than a minute to assemble in the farmhouse's spacious living room. She stood in the back while Andrews issued orders. The cannon fire outside increased in intensity, and it was obvious what was happening.

"The krauts are attacking the Sixth's motor pool. We're closest, so we'll need to defend it with everything we've got until reinforcements arrive from across town." His gaze went to three men standing to the side of the room. "Smith, you know what you must do. Hit those Panzers with everything you've got. How many mortar shells do you have?"

"About twenty, sir. Should be enough to cause some mayhem until the bazookas from across town arrive."

Andrews looked doubtful. "It'll have to do. Make sure you find a sheltered position."

He then pointed at two men carrying a large machine gun. "I want you to set up on the western flank, north from the barn, and take out any infantry you see. Provide cover for the mortar squad. Fire at anything that moves." The men nodded eagerly. "The rest of us will split up to provide cover around the mortar and machine gun. I want uninterrupted mortars hitting those bastards." He looked around and his eyes met Lisa's. "You'll stay with me, Abrahams. Move out!"

———

Lisa's heart was pounding in her throat as she followed Andrews and the other men outside. Smoke filled the air, and it sounded like the German assault was gaining traction, the cannon fire sounding closer and more frequent.

"Lewis, take position over there," Andrews yelled at the man carrying the mortar, pointing at a low wall that was once part of a house. "They won't be able to make you out right away." The soldier nodded and made a beeline for the wall, two squad members following him.

The rest of the soldiers turned the corner, and Lisa gasped at the fires illuminating the area where the tanks of the Sixth Armored Division were parked. The Germans had hit three tanks, and the area was bright as day. She could make out the shapes of the German Panzers in the distance, shrouded in the darkness of the night. Another explosion sounded as one of the German cannons spewed fire. Lisa instinctively hit the ground, as did the men around her. The shell overshot its target, instead hitting a small house behind the motor pool. One of the house's walls was completely blown away, and the roof collapsed with a loud groan. Lisa prayed there were no people inside.

Andrews rose again, barking instructions. Four soldiers headed toward the mortar squad, while the rest fanned out around the machine gun. He positioned himself between the squads, and Lisa remained by his side, watching. This was why she'd volunteered to join the ground troops, wasn't it? She wanted to be involved in the liberation. Another shell missed its target, exploding harmlessly in the street, cobblestones flying everywhere. Lisa's hands were shaking, but she kept her eyes on what was happening around her. *They might need me.* She felt for the first-aid bag. It was still there.

The German tanks kept moving and would soon reach the motor pool, where the parked tanks were. Lisa heard a clonking to her right and moments later, a mortar shell hit about three meters ahead of the approaching forces. She clenched her hands into fists: not bad for their first try, even if they didn't hit anything.

The response was instant. The German tanks sped up and fanned out, engines roaring, their drivers no longer concerned about stealth. Two of the cannons spewed fire, and an instant later a truck in the motor pool was lifted from the ground, exploding in a ball of fire and metal. The heat from the explosion scorched Lisa's face, and she closed her eyes. Andrews cursed next to her.

Then one of the Panzers in the front lit up as a mortar shell found its mark. It crunched to a halt, momentarily blocking the path of the tanks behind it. A few seconds later, another Panzer was hit— engulfing its front in flames—but continued rolling forward. Lisa looked to Andrews, whose face was lined with concentration. His eyes glinted in the hazy light of the fires, and she thought she spotted a hint of worry.

The machine gun to their left sprang into life, and Lisa followed the line of tracer rounds flying in the German forces' direction. Cries of anguish filled the air as German soldiers hit the ground between the tanks. *They must've spotted the mortar squad.* All the while, the mortar shells kept raining down, and they were indeed, as Smith had predicted, wreaking havoc and mayhem between the German lines. Despite that, Lisa could see they were rapidly burning through their supply and had only taken out three Panzers.

Machine guns mounted in the fronts of the German tanks returned fire in the direction of the American machine gun position, and the Americans momentarily halted fire. The German infantry seized the opportunity and poured forward, making alarmingly quick progress toward the American positions. Andrews didn't have to tell the well-trained soldiers spread out between the mortar and machine gun positions what to do. They waited for the German soldiers to advance before opening fire from close range. Many German soldiers fell, but more emerged from the darkness.

"We won't be able to stop them all," Andrews said, more to himself than Lisa. Another mortar shell found its mark, incapacitating a tank in the middle of the column. It wouldn't be enough, though, as the stream of German tanks and soldiers continued. "We'll need to pull back soon, or we'll be annihilated," he offered in a pained voice. The Germans would be able to destroy the entire motor pool of the Sixth Armored, severely crippling the Third Army.

The German soldiers returned fire, and a bone-chilling cry nearby pierced the night. She turned her head and saw one of the American soldiers writhing in pain. He was only twenty meters away from her, but it might as well have been two hundred. The Germans advanced quickly, and bullets flew in all directions. Much to Lisa's horror, the rhythmic clonking sound of the mortar shells being released from the tube had ceased. The German tank drivers must've noticed as well, for they pressed forward with renewed optimism. She looked at the soldier, who was shaking and crying. *I have to help him! It's why I'm here.*

"Sir, permission to assist over there."

Even before she'd finished speaking, Andrews nodded. "Stay low, there are so many of them! And keep your ears open. We'll need to retreat soon."

Lisa took a deep breath and grabbed her first-aid bag. Then she bolted, keeping her eyes on the downed soldier. No matter what happened, she was going to reach him, and help him as best she could. She covered the first five meters without drawing any attention. Then she heard the bullets impacting the ground behind her. They were dull thuds as they hit the thick clay soil. Lisa pushed her legs harder, her muscles aching at the effort. More bullets zipped by, and she was certain one would strike her and end everything. Her heart was throbbing in her head, but she was so close she could almost touch the soldier. In a massive effort, she jumped and rolled the last few meters, landing next to him. He greeted her with admiration, and winced.

"Where were you hit?" Lisa shouted, opening her bag.

"Leg. Knee. Hurts like hell." He pointed at his blood-soaked pants. Lisa didn't hesitate but took a pair of scissors and cut the fabric, revealing a shattered knee. She swallowed hard and did her best to numb the pain. "How does it look?" the soldier asked, his eyes now filled with fear.

"I'm going to give you a shot of morphine," Lisa said, already removing the plastic cover from the syrette. "This will hurt at first, but it gets better real fast. You ready?" She didn't wait for the soldier to respond as she jammed the needle into the soft tissue just above the man's knee. His upper body jerked rigid as he howled. "Hang tight, it will kick in soon!" Lisa yelled, feeling his anguish. Ten seconds later, he relaxed, his head falling back on the soft earth.

The ground shook violently and Lisa covered her head as one of the Panzers struck a nearby building. Their position was getting worse. The Panzers were only a hundred meters from the motor pool. The German soldiers had fallen back, taking cover behind the tanks. With the threat of mortar shells gone, there was no need for them to break cover. It would be a matter of minutes. Lisa looked in the direction of Andrews, but she couldn't read his face. His eyes went between the German tanks and his own troops. *He's got to call the retreat, or we won't get a chance!*

Out of nowhere, a deafening whistle filled the air. Lisa closed her eyes and covered her ears as it screeched overhead. She braced for impact, waiting for the blow that would tear her to pieces. The ground shook and the force of the explosion hit her face, the heat scorching her eyebrows. Burned metal penetrated her nostrils, and she wrinkled her nose. She opened her eyes, and the most majestic sight greeted her. Two Panzers lay overturned in a crater, consumed by flames reaching ten meters into the sky. More shells whistled overhead, and Lisa realized they were coming from behind. They landed between the German lines, the explosions launching man and machine into the air.

To her right a familiar whooshing sound announced the arrival of their reinforcements. Lisa sighed with relief at the sight of more American soldiers launching bazooka rockets at the Panzers. The tide of the battle shifted dramatically within ten minutes. Under the onslaught of artillery fire, the German tank drivers scrambled to turn their tanks around, with only a few remaining out of the original thirty. Soldiers no longer cared about staying in formation and ran for cover from the aerial bombardment.

The assault on the motor pool was over by the time the sun started its ascent behind the trees to the east. Lisa rose from her position with the injured soldier, who had passed out after she'd administered an additional shot of morphine. She had bandaged his injured knee as best she could, having at least stopped the bleeding.

There was still gunfire in town, with several hardheaded German soldiers refusing to surrender, but their position near the motor pool was safe. She approached Andrews, who nodded at her.

"Well done, Abrahams. That took guts. You may well have saved his life."

She was exhausted but managed a thin smile. "Thank you, sir. I'm just glad to be alive myself. At one point, I didn't think we'd make it."

"Same. I was about to call the retreat when the artillery finally hit. Come, let's check on the others. From what I could see, nobody else got seriously injured, but you may need to bandage a few cuts here and there." He turned toward the farmhouse, a conspiratorial look on his face. "Either way, they'll be happy to see you. Don't tell them I've told you, but they've been referring to you as the squad's guardian angel."

"Are you serious?"

He shrugged and smiled. "You're truly one of us now, Abrahams."

CHAPTER FORTY-TWO

Nora stepped out of the crowded block, relieved to inhale fresh air. Looking up, she smiled at the clouds hanging overhead. After arriving in the Sanitätslager, she'd taken the clerk's warning to heart and had gone around a number of the blocks, observing the people in their bunks. Many of them looked more dead than alive, and Nora shuddered at the thought of joining them.

Nora wished she could have taken her time to look for a suitable place for Sophie to lie down and rest, but it hadn't been an option. Sophie's condition had deteriorated by the second as they entered the infirmary camp. Out of the blue, a woman around the same age as Nora approached them inquiring whether they needed shelter. Nora was initially wary; it was every woman for herself in Ravensbrück. However, she glanced at Sophie and recalled how, without any questions asked, she had welcomed Nora into her cell battered and bruised. Deciding that this woman deserved the same courtesy, Nora thanked her profusely.

The woman had guided them to one of the blocks in the back. When they entered, Nora was surprised to find it remarkably clean compared to the interiors of the earlier blocks. It was just as crowded, though, and at least a hundred pairs of eyes followed Nora and Sophie as they passed along a narrow walkway with bunks on either side. The women had dark rings around their eyes, but they looked mostly tired, rather than half-dead as she'd seen in the other blocks. They reached the back, and the woman pointed them toward the bottom bunk, where two other women looked up with glassy eyes. They were clearly also not well. A wooden bucket stood next to their bunk, and Nora wrinkled her nose.

"It's not much, but this is the best I can do," she said, gesturing for the women in the bunk to move over. "We try to keep this block as clean as we can, with the means we have." She helped lower Sophie next to the other two women. Sophie looked up at Nora, fear in her eyes. Nora stroked her friend's hair. Sophie moaned softly and reached for Nora's hand.

"Rest, Sofe. We won't have to go anywhere anytime soon. I'll be right here beside you."

Sophie relaxed and closed her eyes, the grip on Nora's hand easing gently as she drifted to sleep. Nora turned to the woman, who stood looking on. "Thank you for this. I don't know why you reached out to us out there, but I'm grateful. I don't really care if I don't have a bunk tonight, but Sophie, well, she really needs this."

The woman waved her hand in dismissal. "The only way we can survive this place is by sticking together." Her eyes drifted between the women in the bunks around them. "Almost all of us work in the quarry every day. When you work, you're given food at the end of the day. Those people aimlessly wandering around outside? Most of them can't or won't work, and they won't last long. You look strong enough to work—that's why I picked you. And you were looking after your friend, which makes me think you'll be an asset to this block." She held out her hand. "I'm Maria, and I'm the *Blockälteste*, the block elder. I'm in charge of this block, for as much as a prisoner can be."

Nora shook her hand and introduced herself. "Is there any way I can get water for my friend?"

"There are a few faucets in the front, which may or may not work depending on the time of day. When they do, you'll usually find everybody crowding around them." Maria looked troubled. "As you can tell, everybody is in their bunks, which means there's probably no water. But we normally keep a few buckets around the room. Have a look around. Meanwhile, I'm going to assign you to work in the quarry tomorrow. It's hard work, but if you keep your head down and avoid the attention of the guards and Kapos, you'll be fine. There will be food at the end of the day. It won't be much, but from what I've heard we only need to hold on a little while longer."

Nora's interest was piqued. "You really believe we'll be liberated soon?"

"The guards have become less strict, and I've seen more than a few of them disappear in the past weeks. They're not as zealous about controlling us when we're not working anymore, either. Some of the women even told me the guards have been handing them extra rations in exchange for a good word when the Russians come." She nodded encouragingly. "Hang in there, Nora. We might just survive this."

———

Two weeks passed, and Nora had gotten used to the routine of waking up early, reporting for roll call, then spending the day pushing heavy carts of granite chunks from one side of the quarry to the other. The work was exhausting, but she had kept her eyes open. She had been horrified when she first witnessed people tumbling down the stairs, and when she saw a man pushed off the top of the ridge. Others collapsed in the middle of the quarry, their broken bodies giving in to the constant backbreaking labor and abuse from the guards. But Maria had been right about one thing; the guards hardly ventured inside the infirmary camp. Once they were done working and were handed their paltry rations for the day, they were mostly left alone. It was unlike what she was used to from Ravensbrück, where the Kapos tormented them in their bunks.

"How are you feeling?" A familiar voice sounded behind her, and Nora turned to find Sophie there. Her friend had recovered remarkably well and had even joined the work detail to the quarry two days ago. Nora was beyond relieved when Sophie's fever broke a week earlier, even more so when her friend started eating her rations.

"Pleased to see we won't be working in the sun today," Nora said, looking up at the cloudy sky again. "It will make for a nice change."

"Hopefully it stays like this," Sophie said, her eyes shifting to the prisoners making their way toward roll call. "Let's go, we don't want to be late."

———

After roll call, Nora and Sophie found out they wouldn't spend their day in the quarry. Maria had volunteered them for a different job, and they were now escorted out of the camp, along with some thirty other prisoners, by half a dozen guards. Maria wasn't among them as she was needed back in the camp. When the block elder disclosed the job, Nora felt nauseous, but Maria had ensured her it would be less strenuous than their usual work in the dusty quarry. Less dangerous, too, as the quarry always carried the risk of a guard deciding it was their turn to climb the stairs. Despite Maria's assurances, Nora reluctantly followed the prisoners ahead of her as they cut through a meadow, soon leaving the camp behind.

The air was cool and there was still a bit of morning dew on the grass surrounding them. Nora's spirits lifted, despite the knowledge of the gruesome task ahead. Sophie walked next to her and looked remarkably fresh for the first time since leaving Ravensbrück. If she could beat a fever in these conditions, perhaps there was a chance of survival for them, after all?

They had walked for another half an hour when she spotted the trucks. They were parked in a clearing at the foot of a small forest that stretched beyond the hills in front of them. Nora swallowed hard as they neared, the drivers turning toward the group, shouting something at the guards escorting them.

Even before they reached the trucks, the smell overpowered all other senses. Nora choked and almost threw up the contents of her empty stomach. The other prisoners also struggled as they slowed down, some covering their faces with their hands. The smell increased in intensity as they stopped next to the trucks, and Nora focused on breathing through her mouth.

"Listen up. We've got quite a bit of work to get through today, so I don't want to see any of you slacking." A middle-aged guard with a thick accent addressed them, glaring as he did. There was no indication he was at all troubled by the penetrating smell that originated a few meters behind him. "Everybody will start digging, and then we'll fill the graves and cover them up." He pointed at the muddy ground behind him. "You should be able to get through this quite easily, and I expect we'll be finished before dusk. There will be extra rations if we get this done quickly."

Encouraged by the promise of extra food, the prisoners picked up shovels and started digging. Nora held her breath as she passed the trucks, but she couldn't resist looking up. Corpses of men, women, and children, old and young, were piled atop each other. The lifeless, hollow eyes of a woman of around her own age stared back at her in surprise, as if she didn't know what was about to happen just before a bullet ended her life. Nora averted her eyes and moved on quickly, feeling guilty about looking at the exposed bodies of the dead.

They dug the entire morning, only pausing for a quick water break. The group made steady progress under the watchful eyes of the guards. Maria had been right about the assignment: the guards were vigilant, but they also appeared slightly more relaxed. Amazingly, there were a few shouts of *encouragement*, there were no beatings. In the quarry, the first cart of corpses would be making its way up to the crematorium by now. No, Nora corrected herself, they must be collecting the bodies somewhere else. It was why they were here, digging a mass grave for the bodies in the backs of the trucks. *The ovens can't keep up anymore.* Spurred on by the promise of extra rations and determined not to end up like those poor souls in the trucks only a few meters away, Nora dug her spade deeper into the earth.

The howling of the air raid alarm in the distance made everybody pause. The guards turned to the most senior: the middle-aged man who'd instructed them earlier that morning. He looked around for a second, then pointed to the nearby woods.

"Take your spades and head for the cover of the woods, now!" he yelled at the prisoners before barking instructions at the other guards. "Move the trucks as close to the trees as possible. And make sure none of the prisoners disappear into the woods!"

A few minutes later the prisoners sat on the mossy ground of the small forest, the guards surrounding them. The air raid alarm continued howling, and Nora thought she heard the rumble of engines in the distance. A tingle of excitement shot up her spine. It was the first time the alarm appeared to be genuine. Surely whoever was looking down couldn't miss the massive camp? Her hopes about their possible liberation surged, and she had to suppress a smile. She glanced at Sophie and saw a flicker of hope in her friend's eyes. *She feels it, too.*

The sounds of the engines increased. Nora couldn't see anything through the thick canopy of leaves above her, but she prayed planes were flying overhead. Then she realized the clouds would obstruct any views of the camp. She forced herself to remain hopeful; if the planes were this deep into German territory, they would surely return.

"You've been making good progress this morning." The leading guard faced the group of prisoners. "When the all-clear from the air raid alarm sounds, we'll continue. I think we can start moving the bodies into the pit." More planes roared overhead, and Nora doubted they would return to their labors anytime soon. The guard reached for a large linen sack and placed it in front of the group. "Why don't you have your extra rations now? You'll have some extra energy to get the job done quicker once the planes have passed, no?" His voice was surprisingly gentle, and the prisoners looked at each other in confusion. Was this a trap?

The guard turned around and moved to the edge of the tree line, leaving the sack with the prisoners. The men in the front eyed it suspiciously, and one of the younger guards moved toward the sack, picking it up. Opening it, he took out a hunk of bread and held it out to a man in the front. "Come, eat. You're going to need your strength." The prisoner accepted the piece of bread hesitantly, but then took a bite. The guard moved on to the next prisoner, and soon they all had a large piece of bread. They were silent as they ate, and Nora scanned the faces of the guards, who looked on at the starved prisoners. There were no looks of malice, no hint of deception. It appeared the guards had simply decided to do something humane and allow them something extra when they really needed it. Nora took a large bite of the surprisingly fresh bread and chewed furiously.

When the all-clear sounded fifteen minutes later, Nora felt energized and ready to finish the job. Perhaps things really were about to change in Mauthausen?

———

Nora lined up for roll call the next morning, a chill in the air as the sun was hidden behind dark, threatening rain clouds. They were among the first groups to arrive, and they had to wait another fifteen minutes before all prisoners were in place. She kept her gaze on the ground in front of her as the guards walked by, counting the prisoners. Nora hoped they wouldn't find anything wrong this morning; she hoped to be at work before the rain came down. It was one thing working in the rain, but quite another to stand rigidly straight for roll call. As if on cue, the wind picked up, sending her shivering.

Her attention was drawn to the scaffolding in the front, where she recognized the figure of Hauptsturmführer Bachmayer reaching for the microphone. Her heart sank at the man's appearance. She'd seen him at roll call three times before, and he never brought good tidings.

"Prisoners. I'm pleased to announce we've finished the count in record time." The metallic distortion of his voice through the speakers did nothing to mask his obvious glee at his announcement. Nora frowned. Bachmayer wouldn't make an appearance to announce a successful roll call. Quite the contrary; he loved to show up when something went awry. An uncomfortable feeling built in the pit of Nora's stomach.

"Before I send you off to work this morning, I'd just like to draw your attention to something that happened yesterday. Even though this wasn't in the main camp, I still believe it's important you're all aware of this." He snapped his fingers in his customary matter, and two guards appeared. They had been waiting behind the scaffolding, and Nora gasped when they mounted the small platform. They escorted a third uniformed guard that Nora immediately recognized. It was the man who led their work detail the day prior. She held her breath as they forced him onto his knees and started to bind his hands and feet to a pole in the center of the scaffolding.

Bachmayer stepped down from the scaffolding and roamed the first row of prisoners. He quickly identified a young boy no older than ten and gestured for the youngster to follow him. The boy hesitated for a moment, but when Bachmayer gave him a thunderous glare, he shuffled after the SS man, who helped him up the scaffolding. *What madness is this?* The guards had finished securing their colleague to the pole and now stood next to the young boy, who looked terrified. Bachmayer returned to the microphone.

"Mauthausen is a place of rules. All of you who obey them have nothing to fear." His voice was pompous. "These rules are put into place for your safety. When prisoners break the rules, they must face the consequences. The same goes for guards. We expect them to behave according to the high values we set as camp leadership."

The area was deathly quiet as Bachmayer paused. A few prisoners shuffled on their feet. Bachmayer turned and pointed at the guard, even though most eyes were already glued to the sight of the man tied up on the platform.

"This man betrayed the trust placed in him by the führer during his duty yesterday. Instead of looking after his prisoners, he allowed them to roam freely among themselves in the woods during an air raid alarm." Bachmayer's tone was overly dramatic, and Nora couldn't believe what she was hearing. She glanced at Sophie, who barely managed to suppress her own surprise as well. "These prisoners could've been killed if they were spotted by the planes overhead!"

Nora studied Bachmayer. He looked flustered, his lips trembling, sending spittle flying as he spoke. He shook a fist in the air. "Mistakes like these can't go unpunished!" He addressed the young boy in front of him. "You will carry out the punishment, which is death." The boy looked at him incredulously, seemingly not understanding what the Hauptsturmführer requested from him. Bachmayer took away all doubt as he unbuckled his pistol and handed it to the boy, careful to step behind him. "Shoot him." The guard tied up to the pole had closed his eyes, and Nora felt for him. The man's only crime had been to show compassion to the prisoners. She wondered which of the younger, ambitious guards had betrayed him.

The boy's hands were trembling as he lifted the gun. The other prisoners held their breath as they waited for the bang to end the twisted mockery of disciplinary action. Nora's eyes shot to Bachmayer's, and she saw a savage satisfaction written over his face. The boy closed his eyes, and Nora looked away.

"I can't do it." The small voice echoed across the roll call area.

Nora looked back to see the boy standing on the platform with his hands by his sides, loosely holding the gun. His shoulders were slumped as he looked down at the wooden base of the scaffolding.

Bachmayer responded instantly, grabbing the gun from the boy's hand. He pointed the gun at the boy, drawing a collective gasp from the prisoners. His eyes momentarily shot in the direction of the prisoners, and it was evident he was savoring the moment. "You will shoot him, or I will shoot him first, and you after!" There was no need for a microphone as his voice boomed through the yard. "Kill the man and save yourself!" Bachmayer held out the gun to the boy again, but the boy was frozen from fear.

"Sir, please allow me to shoot the man." A man stepped forward from the first row. "Please, don't kill my son." The desperation in the man's voice shattered Nora's soul into a million pieces.

Bachmayer's eyes lit up at the sight of the prisoner stepping out of the lineup. He waved the man toward him, up onto the scaffolding. "You're his father, then?" When the prisoner nodded, a sinister smile appeared on Bachmayer's face as he turned back to the boy, holding out the gun once more. "Last chance. Shoot the guard, or I will kill your father." He flicked his wrist and four guards appeared out of nowhere, grabbing the father before he could do anything. The man protested, but he was quickly moved to the side of the platform, where one of the guards tossed a rope over a beam running a few meters above the ground. He expertly tied a noose and secured it around the father's neck. The guards kept him close to the edge of the platform. A push to the right would see him struggle to his death on the rope.

"What's it going to be, kid? You and your father die, or you pull the trigger and carry out some justice?" Bachmayer's voice was like a serpent's, and it made Nora's skin crawl. The boy turned to his father, who looked back at him stoically, masking his fear as the noose tightened around his neck. The boy took a step closer to the condemned man on his knees. Slowly, he lifted the gun and pointed it at the guard's forehead. He mumbled something Nora couldn't hear, then closed his eyes. As Nora did the same, a loud bang reverberated around the roll call area.

———

Five minutes later, Nora walked from the roll call area, her body shaking. She marched alongside the other prisoners, past the corpse of the guard slumped against the pole. The bodies of the father and the young boy hung next to him, like laundry on a clothesline, swaying in the slight morning breeze. It had come as no surprise to anyone when Bachmayer hadn't kept his promise.

Nora had wanted to scream when the noose was placed around the boy's neck. Instead, she stood in silence, like everyone else, looking on while two more souls left this world at the end of a rope.

She passed through the gate, barely registering the faces of the prisoners preparing to head out. After what she witnessed this morning, the assignment in the quarry felt almost normal. At least she knew what to expect there. She felt a tug on her wrist.

"Are you all right?" Sophie looked at her with concern.

"I'm not sure I can witness more of that. That was such a senseless killing. And that boy could hardly have been older than ten." Her heart felt heavy.

"I know. But aren't they all?" Sophie looked at her with compassion. "Senseless, I mean. There are no principles in this place beyond making sure you lie low as much as possible. The moment that father stepped forward, you knew what was going to happen." Nora listened to her friend and found herself nodding. *Perhaps they are in a better place now. Can't be any worse.*

They passed through the SS camp and came to a fork in the road. One way led to the quarry, and the other to their barracks and the outside. A large group blocked their passage, and they stopped while their guards yelled at the other guards to keep their prisoners moving. The other group consisted of men, and Nora found herself studying them with interest. Most looked relatively strong, by Mauthausen's standards. Each carried a shovel, and some even pushed large wheelbarrows in the opposite directions from the quarry. Nora frowned; where were they headed, if not the quarry?

One of the guards farther down the road barked commands and the men started moving. Nora was watching as they slowly cleared the junction when someone caught her eye. There was something familiar about one of them. His head was shaved just like the others, but his gait forced her to look more carefully. She couldn't make out his face as two others blocked her view. Nora craned her neck and wished for the men to move. The group kept going, but then the two men slowed down, revealing his face.

The voices of the people around her faded into the background. She felt lightheaded as she struggled to process what she saw in front of her. *It can't be.* Nora blinked hard and rubbed her eyes. She was vaguely aware of someone calling her name, but it sounded muted, like she was underwater. The group of men was moving from sight, and Nora opened her mouth to scream, but no sound came out.

"Nora!"

The sounds rushed back to her, and she looked into the worried eyes of Sophie. "We need to move!" The rest of their group had walked on toward the quarry, and they stood alone. A guard was already heading their way, a scowl on his face.

Nora nodded and hurried down the road. She looked back to the other group one more time, but all she saw were the identical backs of the heads of men marching away from her.

As she caught up with the rest of her work detail, she questioned her sanity. *It can't be him. It's impossible.* Was her mind playing tricks on her? It was the only logical explanation. Yet, as she descended toward the quarry floor, she couldn't quite shake the feeling that it really had been Christiaan.

CHAPTER FORTY-THREE

Christiaan's day started a bit differently. He hadn't gone back to the administration's office after returning to Mauthausen two weeks earlier. The block elder was surprised to see him but set him up in a work detail digging trenches outside the camp. It was clear the SS were expecting an Allied assault, and Christiaan dutifully did as he was told. He couldn't wait for the Americans or Russians to arrive. Looking at the guards milling about the worksite, he doubted they would put up any sort of resistance against the well-trained Allied soldiers. *If they even stick around long enough to put up any fight.* Christiaan wouldn't be surprised to see them run well before the liberators arrived. The only thing that worried him was what they would do with the thousands of prisoners in the camp. They couldn't kill them all, could they?

This morning, however, the block elder announced none of them would be heading to work. Instead, they were to gather their belongings and prepare to leave the camp. The man was bombarded with questions, but all he could say was that they were scheduled to evacuate Mauthausen and move to a different camp. All would be revealed later, after roll call.

Christiaan wasn't really surprised. Groups of prisoners had been marched out of the camp every day since his return. He suspected they were sent to KZ Gunskirchen as well, or perhaps even farther west. Once again, he packed his meager belongings in a small sack and slung it over his shoulder. The memories of the last time he was picked to leave the camp came back, but he knew the chances of striking it lucky like last time were almost nonexistent. There was another problem, though, which made him worry about the trek.

When he set off from the camp two weeks ago, he was in relatively good shape. His job at the administration was manageable on Mauthausen's starvation rations. Digging trenches was a completely different matter; his body wasn't used to the strenuous effort suddenly required for twelve hours a day. The only reason he was still alive was that the guards weren't quite as observant as they should be, and it allowed him to take frequent breaks. Nevertheless, there was no escaping the toll the labor took on his body. He'd become a shell of the man he used to be, and he wasn't sure he'd be able to march the fifty kilometers to Gunskirchen. *If that's even where they're taking us.*

He stepped out of the block, where he found two guards and a clerk waiting. He didn't recognize the clerk, and the man checked off his number. The guards grunted at him to move to the area outside the gate and wait there. Another clerk handed him a hunk of bread and some margarine. Christiaan had to control himself not to finish it right there and then. The journey to wherever they were being taken would be long, and it would be best to ration the food. Despite himself, he took a quick bite, savoring the feeling of the bread in his mouth.

It was crowded near the gate, with hundreds of prisoners in the same state patiently awaiting instructions. Most of them stood, a number talking among themselves, and a few sat to the side of the road, silently nibbling at their bread. Christiaan spotted a few men from his work detail and joined them.

"Looks like we're finally getting out of here." The man who spoke was Jaroslav, a friendly Czech from Prague whom Christiaan had spent many days digging trenches with. They had rotated keeping watch for guards while the other took some much-needed rest. "Although things will most likely be worse where they're taking us."

"Worse than Mauthausen? You think that's possible?" Christiaan tried to keep a light tone.

"Well, they're certainly not moving us for our own benefit. I suppose they don't need us anymore now that the trenches are done."

"I guess so." Christiaan cast his glance to the eastern walls of the camp where they'd dug the trenches. "Those trenches won't do them much good if the current guards are supposed to defend the camp."

"Maybe they'll get the Wehrmacht in? They're probably retreating from the front."

Christiaan shook his head but didn't respond. He could still picture the defeated soldiers marching alongside the refugees. Those men weren't going to stop to defend an SS-run prison. He looked up at the guard towers looming overhead. If anyone was going to defend the camp, it would be the SS guards, perhaps assisted by some of the Waffen-SS. *It's not my problem anymore.*

A shrill whistle sounded down the road. A guard barked for the prisoners at the front to follow him. Slowly, a couple of hundred tired men got up and followed the guards' lackluster instructions. Christiaan and Jaroslav remained seated on the side of the road as they waited for guards to tell them what to do. To their surprise, they were left alone, along with another forty men near the gate. The large procession of prisoners disappeared around the corner.

"Did they forget about us?" Jaroslav looked around in surprise. "They must've seen us sitting here, no?"

Christiaan craned his neck to look up at the guards manning the towers atop the gate. They looked back stoically. He then peeked through the large gate, where he saw a group of guards chatting in the sun. "Why don't we just wait here and see what happens? I'm sure they'll realize their mistake soon enough."

With the sun beating down on them, Christiaan stretched out and took another bite of his bread, using a bit of margarine this time. He turned to his friend.

"Do you believe the Americans or Russians will get here in time?"

"Save us, you mean?" Jaroslav shrugged. "I've been hearing about my supposed rescue for over six months now. Just before I was put on transport from Auschwitz, I could hear the Russian artillery getting closer every day."

Christiaan understood. "This must feel similar, in a way?"

"A little. But you know what's different this time? I believe the reports about the Americans and Brits approaching from the west. That means we've got them coming from one side, and the Russians from the east. One of them is sure to reach us. I just hope we'll be alive to see it." Jaroslav's voice was strong, his eyes showing determination. "But once we're freed from the Nazis, what's next? My wife, my daughter, they were taken to Auschwitz. I have no doubt they were murdered there." A shadow passed over his face. "I'll be alone."

"But you'll be alive." Christiaan couldn't think of anything else to say. "You'll have beaten them."

"Really? I've lost everything dear to me. I don't even know if my house is still standing. Have I really won?" They were silent for a moment, before Jaroslav turned to him. "What about you? What will you do?"

His thoughts immediately went to Lisa and he couldn't help but smile. "The woman I love is safe in England." Then he thought of Nora, and a pang of worry gripped him before he dismissed it. "And the other woman I care for deeply has surely made it to Geneva." He put his hand on Jaroslav's shoulder. "We're going to make it through this, Jaro. We've come too far to give up now."

The corner of the Czech's lips edged up in a small smile and he embraced Christiaan. They stayed like that for a moment before they heard the echoing clomp of feet coming closer. When they looked up, eight guards stood in front of them. The tallest and most muscular one spoke to the group of prisoners.

"You've got three options: follow us on our journey to Gunskirchen, go back to the camp, or meet your end right here."

Christiaan and Jaroslav exchanged a look and got to their feet. All but three of the others did the same. Christiaan looked at the men on the ground. They had already devoured their bread, but it was obvious they were in no state to march to the bottom of the hill, let alone make it to Gunskirchen. The tall guard led the way and Christiaan fell in line. Even before they turned the corner there were three shots behind them. Christiaan didn't look back and kept his eyes firmly on the heels of the man in front of him. He clutched his piece of bread firmly and prayed this was the last time he would have to make the journey down the hill.

———

When the group reached the crossroads where Christiaan had made his break for freedom last time, the number of prisoners had diminished to just twenty. Men who had kept up with the march so far had stopped and eased themselves to the side of the road, unable to continue. The SS guards followed them, tasked with delivering the final blow. Christiaan noticed a few of the younger troopers struggling with their orders, some even trying to urge the prisoners back on their feet to no avail; their broken bodies had endured too much.

Any hopes of repeating his escape were dashed: the intersection was deserted. The group slowly continued as it started raining. A drizzle at first, but it quickly turned into a downpour. The troopers wore comfortable raincoats, but the prisoners in their ragged clothes were horribly unprepared. Christiaan was drenched within seconds, the cold seeping into his bones, draining the little energy he had left. A wind picked up, and the rain now came at them horizontally as they struggled through the open countryside.

Christiaan's teeth chattered, and it became harder to breathe. A pressure unknown to him was building inside his chest, and panic gripped him. He gritted his teeth and focused on putting one foot in front of another, like he had done so many times. A small patch of trees loomed up a few hundred meters ahead of them, promising some refuge from the elements. The pace of the group picked up, guards and prisoners alike eager to reach the trees.

Christiaan's breathing became shallower, and his feet dragged every few steps. The pressure increased to a sharp pain in his chest, and he was falling behind. Jaroslav walked a few paces ahead and turned around, giving him an encouraging glance. Christiaan put on a brave face.

"Keep going at your own pace, I'll follow."

"You sure?" There was worry on Jaroslav's face. "Do you need some help?"

Christiaan shook his head, biting on his lip to mask his pain. "No, I'll be right there."

The wind howled around them, the tree line almost within grasp. With an immense effort, Christiaan covered the final meters. The trees provided some cover, but the pain in his chest continued to build. He turned around to find only three other prisoners lagging behind. They were escorted by two guards who looked annoyed to be in the rear and the rain. The prisoners ahead of Christiaan moved forward slowly, and he was pleased to see Jaroslav keeping up.

A searing pain streaked through his chest and up into his head, leaving him momentarily blinded. Pain coursing through his body, he felt unsteady and lightheaded. He slowly lowered himself onto the cold, wet ground and squinted to catch a glimpse of the men ahead of him. He could no longer make out Jaroslav; there was no way to turn back without risking a bullet.

This was the end of the line. The guards in the rear would be here soon. Christiaan tried to push himself up, but his chest constrained his movements. His own body was betraying him. The sticky mud between his fingers felt good, and Christiaan bowed his head and closed his eyes. He had survived longer than any of the SOE agents. His comrades were murdered within a day of arriving in Mauthausen. The odds of survival were stacked against him from the moment he was captured. His eyes stung, and hot tears welled up. To have come so close to surviving within the walls of Mauthausen, only to fall a few kilometers from the camp was a bitter pill to swallow, no matter what he tried to tell himself.

The unmistakable sound of boots splashing and trudging through the sticky mud sounded behind him. Christiaan didn't move. Lisa's face flashed in his mind, her beautiful smile the only light in the darkness. His sole regret was that he would not be able to fulfill his promise of coming back to her. That and not being able to tell her how much he loved her one last time.

The footsteps stopped, and Christiaan felt a presence behind him. *Make it quick.* He dug his fingers into the mud.

Cold steel pressed against his neck, and a surge of adrenaline shot through his body. The pain in his chest cleared, his eyes bursting open in shock. The haze in his brain was gone, and Christiaan jumped to his feet. He turned around to find a trooper looking at him in surprise and annoyance. The exhaustion Christiaan had felt only moments ago had been replaced by a fiery will to survive. He wouldn't meet death on his knees. *If I am to die, it will be with my head held high.*

The trooper holstered his pistol and returned to the road, muttering at Christiaan to keep moving. Christiaan was fully alert to his surroundings. The touch of the pistol's barrel in the back of his neck had triggered an instinct to survive he didn't know he still possessed. He looked up the road, where the trooper who had almost ended his life moments earlier was now harrying another prisoner forward. Turning back, the two guards bringing up the rear had their backs to him, yelling at the stragglers to keep up.

Nobody was paying him any attention. Quickly glancing back and forth, he confirmed the guards had seemingly forgotten about his presence on the side of the road. Without another thought, he took a couple of giant leaps and launched himself into the bushes behind him.

His heart pounded in his ears as he waited for one of the guards to realize he'd disappeared. Rain came down hard, the rushing sound of water running through the trees' canopies muffling the voices of the two guards escorting the final prisoners. Christiaan could sense the impatience in their voices, but not catch the words. A few moments later, three loud bangs sounded. Their patience had run out.

Christiaan tried to crawl farther back. He was only a few meters from the road, and if either of the two guards would look carefully, they would spot him. He was determined to put as much distance between himself and the road as possible.

It took less than a minute for the guards to appear. Rushing to catch up with the rest of the procession, they didn't as much as glance in Christiaan's direction. Still, he didn't move a muscle. He remained flat on his stomach for at least half an hour, until he was certain no one was coming back for him.

It stopped raining, and he carefully climbed to his feet. He stayed deathly still and listened for voices, for any hint that someone was still lingering behind. When he was convinced there was no one on the road, he stepped out. The area was deserted. All that remained were the bodies of the three prisoners about thirty meters back. Unsure what to do next, he approached the corpses. These men didn't wear the camp uniform. The SS no longer bothered handing out uniforms to new arrivals from Hungary, as they hardly spent more than a few days in Mauthausen before being shipped off farther west. It made Christiaan acutely aware of his own outfit: the striped uniform of Mauthausen. That would not do. He quickly stripped the man closest to him in size, took off his own uniform and changed into the dead man's clothes. He briefly considered dressing the man in his uniform but decided against it. It would take too much time, and he needed to get off the road. He took his uniform and disappeared back into the relative safety of the bushes.

Where do I go now? The answer was simple. As far away from the road as possible. Christiaan ran into the forest for ten minutes, dumping his prisoner garments along the way. When he found a small clearing with a stream, he quenched his raging thirst and sat down. Exhaustion finally overcame him; he needed a rest. Christiaan crawled under the cover of a small bush and closed his eyes.

———

Christiaan awoke feeling oddly refreshed the next morning. The forest floor had been comfortable compared to the hard wooden bunks he'd slept on in the camp. His muscles still ached, and he shivered in his wet clothes. The thick coat he'd taken from one of the murdered prisoners had provided some warmth.

He sat up but froze in place when he heard voices. He strained his ears, making sure it wasn't just his mind playing tricks on him. No, they were definitely here, and they were getting closer. He couldn't make out the words, but the tone sounded peaceful and casual, as if they were enjoying a leisurely stroll. To his surprise, he noticed that the ground around him was trodden down and realized he had collapsed close to a walking path.

Run or hide? He dismissed the first option; they were already too close. They would certainly see him if he ran. And he had no idea who they were, or if they might be armed. There was only one thing to do, and that was to play dead. He lay down on his stomach and focused on the approaching voices. He slowed his breathing and prepared to hold his breath once they spotted him. It didn't take long.

"Oh my! Look at this man!" a woman shrieked in a high-pitched voice, and Christiaan nearly flinched. Feet shuffled closer, and he could feel their gaze on the back of his head. "Do you think he's dead?"

"He's not moving, is he? Certainly looks that way." The man's voice was deep and self-assured. He spoke with an authority that unnerved Christiaan. It reminded him of the guards in the camp.

"How do you think he ended up here? Doesn't look like he was well prepared for a stroll. Did he get lost?" The woman sounded concerned. The man's shoes almost touched his face as he circled Christiaan.

"Maybe it's one of the refugees that got lost along the way? There have been so many passing through. Perhaps this poor sod went for a toilet break and got lost?"

"Hmm. Seems a bit out of the way."

"Fine, I don't know where he came from, either. Let's move on. There's nothing we can do for him. We don't want any of the SS patrols to catch us with him. God knows where he came from. I don't want any trouble." The man sounded slightly irritated. Christiaan wished for them to move on. He was having trouble holding his breath.

"Well, okay, if you say so." There was hesitation in the woman's voice, but Christiaan felt relieved when he heard them moving on, their footsteps and voices fading. He breathed out but stayed on the ground for a few more minutes.

He sat up, his mind racing. Who were these people? Had he really convinced them he was dead? More importantly, were they going to come back with SS soldiers? *I can't stay here.* Christiaan stood and stumbled to the small stream, his legs a little shaky still from his night on the cold forest floor. He scooped water and drank his fill. The cold water refreshed him, and he turned to the path. One direction led back to the road, where no doubt SS soldiers would soon appear with more prisoners headed for Gunskirchen. He turned in the other direction and walked at a brisk pace. The air was humid, the thick morning dew combined with the previous day's rainfall giving off an earthy scent. The smell of trees and shrubbery was almost alien to Christiaan, having spent most of his time in the past year in prison cells, the dusty quarry, or the cramped indoors of the administration block. He breathed in the fresh air and vowed he wouldn't let the Nazis take him alive ever again. If he ran into any troopers now, he would fight them, no matter the consequences.

He continued for another ten minutes before he reached the end of the forest. Vast fields and rolling hills stretched out ahead. Colored houses dotted the landscape, a town to his right. His best chance at surviving until the Americans or Russians arrived was to try to link up with a stream of refugees. Surely he wouldn't be the only displaced person without any papers to his name? He took a deep breath and stepped out of the safety of the trees.

A few seconds later, he regretted his decision.

"Hey, isn't that the same man?"

Christiaan recognized the voice even before he turned. Standing on the edge of the forest only ten meters away was the couple from earlier, eyeing him with shocked faces.

CHAPTER FORTY-FOUR

The day's labor in the quarry finally ended and Nora secured the cart on the far side of the track. Together with the other women in her work detail she made her way to the guards waiting near the quarry's entrance. They quickly counted and confirmed all their charges were there and started the twenty-minute trek back to the infirmary camp. Nora spotted Sophie walking a few steps ahead and caught up with her. Even though Sophie had recovered well from the bout of illness she had on arrival, it was always a relief to see her on the way back. There were so many ways to die in the quarry. Anything could happen at the whim of a guard or Kapo.

"Can't wait to get back to the block. I'm absolutely spent." Nora said as she pulled alongside Sophie.

"Our Kapo beat four men to death for no reason at all. Said he didn't like the way they looked at him." Sophie's voice was trembling, her hands shaking.

"So sorry to hear that, Sofe. Sounds like you've got the rotten luck of having one that still seems to care." Nora grabbed her friend's hand and gave it a little squeeze. She didn't mention that she'd witnessed a few of the Kapos in her section doing the same. "Just make sure you keep well away from him, yeah?"

Sophie shook her head, regaining her composure. "It's fine, he tends to pick only on the men. He's been quite nice to me and the other women in the detail. I'm just being friendly to him, but I feel a bit guilty about it. He's the enemy."

"You're just doing what you need to, to survive, like everyone. The Kapos chose their own path, and if pretending to be nice to him is what you need to do, you don't think about anything or anyone else, okay?" Nora caught the harsh tone in her voice and spoke her next words more softly. "We will make it out of here, Sofe. That Kapo won't be in power much longer."

Sophie responded with a shrug, and they continued in silence. The path from the quarry rose steeply, and the women huffed and puffed as they slowly crept forward. After a day in the quarry, few had enough energy to move faster than their current crawl. Thankfully, the guards appeared in a generous mood, silently walking alongside the women.

They reached the top and walked along the ridge. The walls of the main camp loomed only a few hundred meters ahead. Down on the quarry floor, the last prisoners were leaving.

"How long do you think this will last?" Sophie's gaze was on the guards ahead. "I overheard a few of the guards this morning. They said the Americans are already in Austria. They were discussing whether they should make a run for it."

Nora chuckled. "Where would they go, though? I'm sure their more zealous colleagues would hunt them down."

"True. But if they're right, and the Americans really have entered the country, it can't be much longer."

Nora looked around, making sure nobody was eavesdropping on their conversation. "Maria told me some of the guards had approached her, asking if she'd be willing to put in a good word for them once the Americans arrived. They're terrified of being convicted for what's happened here."

"As they should be. They deserve no less than a rope around their necks." Sophie's words were uncharacteristically venomous. "Along with the Kapos."

Nora was about to respond when there was movement in the ranks before them. Two women broke free from the procession, surprising the guards. They shrieked incoherently while they waved their hands above their heads, their faces turned skyward.

Nora looked on in horror as the procession stopped. Both prisoners' and guards' attention was focused on the two women venturing dangerously close to the cliff's edge.

"Who are they calling to?" Sophie's voice was soft, the earlier venom replaced by compassion.

Nora followed the women's gazes, looking up at the clear sky. "They must think they've spotted planes overhead."

"They've gone mad." Sophie's words were heavy. Guards ran toward the women, yelling at them to stop and return to their places. Their words fell on deaf ears, as the women's waving and shouting only increased with every step. They were only a few meters from the cliff's edge—the drop to the quarry floor was at least ten stories.

Nora held her breath as the guards closed in, two drawing their rifles. *That's not going to help.* The women were delirious, chanting at the imaginary visions in the sky. Suddenly one of them noticed the guards and snapped out of her trance. Her eyes went between the guards and the edge of the cliff, only a couple of meters away now. Without hesitation, she took a few steps and launched herself off the cliff. Nora looked away but couldn't block out the dull thud of the body hitting the uneven floor below. It seemed to shock the other woman back to reality. Her eyes went wide at the sight of the guards. With a final shriek that chilled Nora's bones, she followed the other woman over the edge.

The guards halted in their spots, and it was quiet for a few seconds as everyone processed what they had just witnessed. Mauthausen did this to its prisoners. If they weren't killed by the guards, hunger, or exhaustion, they might crack and end the torment themselves. The procession continued in silence, and more work details joined them from all directions. Nora scanned the faces of their prisoners.

For the past few days, she'd furiously searched for another glimpse of Christiaan. Had she made up the image? The chances of Christiaan being in Mauthausen were slim. No, she thought, they were close to nonexistent. Nevertheless, she kept scanning the faces. *I'm not going mad. I know what I saw.*

CHAPTER FORTY-FIVE

A few kilometers south of the camp, Christiaan shivered in the bushes. Darkness had set in, and he'd spent most of the day in this spot a few meters from the road. It had mercifully remained dry, but with dusk the April cold set in. At least he wasn't hungry anymore.

When he walked out of the woods in the morning, the couple who'd seen him playing dead had been only a few meters away from him. There had been no avoiding them, and they had waved him over. He'd considered running, but quickly decided there was nowhere to go. And what good would it have done? They could simply report his sighting. Surviving in these foreign lands while the SS conducted a manhunt for him seemed unlikely, and he'd headed over to the couple.

They introduced themselves as Barbara and Ignaz Friedmann, and they lived in a nearby farmhouse. He'd been surprised by their ages. Judging by their voices, he thought they were in their forties, but they were at least in their late fifties, early sixties.

"What were you doing in the forest back there?" Barbara had

taken the initiative in their questioning, while Ignaz's eyes scanned Christiaan. "Why did you pretend to be dead? It was obvious you weren't, but we didn't know what to do with you."

Christiaan had been surprised by her frankness and couldn't suppress a nervous smile. Of course, it had been obvious he wasn't dead. He'd probably moved involuntarily. "I couldn't think of a better thing to do. You surprised me."

Barbara raised an eyebrow. "What's that accent?" Before Christiaan could answer, realization dawned in her eyes. "You're from the camp, aren't you?"

Christiaan considered making something up. But what was the point? What other explanation than admitting to what he was—an escaped prisoner—was there? Whatever happened next would happen. If these people wanted to report his escape or turn him in, he was in no state to stop them.

"Yes, I escaped from one of the marches. I'm from the Netherlands, and it's been a long journey getting here." The exhaustion set in as he spoke the words, a pang of hunger in his stomach. He saw the surprise in Barbara's eyes, then looked to Ignaz. His dark brown eyes revealed nothing as he stared back at him.

"Are the SS looking for you?" There was a slight tremor in Barbara's voice.

"I don't think so." On a whim, Christiaan decided to share the events of the previous day. He left out some of the more gruesome details, but made sure to include his close brush with death. The Friedmanns listened without interruption, Barbara occasionally gasping. "And then I walked out of the woods and found you waiting for me."

It was quiet as Barbara and Ignaz processed his words. Christiaan felt his hands shaking as he waited for their response. Ignaz had yet to speak, and Christiaan couldn't read him. Yet, it was the man with the piercing brown eyes that broke the silence.

"You've been incredibly lucky. It's hard to believe the guards let you out of their sight. To have the presence of mind to make a run for it and hope for the best shows courage." The man's words sounded sincere, even if Christiaan thought he detected a trace of doubt. "You have nothing to fear from us. We mind our own business, and we're certainly not members of the party."

Christiaan's heart skipped a beat, and the relief on his face must've been evident, for Barbara lifted her hand, raising a finger.

"But that doesn't mean we don't care." She gave him a hard look, scanning his clothing. "You won't survive out here like that. And have you thought about where you will go next?" Christiaan shook his head, and she exchanged a quick look with her husband. Ignaz nodded curtly. "You're going to stay here. Tonight, when darkness falls, Ignaz will return with our horse-drawn cart, and he'll take you to our home. You can stay in the barn. We can't have you wandering around here; people will see you. And trust me, plenty support the party."

Christiaan was torn. He wanted to trust the Friedmanns, but he was hesitant to take them at their word. For all he knew, they could return with the SS in a few hours. He looked at them again and decided he had no choice but to trust these people.

"You must be hungry," Barbara said. "I'll come back in an hour or two and bring you some bread and milk. How does that sound?"

"Wonderful." Christiaan couldn't think of a better response. When Barbara and Ignaz left, he spent the next couple hours sitting on a stump, every small sound startling him. He considered running away, terrified SS troopers would show up instead of the seemingly amiable Barbara Friedmann.

When he heard soft footsteps approaching, his body tensed, and he prepared for the worst. But it was Barbara with a small basket containing fresh bread, cheese, and sausage, along with a large bottle of milk. He couldn't recall ever feeling more relieved—or grateful—as he wolfed down the food.

That was almost six hours ago, and the anxiety grew with every passing hour waiting for Ignaz to show. Barbara had explained they couldn't risk transporting him to their home by daylight. Plenty of nosy neighbors, she'd said.

He rubbed his hands together while keeping his eyes on the dark road. It was silent, and he considered the possibility of Ignaz not showing up. Something might've happened that didn't allow him to head out. Or someone may have spotted Barbara leaving with her basket of food earlier, and the Friedmanns had run into trouble themselves? His heart went cold at the thought. There was still a sliver of doubt at the Friedmanns' intentions, and they could have had a change of heart in the end. Christiaan cursed his negativity. There was no sense in thinking like this. *These people wouldn't have brought me food this afternoon if they wished me harm. They'll come through.* And if they didn't, he could always leave his hiding place tomorrow.

His thoughts were interrupted by the sound of movement down the road. Christiaan strained to hear. A distinct clacking sound was moving in his direction. *Hooves.* Hope rose in his chest, a flutter of excitement shooting through his stomach. *Click clack. Click clack.* The cadence was regular as the clacking of hooves neared and finally slowed down.

"Christiaan." Ignaz's voice was no more than a whisper, but Christiaan needed no further encouragement. He crawled from the bushes, and Ignaz jumped from the simple cart. He moved to the back and signaled for Christiaan to climb aboard. "Quickly, hide underneath this, and don't move or say anything until I tell you it's safe." Ignaz lifted a pig trough, and Christiaan crawled underneath without another word. Seconds later, the cart started moving again, the clacking of hooves music to Christiaan's ears.

———

The fifteen-minute ride felt like an eternity. Christiaan didn't move a muscle as he lay resolutely still. Ignaz was humming in the front, frequently addressing his horse in a gentle manner. For most of the time, there was nothing but the light shaking of the cart as it bounced down the road, and the sound of the horse's hooves clacking at a steady pace.

Christiaan's couldn't shake the thought of Ignaz turning him in to SS troopers waiting in town. A moment later, he would return to his senses. *Why would Ignaz go through all this trouble to pick me up in the darkness if he was just going to turn me in?* He could've just returned with the SS earlier that day.

The cart took a sharp turn and the bumps it encountered made it shake even more. Soon, he heard the creaking of a door opening. The atmosphere shifted; it was now much warmer and there was an unmistakable smell of hay and animals. The cart came to a stop, followed by Ignaz patting the horse before he got off and onto the back of the cart. A second later, the pig trough was lifted, exposing Christiaan's faintly lit surroundings.

He was in a large barn, with hay stacked roof-high against the wall next to them. Ignaz smiled and Barbara appeared by the side of the cart.

"Welcome to your new home. It's not much, but you'll be safe and warm."

Christiaan climbed down from the cart, still struggling to believe where he was. Barbara took his hand and guided him to a small ladder in the corner.

"You'll sleep up there, where we keep the hay. We've put down some blankets for you, so you'll be comfortable enough. Feel free to rearrange the hay. Just stay out of sight. We usually don't get any visitors here, but let's play it safe anyway."

Christiaan was overwhelmed by emotion as he climbed up. It was comfortably warm in the loft, and he could barely contain his tears. "Thank you so much," he managed as he looked down at the Friedmanns. "You can't imagine how much this means to me."

"I'll be back to bring you some dinner in a bit. For now, rest.

You're safe here, Christiaan." Barbara smiled before moving toward the door. Ignaz gave him a nod and followed her.

Christiaan nestled down into the fresh-smelling hay and tucked the scratchy woolen blankets around him. All his worries and fears melted away, and tears of relief welled up in his eyes. For the first time he could remember, he felt safe.

CHAPTER FORTY-SIX

The sound of the Danube River flowing by just fifty meters away was the only thing Lisa heard. She sat by the open window, looking out into the darkness, aware of the hundreds of men crouched near the grassy, muddy riverbank. It wouldn't be long until the calm was broken. The soldiers of the 260th and the 261st—she was proud to call it "her regiment"—had spent the day preparing their assault across the Danube. Anything that floated was requisitioned, and the American army now possessed two dozen small craft to make the short journey across. When darkness fell, the soldiers had silently repositioned them slightly upstream. They would then use the Danube's strong current to help them paddle across as silently as possible. It was a bold plan. Intelligence reported the riverbank on the other side was well fortified, and the first crossing would be pivotal to the chances of American success. If they could get a foothold on the other side of the river, the engineers on Lisa's side would be able to build a temporary bridge. That would allow tanks and trucks to cross.

After breaking through Hitler's Westwall fortifications a good three weeks ago, the Third Army had made steady progress into

Germany. News from the east was promising as well; the Russians had entered Austria and were rapidly heading west. If Patton's army could cross the Danube, they would be able to link up with the Soviet army much quicker, effectively attacking the German positions from both directions. Reports of more and more German troops surrendering filtered through, giving Lisa further hope the war would soon be over. The German soldiers on the other side of the water had different plans.

She had also received encouraging news from back home. Most of the Netherlands had been liberated, with only the most western part still occupied. Somer's message had been full of hope, and he appeared convinced they would soon recapture the western cities, including Lisa's hometown of Amsterdam. She could hardly wait to return and search for Christiaan and Nora. She refused to give up hope that the man she loved was still alive.

The silence on the riverbank was interrupted by a soft, urgent clicking sound. It was soon returned from all along the riverbank, the soldiers confirming they had received the order. Lisa could make out shapes quickly moving toward the river. The assault had started, and soon the soft splashes of the soldier's paddles hitting the water could be heard.

Lisa's squad was not part of the first crossing but would be part of the second wave. She would remain in the small village of Kapfelberg while the soldiers attempted to clear the path east. She was slightly frustrated as she waited for the first wave of soldiers to reach the other side. It was difficult to sit by and wait while the men she'd traveled through France and Germany with disappeared across the dark water. There was no other way, though. Once a foothold was established, she would be allowed to cross and provide aid. Lisa had no illusions that there would be plenty of need for that.

The sound of the first gunfire traveled down the river, a distant indicator that the soldiers had reached the other side. As Lisa hunched out of sight, her heart raced with both excitement and dread. The plan was so simple yet so risky; the success of their mission hinged on the boats returning.

In the darkness, it was hard to make out anything beyond the small muzzle flashes in both directions. If all went according to plan, the boats would return soon, and her squad would paddle across next. With a bit of luck, she would follow in a few hours.

———

It wasn't until well into the morning that Lisa boarded one of the small boats. The sun was high in the sky, and the sound of fighting had moved much farther east. German resistance had been heavier than expected, and the American soldiers had to take out a number of well-defended artillery positions before it was safe for Lisa and the other relief troops to cross.

Engineers were hard at work constructing a Treadway bridge, and Lisa watched them as the soldiers in her boat paddled across. The bridge was built by effectively tying large pontoons together, creating a surface strong enough to support vehicles crossing. The engineers had started earlier, but German artillery fire had forced them to pause. Now, they appeared to be making steady progress.

"How long will it take them to have the bridge up?" Lisa asked one of the soldiers sitting next to her.

"At this rate, they should be done early in the evening, I think." He looked across the water with a frown. "As long as the Jerries don't decide to start shelling us again."

Lisa understood his concerns, but judging by the distant gunfire, the chances of that happening seemed small. "I think we're keeping them pretty busy over there, no?" She pointed farther down the river, and the soldier cracked a nervous smile.

"Never know if they might've called in reinforcements." He gripped his rifle tighter, his eyes constantly scanning the riverbank. Lisa's mind went to what she would find on the other side. It had been impossible to follow the fighting in the darkness. She hoped she wasn't too late.

The boat gently bumped to a stop. Lisa was already on her feet, moving forward and jumping onto the muddy riverbank. She was surprised by what she found. Soldiers disembarked from boats much like hers, quickly forming up with their squads before setting off east. Body bags were lifted into the boats as they returned to pick up more soldiers. A tall soldier greeted her and pointed her in the direction of a farmhouse.

"The injured are in there, in the large barn. Some of your colleagues are already there."

Lisa hurried to the barn, impressed by the well-organized, orderly situation. She wasn't sure what she'd expected, but it wasn't this. From what she could make out, the American soldiers had set up a strong foothold.

She entered the barn, where dozens of men lay on the ground or in the hay. Lisa recognized three of the doctors she'd been working with for months, and one of them waved her over, relief on his face. "Lisa! You're a sight for sore eyes. I need you to help bandage those men, and once you're done, help the nurses outside. They're preparing something warm to eat, but they'll need some help handing everything out." His words were clipped, and he spoke quickly. "We don't have enough people on this side of the river to look after everyone. Please tell me we've got more nurses coming in?"

Lisa shook her head. "I don't know, but I'll get started right away!" The doctor hurried off, and Lisa approached the first soldier. He had a large gash on his shoulder, and Lisa greeted him with a smile, grateful to make herself useful.

———

The bridge was up at nine in the evening, with tanks and troops pouring across minutes later. The German forces had retreated to the town of Bad Abbach, about two kilometers from Lisa's makeshift field hospital. She spent the next days caring for the soldiers that were brought in, finding little time to sleep. It didn't matter, as every man she bandaged said the same thing: German resistance was crumbling, and it wouldn't be much longer.

The good news came two days after the crossing. The Wehrmacht had surrendered Bad Abbach. Lisa was moved to the riverside town to assist in the questioning of the German POWs and citizens. When she arrived, she was overjoyed to find her squad leader, Andrews.

"Abrahams! You finally made it!" He sounded cheerful, but there was no masking the tiredness filtering through.

"Did everyone survive?" Lisa's voice trembled a little, despite her relief to see Andrews.

"We're all here. The rest of the boys are stationed a bit farther into town. We can go see them if you'd like."

"I need to talk to some German soldiers first, then I'll come find you. Brass wants to make sure we get their statements and intel before it's too late."

"Makes sense." Andrews pointed down the road. "We're in a large house in the center. Number twenty-four. The boys will be excited to see you."

Lisa continued through the town, where evidence of the heavy fighting was everywhere. Houses had collapsed and bullet holes punctured walls. Some of the townsfolk sat outside their homes, looking on with despondent faces.

Lisa approached a larger building in the middle of the town. Two soldiers stood outside, and she nodded at them while she entered. Inside, a familiar setting greeted her. Six German soldiers sat with their backs to the wall, guarded by the same number of American soldiers. The Germans were in their late teens and looked terrified. Lisa took a deep breath as she sat across from them. She hoped she wouldn't have to do this for much longer.

CHAPTER FORTY-SEVEN

Christiaan had been in the barn for six days, and it had done wonders for his health. Barbara and Ignaz had provided him with three hearty meals a day, and he'd regained much of his strength, the vigor in his limbs returning. Unable to go outside, he spent his days resting in the hayloft as his broken body healed with every passing day.

Barbara had brought him a few books, and he was reading in the corner of the barn when the back door opened, and Ignaz walked in. He carried a tray with a large bowl of steaming soup and a crusty piece of dark rye bread. Christiaan put the book away and sat at the table in the corner. Ignaz placed the tray down and sat across from him. His mouth watered at the smell of the soup; Barbara was an excellent cook. Before he could take a bite, he noticed the troubled expression on Ignaz's face.

"What's wrong?"

"Well, I have good and bad news." Ignaz shifted in his seat and looked at the soup. "Please eat, or it will get cold. I can tell you while you're eating."

Christiaan had lost his appetite and put his spoon down. "What's going on, Ignaz?"

"I spoke to one of my friends in the gendarmerie yesterday, and he told me the Americans are almost in Austria. The latest news is that they are near the border and will cross soon. The Wehrmacht resistance has been well and truly broken, and they think it's a matter of days, a week at most, before they reach Enns." His words were heavy, and Christiaan wasn't certain what to make of his host's feelings. *Is he worried the Americans will consider him a collaborator?*

"But that's great news, isn't it? That means the war is almost over."

Ignaz nodded slowly. "The Soviets have already made it to Vienna. I wonder if they'll beat the Americans to Enns." Christiaan had heard the stories of how the Soviets treated those they considered Nazi collaborators.

"Are you worried about the liberation, Ignaz? You've been hiding me for almost a week now. I'll tell them you're not a Nazi."

The older man shook his head. "It's not that. My conscience is clean." He looked up with sadness in his dark brown eyes. "The Wehrmacht aren't putting up too much resistance anymore, but that doesn't mean all the Nazis are willing to give up so easily. The Waffen-SS are moving to meet the Americans. The gendarme informed me I'll have to house a few of them here."

Ignaz didn't have to explain what that meant. Christiaan's spirits sank as he looked into his bowl of soup. "I can't stay here."

"No, it's too dangerous. But we have a new place for you." Christiaan looked up in surprise, and Ignaz smiled thinly. "We have another barn just down the road. It's not quite as comfortable as this, but it will have to do. Hopefully, you won't have to stay for too long, if the Americans are really on their way."

Christiaan didn't care about comfort. "When do I leave?"

"Tonight, when it's dark. I'll come get you."

———

"Are you ready to go?" Ignaz and Barbara waited by the door as Christiaan climbed down from the little loft that had been his refuge for almost a week.

"I can't thank you enough for what you've done for me." He looked in the dim light at the people who had saved his life.

Ignaz shook his head. "Anyone would've done the same." Barbara smiled and nodded.

That wasn't true, but he wasn't going to push the issue. Ignaz handed him a small sack and a blanket.

"These are potatoes for the first two nights. I don't know how easy it will be for me to sneak out once the SS troopers are here, but this should last you through the first days. Now, to get to the barn."

"You're not coming with me?"

Ignaz shook his head. "It's better to go alone. If anyone sees you, they won't recognize you. If they recognize me, there will be questions." He gave Christiaan directions to the barn, and made him repeat them. "Okay, we'll come and check on you as soon as we can. Stay safe, Christiaan."

Ignaz opened the door and Christiaan stepped into the darkness. He stayed close to the walls of the barn as he navigated toward the main road. He stopped and listened to make sure there was no one on the road before stepping out. Without hesitation, he turned left, the dark shape of the Friedmann home to his side.

Christiaan was surprised by how dark and quiet it was. At Mauthausen it had never been completely dark, and certainly never this quiet. He made sure to walk on the side of the road, keeping his gaze a few paces ahead of him. It was the only way not to lose track of where he was going. He passed a dwelling to his left, its windows dark. It looked uninhabited, but it wasn't the barn Ignaz had described. It should be a bit farther ahead. His mind wandered back to the march to Gunskirchen a week ago. He thought of his friend Jaroslav and hoped he had made it. Christiaan had felt guilty for leaving him behind when he jumped into the bushes. His friend was a fighter, a survivor. After surviving Auschwitz and

Mauthausen, he would hang on long enough in Gunskirchen, surely.

He looked at his feet and stopped in surprise. The road had turned into a dirt path. There wasn't supposed to be a dirt path. He tried retracing his steps but found nothing but grass under his feet. *Where's the road?* Christiaan took a few more steps in the direction of the road, but only found more grass. The darkness engulfed him, and he listened closely. Silence. He stood in a field, and Ignaz had made no mention of a field. Controlling the urge to panic, he considered what to do next. The late April night was cold, and he was already shivering. The only thing he could do was to continue and hope for shelter along the way. The barn could be right in front of him, but it was impossible to tell in the darkness. He moved slowly, careful not to lose his footing in the uneven field, the thick mud tugging at his shoes. He counted his steps and when he reached fifteen, he heard something. He stopped and pricked up his ears. There was no mistaking the soft trickle of water ahead of him. *A stream?*

The sound increased as he carefully made his way toward it. After another fifteen steps the grass thinned, and the ground became grainy. He crouched down and ran his fingers through sand. It was dry, and he inched farther forward, the sound of the water running by very close. His fingers touched the cold water a few steps later. Christiaan also noticed the temperature around him had changed. Despite the water's proximity, it was slightly warmer in the sand. He was puzzled, but decided this was as safe a place as he was going to find in the darkness. There was access to water, and the sandy ground was dry enough for him to lie down somewhat comfortably. *I'll wait for the morning to make out my surroundings.*

———

Christiaan woke up as the first rays of dawn painted the sky blood red. He blinked a few times, his vision slowly taking in his surroundings. The water he'd heard in the darkness turned out to be a narrow stream running by his small patch of sand. The edge of the field was slightly higher than his spot of sand and it had two big trees, creating a protective shade above him. *That's why the air was somewhat warmer here.* It also hid him from sight, and he rose to peek over the edge. He was surrounded by fields, bare but for the grass he'd walked through the previous night. In the distance he spotted several houses, but he didn't recognize the Friedmann house. How would he? He'd only passed it for the first time last night, but that was in pitch darkness. Turning his gaze in the opposite direction, he saw more farmhouses dotted the horizon.

There was no way for him to get back to the Friedmanns. He didn't even know what the barn he was supposed to be in looked like. All he had were the instructions Ignaz had provided, but those did him little good now.

He drank from the stream. The cold water tasted good, and he splashed some water on his face. It refreshed him, springing his brain into action. *What next?* It made no sense to start wandering aimlessly. The chances of getting lost or running into the wrong people were too high. He looked around while he considered his position. He had fresh water, was somewhat sheltered and still relatively close to Ignaz and Barbara. Surely, once they came to check on him in the barn and didn't find him, they would assume he'd gotten lost? Christiaan opened the sack of potatoes and counted them. Nine. If he rationed them well, he could probably survive here for a few days while he waited for the Friedmanns.

There were voices in the distance, and Christiaan peeked over the edge. He couldn't see anyone, but the sound appeared to come from one of the farmhouses. The field were bare, and Christiaan suspected very few—if any—people would venture in his direction. That sealed his decision. He would stay here and wait for the Friedmanns. *It can't be long.*

CHAPTER FORTY-EIGHT

From the moment they rode into the center of Passau, Lisa was struck by the city's beauty. It was positioned on the banks of the Danube, nestled among lush green trees, and houses lined the riverbank in a rainbow of colors, from soft pinks to earthy browns and yellows.

The Second Battalion of the 261st Regiment arrived early in the day and quickly disposed of some determined Waffen-SS resistance. Lisa had waited impatiently on the other side of the river and was relieved to find all the men of her squad alive after she crossed. Reports quickly filtered through that the First Battalion of the regiment was stuck farther north, but they were confident they would make it to Passau within the next few days.

After securing Bad Abbach less than a week ago, the 261st had been given some time to recover from the fierce fighting. There had been precious little time for Lisa to do so as she tended to the wounded and assisted in questioning the German soldiers and civilians. She much preferred the former task, but she knew there would be plenty of interpreting ahead.

This evening, though, she had a rare few hours off, and she was meeting with her squad leader Andrews and a few of the men in the city. She looked forward to catching up. Even though she had traveled alongside them between Bad Abbach and Passau, there was little time to talk as they remained alert for German ambushes. There had been only a few skirmishes with overzealous SS troopers as they made their way to Passau. Even then, it took only a few hours to force the SS soldiers into surrendering.

Lisa walked into a small tavern, where she found Andrews and three other men at a table in the back. They greeted her rapturously as they hurried to make room. Empty beer mugs littered the table and Andrews was quick to signal for a new round. The woman owning the establishment smiled and seemed pleased with her rowdy customers.

"I'm only having one, boys. I can't remember the last time I drank anything, and I'm on duty tomorrow morning."

"I expect the First will arrive somewhere tomorrow as well, and we'll continue our way east," Andrews said, still sounding remarkably sober, despite the evidence in front of him. "We can't have the Russians get to Linz before us now, can we?"

The barkeep appeared, setting down five large beer mugs. The men picked them up and Lisa did the same as they clanked them together. "To Lisa, our guardian angel!" one of them shouted. Lisa felt her cheeks flush and quickly took a large sip. The beer tasted great, the crisp, bitter taste relaxing her. She quickly took another sip before placing the mug back on the table. *Slow down.*

"So, Lisa, you are joining us when we head for Linz, right?" one of the men, Hugh, asked her, a large grin on his face.

"I don't see why not," Lisa said, picking up her mug with a smile. She took another sip, then caught Andrews looking at her with a serious expression. *Something's wrong.* "Am I not?" The other men also turned to Andrews, who placed his hands around his mug and leaned forward.

"I don't know. There's talk about setting up a large, more permanent field hospital in town. From what the brass told me, Passau is a perfect spot, with Austria just on the other side of the river. I think they might well need you to stay here and help coordinate, Lisa. You speak the language, after all." There was hesitation in his voice, and he looked mortified. "I'd much rather have you come to Linz with us, but it sounded very much like they wanted to keep the experienced Red Cross people here in Passau."

Lisa felt numb. She had become so used to her job in the 261st Regiment. After everything she'd seen and done, she felt more like a soldier than a nurse. "Is there anyone I can speak to about coming along with you instead?"

Andrews raised an eyebrow, the hint of a smile on his face. "It'll be safe in Passau."

"I don't care about that. I want to see this through 'til the end. When we capture Linz and meet with the Soviets, that's Austria liberated, isn't it?"

"Pretty much. There will be some die-hard SS squads roaming the country, but we'll mop them up in the next few weeks, if Hitler hasn't surrendered by then."

Lisa took a large gulp of her beer. "If Passau is so safe, I'm sure the Red Cross can send more nurses down here soon enough. But those girls won't speak German, and there will be plenty of Germans and Austrians between here and Linz. And wherever you're headed next." She put her mug down with a loud clunk, the alcohol emboldening her. "You need me with the regiment." Her words drew grunts of support from the other men. Andrews looked at her with respect.

"You're not letting this go, are you?"

Lisa shook her head. "I never told you why I joined the Red Cross and shipped out from England." She held the attention of the four men at the table and continued. "When Hitler invaded my country I was gradually relegated to being a second-class citizen. For you, Europe is a place to liberate. For me, it's my home. My last memories of home are hiding in the shadows, living in a dusty basement." Her heart ached at the thought of her parents being hauled away, hours after she'd escaped. She took another sip and steeled herself. "Then I was fortunate to meet a man like no other, who risked his own life to bring me to safety. Together, we made it to Geneva. But on that trip, I saw what the Nazis had done to the rest of the Continent. People lived in fear everywhere we went. As I moved in the shadows, praying my papers would be good enough with every inspection, that fear sometimes overwhelmed me. When we finally arrived in Geneva, I felt safe. Finally. I helped other refugees arriving, getting them jobs and homes. But after a few months, something was nagging in the back of my mind."

"It wasn't enough?" Andrews said, his voice soft.

"I needed to be more involved. And I made for London. But then, after D-Day, I knew I had served my purpose there. I wasn't sure how, but I knew I needed to be on the ground. Now I know why. I needed to be here, with you. And I want to be until we're done, until they're all pushed back into Germany and forced to surrender."

The men around the table looked at her in silence. Sharing her story felt good. Ever since she survived the German assault on the motor pool in Struth, the men in her squad had felt like brothers. They looked out for her without ever being condescending or overbearing. They respected and treated her like she was one of them.

"Well, Abrahams. When you put it like that ... Let me see if I can convince some of the brass tomorrow," Andrews said with a big smile, already signaling to the barkeep for another round.

———

Lisa spent the next morning working in the temporary field hospital. The workload was light, especially compared to that in Bad Abbach, where the fighting over two days had yielded far more casualties. At the end of the morning, she was approached by a young corporal, who handed her a message.

She smiled while she read its contents. Andrews had come through.

Two days later she climbed aboard one of the trucks headed for Linz.

CHAPTER FORTY-NINE

Nora sat outside her block in the Sanitätslager. Up on the ridge another large group of prisoners slowly marched toward the road leading down to the village and riverside. Nora tried to make out their faces, but it was almost impossible. They all looked alike with their shaved heads and ragged clothes. Very few wore the camp uniform. When she looked around in the infirmary camp it was much the same. New arrivals hadn't been given Mauthausen prisoner clothing for a few weeks now. Instead, they were told to keep what they were wearing on arrival. For many of the Hungarians arriving, it had been their own clothes, but there was a large number of prisoners wearing the uniforms of various other camps as well.

"Lots of guards walking alongside the prisoners today, don't you think?" Sophie's gaze was also fixed on the group, her eyes darting quickly between the guards in their comfortable uniforms. "Just like yesterday, and the day before."

"They won't be returning to the camp." Maria leaned against the building behind them, a curious expression on her face. "It wouldn't surprise me if many of them disappear along the way."

Nora frowned. "You think they're deserting?"

"I suppose you could call it that. I overheard some of the guards saying they should find a way to get away and dump their SS uniforms. They seemed convinced the Americans would be here soon." A smile crept across her face. "Probably why they're all volunteering for the prisoner marches."

"Are they still taking them farther west?"

"They don't tell me much, but yes, from what I've heard they're still taking the prisoners to the new camp at Gunskirchen."

The new camp was rumored to be more than sixty kilometers from Mauthausen. Nora turned back to Maria.

"When will we be forced to make the trek?"

"Have you looked around our camp? I'm not sure they'll bother. Few will make it down the hill. Even if the Americans get here within a few days, most will have died by then."

The guards didn't appear to care much about what was happening in the camp anymore.

"How are you feeling, Nora?" She looked up to find Maria standing next to her, a fiery sparkle in her eyes.

"Good enough. I'm still worried we'll be told to march to Gunskirchen one of these days."

"I know. But I don't think you should worry about that too much." She crouched down in front of Nora and Sophie, leaning on her heels while lowering her voice. "What if the SS decide to abandon the camp? They just leave us here to fend for ourselves. What would you do?"

Nora was taken aback. "I haven't really thought about it. I always figured they would defend the camp."

"That's what I thought as well," Maria said. "But when I heard those guards the other day, I thought it more likely that they would try to save their own skins. Why would they stay and fight to defend a camp? There's no way they could hold off a proper siege by the Americans or Soviets."

"What if they decide they don't want any witnesses before they leave?" Sophie broke her silence, her gentle voice softening the weight of the terrible words. "They're making sure the people up there won't be here when the camp is liberated." The last of the day's prisoners selected for the march to Gunskirchen were slowly exiting the camp. "If they can't march all of us away, who says they won't dispose of us in another way before they abandon the camp?"

Nora caught Maria's look as Sophie spoke calmly. They both realized her friend's words were a frighteningly real possibility. A thought struck Nora, and she turned to Maria. "Could you get us on a march to Gunskirchen?"

Maria gave her a perplexed look. "Wait. I thought you wanted to avoid the marches?"

"What if Sophie's right?" Nora paused. For weeks, it had appeared that all she had to do to stay alive was survive her days in the quarry, keep her head down, and make sure she lined up for her paltry bowl of watery soup in the evening. It was perverse to think that the impending liberation might mean death. She gritted her teeth and shook her head as she met her friend's eyes. "I'm not going to sit and wait to die. Getting on one of those marches is the only way we can somewhat control our destiny." She gave Maria a hopeful look. "Do you think you can do it?"

Maria looked thoughtful, not immediately answering. After a few seconds, she nodded, but she still looked reluctant. "Maybe. But do you think you could survive the march?"

"We might not have to."

Sophie looked puzzled. "What do you mean?"

Nora took a deep breath. Her plan was risky, and so much could go wrong. She glanced at her two friends standing beside her, knowing that she needed them if this plan was to succeed. "We're not going to finish the march. We're going to escape along the way."

CHAPTER FIFTY

C hristiaan opened his eyes to the now-familiar trickling sound of the stream near his feet. It was dark and he could smell the sweet dew on the fields. Not a trace of the sun could be found on the horizon. He'd become used to waking several times at night. It was from either the cold seeping into his weary bones or his nose and mouth being covered in sand from his tossing and turning. He crawled from under his blanket and took the five steps toward the edge of the stream. He knelt and scooped some of the cold water in his hands and drank thirstily. It was such a luxury to be able to drink at any time he wanted to.

The potatoes had run out the day before, despite his strict rationing. When he took the last bite, he'd cursed himself for not being more careful, and perhaps even being too optimistic. Christiaan had been convinced the Friedmanns would find him within a few days, but apart from a group of farmers giving him a scare when they inspected their fields a couple hundred meters away, no one had ventured anywhere near him. His stomach gurgled, and he felt an uncomfortable sensation spreading from his belly to his limbs. He needed food, and soon, or he'd have to abandon the shelter and risk venturing into the fields and beyond, something he could not do during daylight. For now, he had to wait, and endure the hunger's slow but insistent gnawing.

———

The warmth of the sun shone brightly on his face. He decided to stay put for one more night and, with a new sense of determination, rose and bent down by the stream. Splashing cold water over his face, he dunked his head beneath the surface. He couldn't hear anything but the stream's soothing melody. After resurfacing, he shook off the droplets running down his newly growing stubble before coming to a standstill as his surroundings returned into focus.

Apart from the familiar bubble of the stream and the gentle rustle of the leaves in the canopy overhead, he now heard something else. The sound of crushing earth, rustling grass. It was very faint, but for someone so in tune with his surroundings, it might as well have been a trample of horses. Someone was approaching.

Christiaan slowly crawled back to his blanket, near the edge where the field started. His mind was in a frenzy as he considered his options. Whoever was coming in his direction was most likely in much better shape than him. Running seemed foolish and, if it was an SS patrol, would most likely see him shot and killed seconds after revealing his position. *What if I simply stay down?* Christiaan tried to control his shaking hands as his throat went dry. He slowed his breathing as his heart pounded in his chest.

The rapid footsteps were very close. Christiaan frowned; something didn't sound right. They sounded light, like those of children.

The footsteps were only a few paces away, and Christiaan knew that he would soon be discovered. He balled his hands into fists and squeezed his eyes shut. A second later, the footsteps paused just above his head. He sensed a presence, but before he could look up, he felt a warm and wet sensation on his cheek. Confused, he opened his eyes and found a small dachshund wagging its tail as it jumped on him, continuing to lick his face. An instant later, a larger shadow blocked the sun.

"I can't believe it!"

The familiar voice shocked Christiaan back to his senses. *It can't be.* He looked up and blinked. Standing at the edge of the field, looking down on him, stood a beaming Barbara Friedmann.

———

That evening, Christiaan found himself back in the Friedmanns' barn. After discovering him, Barbara had returned with food and fresh clothes. Christiaan then waited until the cover of darkness, when Ignaz guided him back to the barn. They now sat together by candlelight, and Christiaan could hardly believe what was happening.

"We thought you'd ran away," Ignaz said. "I came to check on you the second evening, but it was clear you'd never made it to the barn."

"I got lost. It was so dark," Christiaan said, taking a bite from the large plate of eggs and ham.

Ignaz cast his eyes downward. "I should've come with you, shown you where it was."

"No, no." Christiaan shook his head and smiled. "You were right. If anyone had seen us, they would've been suspicious. Besides, I made it back in the end." Ignaz looked unconvinced, and Christiaan changed the subject. "What happened to the SS soldiers? Weren't they supposed to be staying with you?"

"They were only here for a couple of nights." Barbara took Christiaan's mug and refilled it with steaming tea. "They were called west, and I doubt they'll be back. The news from the front is encouraging. Since you left, the Americans have been making great progress."

"You spoke to the gendarme?" Christiaan wanted to believe Barbara's words, but he had heard the story of impending liberation and freedom too many times before. He glanced at Ignaz, who seemed more confident as he looked up.

"Yes, they're receiving wireless updates, and our friend was told to prepare for the American arrival in Enns soon. The last we heard they've advanced as far as Linz. That's only thirty kilometers away."

"Prepare? What does that mean?"

A smile crept onto Ignaz's face. "Officially? Probably that they're supposed to offer resistance. But I can assure you nobody but the SS troopers will do anything like that. The war is almost over, and everybody in Austria knows it. Even Hitler's staunchest supporters aren't going to forfeit their lives in a losing battle."

"You just need to stay put here, Christiaan. It will all be over soon," Barbara added.

As much as he wanted to believe the Friedmanns, Christiaan's hopes had been dashed too many times in the past year. "If you don't mind, I would like to get some sleep." The thought of sleeping in the warm hay had been on his mind as soon as Barbara discovered him and said she'd return with food and clothes.

The Friedmanns closed the barn door and Christiaan climbed up to the small loft. With a sigh, he collapsed onto his simple bed. He was gone as soon as his head hit the pillow.

CHAPTER FIFTY-ONE

Nora watched in astonishment as a procession of trucks drove away from the camp. A few hours ago, these vehicles had brought men dressed in unfamiliar uniforms; now, they were leaving with SS guards crammed inside, their arrogance gone and replaced by a palpable nervousness. The drivers seemed desperate to flee from Mauthausen—engines racing before they disappeared from sight.

"You think that's all of them? Any idea who those men that came up earlier were?" Sophie looked out from their position near the barbed-wire fence, a frown on her face.

"Can't imagine they're all leaving. Who's going to guard us?" Nora was perplexed as she focused on a few Kübelwagens bringing up the rear. They had their tops down, making it easy to spot the officers in the back seats. Nora gasped when she recognized one of the faces. "That's Bachmayer."

The Hauptsturmführer sat hunched in the back seat, his eyes cast downward, as if he was reading something. Hope surged in Nora's heart at the sight of the man responsible for so much death and suffering leaving.

"I guess we won't be going on any marches." Nora turned to find Maria standing behind her. "The rats are fleeing the sinking ship."

"Do you know who those men in the backs of the truck coming up earlier were?"

Maria shook her head. "I'm sure we'll find out soon enough." She nodded toward the last car racing away from the SS quarters. A man and a woman sat in the back; their faces were devoid of emotion. "That's Kommandant Ziereis and his wife."

The commander's car soon disappeared down the hill, leaving a cloud of dust in its wake. The women looked at each other.

"Now what?" Sophie said, hope and confusion in her eyes.

Nora tried to process what she'd seen.

"Ziereis and Bachmayer wouldn't abandon the camp unless they were absolutely certain all hope was lost." She looked to Maria, whose eyes were focused on the high granite walls of the main camp on the hill. Nora raised her voice, sounding a little firmer. "Right?"

"I can't think of another reason." Maria moved toward the gate, about fifty paces away. She ignored a small group of women lying on the ground, begging for food. Nora followed her friend and shook her head at the women. They were like many in the infirmary camp: too weak to fight for the scraps handed out in the evenings, they had withered away to become apparition-like figures. She ran her hand over her chest and felt her ribs protruding. The only reason she was still alive was because she stuck with Sophie and Maria.

There were no guards at the gate, but it was locked all the same. Maria rattled it, but the heavy lock didn't budge. They were trapped inside.

"If the SS really abandoned the camp, we need to find a way out, and quickly. I can't imagine they'll just leave us here," Maria said, a scowl on her face. "We know too much."

"You think they'll come back?"

"Not the guards. Those cowards are racing back to Germany as fast as they can. No, when I was in Auschwitz some of the prisoners told me about special killing commandos traveling with the Waffen-

SS on the eastern front. They would follow the soldiers, if you can call them that, and murder entire villages they suspected of collaborating with the Soviets."

Nora's blood froze, and she watched the locked gate. As she did, a group of men came down the hill from the main camp. "Look! Those are the men from the trucks earlier." They walked purposefully, and Nora squinted against the sun, trying to make out their uniforms. To her relief, they weren't SS. When they were some fifty meters away, Nora was stunned to see but a few wearing uniforms. The men were much older—in their late forties—than the SS guards she'd become accustomed to. Nora frowned and turned to Maria. "Who are they?"

Maria answered with a shake of the head, keeping her eyes on the men, who were now close enough to make out their faces. *They're surprised. Or ashamed?* Nora caught the eye of one of the men wearing what looked like a fireman's uniform. He tilted his head ever so slightly as he held her stare. They regarded each other for a few seconds, then a cautious smile appeared, wrinkling his face. For the first time in over a year, Nora found kindness in the look of someone in power. She couldn't help but return the smile, a feeling of relief building inside. *These men aren't here to hurt us.*

The group reached the gate, where more prisoners gathered. Nora could feel the press of bodies while one of the men on the other side held up his hands. A hush slowly filtered through, quieting the crowd, and the man spoke in a calm, clear voice.

"Ladies and gentlemen. You've probably seen the trucks moving about the past few hours. The SS has transferred command of the camp to us. We are part of the *Volkssturm*, and we need to keep you safe until the Americans get here."

Murmurs rose among the prisoners, unsure what to make of the men at the gate. Were they Nazis? Were they like the SS, just older, wearing less fancy uniforms? After years of being lied to and seeing their friends and family killed, the prisoners were hesitant about believing these German-speaking men would safeguard them until the Americans arrived.

"We need the block elders to come up to the main camp with us. Please come forward. The rest of you, please stay where you are. We will come back with food very soon."

The promise of food sent a wave of hope through the crowd of hungry prisoners.

"Nora." Maria tugged at her shirt, Sophie by her side. "Come with me. This is our chance to get out. I'll tell them you're also block elders." She pointed at the white armband marking her as block elder.

"Will it work?" Nora said with little conviction as they pushed through the crowd. One of the Volkssturm men opened the gate, and the first prisoners passed through. They reached the gate and Nora held her breath. Maria was right; whatever happened next, they needed to get away from the Sanitätslager.

The inspection was nothing like what they were used to. Two men gave them a cursory glance, and when Maria indicated all three of them were block elders, they were allowed through.

Nora exhaled deeply as she took the first steps outside the infirmary camp in over a week. It took another ten minutes for all block elders to report before the gate was locked. This time, two guards remained as Nora, Maria, and Sophie followed the men up the road leading to the main camp.

It was odd to walk past the abandoned SS living quarters as they approached the main gate. Nora had made this trek at least twice a day for the past month, and there would always be plenty of SS guards going about their business. They would be getting ready for the day, sitting around having their meals and chatting to one another while the condemned prisoners headed out for roll call or another day in the murderous work details. Now, the area was quiet as a cemetery. Everything was different. Prisoners in tattered clothes milled about everywhere. The doors to the administration building to her left were open, but instead of clerks clacking away inside, the building was empty.

Nora looked on in amazement as the men of the Volkssturm

appeared unconcerned. She glanced at Maria and Sophie, whose surprise was evident from their faces as well. *What's going on?*

They walked all the way to the back of the camp, where they were directed into the hospital. Inside, another surprise awaited them. One of the wards had been cleared, and it was filled with prisoners. From the armbands and prisoner identification on their chests it was soon evident there were people from all walks of life here. Kapos and block elders stood with their armbands, while others were identified as political or even criminal prisoners. At the front of the room stood a group of men in uniforms identical to the ones the Volkssturm men wore. Nora made out various police and fire brigade uniforms. Her eyes then paused on one that looked slightly more military, startling her.

"It's a gendarmes uniform." She looked to her side to find the man she'd locked eyes with earlier next to her. "Don't worry, nobody in this room is a Nazi. We're not here to harm you." He spoke with a heavy accent, but his voice was soft. Nora wanted to believe him.

"I'm sorry, I'm a little confused. Where did the SS go? And who are you, exactly?"

"I don't know. All we were told was that we had to report to the camp to look after the prisoners. I suppose the SS went west to fight the Americans. Not that it will do them much good. From what I've heard they've been making steady progress." The man spoke matter-of-factly, and Nora couldn't detect how he felt about the supposed American advance. He cast his eyes downward, a shadow passing over his face. "What I do know is that many of the people in this camp aren't going to last much longer. Before we came down to check on you, I walked around the camp. There are bodies everywhere, and many more will die in the next few days, if not hours."

"It's like that in our camp as well," Nora said, casting her mind back to the apparitions passing for women. "Can you get more food to the camp?"

"I'm not sure. I don't think we could feed the thousands of people in here. The SS left nothing behind."

"They were starving us to death."

He nodded sadly. "That they were."

"What happens next?"

There was movement at the front of the room, and the man indicated the two men in police uniform. "I don't know, but I'm sure they're about to tell us."

———

The next morning, Nora stood atop the guard tower, which offered a stunning view of the surrounding countryside. In the main camp behind her, prisoners tried their best to conserve their energy. Many had perished overnight, and those still alive hadn't bothered to clear all the bodies. Hundreds of men and women had closed their eyes for the last time, their broken bodies and souls devoid of the energy required to survive another day. Most were left where they were. Those alive were convinced the Americans or Soviets would be here soon, and everybody was determined to live long enough to witness it.

Nora thought back to the odd gathering in the hospital the day prior. The Volkssturm soldiers had surrendered control of the camp to the prisoners. They wanted to help them as best they could and harbored no ambitions about controlling the population the way the SS had. It was obvious they were shocked and overwhelmed by what they'd encountered behind Mauthausen's imposing granite walls. The Volkssturm men were adamant the Americans and Soviets would soon take over Austria, and certain they would liberate Mauthausen soon.

At the meeting, a select few prisoners asserted themselves as leaders. They discussed the threat of the SS murder squads potentially coming to Mauthausen. With the consent of the police, gendarmerie, and fire brigades, all able-bodied prisoners found weapons and stationed themselves on top of watchtowers and on the walls of the camp. Nora and Sophie had volunteered to be lookouts. Maria had returned to the infirmary camp, where she would try to keep order as best she could. A number of the Volkssturm men had joined her, and Nora hoped she could convince the prisoners to stay put for a little longer.

Nora peered along the horizon, scanning the green rolling hills to the south. It was a clear day, and she could see the towns dotted across the landscape well beyond Mauthausen. This was the first time she had such a panoramic view of her surroundings. She found it overwhelming to consider that the guards had always had this majestic view while the prisoners worked themselves to death in the now-deserted quarry only a hundred meters to their right.

"Do you think the Americans will make it in time?" Sophie interrupted her thoughts, her eyes on the single road snaking up. "Do they even know we're here?"

"The people in the villages know." Nora spoke with more conviction than she felt. It was something she worried about herself as well. What if the Americans simply continued on, following the Danube farther east? Would the villagers tell them about the monstrosity up the small side road? It was easy to miss, and Nora remembered their indifference when she passed from the train station through town. She shivered at the thought of none of them speaking up. Then she shook her head; there were still good people here as well. The Volkssturm men proved that. "They'll find us."

———

Nora stifled a yawn. She had been on the lookout for over three hours now, and other than a few of the Volkssturm soldiers moving between the camp and town, nothing had happened. She admonished herself; she was one of the lucky ones sitting in the relative comfort and safety of the ramparts. A good number of fights had broken out in the camp below as prisoners fought over scraps of food. They were quickly broken up, but tensions were growing by the hour. Nora doubted the leading prisoners and Volkssturm would be able to keep the peace much longer.

"Hey, do you see that?" Sophie pointed in the direction of the SS barracks to their left, on the other side of the ramparts. "I thought I saw someone moving about."

Nora focused her attention on the building Sophie pointed at. "Nobody's supposed to be there."

"That's why I thought it was a bit odd. Maybe I'm mistaken. I'm having trouble focusing."

"Me too." Sophie's words only reminded Nora of her exhaustion, and she closed her eyes. It felt blissful for a few seconds, but her rest didn't last long. Excited yelling brought her back to the present. Seconds later, a deafening blast trembled the ramparts. The smoke and dirt flying high up in the air from fifty meters away confirmed something had happened. Before Nora could process what was going on, the earth rumbled beneath her again, followed by the sound of automatic gunfire. Her eyes widened as twenty men wearing SS uniforms emerged from the SS barracks Sophie had pointed out earlier.

"Get down!" A man pushed Nora down behind the thick granite wall. It was only just in time as bullets zipped overhead, striking him square in the face. Nora screamed in horror as his head violently jerked backward, his limp body tumbling down the side of the wall. A dull thud was followed by shrieks of prisoners below. Nora pressed herself against the wall, her hands over her ears. Sophie sat next to her, her whole body shaking as she sat with her eyes closed. Nora entered a daze, the sounds around her muffled, barely acknowledging the men with rifles running by. Automatic gunfire from the barracks below continued but was now answered in turn from the ramparts. Nora turned her head to see a dozen men spread out, their guns pointing through the gaps in the ramparts. More were climbing up, carrying a mix of rifles and handguns. Nora snapped out of her daze, the rattle of the gunfire instantly amplified. Men screamed instructions at each other as more prisoners took up positions. SS troopers yelled at each other below as they reloaded their machine gun. Then she saw the rifle at her feet. It was the one carried by the man who'd sacrificed his own life to save hers. Without another thought, Nora picked it up. It felt heavier than expected, and she cradled it in her hands.

"Do you know how to fire a gun?" Sophie looked at her wide eyed.

"No, but I'll just have to learn along the way." Nora felt possessed by a force stronger than herself as she started moving toward the men firing down at their assailants. *Someone died for me. This is the least I can do.* She kept her head safely behind the ramparts. The sound of gunfire pounded in her ears, increasing with every step. Still, she pushed on, determined to make her stand. She hadn't survived two concentration camps to die at the hands of an SS murder squad. Not while she grasped a rifle and drew breath.

She reached the first man, who looked only momentarily surprised to see her. His expression soon changed to one of admiration when he saw the determination in her eyes.

"We've got them pinned down between the first rows of barracks to the left. They're not going anywhere!" He looked at her rifle. "You know how to fire one?"

Nora shook her head. "No, but it can't be that hard, can it? And they're quite close." She clenched her jaw. "Let me at them."

The man gave her a quick smile and pointed at the rifle. "Pull the trigger, then pull that bolt back to reload." He quickly inspected the magazine. "You've got five shots there. Make them count. Oh, and rest the butt against your shoulder. It packs a punch."

The instructions would've been easy enough to understand if it wasn't for the bullets zipping by overhead. The SS troopers had reloaded their machine gun and were spraying bullets at the defenders. Nora swallowed hard as she peeked over the edge of the ramparts. The machine gun was assaulting the guard tower a bit farther down, and she spotted the soldiers hiding behind the barracks. She aimed the rifle in their direction but didn't have a clear shot. She waited, her hands shaking. There was movement, and she instinctively pulled the trigger. The rifle exploded into life, the force almost knocking it from her hands. *Did I get one?* She quickly crouched down behind the ramparts, trying to control her breathing as she pulled back the bolt. It appeared stuck, and she cursed while she applied more force. *Come on, come on.*

The man turned toward her. "Let me help you." He strained and jiggled the bolt, but it finally clicked, and he handed it back before focusing his attention on the SS troopers. There were multiple cries of anguish from below, confirming the shots from the ramparts were finding their targets. Still, the incessant rattle of the machine gun continued.

A shout came from the guard tower. "Provide covering fire now!" Nora looked across to see a man holding a tubelike object. *Grenade?* There was no time to think as more than a dozen men lifted their guns and pointed them down at the troopers. Nora took a deep breath and did the same. She looked down the barrel of her gun and caught sight of a single soldier whose head was slightly exposed. She pulled the trigger, leaning forward to compensate for the recoil. The gun went off, the force of the rifle again startling her.

She never saw the bullet impact. A tremendous blast followed by a glittering, fiery cloud of wood, glass, and smoke obscured the area where the SS had dug themselves in. A part of the barracks collapsed, exposing the troopers. The men on the ramparts fired blindly into the smoke, resulting in loud cries as the SS troopers sought new cover.

"Hold your fire, stop shooting!" came the command from the guard tower. The words didn't immediately register as some of the men fired a few more shots before it became oddly quiet. Nora sat with her back to the wall, gripping her rifle tightly, waiting for the rattle of the machine gun to return. After a minute of eerie silence, the smoke cleared, and some of the men peeked over the ramparts.

"They're gone! The bastards have fled!"

CHAPTER FIFTY-TWO

L isa was up early and stepped outside the large tent where most of the others were still asleep. The sun had yet to crest the hills to the left, bathing their tops in umber, and there was just enough light from the east to swallow up the night's darkness. To her left was a dense patch of forest with small houses dotted along winding roads. She enjoyed the feeling of space in the Austrian countryside. It was very different from Amsterdam, where space was at a premium and houses were built alongside each other, with only the wealthy able to live detached from their neighbors. Even then, the space between the homes was no more than a small stretch of garden or an alleyway. In the Austrian towns they'd passed, large houses with well-kept gardens stood near the Danube River and farms were visible farther inland.

She turned to her right, where the city of Linz glistened in the weak morning sun, the last remnants of dew glistening on some of the roofs. Situated on the banks of the Danube, Linz was similar to Passau, the German city they'd left a few days ago.

Their journey had been smooth, with very little resistance but for a few SS squads hiding along the road. Most had surrendered upon seeing the well-equipped American forces approaching, and it had pleased Lisa. Not in the least because she'd become battle weary. Her tenth month with the Third Army had just started, and she'd seen enough death, treated enough injured soldiers, and perhaps most importantly: she'd seen the state of their enemy. These young German soldiers were done. Very few of the men she spoke to seemed to believe in the Nazi cause, most stating they never really had. Andrews had been hesitant to believe them at first, but as they made their way through Germany and Austria, even her squad leader had come around. It was time for this war to end.

She could feel her stomach growling and realized she had to head toward the mess tent. To her surprise, it was more crowded than usual at this time of day—just past five in the morning. Usually, there were only a handful of people up at this hour—soldiers coming back from their shifts, or doctors and nurses working odd hours. But now, there was a line for coffee. She scanned the early breakfast crowd looking for familiar faces. A few of the soldiers nodded at her, and she recognized a large group of nurses in the back. They chewed in silence and looked like they had just finished their night shift. Lisa could relate; it was nice to eat before turning in for a few hours of sleep. *You never know what might happen in the next few hours.*

She was startled when she felt a tap on her shoulder. Turning, she looked into the surprisingly fresh face of Andrews.

"Morning, Abrahams. Glad to see you're up early as well. Did you sleep all right?" His tone was friendly, but he looked troubled.

The line moved forward, and Lisa poured a cup of coffee. "It's not too bad around here. Bit cold, maybe, but I've become used to that near the river. Do you know if we'll be moving farther east today? Any news on the Russian positions?"

"Last I heard they were making good progress, and part of the battalion is heading down east today, to secure our side of the Enns River. The Russians should make it there today as well."

Lisa's spirits rose. "That's great, isn't it? That's pretty much the northern part of the country secured?" She buttered a piece of toast and took a bite. "Wait. You said part of the battalion. Does that mean you're not going? Am I?"

"It's up to you."

"How so?" Lisa frowned. Where she went or what she did was hardly ever up to her. "What's the other option?" She suspected it would mean staying in and around the camp and perhaps the city of Linz, taking care of the sick and injured.

Andrews pointed toward a free table, and they sat opposite each other. He leaned forward and lowered his voice. "One of the reconnaissance units came back late last evening. They found something horrible. Some sort of camp."

Lisa's heart skipped a beat. They were the words she'd dreaded to hear for months, and she had been relieved they hadn't run into any of the camps yet. Even back in Amsterdam she'd heard of the horrors. "A concentration camp?" Her voice was soft; she was almost hesitant to speak the words out loud.

"I've never seen the boys this upset. I overheard a few of them speak of hundreds of starving people crowding behind barbed-wire fences. Others said there were thousands. They need help, Lisa."

Lisa's chest constricted and she averted her face, closing her eyes. After leaving Amsterdam, she had somehow managed to put the thoughts of what happened to her parents to the back of her mind. A tiny sliver of hope remained; perhaps the rumors of the camps to the east were exaggerated. She opened her eyes and met Andrews' look. The normally good-humored, confident man looked sad and fragile, his shoulders somewhat slumped. She had to face her demons head on.

————

The Danube glittered in the morning light as Lisa looked out of the truck. In any other situation, Lisa would've enjoyed the ride. She looked at the faces of the men around her. Most had their eyes closed, trying to steal a few more minutes of sleep. They had all been roused early and most managed to grab a quick breakfast of toast and coffee on the go while they hurried to the waiting trucks. When they boarded, Lisa had been pleased to see soldiers carrying large crates of supplies to two trucks parked in the rear. They wouldn't arrive at the camp empty handed, although she worried whether it would be enough. *It would have to do for now.*

Lisa felt restless and anxious and tapped her foot on the wooden floorboard. Andrews' words had hit her hard. When she awoke, she'd been optimistic about her prospects for heading home soon. The war wouldn't last much longer. But now she realized she hadn't fully considered the aftermath of the war. She shook her head at her naivete. There would be so much to do after the Germans surrendered. The destruction of the war had been right in front of her ever since landing in Normandy. Millions of people had lost their homes, their families, their livelihoods. Many were scattered around Europe, imprisoned in camps like the one she was heading toward. Her blood ran cold at the thought of what she was about to encounter. Andrews sat across from her, his eyes closed, his breathing regular. She'd never seen the squad leader as worried as at breakfast. It had unnerved her more than she liked to admit.

The truck slowed down and turned onto a side road, away from the river. The engine protested as the driver shifted gears and they started crawling up a winding road.

A few minutes later, the road flattened out. Some of the soldiers had also awakened and looked around in surprise. They drove through a beautiful meadow surrounded by large birch trees. A soldier across from her frowned and leaned forward, his eyes wide as he stared past her. "What in God's name is that?" Lisa turned see, and her mind struggled to process what she saw.

About fifty meters beyond was a collection of flimsy-looking wooden barracks surrounded by a high barbed-wire fence. There was little space between the buildings, but what struck her most was the number of people crowding behind the fence. They stood silently watching the trucks pass. A few called out in ragged, weak voices, in languages Lisa didn't understand. Lisa tried to distinguish faces in the crowd of identically dressed, bald individuals. She couldn't tell men from women. They all appeared similarly emaciated, with white skin and sunken eyes surrounded by dark rings. Even at a distance, Lisa could see their cheekbones jutting out unnaturally. All the way in the back she noticed there were no people crowding around. She blinked to make sure her eyes weren't deceiving her, but there was no mistaking the mass of bodies piled unceremoniously on top of each other. It was too far away to count them, but she estimated at least fifty corpses. An overpowering sadness filled her. The faces of Papa and Mama flashed in her mind, and she felt her eyes burning at the thought of them having ended up like that.

"Are we not going to help these poor souls?" The words shook her back to the present. Most of the soldiers were awake, their gazes fixed on the otherworldly situation behind the fence.

"Not just yet." Andrews kept his composure, although Lisa could see he was equally shaken by the human misery on display. He pointed ahead. "We need to report up there first."

The towering grayish-black walls rose like a blight in the pleasant green countryside. Lisa's breath caught in her throat as the truck rolled on toward the monstrosity in front of her. Whatever she'd expected a concentration camp to look like, this wasn't it. The walls were at least ten meters high, built from solid, dark stones. Watchtowers were perched atop it at regular intervals, although Lisa was relieved to see American soldiers looking down. On the ramparts she spotted faces following the approaching convoy as well. She scanned the area around the camp perimeter. More barracks appeared to her right, these of much better quality than the ones she'd seen earlier. Several of them were damaged.

Their truck reached the top of the hill and drove alongside the wall toward a large gate. Voices filtered through over the wall. Hundreds of voices; English, German, French, and even some Dutch. She looked up again, now clearly able to link the faces to some of the voices as she watched the people's lips moving. Some waved their hands and fists at the American trucks, a number running along the length of the wall. Most of the soldiers waved back, and Lisa couldn't help but join in. They passed through the gate into a large courtyard, where soldiers jumped from their trucks and started unloading packages filled with water, canned food, and chocolate. Lisa climbed down and saw more curious faces appear atop the ramparts. She noticed a large stairway to the left, barred by American soldiers. Behind it, droves of prisoners crowded around, eager to descend. She didn't blame them, considering what the men were unloading. Andrews appeared next to her.

"We should be ready to hand out food and water to these people soon. It will be crazy. I think it's best if you hang back, okay?" He'd regained his usual commanding voice and posture. "There will be plenty of time to look after the wounded and malnourished once the rest of the Red Cross arrive."

Lisa frowned, unable to mask her disappointment. "What am I supposed to do before that? Just stand around and do nothing?"

Andrews looked ready to give her a dressing down when he caught himself and smiled. "All right, Abrahams." He pointed at one of the trucks in the back. "Why don't you help over there? Just stay in the truck, okay? We won't know how they'll respond. As far as we know, these people haven't eaten for days. It could turn ugly."

"I can handle myself." Lisa was already headed toward the truck when she heard a rumble behind her. Glancing back, she saw the host of prisoners break through the American cordon and rush down the stairs. The first men reached the clearing before any of the soldiers unloading the trucks could respond.

"Huddle around the trucks!" Andrews shouted. "Let them through, but one package per person!"

Lisa climbed aboard one of the trucks and had a perfect vantage point. The soldiers formed a human shield around the backs of the trucks while a number climbed aboard, ready to hand out the precious cargo. Prisoners continued to stream down the stairs, the first finding their way to the trucks. They looked in a reasonable state as they held out their hands and begged for food and water. A few of the women wailed as they clutched children to their chests. Even though they wore a mix of torn, mismatched clothes, they all had one thing in common. Their faces wore the pale, blueish hue of starvation, further accentuated by their cracked lips, croaking voices, and hollow cheeks. The courtyard echoed with a cacophony of voices. Their message was clear, though, and Lisa started handing out the packages from the truck as quickly as her arms would allow.

The stream of hands reaching out was never ending. Lisa ignored her sore arms as she handed out package after package to the starved people below. She had a short moment of respite as the soldiers moved more boxes from the front, and she looked out over the courtyard. It was filled with people. Some sat on the ground, savoring the chocolate, or smoking their cigarettes. Others moved in the direction of the trucks empty handed as they stole glances at those that had already secured their lifelines. The stairs on the far side were still crowded with people making their way down, but now some appeared to move in the opposite direction as well. Lisa sighed and prayed they would have enough supplies to feed all these people. She grabbed another package and returned to the rhythm of handing food to the prisoners. No, she corrected herself. They're no longer prisoners. They're refugees.

"Lisa!"

The shout was faint and muffled by the sound of the people in the courtyard. Lisa wasn't certain if she'd heard correctly and scanned the area near her truck. The faces of the soldiers guarding the truck were all turned in the direction of the crowd. She looked for Andrews, but she didn't see him, either. *I must've misheard.* She was about to turn back when she heard her name again. The voice was louder, more determined, and familiar. Lisa stood frozen, her eyes narrowing as she scanned the faces in front of her. She tried to block out the hundreds of other voices as she searched for the one that just called out her name.

"Lisa, over here!"

She spotted someone furiously waving their hand about ten meters from her truck. Their face was hidden in the sea of outstretched hands in front of her. Lisa leaned slightly forward. Her heart was thumping in her chest as she waited for the face of her caller to be revealed. The crowd moved in waves, more hands now reaching toward her, voices pleading for food. Lisa ignored them, the mystery of the person's identity making her mind race.

Suddenly, the hands parted just enough to catch a glimpse of a face. Lisa's heart skipped a beat, her throat going dry. *It can't be. I'm imagining things.* Still, she didn't look away.

"Lisa! I'm coming to you!" The voice was loud and clear, and she saw some people move out of the way. When they did, all doubt was removed as the person's face was revealed. Lisa felt lightheaded and reached for the side of the truck. A strong hand grabbed her shoulder.

"Miss, are you all right? Do you need a break? You look a little pale."

She looked at the soldier supporting her. "Yes, thank you." She closed her eyes for a moment, her head still spinning. When she opened them again, she turned back to the crowd. The figure she'd spotted moments ago had disappeared, and she felt a mix of relief and disappointment. *I imagined it, after all.* She turned back to grab one of the packages.

"Abrahams?" A voice came from below, and she looked into the face of one of the soldiers guarding the truck. "Prisoner here says they know you. Asked for you by name." He moved aside to reveal the beaming face of the last person she ever expected to find here. Her heart almost exploded from relief, and she didn't try to stop the tears that were forming in her eyes. Lisa jumped down from the truck and threw her arms around the frail figure. She then moved back and looked into their eyes. In a frail voice, she only managed to croak a few words. "I can't believe it's you. How did you end up here?"

CHAPTER FIFTY-THREE

C hristiaan had been back in the barn for three days, and he could hardly recall the first night and day, which passed in a blur. Only the food from the Friedmanns brought him back to reality. But otherwise, he cherished his private loft of hay. On the morning of his second day, Barbara came to bring him good tidings from nearby Linz, where the Americans had taken over the city. Christiaan had spent the whole day on tenterhooks, waiting for news of an American arrival in Enns. When Ignaz brought him dinner, he came in with a beaming smile. Christiaan had almost jumped down from the loft in anticipation.

"Are they here?"

"No." Ignaz put the tray down, and Christiaan's hopes sank, his enthusiasm waning. Ignaz looked up, still smiling. "But there was something else on the wireless that I think you'll want to hear about."

Christiaan sat down at the small table, Ignaz's optimism hardly lifting him. "What is it?" He picked up a fork and scooped up some noodles.

"Your country is free."

Christiaan's hand froze halfway between the table and his mouth, noodles spilling from his fork. "What?" He felt a tingle in his stomach.

"The Germans have surrendered the Netherlands. The news came through just before I headed out to bring you your dinner. The country is celebrating!"

Christiaan looked to Ignaz, who seemed genuinely thrilled. The tingle in Christiaan's stomach remained, but he felt mostly relieved to hear his country was finally freed from Nazi reign. He was still more than a thousand kilometers from home, hiding in a loft. Ignaz seemed to pick up on his somber mood.

"Don't worry. They will be here soon. And then you can go home. Most importantly, the SS have fled the area."

He spent the night dreaming vividly of home. There were no German soldiers or police officers patrolling the streets, he wasn't once asked for his papers. In the canals, children paddled on small rafts while their parents looked on from the side, sipping drinks and enjoying the summer afternoon. Christiaan could even smell the smoke coming from the numerous grills set up outside the houses.

He awoke with a start when the door of the barn opened with a loud clang. The hurried steps alarmed him, and he sat up in his bed, peeking over the edge, his eyes hurting as they adjusted to the bright sunlight. He let out a relieved sigh when he spotted Ignaz and Barbara hurrying toward the ladder leading up to the loft.

"Christiaan! Wake up!" There was excitement in Ignaz's voice. He sounded much like he had the evening prior. Before Christiaan could respond, Barbara's voice sounded.

"The Americans are here! They've arrived in Enns! It's over, Christiaan. The war is over!"

The words didn't fully register as Christiaan stared at the couple below. *Did I hear that right?* After the news of the Dutch liberation, it almost sounded too good to be true. "The Americans? Really? In

Enns?" He caught himself stammering but didn't care. His head was spinning, and he dug his fingers into the soft hay.

"Yes! They arrived in the early morning and are setting up camp in Enns."

"You're absolutely sure?" Christiaan's head cleared, but he was still reeling from the news. It sounded so simple, like the Americans had just rolled into town. *Is it over?*

"We saw a few of them moving down the main road into Enns." Barbara's voice was slightly higher pitched than usual, betraying her excitement. "Come, let's get you cleaned up and ready to go!"

Christiaan looked at her dumbfounded. "Go?" *Go where?*

She nodded enthusiastically. "I'm sure they can help you get home."

He looked around the loft that had been his refuge not once but twice in the past weeks. The simple bed he'd made with the hay had been so comfortable and safe. He felt apprehensive at leaving the safety of his hiding spot as he looked to the open barn door. The sounds of the chickens clucking around in the back garden was so much louder now, and he spotted the clear blue sky outside. He placed a foot on the little ladder and looked at Ignaz and Barbara, patiently waiting for him to come down. He smiled at them as he took one last whiff of the sweet smell of the hay. These people had saved his life not once, but twice, and he had no idea how he would ever be able to repay them.

————

Christiaan stood in the Friedmanns' back garden an hour later. He'd had his first hot shower in weeks and wore a set of fresh clothes Ignaz insisted on providing him. They'd eaten breakfast in the Friedmanns' kitchen, another first. Now he was ready to head into town to find the Americans. As he turned to Ignaz and Barbara, he felt awkward, struggling for the words to express his gratitude.

"You don't have to thank us, Christiaan. We only did what any decent person would do."

Christiaan shook his head. "It's not that simple. You risked your lives to save mine, a stranger you found in the woods. I am forever in your debt."

"Nonsense. You would've done the same." Her tone was sharp, ending the discussion. Her face softened as she took a step closer. Christiaan instinctively hugged her, and while she tensed for a moment, she soon relaxed as they stood for a few seconds. Christiaan wondered if the Friedmanns had any children of their own, but decided now wasn't the time to ask. They broke their embrace and Barbara gave him a warm smile. "Now go. It will be a long journey home."

Christiaan turned to Ignaz, who held out his hand. He grabbed it with two hands and inclined his head. "Thank you, Ignaz. I wouldn't be here without you."

The older Austrian man looked a little embarrassed and avoided his eyes. "Please, we were just glad to help." He let go of Christiaan's hand and stepped back. "Stay safe. And perhaps let us know when you've returned to Amsterdam? I hope you find your loved ones safe and well." He pointed at the road. "Head right and you'll find the main road leading to town after about a kilometer."

Christiaan nodded his thanks once more, then set off on the quiet road. Ignaz's final words echoed around his head. The last hour with the Friedmanns had been a blur as he prepared to leave. Now, alone with his thoughts, he thought of Lisa. Would she return home right away, or would she need to take care of things in London? And how would he find her, once he was back in Amsterdam? As the junction with the main road came into view, his spirits lifted. Parked in the middle of the intersection stood a large truck bearing not the German *Balkankreuz* but a large white star he hadn't seen before. Nearing the vehicle, he spotted two soldiers standing by the driver's door. They wore olive drab–colored uniforms, a small American flag prominently displayed on their shirt sleeves. Christiaan felt immense relief but was careful as he approached them. The men spotted him and turned with curious glances. They were a few years younger than Christiaan.

"Is it true what they said? Have you liberated Austria?" It felt odd to speak English after such a long time. "Is it safe?"

One of the men raised an eyebrow, then smiled. "We sent those krauts packing. Where did you come from? You look exhausted. You better head up the road into town and report to the medics. They'll take care of you." He jerked a thumb to the road behind him. Christiaan nodded and continued down the deserted road. The soldier wasn't wrong; Christiaan's legs were burning, and his breathing was labored. His stay at the Friedmanns had helped put a couple of kilos back on his thin frame, but it hadn't erased more than a year of imprisonment. Traversing through safe territory strengthened his resolve, and he continued to put one foot in front of another. *I survived Mauthausen, I can make it to Enns.*

It took him half an hour to make it into town. Everything was different from the last time when he'd been hauled in by the two SS troopers. The square was crowded, tents covering almost every cobblestone. American soldiers of all ranks were either working in or going between the canvas structures. Christiaan was overwhelmed by the activity, and it must've shown, for a young man wearing a helmet with a red cross approached him.

"Are you all right?" The man inspected him with trained, calculating eyes. "Do you understand me? Do you speak English?"

As Christiaan nodded, his head felt unusually heavy, and an overpowering urge to close his eyes took control of him. "I came from the camp."

The man nodded and took him by his shoulder, gently guiding him toward one of the tents. "What camp?"

"The one atop the hill. Mauthausen."

The man stopped in his tracks and turned to him, surprise on his face. "How did you make it down here?"

"I was ..." Christiaan closed his eyes as his legs felt heavy as lead.

He feared they would give out under him and was grateful for the support of the medic.

"Come, sit down over here. Let me get you something. Do you want something to eat? Drink?"

Christiaan could only nod as he sank into a simple chair inside. The medic rushed away, Christiaan just catching the man's words that he would be back in a minute, and that he shouldn't go anywhere. The man needn't have worried, for Christiaan couldn't move even if he wanted to. The sound of the many voices around him faded as he drifted away.

———

Christiaan's eyes fluttered open, and he was greeted by the relief of a cold cloth on his forehead. The medic looked at him sympathetically.

"Hey, you're back. Good. Have some of this. Careful, it's still pretty hot." He handed him a large tin mug, and Christiaan struggled to recognize the smell at first. "Do you mind if I quickly check some of your vitals?"

Christiaan shook his head and brought the cup to his mouth. Then he recognized the dark liquid. *Coffee.* He inhaled deeply, the aroma reminding him of better times. He carefully took a sip, the richness of the flavor almost overpowering. The medic pressed a stethoscope to his chest, the cold metal jolting his attention back to the man.

"Breathe in deeply for me, please." Christiaan did as he was told. "Now breathe out." He removed the stethoscope and nodded. "Nothing wrong with your lungs. You just need a lot of rest, and plenty of food. But you should be fine." He put his tools away, then turned back to Christiaan with an inquisitive look. "Now, where did you say you came from again?"

Christiaan cradled the mug between his hands. "The camp a little farther up the hill. Mauthausen." The medic tried to hide his surprise, but he flinched enough for Christiaan to know. "You've found it, haven't you?"

The man looked away at first, then nodded. "We have. But, well ..." He averted his gaze, a troubled look on his face. "I'm a little surprised to find you here in town, in your condition. Most of the people we found up there wouldn't have been able to walk more than a hundred paces, let alone make it down that hill and into town." The man leaned forward, compassion in his eyes. "You're tired and shaken. Why don't you grab a few hours of rest, and we can talk about what happened." Christiaan was about to reply when he felt a presence behind him. He turned around to find a young woman in a nurse's uniform smiling pleasantly.

"I'll show you to a bed." She spoke with a heavy drawl while she held out her hand. "You look like you could use it."

Christiaan glanced back at the medic, who simply nodded as he got up. "We'll catch up later." Christiaan rose to his feet a little too quickly. Small specks obstructed his vision and he wobbled on his feet. The nurse grabbed his arm, and he was grateful for her support.

"There's no rush. Take your time, I'll walk you to a bed. We've got some hot soup if you like." Her voice was tender and soft. The nurse guided him through what felt like a maze of tents. Soldiers and nurses rushed by, but she appeared to have all the time in the world, slowing down to match his pace.

They reached a large tent and stepped inside. Rows of field beds dominated the space. Most were empty, and Christiaan was pleased when the nurse stopped at one in the corner, next to the wall of the tent. "I think this is a good spot." She produced a clipboard while he sat down on the bed. It was the softest bed he'd felt in over a year, the sheets crackling as he moved. "I'm going to need your name for your file. And it will be nicer to call you by your name as well." She winked at him, and Christiaan felt instantly more comfortable.

"Christiaan Brouwer."

The nurse jotted his name on the sheet of paper, then stopped and looked up. "And where are you from, Christiaan?"

"Amsterdam, the Netherlands." He looked up to see her glance at him curiously, then appeared to catch herself, her smile returning.

"Great! I'm going to fetch you something to eat, and I'll be right back. Make yourself comfortable. You're going to spend a bit of time here, and I'll make sure we'll get some meat on those bones again."

He watched her walk away and looked around. About a quarter of the fifty beds were taken, and most patients were asleep. He kicked off his shoes and stretched out on the bed. The pillow felt heavenly, and he closed his eyes. *Just a few seconds, then I'll get up.* He started counting to ten, but never reached beyond five as sleep took him.

———

Christiaan awoke to a bright light and the sound of nearby voices. He looked around, uncertain about his surroundings before remembering where he was. Some of the nearby patients spoke in hushed voices, one or two looking up as Christiaan sat up in his bed. He shook off the blanket that had been placed over him, revealing the clothes he was wearing when he came in. Someone entered the tent, the same bright daylight that had awoken him streaming in again. *How long have I been asleep?* He felt surprisingly rested; the overwhelming weariness he'd felt when he was brought into the tent had faded.

"Hey! He's awake!" A voice at the front of the tent called. The tent flap opened again, revealing the silhouette of someone entering against the bright light. He quickly shielded his eyes, the pounding in his head reminding him all wasn't well with him just yet.

He reached for a glass of water on the small bedside table and gulped it down in one go with his eyes closed. Anxious for a refill, he opened his eyes to find a figure standing by the foot of his bed. The light coming in from outside made it hard to make out the person's face, but as he blinked his eyes, he noticed it was a woman wearing a nurse's uniform.

"Christiaan."

His entire body tensed, and he almost dropped his glass. *Am I dreaming?*

The woman's hands went to her mouth as she gasped. "It's you. It really is you." She spoke shakily, but there was no longer any doubt. He would recognize this voice out of thousands.

"Lisa?" Her name came out as a croak, his mouth dry and constricted from emotion. "Where ... How did you ... ?" The questions tore through his mind, but he was unable to put a sentence together.

In what felt like slow motion, Lisa stepped to the side of the bed, her every step agonizingly slow as she moved toward him. The light hit her from the side, revealing tears streaming down her smiling face. She looked just like in his dreams. For a moment, Christiaan was convinced she was but a vision.

Then she touched his face. Her hands were warm, her fingertips carefully caressing his cheeks. She leaned down and kissed him, her soft lips meeting his. Afraid the dream would soon end, Christiaan stretched his arms and ran his hands through her hair, stroking the back of her neck.

When they broke their kiss, Lisa kept her face close to his, their eyes close, noses touching. He felt her warm breath on his cheek and tasted the saltiness of her tears.

"You're real, aren't you?" He spoke hesitantly, afraid his words would break the spell.

Lisa smiled and nodded. "I'm as real as can be. And I'm not leaving your side ever again, Christiaan Brouwer." She kissed him again, removing all doubt.

When he opened his eyes again, he felt the strange sensation they were being watched. Lisa frowned, concern in her eyes while she sat down and placed her hands in her lap. "What's wrong?"

Christiaan sat up a bit straighter, his focus on the person watching them from a few paces away. For the second time in as many minutes, Christiaan's heart skipped a beat, his breath taken away. He couldn't believe his eyes and was completely taken aback.

Nora hurriedly ran up and embraced him tightly, beaming from ear to ear. He had so many questions, but when he opened his mouth, Nora placed a finger on his lips.

"There will be plenty of time to talk. Let's go home."

AUTHOR'S NOTES

Thank you for finishing the Orphans of War trilogy. When I wrote the first book, I thought it would be a stand-alone story. But, by the time I finished, I realized I wasn't done with Nora, Christiaan, and Floris. And judging from the responses to the first two books, neither were you, my readers.

Having spent the past eight years living in Vienna, it was inevitable I would write about what happened in Austria during WWII. After visiting the very well-preserved Mauthausen camp— only two hours from my home—I knew this would be the setting for the finale of the trilogy.

Before anything else, I need to credit the inspiration for Christiaan's escapes from the camp to a true story. While researching Mauthausen, I found Jack Hersch's fantastic *Death March Escape: The Remarkable Story of a Man Who Twice Escaped the Nazi Holocaust.* In this book, Jack retraces the steps of his father, David, a Hungarian Jew imprisoned in the Mauthausen and Gusen camps from June 1944 until his escape in April 1945. In an account where truth really is more remarkable than fiction, Jack vividly describes his father's struggle to survive Nazi Germany's most brutal camp to escape against unbelievable odds.

There is little I love more than using true stories of people's heroism in my books. And here was a detailed account of someone who hadn't escaped Mauthausen just once, but twice. I was able to find Jack Hersch's email address, and my hands were shaking from excitement and trepidation as I requested permission to use his father's story as inspiration for the series' grand finale.

Jack responded within hours.

To my immense relief, he was excited about the idea, and he offered to assist in any way he could. He ended up reading the very first draft of the book, providing numerous improvements and encouragement along the way. I'm deeply grateful for his enthusiasm in allowing me to share David Hersch's story. I highly recommend reading Jack's book, a captivating biography describing his father's journey in 1944 mixed with his own experience visiting the same places many decades later. Thank you, Jack.

Mauthausen is not as notorious as Auschwitz-Birkenau, and certainly hasn't received the same attention. The 190,000 prisoners passing through the Austrian camp's gates between 1938 and 1945 are dwarfed by Auschwitz-Birkenau's 1.3 million. However, its role in the Holocaust cannot be understated. Where Auschwitz-Birkenau was a true extermination camp, Mauthausen's purpose was first and foremost economical. The most obvious examples were the Wiener Graben—the granite quarry—and the underground Messerschmitt factory constructed at St. Georgen in 1944, but there were many companies in the area profiting from the cheap labor. Mauthausen was more profitable than the five other large slave labor camps in the Reich. That includes Auschwitz-Birkenau, which still boasted a large prisoner labor population, despite the many hundreds of thousands that went straight to the gas chambers. In 1944, Mauthausen reported profits of 11 million Reichsmark, amounting to more than $90 million in 2023's money.

That the prisoners were treated so abhorrently had everything to do with the Nazis' utter disregard for the lives of those considered subhuman. That, coupled with the endless supply of new slaves arriving in cattle cars, made Mauthausen and Gusen the only camps in the Nazi camp system classified as Category III, reserved for "incorrigible political enemies of the Reich." Assignment to Mauthausen was essentially a death sentence through hard labor.

The treatment of Russian prisoners of war was just as bad, if not worse. Confined to Block 20, they were literally left to die of starvation and dehydration. The instances I described in my book all happened, including the film where the prisoners were forced to pretend they were treated well, only to end up dead from overeating. The revolt of the prisoners in Block 20 also happened. Of the 500 prisoners that participated, 419 managed to escape, but only 11 survived. Aided by a local population keen to help, the SS set up a massive manhunt. If you're interested in reading more about this shameful episode in Austria's history, I suggest reading up on the "Mühlviertel Hare Hunt."

From everything I've read, Georg Bachmayer really was the sadist I've portrayed him to be as he wielded his iron fist over the prisoner population. The events I've described in this book are all based on memoirs written by prisoners. For me, Bachmayer was the personification of evil. He did not survive the war, committing suicide days after abandoning the camp, but not before shooting his wife and two children.

On the Allied side, I was keen to highlight the efforts of legendary General George Patton and his Third US Army. When the German Wehrmacht countered unexpectedly and with great force in the Ardennes on 16 December 1944, the Allied commanders were surprised and pushed back west. It was Patton who quickly turned his massive army north to smash through the German forces, free Bastogne, and create the initial breakthrough required for the eventual Allied victory in the Battle of the Bulge.

I especially enjoyed placing Lisa with the Third Army to give an insight into their rapid liberation of Europe. The battles she witnesses all happened, although I've taken some creative liberties with the details. Nevertheless, I believe it gives a good impression of the confidence the soldiers of the Third Army had in themselves and their commander, General Patton.

Lisa's and Nora's roles in the preparation and execution of the D-Day invasion were also a lot of fun to write. There are many accounts where the events on the Normandy beaches take center stage, and I wanted to show a slightly different perspective. It's easy to focus merely on the soldiers fighting at the front and forget about the efforts of those working in the background. The Women's Auxiliary Air Force in the UK played a crucial role in guiding Allied pilots across the North Sea and Channel, not to mention keeping the British shores safe.

I'd also like to believe Floris Brouwer showed his true face in this final book. Powerful, ambitious, and ruthless as a policeman in Amsterdam, safely detached from the horrors he sent his Jewish countrymen to, Floris began to show cracks on the eastern front. Witnessing the war crimes committed by his comrades of the Waffen-SS, his conscience started playing up. In Mauthausen, he needed to pick a side. Join in the senseless killing and torture of the prisoners, or try to get by without? In the end, the arrival of Christiaan changed everything, and he returned to being the self-serving opportunist operating in the shadows. He was never going to survive the war, and having him take his own life felt completely in character to me.

Christiaan's journey in this final book is based on that of the 40 Dutch SOE agents after they left Haaren prison in the Netherlands. Christiaan's lucky escape was entirely fictional, as these men were murdered in the quarry the day after arriving at Mauthausen. I've used a combination of former prisoner accounts to shape his life in the camp. It won't surprise you to learn a prisoner working in the administration had a much higher chance of survival than those slaving away in the quarry. Few prisoners survived longer than a couple of weeks.

Finally, Ignaz and Barbara Friedmann. These brave people really existed, and they hid David Hersch in their barn after finding him on their hike in the woods near their home. They demonstrate the very best of human nature: that there are always people who will help, even if it means risking their own lives. It only made sense to include them in Christiaan's escape as well.

As always, I'd love to hear what you think of the book. Feel free to drop me a line through my website, michaelreit.com, and sign up for my newsletter to stay up to date on new releases and exclusive offers.

All my very best,

Michael

A NOTE TO THE READER

Dear Reader,

I want to thank you for picking up your copy of *Crossroads of Granite* - the final book in the *Orphans of War* series. Readers mean everything to authors, and I appreciate you more than I can say.

As an author I depend on you to leave an honest review on your favorite (online) bookstore. If you've got the time to do so, I would be very grateful.

If you would like to reach out to me with questions or comments, please feel free to contact me via my website – michaelreit.com or reach out to me on Facebook – www.facebook.com/MichaelReitAuthor. I love hearing from readers, and look forward to hearing what you have to say about *Crossroads of Granite*!

Warmly and with Gratitude,
Michael Reit

ABOUT THE AUTHOR

Michael Reit writes page-turning historical fiction. His books focus on lesser-known events and people in World War II Europe.

Born in the Netherlands, he now lives in beautiful Vienna, Austria, with his partner Esther and daughter Bibi.

Connect with Michael via his website:
www.michaelreit.com

Or via:

f facebook.com/MichaelReitAuthor

a amazon.com/stores/Michael-Reit/author/B08F2DBT3C

BB bookbub.com/authors/michael-reit

ALSO BY MICHAEL REIT

Made in United States
Orlando, FL
26 July 2024

49445342R00246